SPELLBOUND

Damian scooped Sarabeth up, cradling her. Swiftly he strode from the room and carried her into the hall. He set her down. Sarabeth remained silent.

Damian knelt in front of her, his eyes solemn. "You will not go into that room ever again."

Sarabeth gazed at him, her very soul bleeding. He did not believe in magic, yet only magic could release her. "No," she said softly. "I shall not. I—I shall not if you do not want me to."

"I do not want you to," Damian said. "Never shall I want you to."

"I am sorry!" Sarabeth rasped. "Sorry for—" She killed the very words upon her lips. She could not say she was sorry for lying to him, for being spellbound, for loving him and being helpless.

Damian smiled slightly and lifted his hand toward her cheek. "No, 'tis I who am sorry. I do not know what came over me." He shook his head. "I no longer even know the man I am. Always looking for phantoms."

Sarabeth's own hand reached out to him. She wanted to touch him, to confess that she was indeed his phantom, but not of her own choosing. "I should be going."

"I frightened you," he whispered.

Yes, he had frightened her, frightened her deeply. She needed him, loved him. She was more spellbound by him than by Maudar's curse . . .

—from LOVE'S MAGIC, by Cindy Holbrook

WATCH FOR THESE ZEBRA REGENCIES

LADY STEPHANIE   (0-8217-5341-X, $4.50)
by Jeanne Savery
Lady Stephanie Morris has only one true love: the family estate she has
managed ever since her mother died. But then Lord Anthony Rider
arrives on her estate, claiming he has plans for both the land and the
woman. Stephanie soon realizes she's fallen in love with a man whose
sensual caresses will plunge her into a world of peril and intrigue . . .
a man as dangerous as he is irresistible.

BRIGHTON BEAUTY   (0-8217-5340-1, $4.50)
by Marilyn Clay
Chelsea Grant, pretty and poor, naively takes school friend Alayna
Marchmont's place and spends a month in the country. The devastating
man had sailed from Honduras to claim his promised bride, Miss
Marchmont. An affair of the heart may lead to disaster . . . unless a
resourceful Brighton beauty finds a way to stop a masquerade and keep
a lord's love.

LORD DIABLO'S DEMISE   (0-8217-5338-X, $4.50)
by Meg-Lynn Roberts
The sinfully handsome Lord Harry Glendower was a gambler and the
black sheep of his family. About to be forced into a marriage of con-
venience, the devilish fellow engineered his own demise, never having
dreamed that faking his death would lead him to the heavenly refuge
of spirited heiress Gwyn Morgan, the daughter of a physician.

A PERILOUS ATTRACTION   (0-8217-5339-8, $4.50)
by Dawn Aldridge Poore
Alissa Morgan is stunned when a frantic passenger thrusts her baby into
Alissa's arms and flees, having heard rumors that a notorious highwayman posed a threat to their coach. Handsome stranger Hugh Sebastian
secretly possesses the treasured necklace the highwayman seeks and
volunteers to pose as Alissa's husband to save her reputation. With a
lost baby and missing necklace in their care, the couple embarks on a
journey into peril—and passion.

Available wherever paperbacks are sold, or order direct from the
Publisher. Send cover price plus 50¢ per copy for mailing and
handling to Penguin USA, P.O. Box 999, c/o Dept. 17109, Ber-
genfield, NJ 07621. Residents of New York and Tennessee must
include sales tax. DO NOT SEND CASH.

BEWITCHED BY LOVE

Teresa DesJardien
Cindy Holbrook
Valerie King

Zebra Books
Kensington Publishing Corp.

ZEBRA BOOKS are published by

Kensington Publishing Corp.
850 Third Avenue
New York, NY 10022

First Printing: October, 1996
10 9 8 7 6 5 4 3 2 1

Printed in the United States of America

CONTENTS

The Haunted Bride

Teresa DesJardien

For:
Noreen Brownlie and
Patricia Simpson

Thanks for always raising
my flagging spirits (pun intended!)

One

While smiling benignly at the sight of Cousin Susannah, wed just four hours past, Henrietta Louise Carson's attention was captured by a touch on her elbow. Etta turned her head to find a pair of deep brown eyes staring intently into her own, knowing the moment she did so that there was something familiar about the unknown man whose touch had sought her attention. She felt a tingle of awareness dance across her shoulders, the kind of awareness that her nanny had always said came with the fact that Etta was fey.

"I know we have not been introduced, but I must speak to you," the brown-eyed man said, the urgent note in his voice cutting through the cluttered noise of music and laughter.

Without waiting for her response, he gripped her elbow a little more tightly than was necessary and propelled her through a doorway leading out of the crowded parlor where the wedding guests frolicked through a country dance. He ignored her small sounds of protest.

Finding herself alone with him, Etta pulled her elbow free of his touch, retreating a few steps. "I beg your pardon!" she said. "I think you would be well served, sir, to take a cool stroll outside to clear your head."

"I am not intoxicated," he said with a scowl. He pressed a hand to his waistcoat and made a quick, almost rude bow to her. "I am Lord Healey," he introduced himself. "And I know your name is Miss Henrietta Carson. My friend Thayer was so good as to give me your name," he said, naming the groom.

Etta eyed the stranger. She had met Cousin Susannah's betrothed only a few times, and certainly never this gentleman, although she knew by where he had been seated for the wedding breakfast that he must be a friend of Mr. Thayer's. Perhaps this was the friend who had traveled from Bath for the sole purpose of attending the wedding, the one Susannah had said must be leaving almost as soon as the wedding was over? Perhaps so, for this fellow was certainly of such a rude stamp.

"How is it that Mr. Thayer did not come with you to make the proper introductions?" Etta replied.

"Because he *is* intoxicated, and occupied dancing with his bride, in case you have not noted the obvious. Besides, I do not think you want him to know what matter we mean to discuss," Lord Healey said impatiently.

"And what would that matter be?" Etta asked, glancing around quickly to see if anyone had noted the spectacle they were surely making. Fortunately only Aunt Mildred seemed vaguely interested, and even she was torn between watching her niece and the dancers, who in their enthusiasm occasionally thumped into the furniture that had been pushed back against the walls.

"Please," he said, the word sounding as though it were dragged forth from some distant memory of lessons on manners. "I only mean to show you something. Even over the music, any cry you uttered would be heard and attended to. Please come with me."

"I think not," she said with deliberate coolness, turning away.

"It is about your drawings."

Etta stopped at the tightly uttered words and turned back to him, puzzled. "My drawings? Of the bride and groom?"

Lord Healey shook his head and moved to close the door. Etta frowned, but she did not protest when he reached out to again cup her elbow and lead her to the desk situated to one side of the room.

He picked up her sketchbook, extending the pad toward her. "What is the meaning of these drawings?" he demanded.

Etta glanced at the pad, not accepting it. "They are my gift to Cousin Susannah and her new husband, if you must know. I offered to sketch their likenesses on their wedding day. I should think that would be obvious," she said, bristling. Was it that he questioned her talent? She might not be the finest artist ever born, but she knew she had a good eye and a fine hand at the art of sketching. What right had he to insult her choice of a gift?

"Not the bridal sketches," he said, more impatient than ever. He turned the pad so that it faced her fully. "I mean *these* drawings! The ones of me!"

Etta stared at the half-drawn figure on the paper, a profile, and then her gaze flew to Lord Healey's face. "It *is* you!" she said on a gasp. "I can see it clearly now. Oh, my heavens! But only look at your eyes—" She cut herself off abruptly, one hand rising to cover her mouth in sheer astonishment.

He turned the pad toward himself, flipping half a dozen pages. "Yes, I noticed you never gave me more than a simple line to serve as eyes. Did I not stand still long enough for you to catch my image completely?" he asked with a sarcastic edge. He looked up, his gaze riveting. "When did you draw all these? There must be two dozen sketches here! You could not have completed them all today. Have we met before?"

"If we have, I have forgot the occasion as clearly as you have forgot me," Etta replied, arching a brow.

He slapped the sketchbook back on the desk and stared at her. There was exasperation in the set of his shoulders, but, too, there was a hint of curiosity rising in his gaze, as if she had intrigued him despite his inclination otherwise.

"No," he said at length, looking mildly surprised at his own words. "I would not have forgot you."

Etta felt herself blush and wondered why. It was not the first time anyone had hinted that the rich red highlights in her chestnut hair and that her blue eyes had made a lasting impression.

But perhaps she blushed in reaction to this man's overt anger. Her drawings had never angered anyone before, not even the time she had drawn a picture of a broken tree limb; Papa had even laughed a little about the irony of its prediction that not a day later he would trip on a doll Etta had left on the stairs, ending with his arm in a splint.

"Indeed," Lord Healey said, crossing his arms as he glared at Etta, "I am quite sure I have never seen you before. But you must have seen me." His eyes narrowed. "How often? Only once? I would have noted you if it were any more than that. You had to have drawn from memory—I am most impressed, Miss Carson. Your images are good despite an apparent lack of repeated exposure to the subject. But whatever possessed you to draw so many pictures of me?"

What could she say? That she had seen his face any number of time in her dreams?

"How is it you happened upon these drawings, my lord?" she asked warmly, perhaps as much to avoid answering his questions as to gain a reply to her own.

Two red lines appeared along the crest of his cheekbones. "I came here seeking some relief from the heat of the dancing and chanced to note your sketches. The book was on this desk in plain sight," he said as though accusing her of an indiscretion. "The topmost sketch was of a quality such as to propel me, quite naturally, I believe, into turning the pages—"

Despite her annoyance, Etta felt a flicker of gratification at his reluctant words of praise.

"Imagine my surprise when I discovered I had been an unwitting subject of your pen," he said, and now he appeared faintly amused, as if he suspected her of harboring a secret fascination with his person. "Truly, Miss Carson, I believe you owe me an explanation, since you did not deign to first seek my permission. How is it that your sketchbook is filled with portraits of me?"

Etta lowered her eyes, scowling at the carpet below their feet. "I do not suppose there is any point in telling you," she said stiffly, wanting to deny any such fascination existed outside her dreams, but realizing in light of the sketches that a denial could only ring false to his ears.

"Why not?"

She looked up again and pursed her lips defiantly. After a moment she said baldly, "Because you will not believe me."

"Why not?" he repeated.

She merely shook her head. He would think her mad, or at best an outrageous coquette.

"Come, come, Miss Carson! Admit you owe me some manner of explanation."

"To what purpose? I have offered you no insult. You may take the drawings if you prefer I not have them, and that can be an end to the matter."

"And what is there to keep you from drawing more?"

"Such vanity!" she cried on a tight half-laugh. "I have no need to draw any more." She turned toward the door, but he moved swiftly, placing himself in her path.

"Indeed? And why is that?" he questioned.

She thought to order him out of her way, but she knew that would only lead to a further battle of words. The truth, however, might cause him to lose interest in bedeviling her. What matter if he thought her mad?

"I do not need to draw your face anymore, Lord Healey," she said with deliberate calm, "because I have now seen your eyes."

He stared at her, quite mute for a full five seconds. "My eyes?" he said at last.

She felt her blush returning, but she did not lower her gaze from his. "Your eyes, my lord." She lifted her chin as if trying to challenge his greater height. "If you insist on knowing, the truth is, well, that I *see* faces, or things . . . sometimes. I draw them—to clear my mind of the image, you see. I know you must now be thinking me quite mad, and I do not care a fig if you do! But if you had but looked at the dates I put on each page of my sketchbook, you would have noted that I have been drawing that particular face . . . that is, *your* face . . . for over two weeks now."

He stared. "Impossible! I have been in London for only two days!" he exclaimed, frowning down at her. He did not move from her side to the sketch pad to authenticate her claim, but then, she supposed a series of dates could be easily listed regardless of their authenticity. "You have seen me in Bath," he accused Etta.

"I have never been to Bath, sir."

"Why should I believe you?"

"Why should I care to lie about the matter?"

He did not respond, did not reiterate that he thought she might have some reason to lie as she half expected him to do. Instead, a curious expression spread over his face, an odd mixture of understanding and something that resembled confusion. He took a step back, and his arms dropped to his sides.

"Miss Carson," he said, his voice much lower, calmer. "Miss Carson, do you believe there is more to this world than we can see with our eyes?"

What a curious question! It was the last she might have expected of this gruff stranger. So few people believed in what they could not see, could not touch and immediately comprehend. If "fey" was the right word to describe the extra aspects Etta had always seen and felt, those sensations that tingled to life across her shoulders and visualized beneath her pen, she was also used to not letting others know of her experiences, for they only laughed and called her witless. And yet, this man, this Lord Healey, had asked her if she believed in what she could not see!

"I believe in God," she replied cautiously.

"Yes, of course," he said, taking another step back. "You could say that nearly everyone believes in God, and He is certainly beyond human vision. And there is the Holy Spirit, of course, equally unseen."

Etta gave him a steady gaze, not sure what point he meant to make, nor why he chose to make it.

"Miss Carson," he said then, and there was something about the set of his shoulders that relaxed, that lost the angry edge he had shown when he had first brought her in the room. "I humbly offer you my apologies. I have been boorish. What matter, indeed, that you have images of my face in your sketch-book? I tell you now, I am flattered, howsoever they came to be there. Of course I shan't take them away with me. They are yours, to do with as you please. I was merely startled. Do say you forgive me?"

Her reply was a mere curt nod of the head, but the gesture seemed to please him.

He made every apparent effort from that moment forward to be charming, as if to erase the rudeness that had marked their initial meeting.

Etta responded with studied coolness at first, but after an hour or two—when he cast a radiant smile her way that made it difficult to remember how his handsome face looked when fixed in a frown—she forgave him in fact as well as in word. After all, it had to have been startling to see his own face sketched in her book; she could hardly blame him for demanding an explanation. In fact, she relented so far as to give him a dance that afternoon, and another that evening.

Late the next morning, Etta only clicked her tongue a little in impatience when she learned he had not left for Bath and was to be included in the continuing festivities. Cousin Susannah and her groom meant to make their home at his estate in Salisbury. As the journey would take two days to complete, the newlyweds had chosen to postpone beginning their bridal jaunt until the new day. She could not imagine why Lord Healey had chosen to postpone his return home, but here he was, despite the lateness of the morning hour, remaining to see the newlywed couple on their way.

"I am surprised to see you with us yet here in London, Lord Healey," Etta said, pausing beside him for a moment as the gathering of friends and family all waved a farewell to the groom and a happily weeping Susannah.

He gazed at her steadily and said, "I felt no overwhelming need to go just yet, Miss Carson."

Etta smiled and nodded and looked away, feeling an odd little vibration in her breast—one that had nothing to do with visions or premonitions but everything to do with a certain gentleman's steady regard.

When he remained yet another day, Etta found it not too insufferable that he came on this, the third day in a row, to call at her aunt's house. She also had to admit that the offer to go rowing with her cousin Anthony and Lord Healey about the Serpentine in Hyde Park was an offer she was not likely to decline . . . and later that night she admitted to her aunt and Papa that the expedition had proven to be all that was pleasant.

By the fourth evening's gathering for coffee before the fire cheerily blazing on the grate in Aunt Mildred's parlor, Etta found she had never laughed quite so much as when Lord Healey told outrageous stories of exploits he and his brother had engaged in as children. That night he took her aside and asked that she call him by his Christian name of Daniel.

By the fifth evening, in her first letter to the married Cousin Susannah, Etta found herself describing Lord Healey, Daniel, as "witty" and "handsome" and "quite the gentleman." After that she no longer even tried to pretend a lasting annoyance with him.

At the end of a laughter-filled, precious week he asked her to marry him, and she was surprised at how the very idea of accepting such a precipitous proposal failed to shock her. Then again, had she not drawn his face before she had ever met him? Her drawings had foreshadowed events before, and it was not difficult to think his proposal was meant to be.

"Yes," she answered him simply, smiling up into his handsome face.

"Let us be married at once," he said.

"I am flattered, sir," she replied, not wanting to seem missish, but finding her heart beat so quickly, it threatened to carry away any semblance of sense.

"And I am serious. I see no reason to wait."

"But what if I should turn out to be upon further acquaintance the very sort of person you would least admire? Are you not concerned I have yet to show my true spots?" she asked, still half flirting.

"No, I am not much concerned." He did not flirt in return; indeed, he seemed incongruously thoughtful, perhaps even somber. "I think it possible you are the very sort of woman I have been seeking."

"Me or my dowry?" she said, still trying to be flippant.

He looked down at her, and a slow smile spread across his face, erasing his sobriety. "Both," he answered, then laughed. "I need your money as soon as it can come into my pockets, dearest girl. Now, how is that for being absolutely honest and frank?" He lifted his brows, the smile fading as he gathered up her hands in his own. "But you cannot say I have led you to believe anything otherwise. You know ours will not be a life of luxury and leisure. The estate is in dire need of rebuilding. I will do everything in my power, including using every penny of your dowry, to build a comfortable life for us."

"Has any woman ever been offered sweeter words to entice her into marriage?" she pretended to scold, having already weighed the consequences of marrying a man whose funds were in abeyance.

His smile returned. "Perhaps the words lack any enticement, I grant you, but what greater flattery can I offer than to whisk you off your feet into an impetuous marriage? Let us set the date: the Monday after our banns have been properly called."

"Three weeks! I do not know . . ." Etta replied, not sure whether to argue or to laugh with him. "Do you not think it best to be betrothed for a while?"

"No" was his simple answer, which received no reply, for he leaned down and kissed Etta rather thoroughly until she laughingly agreed they must be married sooner than later.

The days floated past, every one filled with Daniel's presence, for he remained in London to marry in her parish. When she thought back to that first week, sometimes it seemed as though time had been folded like a fan, compressed, one day blending into the next without revealing its pattern; but the next instant she recalled every moment in Daniel's presence, every word uttered between them, and when she reviewed them in her mind she marveled that so much delight, surprise, uncertainty, and firm regard had erupted into her life in so short a space of time. Why did it feel as though she had known Daniel for years and years and not the mere seven days it was in truth?

The next two weeks equally proved a blur, what with arranging the ceremony with Rector Johnston, readying Etta's best gown with additions of Brussels lace, and arranging a breakfast feast to be served to the hurriedly invited guests.

"Such haste, Henrietta!" Papa scolded, and not for the first time. "Your mama would never have approved of such haste. People will think I have a grandchild on the way!"

"People will learn otherwise in nine months," Aunt Mildred assured Papa firmly, even though she gave Etta a level look that seemed to command that Aunt Mildred not be proved mistaken.

"We are in love," Etta stated unequivocally to her papa—even if in her heart she could not help wondering, just a little, if she would feel the same fifty years, or even fifty days, from then. She supposed that was a perfectly normal thing for any bride to ponder—especially a bride who had only recently learned that her groom had been married before.

Aunt Mildred had taken her niece aside, at first to whisper in Etta's ear that she had learned from friends that the Baron Healey was all but penniless. Assured that Etta already knew and accepted this fact, she had gone on to share the knowledge that Daniel had already had a wife.

When asked, Daniel had confirmed the truth readily enough.

"We were married only two years. She died . . . an accident . . ." Daniel had explained, his eyes clouding with memories. "She's been gone more than a year."

Etta had not pressed him to say more, for he seemed pained

by his thoughts. She had refused to allow herself to feel hurt that he had not mentioned this former wife. Perhaps he had assumed Etta knew. After all, it was hardly a secret. But never to have mentioned a woman who had married him, lived with him for two years . . .

"I love him," Etta repeated firmly, not having meant to say the thought aloud.

Papa snorted. "God save us all when 'tis love that leads to marriage in haste! Damn fool notion," he said, shaking his head.

But he never protested the point with her again, leading her to suppose he could not argue with the happiness that surely shone forth from the very core of her being, a happiness that could conquer any doubts that lingered yet in the back of her mind when she stepped down the aisle on her wedding day.

Two

Miles from her papa or any family, the giddiness of her wedding three days behind her, Etta stepped down from the carriage to gaze up at her new home, the Bath home she would share with Daniel.

Their three days as husband and wife had proven to be blissful, sweeping away any bridal fears, but now Etta experienced a tremor of uncertainty as she looked upon the handsome, tall building that was to be her new home. There was that old tingle, that singular quality that spoke to her in a wordless language. She ought to be gratified that the house appeared well-appointed, but something struck at her, chilling her despite the afternoon sunlight that fell across her bonnet. The sensation was rather like becoming aware of the scent of food just beginning to spoil, or catching the lingering echo of a sour note of music. There was . . . a problem, but she could not quite see where it lay. Was it the house itself? The grounds? The people waiting within? For a moment Etta felt as though she could not breathe, and when the sensation passed, she shuddered.

Still, the uneasiness that cloaked her shoulders must be shrugged aside for Daniel's sake. He came to stand close behind her, his hands coming to rest on her shoulders as he also gazed up at the house. This was his home, and she must not let him know she felt anything but joy coming here to live with him.

She turned her head to glance up at him, and her uneasiness flickered back to full life, for she thought the smile he gave her was strained. Did he feel it too, this . . . something in the air?

She bit her lip and glanced once more at the house, squaring her shoulders beneath his touch. There was no point in brooding, no point in letting her imagination run away with her. If the house was now filled with a somber air, the two of them would bring joy and laughter to it; Etta vowed it silently.

A maid had looked down from an upstairs window, disappearing at once from sight, no doubt to inform the household that the master had returned home. A minute later she came forth to greet their carriage, curtsying and flickering glances toward Etta.

"Etta, my dear, this is our only maid, Roberta," Daniel introduced the young woman, who had a wary, almost sullen look about her. To the maid he said, "This is my wife, Lady Healey."

The maid's mouth dropped open before she recalled herself and snapped it shut. She looked to the ground, curtsying again as a greeting. "Ma'am," she muttered.

Daniel reached to the floor of his curricle, bringing forth one of Etta's smaller valises. He handed it to the maid. "Take this to the master chamber."

"Yes, sir," the girl said, offering another curtsy and departing, but not without casting over her shoulder one more glance at Etta.

Daniel smiled slightly. "I daresay the news of our marriage will set the household on its ear."

"Understandably," Etta said.

Daniel had hired a post chaise to follow his far lighter curricle, and now all of Etta's belongings had been unloaded by the driver and the outrider. Their fee having already been paid, they tipped their hats and the driver clucked to his team, and the post chaise rolled away.

Daniel glared at their retreating backs. "It seems I must find someone to assist me in moving these portmanteaux into the house," he said, then shook his head as if recalling his manners.

"But first, I have kept you in the dust long enough, my dear. Come, let me show you the house."

He could have added "the house on which my father squandered my inheritance," for Daniel had told her that his father, a man susceptible to demonstrations of vanity, had obdurately decided that aggrandizing his home was more important than improving the fields, stock, and equipment of the holdings. With the property declining from years of indifference to the very source of its income—the crops and cattle—Daniel's father had chosen to beautify the house even while he ruined the estate that supported it.

Perhaps that was what Etta sensed about the dwelling: the former Lord Healey's legacy of desperate bravado. Or perhaps it was seeing the lovely facade of warm, honey-colored Bath stone, the gracious lines of the house, the many windows, the new roof . . . and knowing that despite its beauty it all stood upon a financially crumbled foundation.

Daniel led Etta up the short stairs to the front door as she sighed and turned her thoughts to the greeting they had received. She did not know what she had expected by way of a reception, especially as there had been no advance warning so that the few servants might assemble. But . . . it was that maid. There was something . . . well, peculiar about the young woman. It was not the way the girl held herself, nor even her sullen expression, but . . . something.

"M'lord!" came a call, stopping them on the threshold.

"Ah, here are the very two I needed to see," Daniel said to Etta as two roughly dressed men approached. Daniel introduced the shorter, thinner man as Will, their man-of-all-work. "He sees to all the chores about the house, while Mr. O'Brien here sees to the gardens."

The taller of the two, a big, gruff-looking man with a brushy mustache, inclined his head and touched his hat brim. "Ma'am," he said.

The two servants said they would see to bringing in the portmanteaux, and with a nod of thanks Daniel turned to escort

Etta into the house. She paused for only a moment on the threshold, but then she stepped within, having already determined she would not slight the house that belonged to Daniel.

The entry hall was well appointed with tall windows that let in plenty of sunlight. The curtains were a rich egg-yolk yellow, held back by gold tassels. The room lacked any fine vases, statuary, or portraits, and Etta knew that if there had once been any, they had long since gone to the auctioneer. There was a large gold-veined marble fireplace ready to warm callers, surrounded by tables of white and gilt, and the two settees were striped in silk of matching colors.

"Daniel! It is lovely!" Etta said sincerely, pleased there was so much sunshine, with its play of light to counter the dismal impression she had felt upon first looking at the house.

"Thank you," Daniel said wryly. "For what it cost the estate, and consequently us, it ought to be."

"We may be poor as field mice," Etta said, striving to be light in her tone, "but we have a very nice mouse hole in which to nest."

She must have succeeded, for Daniel laughed lightly, and then offered to give her a tour of the house. He took her around the rest of the ground floor of the three-story house, and then up to the highest floor, where a nursery and servants' quarters lay. Even these latter rooms suggested a graceful architectural style and richness of detail, all of which could have been foregone and still proven entirely comfortable had Daniel's father possessed an eye toward economy.

He saved the middle floor for the last part of their tour, bringing her lastly to the rooms they would share as husband and wife. These rooms consisted of an appealing sitting room in palest yellow and sea green, and connected to it, a bedchamber, charmingly decorated in cream and blue, with pink roses "blooming" delightfully in the matching carpet.

Etta admired the finely carved bedposts of the large bed she would this night share with her husband. She did not quite meet Daniel's eyes, even though she felt his gaze upon her, for she knew she would blush if she did. Their first night of love-making had been . . . well, awkward might naturally be the word, but the two nights since had proven a revelation. Etta had not quite perceived how it might be between man and woman, and was well aware by the lectures in chapel of how she ought to feel about her marital duty to her husband, but the truth of the matter was that she did not mind his presence in her bed, not at all. In point of fact, she thought she liked the activity there rather more than was good and proper, although Daniel laughed and told her he was not likely to complain that she did.

She moved away from the bed and its blush-producing associations, noticing an extra door leading left out of the room. She tried the knob, faintly surprised to find it locked.

"Where does this door lead?" she asked, and then she turned, for Daniel did not reply at once. "It is locked," she told him.

He did not move, but all the same he stiffened. "It is merely the second sitting room that branches off these chambers," he answered, the words brusque.

"But why is it locked?"

She could see he did not wish to answer, and for a moment she thought he might not. Instead, he sighed and shook his head, rather sadly she thought, even though his expression was more forbidding than forlorn.

"Henrietta," he said, putting out his hand to her. She took it, allowing him to lead her to a chair, and he sat in the one opposite. She looked at him expectantly, for it was not often that he called her by her full name.

He stared at her, a nerve jumping along his jawline. "We keep it closed off because my first wife died in that room," he told her flatly.

Etta put a hand to her breast, and for a moment was speechless. "Oh, Daniel!" she said at last. "I knew there had been an accident, but I did not realize it had occurred inside the house. I thought it must have been a riding or a carriage accident, or . . ." Her words faded away, and she glanced toward the locked door. A shiver coursed down her spine at the thought there had been a death in this house, her new home.

"Aileen. My first wife's name was Aileen," Daniel went on, and although his gaze no longer met Etta's, she could see that his brown-eyed gaze seemed darker than ever, as though shadows haunted his eyes as well as his words.

Then he did return his gaze to meet hers, his face taut with emotion. Was that grief? Or could that be annoyance?

"I should have told you about that room," he said, his words clipped. "I did not do so for the very simple reason I did not want to. I did not wish to put any manner of cloud over our wedding. I am sorry that even now we must discuss it, but it must be, and I would be done with the matter here and now." He took a breath and scowled. "We were married for a little over two years. She was an asthmatic. She had one of her spells, and she passed away, and I found her . . . in there."

Etta rose to her feet, not quite sure what aim she had in mind, except that she thought for a moment that she might flee the room. Perhaps it would clear a growing sense of unreality from her head if she went for a walk in the garden. . . .

Daniel stood suddenly and shot out a hand, catching up her own, halting her before she could move away. "This makes a second time you have received surprising news from my past," he said seriously.

His gaze was hooded, and she could believe it was made so by regret, by an expectation of rejection—and not unduly so. It would have been a kindness had he explained to her before bringing her into his home the nature of this Aileen's death. It would have been more in keeping with his usually gracious nature to prepare her to find that locked door.

But now the sight of his tensed body, the misgiving in his eyes, caused the shock to leave her abruptly. Instead of fleeing, she found she raised her other hand to cup the line of his jaw.

"But that is how we ought look at it, Daniel. As nothing more than uneasy news from the past," she said in return.

A light leapt in his eyes, and he nodded once against her cupping palm.

"Still, you ought to have told me, at least before we came into the house." Her hand fell away from his face, but she did not pull the other free of his grasp.

"I know I should have. What if a servant had said something first?"

"Exactly. I would not have enjoyed being shown up in my ignorance. But you *have* told me now," she conceded. She tilted her head at an angle and lifted a brow, and almost smiled. "Is there anything more I should know? Am I now to learn there are a score of children in the house for me to mother? Is the nursery above more immediately necessary than I imagined?"

"No children," he said firmly. He caught up her other hand, giving each of them a quick squeeze. "Can you forgive my reticence?"

Etta considered his shirtfront for several moments, then looked up at him once more. She nodded. "Of course I can."

He squeezed her hands again, pulling her closer, and offered her what could be described only as a relieved grin. "Etta!"

"After all, you *have* made it simpler for me to tell you about my five former husbands," she said, smiling in return.

"Five, eh? All of them infirm, I presume, for I know for a fact that none of them succeeded in the marriage bed before me," he teased.

"Daniel! Such talk!" Etta blushed, but she did not object when he swept her into his arms.

He kissed her soundly, then gave a quick nod toward the locked door. "That room should have been your sitting room, of course, my dear. But I would ask that you not use it, not now. Not for a while. Perhaps, in time, when we have had a chance to refurbish it, to change it. . . ." His request trailed away.

"Of course I will not use it. Not if it distresses you in any way. Later, as you say, perhaps, but I am content for now," Etta assured him.

"Thank you."

He kissed her again, several times, before excusing himself with a need to go to his study downstairs, stating he had business concerns to consider before luncheon was served. "Or before other matters of interest distract me," he said with a wink before slipping out the door.

Left to her own devices, Etta smiled to herself and circled the room again, trying to familiarize herself with her new surroundings, stopping last before the locked door once more. She considered the heavy oak paneling, the small black, empty keyhole, and realized she had never before encountered a secured lock on an interior door. The promise she had made to Daniel had been an entirely truthful one, but now she made one to herself: Her home must not contain locked doors.

She would not use the room until both she and Daniel were accustomed to being married, but eventually she must see that it was opened up. Death must be flushed from the room, from the house, chased out by sunlight and fresh air, and replaced with the bustle and joy of life.

"I will be happy here," Etta murmured to herself . . . and perhaps her comment was aimed, just a little, to the closed, locked door before her.

Three

Two hours later, Daniel and Etta sat at a tablecloth-draped card table in the front parlor, a late luncheon spread before them.

"Are you certain everything that came in the post while I was gone was placed in my desk drawer?" Daniel asked Mrs. Lawton, the housekeeper whose dark hair was now touched with highlights of gray, who had returned to the room to see how the meal progressed.

"Yes, my lord. Everything. I put every bit of the post there myself," the housekeeper assured him.

Daniel pushed a slice of beef about on his plate with his fork, but he made no effort to raise it to his lips.

"And Sean? Has he not yet returned for his luncheon?" Daniel next asked, seeking his brother, who lived also in the house.

The housekeeper shook her head. "Mr. Rifkin is of late increasingly quit of the house for lengthy periods, my lord."

Daniel grunted, not happily.

"Daniel, do please eat," Etta put in, even though her own meal sat neglected and cold before her. The day had been too filled with oddities to leave her now with any real appetite. First had been the drive that morning, followed by the odd sensation of wishing to recoil from the doorstep of her new home, only to lastly learn that the former wife had died within its walls. Small wonder she had little interest in her meal . . . so, perhaps, it was much the same for Daniel.

Mrs. Lawton stood silently by, awaiting any further questions or requests. The housekeeper was the last servant Etta had met, the fourth of the four retainers who remained as part of the household. Mrs. Lawton's hair might be graying, but Etta speculated the woman was no more than fifty. The woman must also be in good health, for Mrs. Lawton served in two capacities. With Roberta's help, she was cook as well as housekeeper. Indeed, unavoidably with a staff of but four, all the servants were committed to service beyond the usual confines of their employment.

To judge by Mrs. Lawton's pursed lips, Etta thought the housekeeper also noted the master's lack of appetite, and was not best pleased to have her culinary efforts shunned. Or perhaps it was the fact Daniel had brought home a new wife, unannounced, that had put that tight set to the woman's mouth. As would all good housekeepers, Mrs. Lawton might not have cared to be caught unprepared to receive a new mistress, and Etta could scarce blame her. She opened her mouth to offer the woman a compliment on how she had found the house to be in a clean and orderly state, but she was interrupted.

"Brother, I am home!" came a carefree cry from the entryway, causing the three occupants of the parlor to turn as one to see a well-dressed man framed in the doorway.

"Sean," Daniel identified the newcomer, although the man's face had already revealed his name to Etta. This Sean was not Daniel's double, but there was a marked familial resemblance, excepting Sean had very light hair bordering on blond, as opposed to Daniel's rich brown. Under the newcomer's left arm a crutch was lodged, and Etta could see after a moment's inspection that the man rested nearly all his weight on his right foot, the left suspended up off the floor.

Daniel stood, cordial if not smiling, and waved his brother into the room. "Come in, Sean. Luncheon has yet to be removed. You must join us."

"I will return with a plate for Mr. Rifkin." Mrs. Lawton excused herself, exiting on a curtsy.

"Us?" Sean asked, one eyebrow cocked as he settled his gaze on Etta.

"Of course, you do not know!" Daniel said, still standing. He looked down at his wife. "Etta, this is my younger brother, Sean. Sean, please meet my wife, Lady Healey—that is, Henrietta, although she prefers Etta."

Sean moved into the room, right foot first, his left leg cocked at the knee, the foot dangling uselessly. It must be the lower leg that did not function properly, she thought, for he still had control over the muscles of the upper leg.

He stopped beside Etta, and she caught the definite scent of spirits about him; he had been drinking.

"Your wife?" Sean asked of Daniel. He did not smile.

"Just so. We were married three days ago, in London."

"Truly?" Sean said, the question rhetorical and perhaps faintly impolite. His gaze was steady and intense, and lasted long enough that it caused Etta to blush.

"How do you do, Lady Healey?" he murmured belatedly, somehow making her new title sound inappropriate. Leaning on his crutch, he put his hand to his chest and contrived to make a surprisingly graceful half-bow.

Etta nodded and lifted her hand, and Sean took it in his own to execute an airy kiss there. Somehow he managed to convey a measure of haughtiness as he did so—or perhaps that was the result of the alcohol he had consumed.

His brother's misfortune was a tale Daniel had not kept from Etta, and so she knew that only a month after Corporal Sean Rifkin had bought his commission, a ricocheting bullet had done a great deal of damage to his left foot—and a surgeon's incompetence even more. Now the foot was all but useless. Unable to hold its owner's weight, it afflicted him with a dull but constant pain.

Daniel had made it obvious that although sorry for his brother's misfortune, he had little enough tolerance for Sean's subsequent fifteen months of bemoaning idleness.

"He would be best served to put his mind and his hands to

some manner of work, but he refuses all my offers," Daniel had told her. "Sean has no head for figures, but he would be a good man to oversee the tillage and crops, for he has a sense for when to plant and when to harvest. But he says there is no place in the fields for a one-legged man, even though I tell him much may be accomplished from horseback. He will not be persuaded."

Instead, Daniel's younger brother had turned to spirits to fill the empty hours, just as he had evidently done once more, and in the middle of the afternoon, no less!

Sean, redolent of the drink in which he presumably sought to hide from pain and injury, released Etta's hand and hopped back. He teetered for a moment before reestablishing his balance—a visual betrayal of his inebriated state.

Daniel then saw what Etta had already scented. "You are disguised again!" he accused Sean, but in the tired manner of one who expects little else.

"Disguised? After only three bottles of wine shared with my friends? I think not," Sean said, his voice steady and controlled, in fact so controlled it reflected the opposite was true. "Merely soaked enough to be able to tolerate, for the moment, my fate."

Daniel's brows drew together to form a scowl. "It behooves you to refrain from joining us at table," he told Sean.

The corner of Sean's mouth cocked up in a rather unpleasant little smile, and he deliberately lowered himself to a chair set before the card table. Daniel's jaw tightened as he leaned his knuckles against the table surface, but Sean ignored him to turn to Etta. "Must I leave?" he asked her in feigned guilelessness. "I am probably quite hungry, you know, if only I was not too *disguised* to know it, my dear Lady Healey."

Etta gave Daniel a quick glance that must have implied the toleration she thought might be best under the circumstances, for Daniel silently resumed his seat.

"Please, Mr. Rifkin," she said to Sean, maintaining a pleasant tone, "as we are now brother and sister, you must call me Etta."

"Etta," Sean repeated. He stared at her, long and hard, again. When he looked away, to her surprise she would almost have said there was a shadow of embarrassment in his eyes. "You must call me Sean, of course," he said, and if this had been the first moment between them, she thought perhaps she might have favored him, for the sarcastic edge the wine had given him was, for the moment, missing.

"Sean," she repeated with a nod and a small smile.

He gave her yet another of his long stares, not haughty and yet, although he scarcely moved a muscle in his face, the brief show of little-boy embarrassment evaporated, replaced by a hooded look.

"You have shown Lady—Etta the house, Daniel?" he asked his brother, the cockiness returning to his tone.

"Yes," Daniel said, pushing his plate away and reaching for his goblet of wine.

"And what did you think of our little castle, Etta?" Sean asked her.

"It is lovely," Etta replied just as Mrs. Lawton reentered the room, the housekeeping ring of keys at her waist jangling as she set a plate of sliced beef and gravy before Sean.

"Lovely?" Sean echoed. "I suppose it is. Except the wine cellar, of course. Is that not correct, Mrs. Lawton?" Sean asked, looking up from his seat at the housekeeper. "Tell Lady Healey how the servants avoid the wine cellar."

Mrs. Lawton's expression filled with reluctance, and perhaps a trace of trepidation as she reached to pull some of the side dishes close enough for Sean to be served. "Stuff and nonsense!" she declared.

"Come now, Mrs. Lawton," Sean coaxed. "You have heard the tales."

" 'Tis only that. Tales," the housekeeper replied, turning to Daniel. "Lord Healey," she said, ignoring Sean's devilish grin at her, "I have come to ask you about—" She cut herself short, glancing toward Etta. "Er, that is, I suppose I must address the new mistress, of course, for I need to discuss the menus for the next week. My lady, if you have a moment after supper?"

"Do you see, Etta?" Sean interrupted. "Even Mrs. Lawton fears to discuss the matter of the cellar, and I have never met a more rational lady than Mrs. Lawton."

Etta nodded her agreement to discuss the menus before turning her attention back to her new brother-in-law, and Mrs. Lawton muttered a thank-you and curtsied with a decided flounce before leaving the room again.

Sean was still amused, offering Etta an ingenuous stare. "But I can see by your expression that you were *not* shown the wine cellar!" he said. He turned to Daniel. "I presume you showed this dear lady the rest of the house, brother. But why neglect the cellar, I wonder, for how is the new mistress to manage the household if she does not know all there is to know of her estate?"

"You mention the cellar only in the hopes that a bottle or two might be brought up for your continuing consumption," Daniel countered. He rose brusquely, snatching up his glass and the half-emptied bottle before him, plunking them down before Sean. "Here, if that is your interest. You may have mine."

Sean gazed at the goblet, smiling slightly. "Do not think I would not."

"Oh, I do not doubt it, but you will take it to your room, Sean. You will confine your drunkenness to your chambers from now on."

"For the lady's sake," Sean said, rising from his seat without touching either the goblet or the bottle. "Of course. We cannot have the mistress of the house unhappy, can we? She must not know of brotherly drunkenness, or of eerie chambers—"

"Get out," Daniel said, his voice lowered, resembling something very near to a growl.

Sean, apparently unabashed, turned his attention again to Etta. "Do make him take you to the wine cellar, my dear. Personally, I believe our 'little problem' resides in the closed chamber above stairs. But you will want to judge for yourself."

Daniel's hand came down hard on his brother's shoulder, but if he meant to say anything, it was lost because Etta spoke before he could. "Little problem?" she echoed.

"Why, our ghost, of course," Sean said on a self-satisfied smile.

Four

"A ghost?" Etta cried, her gaze flying to meet Daniel's.

His jaw tightened, and he cast his brother a dark glance before he spoke. "Some of the servants claim to have seen a specter," he said, his skin growing ruddy.

"Servants, eh? What of the day *you* swore there was 'something' in your room?" Sean countered.

Daniel shook his head, but he did not deny his brother's claim.

To Etta, Sean explained, "He said there was a sudden swirl of cold air, and then he claimed he felt something pass, like when cloth brushes against your clothing—"

"It was nonsense then, and it remains nonsense yet," Daniel interrupted. He crossed to Etta, extending his hand to her. "Come! Let us go down to the wine cellar, most certainly! I will show you there is naught but the stone walls of an old chamber and some racks of wine there."

Sean lifted his eyebrows, looking not so secretly amused.

Etta placed her hand on Daniel's arm and rose to her feet. "Of course," she said, uncertain how to judge the brooding expression on his face. He had once asked if she believed there was more to this world than met the eye . . . but, then again, Daniel was no mere dreamer. His feet were planted in the soil; he would not be one to encourage fanciful tales.

As Daniel led Etta from the room, he said quietly, "You must not mind all Sean says, Etta. 'Tis the drink speaking, you realize, and he tends to repeat servants' gossip."

"Oh, yes!" Sean interjected, coming through the doorway on their heels. Daniel's mouth pursed in consternation at having been overheard. "Do believe I am merely drunk, Etta, if you can," Sean continued. "Do let us pretend everything is as it should be, and the younger son is merely made daft from wine." He spoke airily, but she caught a flash of anger in his eyes.

Etta found herself thinking that Sean had undeniably consumed too much alcohol, but there was in his gaze, too, something particularly lucid. If he had meant to drown his sorrows and his sense, he had not quite succeeded . . . something in his gaze gave Etta pause to wonder if Sean's words held more truth in them than Daniel might be willing to concede.

Daniel shook his head in disgust. "Sean, go and doze away the drink." To Etta he said, "Come," and did not await her permission before pulling her from the room.

He led her through the kitchens, past Roberta, who was scrubbing pans, and to the rear wall, in which resided a heavy oak door. The door was built into a wall of old gray stones, the surface of the mortar between them a powdery and dirty gray from great age. Daniel pushed open the door, revealing a steep staircase descending into gloom.

"We must both take candles," he informed her, handing her one already lit in its holder. He accepted a second light from the maid Roberta, whose expression Etta could not help but note was now somber as well as sullen. What a household!

"The cellar has no other light, no windows. Will uses a torch when he must go down, but I think we will do well enough with these."

Daniel led the way down the stairs, which in addition to being steep and narrow were also well worn with age.

"How old are these stairs?" Etta asked, tightly grasping her candle with one hand, lifting her skirts with the other.

"The entire cellar is over two hundred years old. Family history has it that the Rifkins were once Papists. Fearful of reprisals—whether from the Crown, the Church, or some other adversary, I could not say—I understand they built a house of thick and defensible stone, practically a fortress. This cellar is what remains of that abode." He stopped halfway down the stairs and lifted his candle. "Look back."

She turned, gazing back up at the open doorway above them.

"Do you see that iron support fixed into the wooden frame? And the other on the opposite side?" Daniel pointed toward each.

"I see them. They are intended to cradle a crossbar, are they not?"

"They are. But note that they are on *this* side of the door."

"Ah!" Etta said in dawning comprehension. "The crossbar would be used to keep the invaders *out,* while keeping the family *in* as they waited for the danger to disperse."

"Just so."

"It is faintly . . . ominous. The idea of locking oneself in, that is."

Daniel murmured an affirmative reply, and Etta assumed it was his breath that made her candle's flame leap and sway, although something very like a cool breeze touched the back of her neck. She kept moving, and the sensation dissipated, and she decided she had imagined it. This dank, light-swallowing chamber was the perfect breeding ground for fancies.

Still, Etta gave a nervous little laugh as they stepped down from the last stair to the compacted dirt floor of the cellar. "I daresay we ought to search for buried treasure down here."

"I have," Daniel stated.

Her gaze flew to his face, for he sounded rather serious, but even if his voice held little humor, she found a wistful smile pulling up one corner of his mouth.

"Unfortunately, I never found any," he told her with a mock sigh and a shrug.

"Yes, I can just imagine two little boys digging up their father's cellar floor," Etta said, peering about herself. "But how poorly our candles serve us! I vow I can scarce see more than six feet ahead of my toes. Is that a wine rack there?"

"It is." Daniel guided her to it, and once they were close,

she could see the rack's detailing, with its multiple slots of ornately carved and fitted wooden slats that held in place dozens of bottles, if not hundreds.

"Your papa liked his wine," she observed dryly.

"Well enough to have paid the vintner in full, so these bottles at least do not add to our debt. Given Sean, it is almost too poor a thing that the vintner had no reason to come reclaim his stock."

"You could always pour them out."

"If I must," Daniel agreed. "But why bother when he can always go drinking with his friends?" He apparently required no answer, for he put his hand on his hip, turning with the candle in a slow circle, then spreading out the hand in a questioning gesture. "Well then, what say you?" he asked. "Is Sean mistaken?" He gazed down at Etta, the flickering light from their candles bringing eerie shadows to play across his features. "Do you sense a ghost down here with us?"

She began to answer at once in the negative, only to pause and truly consider the question. There *was* something about this ancient, vast space. . . . Just to know its age was to feel an echo of other times, of other people in the chamber. It took no special gift to sense there had once been laughter here, and tears, and terrible fear as well. Once upon a time, a foreign force had raided the former house that had stood upon these stone walls, and the inhabitants had cowered in the dark, perhaps listening with trembling hearts to a pounding on the door, the door they had barred from the inside. Two hundred years of history crowded the space, pushing at her like the darkness pushed against the feeble light of their candles.

"A ghost?" she said at length, aware her husband quietly watched her features. She shook her head and put her free hand on his arm. "What are ghosts but the souls of those we once loved? Even if your house holds such ghosts, we will count them as friends and relatives, and abide with them. I cannot help but think if we are happy, that happiness will prove infectious, even among what spirits choose to reside here."

Daniel remained still, and perhaps it was the angle of the candlelight that made him appear remote. "You did not learn such sensibilities from any prayerbook," he said.

Etta lifted her chin, perhaps to echo the coolness in his stance, and she took her hand from his sleeve. "You know how we met. You know that some have called me fey," she said.

This time it was his turn to place a hand on her arm, and the spell of remoteness was broken by the action. "Etta," he said, sounding much more like the man she had married. "Forgive me! I am in point of fact relieved you do not . . . that you are the person you are. I cannot quite allow myself to believe in ghosts, but this house . . . you will find the servants believe that Aileen haunts it."

"Servants always believe such things—"

He interrupted her with a cutting gesture, clearly wishing to be sure she understood. "The truth is, curious things have happened, things that are not easily explained away. The servants . . . they say they have seen her, have seen a white, wispy shape in the corridors. They threaten to leave my employ. Many already have, and not just because they know they must wait on my good fortunes to ever be paid their back wages. Mrs. Lawton attempts to maintain rationality in the servants' quarters, but the truth is that you will hear odd tales, and it becomes a simple thing to begin to believe in the unbelievable. I am sometimes half convinced myself that a ghost exists."

Etta gazed around the room once more, searching the dark corners, listening for sounds that were not there, seeking to breathe in scents that did not exist. "Did you love your first wife?" she asked, turning to see his expression as he answered.

He hesitated, but he did not look away. She wondered at his hesitation—what did it signify? She could not say from the expression on his face, other than to know that he found the question to be disquieting.

"Yes," he said at length. "I loved her."

What answer had she wanted to hear? This was the one he ought to have given, the one Etta should want to hear, because it spoke well of the man that he had loved the woman he had taken to wife. It was mere selfishness that she knew a moment's disappointment that he had loved another before her. Etta shook her head once, casting away the unworthy sentiment.

"Then, even if she is here, she will not haunt you. Not if she was loved," Etta said firmly.

He continued to stare down at her, but after a long pause he nodded. "You may be fey," he said, perhaps smiling just a little, "but you are also wise."

Etta slipped her hand along his arm. "Come, Daniel. It is time to return above stairs."

Without debate he took her elbow and led her up the stone stairs, back into the afternoon light streaming through the kitchen windows. They blew out the candles, and she followed his lead as he brought her through the kitchen and front entry, and then up the stairs and to their chamber door.

She smiled shyly and laughed a little as he secured the door behind them. "When I said 'above stairs' I meant to go up only to the ground floor."

"I could have sworn you asked to be brought here," he said, smiling. He caught her in his arms, and while there remained a show of laughter in his eyes, there was also hunger in his touch.

" 'Tis broad daylight. What will the servants say?" She tried to reprove him, but even she heard the invitation in her voice.

He scooped her up and laid her on the bed, quickly lying so that a portion of his weight pressed her into the feather mattress, making escape impossible should she desire it—which she decidedly did not. Propping himself on one elbow, he looked down at her and grinned. "The servants will be wondering about ghosts, I have no doubt, for how else to explain the odd sounds coming from our room?"

"Daniel!" she scolded on a laugh even as she reached up to slip her arms around his neck and pull him to her, to see to it that his prediction came true.

* * *

Etta blushed as the maid settled a breakfast tray before her the next morning. Fortunately Roberta gave no overt sign of being aware why her mistress blushed, even though the maid set about gathering the supper dishes that had been ordered sent up, and which proved the master and mistress had never left their rooms once they had entered them the previous afternoon.

The dishes piled in her apron, Roberta turned back to the bed, where Etta nibbled on a triangle of toast. "I will be back shortly to help you dress, ma'am," she said, bobbing a curtsy.

"Very well, Roberta."

Etta could not miss the flash of . . . what? annoyance? that crossed the maid's face. She set down her toast. "Is something amiss?"

"It is . . . my name. Roberta. It is too grand, my lady."

"Too grand?" Etta echoed. She might have laughed if it were not for the serious expression on the maid's face.

"I been . . . I have been trained to be all that is proper in a lady's maid, ma'am," Roberta explained, and Etta became aware of what had niggled at her concerning the maid: Roberta spoke in accents above her station. Of course, that was it exactly! It was not a natural speech pattern for the girl; it was something learned in later life, not in infancy, for the girl was sometimes awkward about it.

"I see," Etta said, at a loss for a moment, but then she thought she understood. "Well, my goodness, of course you must resent having to serve as not only my lady's maid and the cook's assistant, but also as a parlormaid! If the work is too onerous, I can do my own hair, and I do not expect you to sew or repair my things—"

"Oh, no, ma'am," Roberta corrected her at once, the sullen expression for once erased. "I'm not complainin' about the work." Her careful tones began to slip in her agitation. "It's not workin' that I mind, ma'am. It's the name. It don't sound proper. I am not one to act above my station. 'Roberta' indeed! Like I was some kind of highborn lady! Me mum, she wanted me to have the ways of a queen—" The girl stopped speaking abruptly, and flushed scarlet. "It's not befitting for me," she added in a low mumble.

Etta lay back against the pillows, unsure how to respond to the extraordinary declaration. She had seen servants before who wished to rise *above* their lot in life, but never the reverse. "I see," she said neutrally.

Roberta looked to the floor. "Pardon me, ma'am. I put up these fits sometimes." She must have swallowed her agitation, for once again her words were carefully formed. "I should not have spoken." She made as if to dash from the room.

"Fiddle"—Etta stopped her with a word—"if you do not care for your name, then let us use something else. What of, oh, how would 'Robbie' suit . . . or is that too much a man's name?"

The maid looked up, all sullenness gone as she beamed a smile at Etta. "Oh, yes, ma'am! I mean, no. It'd be right enough for me. 'Robbie.' It would do, do you not think?"

Etta gazed at the girl, and then nodded. "In point of fact, I think it would."

"Robbie," the maid repeated, seemingly pleased.

"I should like to know if Lord Healey is about, if you would be so good as to find out before you return," Etta said as a dismissal.

"Yes, ma'am." The girl curtsied a third time, leaving the room with the smile yet lingering about her mouth.

"What a strange household!" Etta said aloud, thinking of Sean and his belief in ghosts, and now the maid who wished not to rise above herself.

Robbie returned after a few minutes and informed Etta that the master was in the study with his steward.

"I will not disturb them at their work," Etta decided as Robbie removed the tray. She swung her feet over the side of the high bed and slipped to the floor. "This seems a good time to take my first stroll in the gardens. My sprigged muslin and the blue cloak will serve, Robbie."

Dressed, complete with half-boots and gloves, Etta moved downstairs, leaving the house by way of the door leading off the music room. She moved down a gravel walk, which some distance ahead connected to a perpendicular gravel path, beyond which lay the large formal gardens belonging to the house. Here, though, in the house's shelter, lay a small flower garden on her left, and to her right an orangery, its glass panels steamy with morning condensation. She veered her steps to enter the orangery, at once struck by the moist heat as she closed the door behind her. To one side within stood lemon and orange trees, their rich green foliage framing growing fruit the size of walnuts, quite in defiance of the coolish early spring morning without. Their branches reached to the glass ceiling, while below them two long rows of boards set on trestles filled the rest of the room, providing waist-high platforms on which resided a multitude of potted plants.

Etta moved to the nearest trestle table, breathing in the heady scent of soil and foliage. There were late spring flowers already in full and glorious blossom, ready to be moved out to the gardens once the danger of frost was past: yellow daffodils, forget-me-nots, and bluebells, the last of which would probably best be contained in pots, Etta thought to herself, or else they would sweep through the garden in wild abandon. Too, there were plants with hints of the summer blooms yet to come: the exotic Oriental chrysanthemums that were now so sought in many a garden; roses of pink and red and white; and mignonette. The last would be very fragrant once it bloomed, and Etta smiled to see it, for her aunt had taught her the meaning of flowers.

"Never give your beloved the flower candytuft," she remembered Aunt Mildred stating firmly, "for it means 'indifference,' and that is never what you wish. Now, mignonette, on the other hand, means 'your qualities surpass your charms,' and if one's charms have been already praised, who could help but be flattered?" When the mignonette's fragrant buds opened, Etta would have to be sure to put a bouquet of them in the room she shared with Daniel.

There were sprigs of honeysuckle, hyssop, and jasmine already trailing out of their pots, seeking a trellis upon which to twine. In fact, there were quite a few twining plants—prominent among them the curious choice of the trumpet-shaped morning glory.

Etta frowned mildly, for there were several plants nurtured here that she would not have thought to see fostered for a household flower garden. She might choose the bluebells or the morning glory to cover a bank or to ornament some piece of woodland. They would be charming, blanketing those areas where a pretty plant run riot could enchant. But she would not choose them for the garden; there they would, without due and persistent care, instead engulf and smother. Perhaps that was the intent here; however, perhaps they were intended for some space other than the garden. Still, it seemed peculiar to give over to the orangery those plants that would thrive well enough in the open.

"Can I help yer, m'lady?" a deep male voice asked out of the silence, and Etta gasped and jumped. She looked up with startled eyes to see the orangery had a second door at its rear, one apparently with well-oiled hinges, for she had not heard the gardener, O'Brien, enter. He briefly touched the brim of his hat, the action serving only to point up his general air of impertinence. Whyever did Daniel keep the man on?

"I am merely familiarizing myself with the gardens," Etta replied, feeling her pulse beat in her throat.

If O'Brien saw he had startled her, he made no apology. He merely grunted an acknowledgment of her statement, nodded, then set about lifting the water bucket he carried, tipping a portion of its contents into the nearest pot. It seemed for all the world that he had dismissed her presence.

Etta began to speak, only to realize she had nothing to say to the man. What a sullen fellow! Indeed, the few servants they employed all seemed to have that brooding manner about them . . . Etta could not help but remember Sean insisted the servants feared a ghost lived in the house. Could it be a ghost, or even the mere dread of one, that left the servants with such a uniform ill humor?

"I shall leave you to your work," she said, feeling that as the mistress of the house she ought to say something. When Mr. O'Brien did not even look up, Etta turned and slipped out the door.

It was only four steps to cross the gravel path and move into the pretty spring flowers of the garden there. As she willed her pulse to steady, Etta observed again that the garden was not a vast patch, being just large enough to informally supply some flowers for the household. She noted it was also in need of upkeep, for the plants required thinning, and more than a handful of weeds had crept in among the flowers.

This little patch was, she thought with sudden certainty, a private garden planted by or for an individual—and it was no stretch of credulity to presume the individual would have been, of course, the former Lady Healey. Aileen had been her name. This had surely been Aileen's garden.

In keeping up the formal gardens, Mr. O'Brien certainly had more than enough work to occupy him. No wonder this little private patch was uncared for. Still, it seemed odd that no one attempted any upkeep on this with it so close to the house.

Etta moved among the flowers, unsettled by the signs of neglect—it could almost be imagined that no one had cared enough for the former mistress to maintain her garden. . . .

Or could it be that no one had dared to touch it? Had Daniel ordered it left be?

Etta shook off the thought, thinking it did not sound like the man she had married. Daniel might have ordered it dug up, but not left purposefully untended. Perhaps it had merely been forgot, as things often were in a household lacking a woman's touch.

New growth reached up to brush Etta's skirts, last year's brown and untrimmed stems and leaves rustling and crunching under her feet. She touched the violet face of a pasque flower, and stooped to pluck a cone-shaped purple hyacinth, recalling that the hyacinth represented sorrow. For that matter, the pasque flower was said to mean sickness. And here was pinkish-purple bindweed . . . which Aunt Mildred had warned meant uncertainty. . . .

Standing at the little garden's center, Etta rotated slowly, taking in each plant with a dawning dismay. Every one, every single blossom in the garden, had the misfortune to carry a negative connotation. Here was a yellow pink whose ruffled, many-layered petals had been "rewarded" by romantical poets with the ill luck of meaning disdain. And there was scabious, which bore the interpretation of unfortunate love. And here lavender, yoked with the meaning distrust. Insincerity was the message given by the tall, budding spears of foxglove. Even the dahlias, which would soon produce spiky-petaled extravagant blooms, stood for instability. There was nothing here, not a single bud that gardening lore had designated as a symbol of love or peace or hope.

Etta pressed shaking hands to her face, belatedly reminding herself to breathe, and wondered *could it be coincidental?* Had Aileen, the first wife, unwittingly made such an unfortunate selection? There was not a single rose or a chrysanthemum, so favored, so likely, so symbolic of love and affection, among the lot. While it was true some people did not know the flowers' meanings, or knew only a few, still . . .

Or perhaps, Etta thought, feeling the blood leave her face, perhaps Aileen had known exactly. Perhaps Aileen had chosen these flowers most deliberately, meaning to leave behind a message.

Distrust, instability, sorrow, unfortunate love.

Etta turned and fled the little garden.

Five

Etta stood in the doorway of her chamber, staring at the maid, Robbie, as the girl arranged a bowl of flowers.

The maid turned to her, not smiling, although Etta thought perhaps the girl's expression was less sour than before. However, at Etta's stare, the maid reverted to her former long face. "Can I help your ladyship?" she asked in careful, defensive tones.

Etta crossed into the room, divesting herself of her cloak, which she handed to the maid. Etta then reached out, touching the trailing scarlet finger of a love-lies-bleeding, a forced-before-summer blossom taken from the orangery. It was the flower of unfading love, of immortality. "Did you cut these?" she asked Robbie, suppressing a shiver.

"No, ma'am. I just arranged them. I have been told I can arrange any flowers what have . . . that have been cut for the day. Is that no longer acceptable, ma'am?" Robbie asked, looking as though she expected a scold.

Etta trailed a finger down the long, fuzzy-appearing blossom again. "It is perfectly acceptable," Etta assured the girl, and then asked, "But tell me, Robbie, who cuts the flowers?"

"I do, sometimes, when I'm told to. Mrs. Lawton does often enough, and Mr. O'Brien will bring in flowers and greens, whatever needs trimming. He sometimes has Will help him. And even m'lord's been known to cut a posy for his wife . . . the other wife. . . ." Robbie's voice faded away awkwardly, as it obviously occurred to her that she may have committed a faux pas.

"It is all right, Robbie. I do not mind hearing of Lord Healey's first wife. In point of fact, I should like to know if that is her garden just outside the music room?"

"It was, ma'am."

Perhaps Etta had been foolish to ascribe too much meaning to the chosen flowers of the garden patch, but there was something in the narrowing of the maid's eyes that made her withhold judgment yet. "Why does no one tend it?"

The maid looked to the bowl of flowers and shrugged, one hand nervously reaching to rearrange a drooping scarlet tassel.

"Robbie?" Etta questioned. She watched as the maid bit her lip in reluctance to answer. "Has Lord Healey said to leave the little garden be?"

Robbie shook her head and mumbled, "No, ma'am."

"Then does the matter have something to do with the ghost?"

Robbie flushed as red as the flowers, and at Etta's steady stare gave a hesitant nod. "I'm not supposed to speak of that," she whispered. "The master has ordered it so."

"And now the mistress is ordering otherwise. Go on, Robbie."

The maid shuffled her feet, but her resistance was at an end. "Mrs. Lawton says there're no such thing as ghosts, but Will, he seen it . . . her one day, there in that garden." As before, when challenged by misgivings, Robbie reverted to a more rustic pattern of speech. "Will said he woulda thought she were real and alive again, she were that easy to see, standing there all sad-like one minute, and disappeared the next! The master, he says it's all folly, brought on by bereavement, but why's Will got any reason to grieve the mistress? . . . that is, the other one. The first wife." Robbie blushed anew.

"Was she a good mistress, or less so?" Etta asked, watching the girl's face closely.

"I weren't here, ma'am. I only know what I learnt since I

come here, but they say she was kind enough. She were sickly though. She weren't allowed to dance or ride, nor nothing like that. She'd get to coughing and gasping something awful-like, Will says. But she weren't hard in her ways, and they was sad to see her die . . . all alone, like she done."

"I see," Etta said, faintly surprised to learn the first wife had not been thought ill of by the servants. From their general surliness, she had half formed the idea that the first Lady Healey must have been a termagant. That would have been more in keeping with the notion of a haunting too: the evil wife who would not leave the scene of her reign of terror, not even in death. But a kind woman of poor health . . . that was more difficult to reconcile with brooding servants and strange claims of spectral sightings.

Perhaps it was Sean, a soldier wounded in more than body, who stirred up such morose fairy tales. Perhaps, along with drink, such tattle to the servants was how he kept himself entertained?

Either way, it was time she brought such talk to an end. If the ghost were a mere tall tale, then a program of calm assurance would turn things about; and if the ghost were real, then how better to begin to exorcise her lingering spirit than by setting her garden to rights?

"My cloak, Robbie," Etta said.

"You're going out again, ma'am?" Robbie questioned, moving to fetch the cloak from the wardrobe where she had hung it only a few minutes before.

"I am indeed. To speak to Mr. O'Brien."

Robbie gave her a dubious glance, but she said nothing as she helped Etta don the cloak.

Etta found O'Brien still hauling water to the many potted plants in the orangery. He glanced up when Etta entered, and although he did not deign to speak, he reached up and tugged at the brim of his hat, as usual, in acknowledgment.

"Mr. O'Brien," she ordered, "come with me." Etta did not

give him time to either offer a response or give a show of ignoring her, but turned at once, back out the hothouse door.

Somewhat to her surprise, he followed, joining her in the little garden.

"Yes, ma'am?" he asked, and he did not even sound surly for once.

"I want you to begin tending this garden."

He pursed his lips and shook his head. "Beggin' your pardon, but no, m'lady. 'Tis haunted, and I'll have naught to do with tending the flowers of a dead woman."

Etta stared. "You will, because it is your job to tend any garden I tell you to tend."

"It is, until such time as I choose to leave your employ."

Etta began to say it seemed to her he had just made that choice, but then she hesitated. Daniel had already informed her that the servants were nervous and edgy, and if one of their number should depart, it could start a tide that would leave the household without benefit of its already meager staff of servants.

"Come now," she said, attempting to sound conciliatory, "you do not truly believe there is a ghost, do you?" She folded her hands before her calmly, but she could not quite keep from putting back her shoulders.

"I do, Missus, and so do you," he answered, and he surprised her by lifting one corner of his mouth in something resembling a smile. "I kin see it in yer eyes, m'lady. Yer must have a bit o' Irish blood in yer, to be sure. There's a way of seeing things that some people have, and my people were among them. I'm thinking someone passed the gift on to you, whether you admit it or no."

Etta was not as astonished by his words as most anyone else would have been. It was not the first time she had met another who, with scarce a word spoken between them, had been so bold as to state they saw something unique beneath her surface. Perhaps Daniel even possessed some measure of such a gift, to judge by the swiftness of his courtship and their marriage, if for no other reason. Etta had no gift herself for seeing "the touch" in others; her predilection was revealed through her art, through the sweep of a charcoal stick on paper, but she believed others possessed such a talent. She might be what mankind chose to call fey, and O'Brien might be touched in one way or the other himself, but neither case would change the fact that she would be mistress here.

"I will not admit it, for I am not one bit Irish, although my great-grandmama was Welsh, if you must know. But my question to you is, have you seen this supposed ghost?" Etta challenged.

He shook his head. "No, I never seen her, but she's here a'right. I kin feel her about the place, watchin'-like."

"That's as may be," she told him, "but it is not to the point. Ghost or no, I will have things as I wish, and I wish for this garden to be tended."

O'Brien considered her over a long silence, then surprised her anew by grinning, the gesture softening his features to the point where she began to think that he had kept his job this long by making a point of smiling for the master. The gesture certainly went a long way toward making Etta put aside for a moment or two that his demeanor to date had been nothing more than gruff and scarcely hidden rudeness.

"I can only believe you will, m'lady." He shook his head and sobered. "And I'll be obliged to help you in all other ways but to the point of growing flowers here. No, Missus. That's one thing I will not do. I would, however, tear it all up if'n that be yer wish?"

Etta bit back the instant "no" that rose to her lips. She could tend the garden herself, of course, but in truth, even standing among so many blooms with such unrelenting and unfavorable significance for a few moments had caused the skin along her arms to raise in gooseflesh.

"Yes," she said, favoring the answer even as she uttered it. "Yes, let us be done with this patch. If I wish to have it developed later, there are plenty of starts in the orangery from which to choose."

All of which, she noted in a mental review of what she had seen there, were perfectly acceptable. Forget-me-nots for true love, and morning glory for affection . . . yes, those were flowers that might chase a ghost from this little patch of earth, flowers that would not give her gooseflesh. Roses, one day she would plant roses here. But for now it was enough that O'Brien had agreed to pull up the strange collection of innocent and lovely blooms that no one in the household cared to tend or bring into the house.

"She were barren, that other one," O'Brien said, cutting into Etta's thoughts. He bent to begin pulling at the nodding pinkish heads of some bindweed, jerking them so the roots came free of the soil.

"I beg your pardon?" she asked, frowning in confusion.

"That first wife o' the master's. She were barren. They were married two years, and never a babe nor hope o' one. He said it were right enough that she never got with child, as her health grew worse, but babes is what the master needs. Sons. That's what a man lives for, sure enough."

He stood up straight, glancing around with a scowl as he shook off a shiver. "Unhappy place, this patch. She don't like me in her garden, that's what I think." Still, he bent back to the task at hand. "She knows I thought she weren't much in the way of a wife. Pretty and such, but never able to dance much nor otherwise do her duty by the master. Her ghost knows I think he's well rid o' her. Just as we'll be well rid o' this garden now, won't we?"

He glanced up at Etta, his flashed grin seeming out of keeping with this talk of death and ghosts. Etta did her best to repress a sudden shudder by pressing a hand just below her throat.

"You've any brothers, Missus?" he asked.

"No."

"No sisters neither?"

She shook her head.

"Well, that don't always mean naught. You'll give the master sons, eh?" he said, and then he began to whistle, the merry tune in contrast to his task, to the way his hands tugged and ripped the unfortunate flowers from their beds.

Etta turned, chiding herself for giving in to the desire for quickened steps, only lowering her hand from her throat once she had closed the music room door between herself and the little garden.

He's well rid o' her, O'Brien had said. If the first wife had not been exactly reviled, neither had she been adored, certainly not universally. One could even say O'Brien was gratified Aileen was dead. He had deemed her useless to the master. Where had O'Brien been when the lady of the house lay dying? Did anyone know his whereabouts at the time? Had anyone inquired?

Despite the relative mildness of the weather, Etta shivered. How had Aileen died? From her asthma, yes, but how exactly? Why had this attack been worse than any other, enough to kill her?

Who had found the body? O'Brien? No, she remembered now, the first to find Aileen had been . . . Daniel.

Etta shivered again, and shook her head, refusing the instantaneous thought that followed: that if Aileen's death had been anything other than nature's cruel twist, the first to find the body must be even more suspect than a surly, disapproving gardener. O'Brien stood a far greater chance of being noted as out of place in the upper chambers of the house, but not so the master, Daniel!

"No," Etta said, and then gave a tight little laugh. What an absurd thought that Daniel could—no, of course not! She might not have known him long, she might not be able to say what his favorite drink was, or give the names of pets he'd had in the past, but to think he could . . . No man was such an actor as could hide such maliciousness, not from that part of Etta that sensed more than her eyes could see. Daniel's first wife had died a natural death . . . and even if she had not, Daniel could not be in any way responsible.

"How far away your gaze is, my dearest Etta."

Etta gasped, and looked up from where her gaze had been fixed on the carpet, recognizing Daniel's voice even before she saw him.

He moved into the room, extending his hand toward her. "Have I caught you coming in or going out?"

"Coming in," Etta answered, lifting her hand to meet his, the movement slow. If she were inclined to fancifulness, she might have said it was as if the weight of her thoughts had increased the pull of gravity on her motions. However, despite her fey nature (or perhaps because of it), Etta did not consider herself a woman given over to foolish fancies. The simple act of touching her cool hand to his warm one, of glancing into his deep brown eyes, was enough to make her silently admonish herself for thinking the impossible, even for a moment.

After all, as the poets said, guilt lay in a man's soul, and they rightly further pointed out that the eyes were a window to that soul. Etta had looked into a number of gazes and seen the guilt residing there, but either no guilt rested in Daniel's gaze today—or else he was a man utterly without conscience.

That she could not, would not, believe, not without firm evidence to the contrary. Of which she had none, nor any reason to seek it, she told herself.

"I am sorry I was occupied earlier this morning." Daniel gathered up her hand and pressed her fingers to his lips. "There is quite a bit of business to be seen to each day. Vulgar to speak of such matters, I know, but it must be done, even if it causes me to fail at this business of being a newlywed."

"You are quick to condemn yourself," she said, liking both the apology—unnecessary though it was—and the humbling nature of his words. Silly, silly girl, to doubt him even for a moment. For that matter, silly to doubt her own impressions of the man. "But I do not consider that you have failed. Only see, you have left your important business to seek me out. Or do I flatter myself?"

He laughed. "Only a little. Mr. Emmett has set me free for the time being."

"Mr. Emmett?"

"He is my bailiff. He lives close in to the heart of the city, considering a morning walk through Bath's market to be a daily essential in conducting business. I have every reason to agree with that sensible suggestion, as he is a man of sound advice and level head. Since he does not make his home here with us, that is why you have yet to meet him."

"I am sure I will be pleased to make his acquaintance, even though his presence means he keeps you from me sometimes," Etta said on a pretended pout.

"Ah, but not at present," Daniel pointed out, raising her other hand to kiss those fingers as well. His gaze grew warm. "In point of fact," he growled against her fingers, "I do not expect to see him again until after luncheon."

Etta felt a blush rise into her cheeks even as she gave in to the gentle pressure of Daniel's hands, swaying toward him. Perhaps, as the preachers said, it was wrong for a wife to desire her husband the way Etta did, but it was not any preachers' sermons that filled her thoughts now.

"It would seem I am at loose ends," he said, his arms slipping around her waist, pulling her closer yet. "You have already viewed the house, the cellar, and now the gardens. What does that leave? I cannot think of a thing. However shall we pass the time until luncheon?"

"That depends on whether or not you wish to further shock the servants," Etta said. Her voice was pitched low, but she boldly met his heated gaze.

"I believe that shocking the servants occasionally is the very thing," he said. He pulled her close for a kiss, both hands sliding down and over her backside, where he gently squeezed. Etta gave a surprised squeal, which quickly turned into a murmur of appreciation.

"How naughty you are, sir!" Etta said with a giggle against his lips.

"Not as naughty as I intend to be," he assured her, reaching for her hand to pull her toward the stairs.

Six

"So that is Aileen," Etta said. She leaned her elbow on the desk before her, resting her chin in the palm of her hand as she gazed up at the portrait hanging behind Daniel. The late afternoon light from the windows fell across the painting of the lady's comely face, revealing that Daniel's first wife had been something close to a beauty.

Daniel pivoted his head to briefly glance at the portrait. "Yes," he said, but his attention was really given over to Mr. Emmett, who had taken a step back in preparation of departing the room. "You will let me know tomorrow morning whether or not Mr. Damson means to sell that seed drill of his, will you not?"

"Aye, that I will," Mr. Emmett said on a nod. "I can repair it, my lord, or I'm not worth me salt."

"I am confident you can, Mr. Emmett," Daniel said, smiling slightly as he nodded a dismissal, at which Mr. Emmett nodded to Etta and departed.

Etta had come downstairs early, even before the warning bell that preannounced dinner, and joined her husband and the bailiff in his study. Introductions were made, and Mr. Emmett did not seem to take it amiss that the master's lady was to join them while they yet conducted business. She sketched scenes of ripe fields, of barley bending in the wind, while she listened to them talk of Squire Henley's new breeding cows. She had smiled to herself, not surprised, when the subject shifted to the projected price for barley, for she was used to her drawings connecting to the events of her life.

Having grown tired of her own efforts, she had looked up again at the painting of the woman behind Daniel's desk. At leisure to study it, Etta had seen at once by the painted lady's modish clothing that this must be a recent portrait. Simple logic had then supplied that this must be a portrait of Aileen, for what other female had there been to sit for a painting in recent years? Daniel's mama, by name Francine, had been ten years passed away.

This lady—really, not much more than a girl—was dressed in a fashion that could have fitted nicely into Etta's own wardrobe. The painted woman's hair was a soft blond, and her gown was of white silk—a mistake with that wan, pale complexion, although it did show off the fiery red of her jewels to a nicety. The girl might have been an Incomparable were it not for eyes set a little too close and a chin that was a shade too pointy. Still, she was handsome, and would have been fetching if the artist had managed to find a spark beneath her too-pale complexion. She—or the art—lacked . . . luminosity, that was the word. Something in her expression, or perhaps it was her eyes, seemed weary, or vexed. . . .

But why did her portrait hang here all by itself? Why not in the hall with the others, Etta wondered.

So she asked Daniel. "Why do you keep Aileen's portrait here?"

He turned in his seat to glance up at the framed painting once more, his expression unreadable.

"Mrs. Lawton had it brought here shortly after . . . after the services. I had yet to hire Mr. Emmett then, and I did not much use the study, so I always supposed she had it moved to where I would not have to gaze upon it very often. And I still do not, given that my desk faces away." He shrugged, but there must have been something in Etta's expression, for he added, "Mrs. Lawton meant to spare my feelings, I feel sure."

"Were you—" she started to ask, wanting to know if he had

been very upset at Aileen's death, but that was an unkind question. Even though Etta might not be faulted for a curiosity concerning the previous marriage he'd made, she would not ask such a sensitive question so baldly. Instead, she substituted, "Were you intending to move the painting again? I should not mind, of course, to have it back among the other portraits. . . ." She allowed her voice to trail away, for even to her own ears the statement was not completely free of a jealous tone.

Daniel looked away from the painting, directly at Etta. He did not blink, and in fact could almost be said to be studying her features. "Perhaps," he said after a length, and then he stood, tugging his waistcoat into place.

There was a disturbance at the open door, and Etta turned to see Sean had joined them, a half-full glass of spirits in one hand, his crutch in the other.

"Those rubies ought to have been yours, I suppose," he said sourly toward Etta.

She frowned, then looked to where he indicated by pointing with his forefinger. As she had noted before, there, adorning the painted Aileen's ears and throat, glowed an ornate set of red jewels set in finely wrought gold.

Sean worked his way into the room slowly, the liquid in his glass swaying with each move. He turned his direct gaze toward Daniel, his expression becoming as sour as his tone. "I am glad I insisted the rubies must go to the grave with Aileen, although I admit at the time it was not to keep them from going to your next wife," he said nastily.

Daniel scowled. "You are drunk, Sean," he said. It was not an accusation but rather merely an observation, surprising Etta a little with its edge of tolerance.

"Not nearly enough so," Sean said, and Etta was surprised again, for there was a hint of amusement in Sean's voice. He appeared to be drunk, to her eyes anyway, but something in his manner implied he might just be less inebriated than first appearances implied. Perhaps Daniel sensed that too, for he did not ask his brother to do the polite thing and leave.

Sean turned once more toward Etta with an abruptness that made him teeter for a moment before he recaptured his one-footed balance.

"I made him bury her with the rubies," he said more loudly than the distance between them warranted. His eyes flashed, and Etta wondered for a moment if it would take more than mere drink to put such a flash of animosity in his eyes.

"It was a poor enough thing that he put her in the ground in a plain pine box." His voice rose, and now Etta could only suppose he was indeed drunk . . . or mad. "I could not let him bury her without some show of dignity. She, Lady Healey, and yet all she rated for her funeral was a best dress and an ugly box in a hole?" His words ended on a note of incredulity.

"She has a gravestone too," Daniel interjected quietly.

Sean spun to face him, his drink sloshing wildly, his crutch knocking against the furniture. "Oh, yes, her gravestone," he snapped. "But is it made of marble? No, of course not. It's just a dirty old piece of granite dug from our fields. Dug up from the fields! I swear, if you had possessed any skill for it, you would have chipped the letters upon it yourself. To save *money,*" Sean snarled.

Daniel stared at his brother, any temper revealed only by the twitching of a muscle along his jaw. He took a deep breath. "Yes," he agreed, once again quietly. "I would have. To save money, even as you say, Sean. Or would you have rather I sold the rubies?" He spoke to his brother, but it was to Etta that he glanced, and then away again.

Sean made no answer, his mouth working as though he struggled to find words offensive enough to satisfy some burning resentment in him.

"What else did I have to sell to give her a prettier box in which to rest?" Daniel asked with quiet logic.

Sean put aside his glass and closed his eyes. He sighed, in the way of men who are in constant discomfort, and at length he settled back against the crutch, seeming to shrink before their gazes. When he opened his eyes again, his anger was clearly spent.

Daniel made a motion with his hand as though to wipe away their words, meeting no one's gaze. "I cannot see why we must revisit the subject of the rubies again and again. I agreed, and they are buried and gone, and so should the matter be. Etta, I hope you know, if I had thought . . . a woman ought to have some jewelry. I would have kept them—"

"I would not have wanted them," Etta declared at once, and meant it. Even had she not heard the tale before, even if she had not known the discord that surrounded them, she knew she would not have kept them. If nothing else, she would have offered any jewels to Daniel, that he might sell them and better help the estate. What good were jewels when there was no food in the larder? What good was it to adorn herself in gems when she would far rather be surrounded by a happy, contented family?

She turned back to the portrait, and perhaps it was a play of the late afternoon light, but the rubies glowed a bright red, causing Etta to catch her breath. The gems were a color too reminiscent of freshly spilled blood, the thought causing a shiver to crawl up her spine. There was something . . . not right about those rubies; the old familiar tingling across her shoulders, that fey sense that came at the oddest moments, flared to life once more. She shivered again, and the sensation was gone, if not the knowledge.

No, she would not have kept those rubies, and she was only too glad they were buried. She did not care why Daniel had agreed to such an odd, foolish concession in light of his financial difficulties; the only misfortune in the matter was that the grand gesture had evidently brought Sean no satisfaction.

Though, why Sean should care what trappings of splendor— or lack of it—had adorned his sister-in-law when she had been lain to rest was a puzzle, in a day already filled with a series of small puzzles. Perhaps that final show of opulence was important to his sense of ceremony? Etta sighed, and was glad when her brother-in-law thumped slowly and without further comment from the room.

Daniel stood, two bright spots of color on his cheeks. He closed the accounts book on the desk before him a little more forcefully than was necessary.

"Well, that was unpleasant! I hope he did not upset you unduly. I am afraid Sean feels I allowed Aileen to . . . fade away," he said, but then he gave a weak smile. "In case you could not tell that for yourself."

"It is the drink talking."

"I daresay so. You are good to understand that." He cast Etta another half-smile, and just then the dinner bell rang.

"Ah!" he declared with the kind of brusque charm meant to gloss over an awkward moment. "It seems I am running behind schedule. I shall have to make haste if I am to be changed into my dinner clothes in the next ten minutes," he said. "Mrs. Lawton does not take it kindly when I am late to table."

"I will assist you," Etta offered at once.

Daniel cocked an eyebrow at her. "Be careful, Etta," he said, this time with a fuller, more honest smile. "When once again I can afford the services of a valet, I may not be willing to surrender your tender services. I rather fancy having your touch about my person as I ready myself. I cannot imagine why more husbands do not enlist the aid of their lovely wives when it comes to such tasks as tying a proper cravat." He moved around the desk and offered her his arm.

"Because most wives are too clever to be caught at any task that might lead to having to pull off muddy boots, or spend an hour polishing them to the highest shine. Which, by the way, *I* refuse to do."

He laughed, and the odd spell of Sean's anger was broken, at least for the moment.

Etta was reminded of the bloodred rubies that night as they lay in bed. Daniel was restless, and when he propped his arm behind his head to stare up at the bed's canopy and began speaking, she encouraged him to go on by offering small murmurs.

"You would have had other jewels, Etta," Daniel told her. "They were not very grand, but there were some nice pieces, ones that would not have shamed you to wear."

"But you sold them. . . ."

"I sold the best pieces, yes. But these were simple brooches, and a few hair combs. They sported real gems, if nothing wondrous. They ought to have been yours—"

"Hush. I do not care about such things," she soothed. "I am glad you sold them, if it helped—"

"But I did not! I kept some of Mama's things as mementos, as any son might, even though I never intended to marry again." He turned toward her, draping an arm over her waist, his eyes dark pools in his face, scarcely illuminated by the glow of the fire crackling in the fireplace. "But half have gone missing, and the other half are lost."

Etta laughed lightly. "And what is the difference between missing and lost?"

"Let me explain. I believe some of the servants I had to dismiss took some of the smaller pieces as recompense for losing their positions. The items disappeared over time, as the people were let go. I thought I was clever about moving them, but items kept going missing. Finally, one day I'd had enough, and I asked Aileen to hide the rest, thankfully the better pieces. This was shortly before she died. I am afraid she did as I asked, and then she passed on without revealing the hiding spot to me. To that moment it had never occurred to me that both of us ought to know their location. . . . We have looked, of course, but found nothing. I would swear they are nowhere in the house, for we searched every corner. They are no doubt buried in a field somewhere, never to be seen again."

"Buried treasure?" Etta asked, but then she sobered, for Daniel did not smile in return. And a thought, a precious thought, occurred to her: He did not know where his mama's jewels were? What financially strapped man would have had a hand in his wife's death without first finding out such an important detail from her? Certainly no one as clever as Daniel, who was a good man . . . a man who deserved a wife who could not imagine such diabolical thoughts about him. What manner of woman was she, Etta scolded herself, to let such thoughts creep into her mind even as she shared a bed with the object of her deliberations?

"Are you still having difficulties with things being taken?" she asked, glad he either did not note or mistook the humbled tone of her voice for a more intimate emotion.

He shook his head against the pillow. "Although we had spoons and such go missing now and again, which could just as easily have gone accidentally into the dustbins, Mrs. Lawton has not reported anything missing in some months."

Etta wondered for a moment about a pair of jet earrings of her own that she had not seen since arriving there, but decided they had no doubt been merely lost in the move.

"I consider the problem at an end," Daniel went on. "I merely wanted to explain why I have nothing, no bridal gift, to pass along to you."

"Oh, Daniel, what do jewels and such matter? Is it not enough that we found each other? That I have you?" she asked, meaning every word. She draped her arm across his bare shoulder, spreading her hand on his back to urge him closer.

"Many another woman would not think so," he answered, but he gave in to the pressure on his back, pressing his length to hers as he gathered her close.

"Many another woman does not understand there is more than one kind of jewel," she replied.

He grinned, and ran his hands up her legs, causing her nightrail to bunch up around her waist. "Why, my dear, I think you might be right. I can think of something right now that might bring a squeal of delight from those lovely lips of yours, and even though it is quite hard, it is not a gem."

She quirked an eyebrow at him, and then laughed throatily.

If she had thought to disagree, the words were lost once his lips and hands began to move upon her. It seemed, she thought with a final laugh to herself before her thoughts were gone to the moment, there was one other thing that could be as precious as gems when applied at the right moment: silence, or, at least, a lack of polite conversation.

Seven

"You have dark circles under your eyes," Mrs. Lawton noted the next afternoon, causing Etta to lower her face to hide a blush. "Did you not sleep well last night, my lady? This bed-chamber can be dreadfully drafty, and that could lead to a rough night. Should I see to having Will come in and reglaze some of the windows? I know the former Lady Healey used to com-plain of a draft if she stitched by the windows in here."

Etta restrained from frowning down at the stitchery she was working on, even though the thought of a former Lady Healey sitting in this room—the room Etta shared with Daniel—made her feel like frowning. It was petty of her, she knew, so instead she sighed and resigned herself to the fact that at least for some years there would be many an occasion when Aileen's former presence would be remarked upon.

"Or are you just one of those who does not sleep well, my lady?" Mrs. Lawton went on. "Do you care to take laudanum of a night? Shall I send to the apothecary for some?"

"Laudanum!" Etta cried, and now instead of frowning she gave a partial laugh. She could explain she would look more refreshed of a morning if her husband ever allowed her to sleep, but she refrained. "No, thank you, Mrs. Lawton. I am just get-ting used to being in a new house. I shall adjust shortly, I feel sure."

"Ah!" Mrs. Lawton said, nodding. "I daresay you are quite right. Are you ready for a luncheon tray?"

"Indeed I am," Etta said, putting aside the stitchery. She

wondered for a moment if her talent with thread and needle matched or perhaps even exceeded those of Aileen, then pushed the thought aside as petty. She had been told the servants whispered that the halls of this house were haunted by the ghost of Aileen—and there was a ghost, all right, even if it was not one that materialized in any physical sense. The specter of Daniel's first wife might be no more than a memory, but memories had a life of their own. The former Lady Healey would be a resident of this house for years to come through recollection and association—but that did not mean Etta had to fear her. Aileen had been someone Daniel had married and loved, and now he loved Etta. It was no more or less than that, and Etta would be well served to remember that fact.

When Robbie arrived bearing the tray Mrs. Lawton had arranged, Etta directed the girl to deliver it to the music room. "I wish to look out at the gardens," Etta said to the unspoken question in Robbie's eyes.

"But the patch by the house is all torn up, or near all. Mr. O'Brien's been working it steady-like," Robbie protested. "It won't be much of a view, ma'am."

"Yes, I know," Etta replied with a small smile. "I wish to consider what would be best planted there. Roses perhaps."

"Oh, of course, ma'am," Robbie said, and there was something in her expression that reflected approval of the idea.

As they moved to the music room, they encountered Sean. He eyed the tray, winced, and asked, "Food? So early in the day?"

"Indeed. It is a little habit of mine to take a meal sometime around the noon hour," Etta replied crisply. To her surprise, Sean's mouth puckered, coming suspiciously close to smiling. What a curious man! Just when Etta thought she understood something of his nature, he did the opposite of what she expected.

She relieved Robbie, who tried to protest, of the tray, and ordered, "Bring another tray for Mr. Rifkin, Robbie, in the music room. You will join me, will you not, Sean?"

He looked Etta directly in the eye, and if he sought some hidden meaning there, he seemingly did not find it. At any rate, he shrugged. "Join you? In the music room, yes. In the eating of food, perhaps."

Robbie curtsied herself away, and Etta proceeded into the room and deposited her tray on the wheeled tea table, which she then pulled next to a chair in which she took her seat. Sean followed her in, seating himself on an opposite settee and propping his crutch within easy reach.

"Is there some point to your invitation?" Sean asked without preamble.

"None at all, Sean, other than to share your company," Etta replied, shaking out her napkin and spreading it on her lap.

"I cannot think why you should imagine I have company worth sharing after the lovely scene I set you last night."

He had astonished her yet again, this time by admitting his behavior could have stood improvement.

"We have to live in the same house," she said, choosing to be just as forthright.

He watched her pour out a cup of tea, his features guarded, if perhaps also faintly amused. "You will not throw the cripple out into the street?"

Etta gave him a level look. "That would be Daniel's prerogative, not mine."

Now he did smile. "I see I must not treat you as a fool, madam."

She noted that his smile made him look all the more like his brother. "Nor I you," she said.

He inclined his head as though accepting a compliment.

Roberta returned, bearing another tray. Sean indicated with an indifferent air that she was to set it on the sofa table immediately behind the settee on which he reclined. Roberta left for other duties, and Sean proceeded to ignore the covered dishes.

"Do you know, I could actually believe you do not covet those rubies. The ones in the painting of Aileen," he said conversationally as he shifted to a more comfortable position.

"I do not."

"Well, perhaps 'covet' is too strong a word, but surely every lady would like grand jewels to wear?"

"Of course every lady would like that," she said, lifting the cover from her plate to reveal sliced beef sandwich quarters next to a square of Stilton cheese and a cinnamon-brown ring of pickled apple.

"But not you," Sean said, looking skeptical. "You would give them to Daniel to sell, of course, along with your own jewels," he added in a sarcastic tone.

"Had I ever possessed any, I would have indeed. Long since."

Sean gave a snort. He settled back on his seat and lifted his injured foot—clad as always in a kind of half-boot of soft, loose leather—and settled the length of his leg along the settee. He did not bother with so much as a "by your leave," and the look he cast her dared her to tell the cripple he could not put his dirty shoes on the furniture.

Her response was to bite into a piece of sandwich.

He grinned again, not entirely pleasantly.

"Etta . . . but, no!" He shook his head. "I cannot call you Etta."

She swallowed and asked calmly, "Indeed? Do you feel it is too familiar?"

"Too friendly," he responded at once. "I must insist on Henrietta."

"Are we not to be friends, Sean?"

"Henrietta," he said, ignoring the question. "Shall I tell you something that will shock you?"

"Dear me, I thought that was already what you were doing," she said drolly.

"It is sure to agitate you, because it concerns Saint Daniel."

"I assure you, anything you have to say about Daniel—"

"You know we used to have quite a few more servants," he interrupted. He went on, not giving her time to respond. "When it was time to let some of them go, most were happy to leave."

"Because of back wages owed, or because of the 'the ghost,' I suppose." Etta sniffed in dismissal.

"Oh, those reasons, of course, but the real reason they were happy to go was because of the whispers. Do you know what they whisper among themselves, Henrietta?"

She put down the sandwich and stood, offering him one quick, quelling glance as she gathered her skirts in preparation of leaving the room.

"They whispered that it was Daniel who killed Aileen," Sean said, intently watching her face.

Etta grew still despite her best intention otherwise, and wondered if the ringing in her ears was caused by the heat she felt flooding there. "Gossip!" she murmured, now unable to tear her gaze from his.

"They said he allowed her to die because she would not tell him where she had hidden a collection of jewels."

Etta put back her shoulders and lifted her chin. "I know all about the jewels. Daniel told me everything about them. There are not many, and they are not terribly valuable. And besides that, it makes no sense for a man to murder his wife over such a matter, for then he would have no hope of learning where they were hidden."

"I see you have given this some thought, my dear. But have you never heard of a fit of passion? Perhaps one night he demanded to know, and she stubbornly refused, and he—"

"How can you say such things?" Etta cried, her hands knotting into fists where they pressed into her skirts. "What manner of brother are you to accuse Daniel of such things? Aileen was not murdered—"

"Was she not? It was odd, you know, how she was found. Right behind the door, as if she had tried to get out but could not." He glowered at Etta, fixing her in place with the intensity behind his unkind words.

He went on. "Daniel claimed that when he found her, the door was unlocked. But of course we have only his word on that. *I* believe she was locked in, for why else would she be found just behind the door? No, she was struggling to get out, I tell you. And the bowl—she used steaming water laced with oil of eucalyptus to ease her breathing, you see. It was the only thing that helped. When she was found, there was a bowl of yet warm water in the room"—he tilted his head to one side, in a mock gesture of innocence—"but it was found to contain no eucalyptus oil. Even at the time that seemed odd to everyone. She always carried a vial of the oil with her. She never knew when she would need it. I had seen her sniff straight from the vial at times. Dust could cause an attack, or even taking exercise, little things most of us do not note. She had to be prepared."

"She died from her asthma, from a severe attack," Etta said, pointing out the obvious. She sank back down to her seat, for her knees were oddly shaky.

"True, true. Indeed, she had an attack! It was not to be wondered at, of course. She had just returned from a walk in the garden. Mrs. Lawton told us that when Aileen came in, her face was pale—although, to everyone's regret, at the time she did not note that Aileen was in any distress. Aileen used to hide it, though, when she could. She hated being frail, hated how it limited her. Yes, the walk triggered an attack, but you must see that someone capitalized on that fact."

Sean paused dramatically, as if he did not know he already had her entire attention, Etta thought sourly. She refused to ask him to go on, but she must hear the rest, as awful as it all was. She had to know how Aileen had died.

"The odd thing," he drawled, "the thing no one could explain, was all the dust in her room! A layer of it, everywhere. And the maid had just dusted that morning! Yes, indeed, *that* was very strange." His voice slipped into a derisive croon. "Poor Aileen, coming back from a stroll, too often a taxing experience in the first place, only to find a room full of dust."

"Dust? Are you saying someone deliberately threw . . . well, what? Handfuls of dirt about the room? Do not be absurd! The maid lied to cover the fact she was not doing her work. Or perhaps someone shook out a rug without thinking about the consequences," Etta challenged.

"Making up explanations, Henrietta? I wonder that you feel the need to do so. But you are correct, the sudden appearance of dust *was* absurd. And deadly."

Etta pressed her lips together into a thin line. How could she argue that fact?

Sean went on. "Recall that when she was found she lacked her vial. Too, there *was* a bowl of water. Why did she have that, I suppose? Had someone brought it to her? Certainly not Mrs. Lawton, who had not seen that Aileen was in any kind of distress. The servants all denied doing it, but why should they? They were not responsible for Aileen's oil. She carried it for herself. Who then? Ask yourself, did the one who brought the bowl try to convince her it contained the missing oil? Or could they have used the bowl as a ruse, a way to get Aileen to surrender the vial to them? Had it even been hot enough to steam? She required the steam, you see. Even just the steam might have helped her," Sean said, but his voice had grown softer until now it trailed away. He frowned, and Etta thought it a strangely sad frown.

"Perhaps she meant to fetch her oil but the attack caught her up," Etta said. "Perhaps there was nothing amiss but sloppy housekeeping creating the atmosphere for a terrible accident."

"That is how it was ruled by the doctor. A terrible accident," Sean said in a low voice. He shook his head, no longer looking at Etta, but staring at nothing, caught up in memories. "And then Daniel buried her in the simplest possible box, beneath a slab of stone taken from the fields," he said bitterly.

"There was no money," Etta explained even though Sean had to know that truth far better than she. "He did what he could for her. The rubies—"

"I made him bury her with the rubies! He saw no reason to honor her in such a manner," Sean stated. Abruptly he sat up straight, pulling his leg from the settee and snatching up his crutch.

"He was trying to be reasonable."

"Oh, yes, Daniel is nothing if not reasonable," Sean said sourly. He awkwardly pulled himself to stand, settling the crutch in place under his arm. "It was entirely reasonable that he marry the woman whose dowry was to be a hundred acres of land that march along our own! And it was entirely reasonable that he spent so much time away from her, for, as you know, her health was too fragile to keep her at his side."

"Is that why you hate him so? For being more occupied with business than you thought he ought be? Sean, he struggles to keep the estate together. He was trying to ready fields, to invest what little capital there was—"

"You are quite right, my dear," Sean said icily. "He was doing what the estate required, if not the occupants of that estate. I only hope for your sake that you do not mind a husband who is chronically too busy to stop and share an occasional luncheon or play of cards with you. And I certainly hope your health never fails, for then I can guarantee that your busy husband will have absolutely *no* time for you! Just as he had no time for *her."*

With that said, Sean stalked from the room.

Etta sat for a long space, thoughts whirling in her head, her meal forgotten. Had Daniel neglected Aileen? It was entirely possible it had just appeared that way because Aileen's health had prohibited her from much activity. But even if "her abandonment" were true, why did Sean resent it so bitterly? Had he, in his wounded state, been neglected by Daniel too? Or was it a twisted form of jealousy that created Sean's resentments? Jealousy of Daniel's health, of his preoccupation with matters surrounding the estate? Was it possible that Sean was filled with spite because he had too much time on his hands . . . and too much liquor coursing through his veins? Or could it be that Sean had cared for Aileen, perhaps more so than her husband?

Etta rose, her knees not much steadier than before, and went up to her room. She sat at the dressing table, taking the pins out of her hair, and applied her brush to its length.

The movement soothed her, relaxing her enough that she came to a decision: She must ask Daniel about that night, about the time he had found his wife's body. Daniel would tell her the entire story, and, she told herself, these awful innuendoes would surely shrivel in the light of the whole truth.

She nodded affirmation of this idea at her reflection in the dressing table mirror. Even as she experienced a sense of satisfaction at her decision, it was then that her gaze focused on the other thing reflected in its polished surface: the locked door. The door behind which Aileen's body had been found.

Etta slowly lowered the brush to the tabletop, only then turning in her seat to face the one locked door in her new home.

She bit her lip and stared at the door, so solid and so much a symbol of the stranger Daniel was in truth to her. How little she really knew of him! However, she reminded herself as she pulled in a deep, deciding breath, she had determined that he would tell her what she needed to know, and so would the room behind that door. It was time it gave up its secrets.

She rose and crossed the room, not to the locked door but to the one leading to the hallway. She went downstairs and located Mrs. Lawton, and requested the housekeeper provide her with the key to the locked door above stairs.

"I do not have a key to that room, my lady," Mrs. Lawton told her, staring.

"Where is it? Is it lost?" Etta demanded.

"Lord Healey has both keys to that room."

Etta just managed to keep from wincing, even though she felt as though she had just received a blow. Instead, she took a deep, shaky breath. "I see. Well. Yes. Thank you, Mrs. Lawton. I shall obtain one from him."

"Very good, my lady," the housekeeper said.

Etta returned to her room and proceeded to go through every drawer. Why was no one, not even the housekeeper, allowed a key to the locked room? Surely it required airing occasionally, or at least a dusting, and surely it made perfect sense for Mrs. Lawton to have a key toward that purpose. Was the housekeeper required to ask for the key when she needed it? Or was any such need denied and the room left to moulder?

Rather to her surprise, Etta found what she sought in the topmost drawer of Daniel's chest of drawers: a ring of keys.

Of the ten keys, it was the seventh that unlocked the door. Was it an omen? Certainly, if nothing else, it behooved her to pause before she went on, to think this through clearly. She must remember that Daniel had kept the two keys to this room under his particular control. Too, he had asked her not to make use of the room, to let time pass. . . .

But he had never forbidden her to *look* in the room.

She turned the knob and entered, and wished at once that she had thought to bring a candle.

Eight

Etta shivered, not just from the cold, stale air that greeted her, but because of the room's inky blackness. The only illumination in the room came from the bedchamber behind her, pooling around her feet on the threshold, unable to reach far into the cave of blackness before her.

But as her eyes began to adjust to the darkness, Etta began to be able to make out dim shapes, and she perceived she looked at Holland cloths draped over chairs and tables and other bits of furniture such as would fill a lady's sitting room.

If Aileen indeed haunted this house, it would most likely be this room that would host her spirit.

Etta shivered again and crossed the room, her steps hurried. The darkness pressed at her back and gave her impetus, so that she was running by the time she reached to pull aside the drapes. Her fingers fumbled for a moment, struggling with the window latch. Once she grasped it securely, it gave way easily. In a moment she had the window up, and had unlatched the shutters as well. She pushed them open, realizing she had been holding her breath only when she inhaled greedily at the sunlit air that wafted into the room.

After three more deep breaths she set back her shoulders and turned to face the room. In the light from the window she saw wallpaper blocked in a delicate flower pattern, a thick carpet that ran almost to the edges of the room, and six pieces of covered furniture. It was decidedly a woman's room, its white and rose-colored walls and carpet pretty in the afternoon light.

The room was orderly except for a layer of dust visible to the eye where it sat atop the Holland covers. Someone had put the room to rights months ago, or longer. The only set of footsteps disturbing the dust on the carpet were Etta's own. Had Daniel allowed the room to be cleaned just after Aileen's death and never since? It would seem so, to judge by the proof before Etta's eyes, and by the way he had asked her to leave off using the room for the time being.

Why did Daniel wait? Did he keep the door locked to placate nervous servants? Did he carry with him a horror of what he had found here? Or could it be a regret so deep, it had tainted the room forever? Did he keep the room inviolate to honor Aileen's memory?

How much had Daniel loved Aileen? The question slipped into Etta's mind, lingering a moment too long. He honored his dead wife, yes, hopefully, surely, but honor and the memory of love were not enough to displace a new love—Etta and Daniel's love—certainly not! And yet, and yet . . . why did the room remain closed and locked?

Etta moved around the room's perimeter, lifting the Holland covers as she passed, finding a padded rose velvet chair here, a dressing table there, and everything denuded of doily or perfume bottle or any other item to mark who had once passed her hours here. Strangely enough, that was comforting. Etta could not help but think it would be odd to find the first wife's belongings here, enshrined, as it were. This was just a room, no longer in use, and perhaps that was not so odd, so threatening a fact as it might at first seem.

Etta was just about to leave the room, when another thought crept into her mind: *If Aileen did not have her breath-giving oil on her person, where else would she store it but here?* This had been Aileen's sitting room. It was only logical that she would have provided for her comfort here. She should have been able to find a vial easily . . . unless she spent all her time downstairs, in the parlor. . . . She might have been the sort to forget things about the house. But would an asthmatic be so

casual with her only means of relief? And there had been a
bowl of water here, brought up by her . . . or by someone else?
This room ought to have contained a vial, surely, this room
where her body was found. . . .

Etta shuddered and closed her eyes for a moment, feeling
slightly sick. She was making too much of the tale Sean had
told her. She was allowing a few silly, superstitious servants
and a deliberately unkind brother-in-law to fill her head with
outrageous thoughts. Aileen had been increasingly unwell, and
had met an unfortunate end—and that was all the more com-
plicated the matter was.

Perhaps it had been a mistake to come here, for it had served
no constructive purpose. All the same, Etta determined as she
opened her eyes once more, she would leave the shutters and
drapes open. That would be a start to reclaiming this room, to
chasing out what she presumed was an old hurt for Daniel and
a collective dread for the servants.

She faced the door, now nearly swung shut. If she had closed
the drapes she would not have had sufficient light to see the
back of the door. As it was, the afternoon light streamed in,
setting the wall opposite the windows almost to glaring. There,
unmistakably, on the back of the door, Etta saw a series of
nearly parallel marks.

Scratch marks, she thought at once. She stepped forward and
bent down, tracing one of the marks with her finger. Had a
dog been kept in this room, marking his desire to get out by
clawing at the door? Daniel kept no dogs now, but once upon
a time there would have been money for keeping hounds. But
these marks were faint, for all that they were long. Only a short
dog would have left them, or . . . Etta pressed a fingernail into
the door's solid wood and drew it down, leaving behind a long,
thin, light scratch, more a disturbance of the wood oil than of
the grain itself.

She sank down to her knees, her legs gone too weak to support her properly. Human nails, presumably female nails, had
left these marks! It was a simple leap of logic to realize Aileen

must have clawed at this door, Aileen, who presumably tried to get out or get someone's attention, her voice no doubt lost to the fit of asthma that had robbed her of life.

Etta pressed her hands to her forehead while terrible visions filled her head. She fought against the familiar tingling and ached to believe that the pictures forming in her mind were nothing more than fancies, but even so she knew better. Usually she could use her sketch pad to draw out the visions that came to her, usually they did not fill her head to the exclusion of all else, but today, in this room, she was lost to them.

She saw the pretty face from the portrait, saw the eyes grow round with alarm when Aileen realized the bowl of water contained no soothing oil. Perhaps Etta cried out, she could not be sure, or perhaps it was Aileen who cried her alarm upon discovering the bowl of water was not warm enough to offer her the vital steam so necessary to opening her closed lungs. Etta saw a hand reaching for the room's doorknob, perhaps— even quite possibly—finding it locked. Surely Aileen had not yet been so weakened that she could not have opened the door had it been unlocked. Desperation alone would have given her the strength, but the hand in the vision was not equal to opening the door.

Etta saw the woman sliding to the floor, saw her pounding on the door, increasingly feebly, saw her struggle to gasp in air. She saw a hand reach up again, desperately, saw the nails rake the door in a last chance at attracting someone's attention, or perhaps Aileen merely reached out, scratching and snatching at life, at hope!

Etta groaned and pressed the heels of her hands into her eyes, willing the horrible visions away. A dark red light spread through her thoughts, and after a moment the terrible apparitions were gone, replaced only by the darkness seen behind closed eyelids.

Etta moved her hands and blinked, half stunned by the bright sunlight in the room. She trembled, panting, feeling nearly as hungry for air as Aileen had surely felt. She managed to stumble to her feet. Perhaps this was why Daniel had asked her not to come in this room. Perhaps he had not wished Etta to know, to feel the awful vibrations that still clung to its walls. No one knew better than Daniel of Etta's fey nature. Her "gift" was a large part of what had brought them together. She had drawn portraits of his face, and he had found them, and had been angry with her at first. . . .

She had always assumed he was angry to have his portrait made without permission, and that was undoubtedly true enough. But was there more to it? Had there been anything in her portraits that had alarmed him? She tried to remember, but she felt so shaky that details escaped her.

Had she drawn him near a door? Or holding a key?

"No!" she cried out loud, experiencing a quick, sharp dart of pain at her very core. No, Daniel had been devastated when his first wife had died! His every action indicated as much. He could not have had anything to do with her death! How could Etta even entertain such an evil thought?

But someone had locked that door. Someone had baited Aileen into the room with a bowl of too-cool water. Someone had seen to it that the oil of eucalyptus was unavailable, had scattered breath-stealing dust around the room. Etta was sure of it, as sure as the residual tightness in her throat, the shortness of breath that had her panting yet.

She reached for the room's door, pulling it open wide, needing to be quit of the room. She shut the door behind herself quickly, using the key with shaky hands to lock it behind her once more. She took a deep breath, steadying herself, and moved to return the ring of keys to Daniel's drawer, only too glad to relinquish them.

She crossed to the bedchamber mirror, seeing too-wide eyes in a pale face. She pinched her cheeks, but nothing could take the echo of horror from her eyes, nothing but time.

Determining the best thing would be to return to her routine, Etta decided to seek out Robbie, for she had told the girl she soon meant to make an inventory of the household belongings.

How else to be absolutely sure the little thefts were no longer taking place, and, even more practically, to know her household's assets and needs? Etta was a fair hand at stitchery, so she must determine how many linens needed mending and which others might be best put to use as cleaning rags or converted into shifts or other necessary garments for the servants' use.

Regardless of what the inventory disclosed, she thought at once, any items from the room that had been Aileen's private domain would remain as they were for now. She had no need for a writing desk, not if it must mean another venture into that room, not yet and not soon.

She shuddered anew at the thought of reentering that place, only to open the hallway door and find Sean leaning against the opposite wall.

"I thought I heard something," he said, his expression entirely neutral. "Did you cry out? I was just toying with the thought of barging into your room, but here you are. Is everything well?"

"Everything is fine. I . . . I did cry out. I stubbed my toe," Etta lied.

"I see."

"Thank you for your concern," she said, managing to sound almost sincere.

"Oh, certainly. There is little enough for me to do around this place," he said, casting a glance about and resetting his crutch under his arm. He smiled tightly. "Rescuing a damsel in distress might relieve the tedium."

"I see." It was her turn to say the meaningless expression, for she could not think how else to answer him.

"But you need not suffer from tedium," he commented, and now the neutral expression was replaced with a knowing glee.

"I beg your pardon?"

"I heard a jingle of keys, and there is dust on your hem, my dear girl. I daresay it does not take a genius to know you went exploring."

Etta looked down, admitting her guilt by the action. She felt a blush stain her cheeks. She deliberately bent to dust at her hem with her hands, belatedly realizing that Sean seemed to be entirely sober, for his eyes were clear, nor did he sport the smell of alcohol about his person, as she had come to expect. It would seem he was an even more unpleasant person sober than when he was drinking.

"Daniel does not care for anyone to explore a certain room, you know," he taunted.

Etta straightened, and gazed at him directly. "Yes, I know," she said. "Do you think he will be very upset when I tell him what I have done?" she challenged, informing him there was no purpose to be served by revealing the breach, for she would do so herself first.

"I see no reason why he should change his pattern now, since he has always been angered by the act before," he said, but some of his malice had retreated, no doubt out of disappointment.

"I think it might be time for many a pattern to be changed," Etta replied, turning for the stairs, denying him the chance to make a reply.

"I do not think your brother drinks so much as he pretends to drink," Etta said to Daniel over dinner that night.

Daniel raised a brow in question, and he asked in light humor, "Indeed? And, pray, what purpose would it serve him to act a part he does not in truth play?"

"So he can watch," Etta said. She felt as if she demonstrated her own words, for it had been difficult to keep her gaze from Daniel all evening. Who was this man, this husband of hers? Was there any more mystery to him than there was to any person not long known to another? Did he hide a depth—a darker side—not unlike his brother? Was Sean the more honest of the two?

"Are you calling my brother a *voyeur?*" Daniel asked with a small smile.

"Not exactly. I think he likes to pose as an inebriate so he can actually stare and take in all that occurs around him. I think acting a little out of his head with drink gives him an excuse to meddle in events as he chooses. After all, any lapse in good manners can always be explained away."

Daniel put down his knife and fork and sat back in his seat. "An extraordinary observation, Etta."

"You disagree?"

"Not at all. In fact, I concur. I am only surprised you have seen it so quickly in him. No, in truth I am not surprised at all. That is your way, to see things others miss. Sean has something of that same talent, you see, even if he chooses to manifest it in a different way."

Was that praise? Etta could not say for a certainty, so her answering smile was undoubtedly more cool than it might have been.

Daniel pressed his napkin to his lips and then went on. "Sean can tip a bottle with the best, but I am not so blind as to miss that sometimes he spends more time waving his glass about in his affected manner, and very little time actually drinking from it. I cannot say I disapprove the act, however, my dear. I would rather tolerate his play-acting than his actual drunken fits."

"But why tolerate either?" Etta pushed her plate aside and leaned forward to lift her goblet of wine. "Why not put him to some task or other, that he have less hours in the day to idle away?"

"And how does one put a grown man to a task unless he wishes to accept it? Sean chooses the life he leads," Daniel said, a hint of bitterness creeping into his voice and his expression. "He seems to enjoy skulking about, minding all manner of business but his own. Watching, always watching. Sometimes I think he means to punish me by watching everything I do." He laughed shortly, and reached for his own wine. "I daresay it is an effective means of punishment."

"Punishment? For what?" Etta asked, her fingers tightening on the goblet's stem.

Daniel stared at the table linen for a moment. When he finally looked up, Etta found a dark imp of amusement in his gaze. No, not exactly amusement, at least not without a modicum of self-recrimination mixed in.

"Aileen never lived in Bath until she made her come-out. I daresay it made sense for her parents to bring her here from London for the event, because her dowry was to be land only, handed down in the female line from a great-grandmama. There would be no moneyed settlements. Here, someone might value such a dowry. Someone like me, whose property adjoined hers, you see." He gazed unblinkingly at Etta, as if daring her to disapprove the fact he had married his first wife for the property she would bring to the marriage.

Having already garnered some of these facts from Sean's angry tirade that afternoon, Etta nodded. After all, most marriages were based on mutual offerings. It did not bear thinking on to realize that without progeny to inherit it, Aileen's land would remain part of Daniel's estate.

"Sean was the first to meet Aileen," Daniel said softly but clearly. "He has never said one word to me, never admitted what I suspect, but I have come to believe utterly that he developed a tendre for her, most probably before I was even introduced to her. He may even have gone to her father to request her hand in marriage."

Daniel stood up abruptly, tossing aside his napkin, and Etta thought that was to be an end to his explanation, but after throwing the remnants of his wine on the blaze in the fireplace and listening to its hiss and pop, he turned back to Etta.

"Perhaps Sean was refused. Almost certainly Aileen's father would have a thought toward doing better for his daughter than a penniless second son. Certainly Sean knew better than to apply to me for money, as there was nothing to be promised him per annum to set himself up as a bridegroom. You must understand, I knew nothing of that then, I never guessed, not

soon enough. When I offered for her, it was with a clear conscience—how could it be otherwise?"

Daniel stared at his goblet, seemingly watching the play of
firelight across its faceted surface. "As we have spoken of
'watching,' allow me to tell you that once Aileen was my bride,
Sean watched, oh, yes, he watched. Her. Me. Us. If, as I suspect,
he had made his offer, how it must have galled him to see his
chosen lady go to his own brother! *My* only circumstance over
him was that I possessed the title. A penniless title, but it was
enough to make Aileen a baroness, of course. Enough to tempt
her father, it seems."

He spun to face Etta, his shoulders back, his chin up. "She
was not well. Never had been. Her parents were, frankly,
astonished she survived into adulthood. The squire's daughter
was fortunate to marry me, it seems. They were delighted that
I should offer for someone so obviously frail."

Etta looked away, not sure what to make of the sharp-edged
words he uttered. "They saw that you loved her," she suggested,
still not looking to him.

"Did I?" he asked roughly, and the question was followed
by a long silence, a silence that could have been formed from
disappointment or guilt or some other strong emotion.

Then Daniel sighed, drawing Etta's gaze once more. "Yes, I
loved her well enough," he said, the sharp tone gone once more,
his features softening at some memory. "She was a gentle girl
with a sweet disposition. Who could reproach her? She hated
her infirmity more than any of us could ever begrudge it."

He turned back to the fire. "I think you must have sensed
for yourself that Sean loved her. He loved her enough that he
could not abide living with us for long. I gave him what little
I could, and he borrowed from friends and bought himself a
commission. For all the good it did him! He came back injured
and more unhappy than when he left, returning just weeks before Aileen . . . passed away. The poor chub."

Etta rose, crossing to his side. She touched his shoulder, and
knew a thrill of wifely conquest when he turned to her, his

gaze haunted but seemingly searching hers for some form of comfort.

"You could not know. Had you known, had Sean said a word of his affection to you, you never would have pursued the girl," she assured him.

He gathered up her hand and placed a kiss in her palm, closing his eyes as if in pain.

"Aileen herself could have said something to you. I think it must be obvious that her affections toward Sean were not engaged," she went on.

He opened his eyes, pressing her hand to his cheek. "Or she was forbidden to speak of it. Her father was not an easy man. It would not have been in her nature to defy his will."

Etta smiled gently and shook her head. "Daniel, even a woman forbidden to speak would have found a way to let you know something so very important. I am sorry for Sean, but I think it must be clear to all that Aileen made the choice she wished to make."

He shook his head, but he said, "Sometimes I think that way, but other times I think of the lives I ruined without ever meaning to. Perhaps she should have married Sean. He loved her more deeply than I ever did, I confess it. He would have been near at hand. He would have heard her attempts to help herself. I was in my study, napping in my chair. *Napping,* for God's sake, Etta! I had turned down her invitation to walk with her, and then . . ." He shook his head, lost to cheerless memories.

Etta looked into his face, and even though his gaze was turned inward, was it possible to find the tiniest hint of play-acting there? She saw regret and, yes, guilt—but surely not the sort of guilt that blackens a man's soul? Someone had played a hand in Aileen's death, but could it have been this man? And how could Etta claim she loved him, feel this aching sympathy for him, but secretly fear he was capable of executing a dastardly act? Would a longer length of time reveal something of his nature that could kill the emotion she called love? Did she in truth love him, or merely desire him? Was theirs a bond merely made in the bed, or did it live in her heart?

"Oh, Daniel," she whispered, unable to answer her own questions, yet unable to truly think ill of him, not while she touched his dear, handsome face, not while his arms held her close. It was just that this house was so unsettled. Terrible tales needed to be uttered, pondered, explained aloud. With time all the truth could come out; perhaps it was neglect more than savagery that had caused Aileen's death. That agonizing, terrible death. Yes, time. She and Daniel needed time to sort it all out—

Just beyond the closed dining room door, a scream of raw terror rent the air.

Nine

At the horrified scream, Etta jumped, and Daniel's arms tightened momentarily around her, but then he crossed the room and threw open the door to the dining room.

"What is it?" he demanded of a wild-eyed Robbie just as Etta attained his side.

The girl had her back flat across the wall, the single candle whose holder she clenched with both hands flickering. She was white-faced and her mouth worked soundlessly for a moment. "I seen it," she whispered at length. She raised a quivering hand to her face. "The ghost. I seen it, sir!" She began to sob in rough hiccoughs.

"Nonsense!" Daniel said at once, but Etta noticed his face went pale.

Robbie shook her head vehemently and struggled to reconstruct her composure. "It were . . . a swirling sheet of white, m'lord," the girl gasped out. "It . . . it floated, with no feet, but ghostly arms a-wavin'. In the parlor. The room where . . . *she* used to sit and read. Oh, sir! It were so horrible!"

Etta closed her eyes and shook her head, chasing out visions of the scratch marks she had seen on the back of the door above stairs.

"You surely saw a drapery stirring in the evening breeze," Daniel told her firmly. "Nothing more than that." When the girl shook her head again, Daniel announced gruffly, "I shall prove it." He matched his action to the statement, striding at once down the hall to throw open the parlor door.

"Oh, sir, take the candle at least!" Robbie urged, trembling so much that her voice trembled with her. Etta thought it best to relieve the girl of the candle before she dropped it.

Daniel strode into the room, not bothering to heed Robbie's advice, and there followed a handful of exceedingly long and silent moments. Etta felt no particular tingle, no repetition of the awful visions earlier this day, but Robbie's dread was so palpable that it proved contagious. The candle trembled just as violently in her own hand as it had in Robbie's.

Still, Etta stepped forward, her hand outstretched to throw the small light before her as she moved in the direction Daniel had gone. Each breath caught in her throat, sounding loud in the evening stillness. "Daniel?" she asked in no more than a hoarse whisper, and when she received no reply, she began to run toward the dark doorway.

Daniel stepped out just as Etta approached, causing her to gasp in a combination of surprise and relief.

"It was even as I said," Daniel pronounced. "I secured an open window. Everything is in order now." He looked to the maid. "Roberta, I daresay you have had a fright and probably ought best retire for the night. I shall see to the fire in my and Lady Healey's room."

"Oh, yes, sir. If you say, sir. I'm terribly sorry—"

"It is quite all right, Roberta. We all take a fright now and then. But might I advise against putting much stock in the likes of kitchen prattle in the future?"

The maid looked to the floor and executed a curtsy. "Very good, m'lord," she murmured before turning and hurrying away.

"What a fright she gave me!" Etta said on a forced laugh.

"Quite," Daniel agreed shortly.

"Well, that is behind us now, is it not? It is best forgot."

"Exactly so."

"And have I told you? My maid has requested that she be called Robbie. She prefers it to Roberta."

"Does she indeed? I cannot see a great difference myself,"

Daniel murmured, glancing back through the dark, open doorway of the parlor, clearly distracted.

Etta looked too, seeing only a hint of dark edges, presumably furniture, within an inky blackness. "Has the window come open again?" she asked.

Daniel refused to look at her, instead taking the candle from her and grasping her elbow. With gentle pressure he propelled her forward toward the stairs. "No," he answered quietly, never releasing her elbow as they moved upward. "For you see, Etta, I never found it open to begin with."

"What?" Etta cried, halting abruptly.

Daniel urged her onward by the pressure he exerted on her arm, shaking his head until she took another step upward.

"I do not know what Robbie saw," he continued then, "or if indeed she saw anything at all, but the room was secure. If a curtain moved, it was not because of any breeze."

"Oh, well then," Etta said faintly. "Surely then, I mean to say—Robbie imagined it!"

"Of course she did," Daniel said, and Etta could not say whether she heard a lack of conviction in his tone or merely imagined it there herself.

Daniel took her to their room, no more words of explanation passing between them. He set the fire while Etta readied for bed. Her trembling could be attributed to the night's briskness, even though she pulled the blankets up to her chin, but she knew the chill she felt went deeper than that.

A sweet aroma wafted to her nose, already half smothered by the smoky scents of the fire Daniel had set to blazing. Had her bottle of lavender water somehow tipped or come open? But no, a quick glance at her dressing table revealed the bottle stopper in place—and next to it sat a full bowl of lavender sprigs.

Etta tensed beneath the covers. Robbie or Mrs. Lawton or perhaps even Will would have brought them here. Normally that would be all that was delightful, were it not for the flash of memory that ran through Etta's thoughts. She saw the thin stalks, waving heavy-headed in the breeze in the small garden, the garden that O'Brien had torn up at her demand.

The blossoms should have been long consigned to the debris heap, and yet here they sat, casting out their perfume, sending forth to Etta their unfortunate botanical interpretation: distrust. She knew well enough, as did most girls who longed for posies from their sweethearts, that lavender might be made into a nosegay for the sweetheart whose intentions were unclear or clouded by the appearance of misdeeds.

Etta sprang from the bed, drawing Daniel's regard where he sat removing his boots with the help of a bootjack. "Etta?" he questioned.

"These flowers! Their scent, it is making me feel ill," she explained, gathering up the bowl of the fragrant stems. "I shall just put them outside the room," she said, perhaps in too tight a voice.

Daniel said nothing, a quick lift of his brows expressing his consent or, more likely, his unconcern with her decision.

Etta set the bowl in the hall, closing the door upon them with a decided sigh of relief. She leaned her forehead against the cool, hard wood for a moment, silently castigating herself for allowing the day's events to so unnerve her that a bowl of flowers had quite overcome her reason. They were only flowers, poor, harmless flowers, and their meaning an arbitrary appellation given them. She could almost laugh now that they were out of the room, but neither was she tempted to open the door and bring them in once more.

Etta crept back under the covers, silently watching Daniel disrobe and ready himself for bed. He had seen nothing amiss with the flowers, just as he had found nothing amiss in the parlor, although the latter was more difficult to explain away as a trifle. He ought to have seen something that might explain away Robbie's fright, but if he had, he had not mentioned it. And his face! It had gone too pale to prove indifference.

What had Robbie seen? Something that clearly terrified her. She was an excitable girl, true, and it was possible she had let her own fancies run away with her. . . . But for Etta, worse than the thought of *something,* some ghostly apparition, was the thought that perhaps she had played a hand in raising any such specter, whether real or imagined. Did Robbie know what her mistress had done? Certainly Sean did, and he was not above relating Etta's "sin" of invading the forbidden room. If he had told Robbie, it would be easy to assume the girl was simply filled with tales and in an excitable state.

Although, Robbie's terror had been so real. . . .

Oh, why did I ever go in that room! Etta scolded herself even though a part of her knew it had to have been done sooner or later.

Daniel, now dressed for bed, blew out the candle and crawled under the covers. She turned to him, welcoming his warm presence, only to encounter his back.

"Daniel?" she asked in surprise.

"It has been . . . an odd night, Etta," he said, his tone cool and remote, so unlike the deep, caressing tones she was used to of a night.

"Odd?" She gave a brief, halfhearted laugh. "Exceedingly!"

He grunted in agreement. "Good night, then," he said, bothering to roll toward her just long enough to plant a quick peck not quite on her mouth.

"Good night," she murmured, sinking into her pillows. Never before had Daniel settled to sleep without first holding her and warming her with his kisses. He was correct, of course, that the night had been exceedingly odd—and now that he withdrew his usual show of affection, it was odder yet.

When Etta finally slept, it was to dream of a house that had room after room—and every one of them filled with bowls of lavender.

Two nights later Etta almost backed out of the front parlor when she saw Sean seated within, but she had spent two whole days avoiding anyone's company, and she decided she was heartily sick of being on her own. When Daniel had turned his back to her two nights ago, a small rift had turned into a larger one as soon as she woke up alone. He then spent all yesterday closeted with his bailiff, even taking his meals on a tray in his study.

Last night he had not come to bed until after she was asleep, and he had not awakened her. When the first sight she had seen this morning was that of his side of the bed, rumpled but empty, it fueled a growing ire to then glance up and find a bowl of lavender had been returned to the dressing table. Had the maid brought the bowl into the room in the early morning hours while the master and mistress yet slept? What a curious thing to do, if so! Or had an early-rising Daniel given the maid permission to bring it in? That scarcely made more sense than Etta's first conclusion—and she chose not to linger on the thought that Daniel had seen her put the lavender out of the room just the night before and would have known better than to give any such permission.

Miserable and confused, Etta had avoided Daniel's company once more all day, put out by the growing impression that he was avoiding hers as well. She made a point of working for hours in the little garden, which was situated out of sight of the windows of his study.

But now she was tired and a little stiff from gardening, not to mention sick at heart, and even Sean's company was welcome over another minute alone with her hurt and bewildered thoughts.

"Good evening, Sean," she said quietly to his bowed head.

He looked up slowly from his seat on the settee, his eyes rimmed in red. On the table before him stood a bottle, and in his hand he clutched a nearly full glass of burgundy wine. "Henrietta," he greeted her morosely, only to lower his head once more and stare blindly at the bottle.

"What a cheery greeting!" she said, wondering if she appeared half so miserable as he. "But I can see neither of us is in the mood for cheerfulness. What say you? Shall I stay and help you fill the entire room with gloom?" She did not wait for his answer, settling in one of the wing chairs.

"What is this, dearest sister?" he looked up again to ask, not smiling. "No, let me guess, although it takes no stretch of the imagination to come up with a thought. Can it be that the happy flower that is marriage has lost its bloom?"

"No," she said, half convinced her expression must surely declare otherwise. "I am merely bored."

"Which you would not be if your husband attended you properly." Sean looked away, saying softly, "I warned you of as much."

A cold pain stabbed through Etta's center, and she had no reply to make to that. Instead, she said, "Tonight you drink. You do not always, I know, although you pretend at it. I wonder, why do you bother? Whom do you seek to fool? Daniel, or yourself? And to what purpose?"

She expected an angry retort, but instead he sat back in his seat and picked up the glass of wine, inspecting it in the room's lamplight. Suddenly he put the glass to his lips, upending it and emptying it of its contents.

"Ah!" he sighed, and licked his lips. He looked at her with an odd mixture of sharp attention and a seeming playfulness. "I drink," he said, "because drink can help one to forget." He lifted his eyebrows, inviting her to disagree.

When she did not, he went on. "I do not drink as deeply or as consistently as I might choose, however," and here he paused, his eyelids lowering to half mast, as if to ward off pain or to prevent her from seeing anything more than he wished her to see. "Because"—his voice slowed and he chose his words with apparent care—"because I cannot always recall, later, what I have done when I have been too drunk."

When she made no reply, he straightened abruptly, stiff in his seat, and stared Etta in the eyes. "Do you not understand?" he cried out, his voice rising nearly to a shout.

"You are concerned you do not behave as you ought when you have been drinking—?"

Etta's puzzled explanation was interrupted by the click of the parlor room door opening. Daniel stood there, looking from her to Sean and back again.

Sean saw his brother as well, but Daniel's arrival made no apparent impression, for there was no reduction in his volume. "Of course that, you silly baggage!" Sean snapped at Etta, his eyes glittering with either anger or despair. "But what I am really saying is that I do not know if I—" His voice broke, then he shook his head, his jaw working as he stared with a haunted expression at his brother.

Daniel's eyes narrowed. "He is trying to confess that he believes *he* killed Aileen," he supplied.

Etta could not help but gasp.

Daniel quietly closed the parlor door behind himself as Sean collapsed in on himself, his shoulders slumping as they had several nights before, the glitter fading from his eyes.

"I was so unhappy after I lost my commission," he mumbled, shaking his head. "Watching them, Daniel . . . and Aileen . . . I drank too much. I drank myself to sleep every night. I broke dishes and glasses and bibelots in my fits of rage . . . and in the morning I could never remember having done it. Perhaps . . . perhaps that night I could take no more. I was out of my head with drink. I was a soldier. I could kill. I've killed before. And what an easy way to kill her! It would have been so simple to come upon her in that room, to take her vial of oil from her! Even as the half-man I am now, I could have easily overpowered her. I could have locked the door, or even merely held it closed. It could have been me who killed Aileen," he whispered, at last running out of words. He buried his face in his hands, making one wrenching gasp, not quite a sob.

Etta stood, thinking to cross to his side, to put a soothing arm about his shoulders, for his misery was so palpable, so complete that it brought forth the instinct to comfort. Only the fact that he could very well be correct kept her rooted in place. Everything he had said was believable, even convincing.

"Oh, God," Sean moaned, rocking back and forth on the chair. "Oh, God!"

"If," Etta said through lips that felt half numb from shock, "if that is so, then it was in truth an accident, Sean. You would never have harmed her if you had been in your right mind." She looked to Daniel, imploring him to agree.

He crossed the room, not to Sean's side but to Etta's. He gazed down into her upturned face. "He would not have hurt her, not even when he was drunk and out of his head," Daniel told her. His manner was very matter-of-fact, even flat, as it had been these two days past.

"How good of you to find me so utterly guiltless!" Sean cried in biting sarcasm, his hands dropping away from his face to reveal a reborn fury there. "Or could it be that my dear brother, the beloved Saint Daniel, can so magnanimously believe in my innocence because he knows who *really* allowed Aileen to die? Could the wolf be condescending to the sheep?" Sean stood, balancing on one foot, clutching at the high arm of the settee to help him keep his balance. "Is that the way of it, Daniel?"

Daniel made no reply other than to take up Etta's hand, which he squeezed too tightly, presumably unknowingly, as a sea-tossed man might grip a ship's rope.

"You had everything, Daniel!" Sean cried. "Whatever funds there were! A loving wife! A house that you could call your own. What could have made you want to turn your back to it all? Was it that Aileen could not have children? Did you need to leave your mark? Was the lack of progeny enough to drive you to end her life?" Sean nearly howled, his grief plain to see.

When Daniel only stared at him wordlessly, Sean fumbled with angrily shaking hands for his crutch, sending it crashing to the floor.

Daniel bent and retrieved it, handing it to Sean. Sean received it with a clear and jaw-tightened wrath, pausing no more than a moment before tossing the crutch across the room with a snarl, leaving a dent in the plasterwork there. Daniel looked to the damage, then back to his brother, never so much as flinching.

"Dammit, man!" Sean shouted. "Let me hear you say it! Just once!"

Daniel shook his head ever so slightly.

"You miserable bastard!" Sean's voice dropped to a growl. "What am I to think? You have never once denied it! Why will you not just once say 'I did not kill her'?"

A long silence stretched out, but then Daniel took a deep breath and let it out slowly. "Because I should not have to," he said steadily.

Sean stared at him, then reached to grip his brother's shirt-front with one hand. Daniel took half a step back, but only to realign his weight, now shifted by the pull of supporting some of Sean's balance.

"You bastard," Sean repeated, only now his voice had fallen to a whisper, and he blinked rapidly, as though to ward off tears. "You have always left me to believe the worst of myself. Would it have cost you so dear to let me hope you were a liar? That you had done the evil deed yourself? But, oh, no, you never spoke, you never admitted or denied anything, and some-how that ever shifted the blame from you to me. Curious, is it not?" He gave a sickly smile.

"I have never blamed you. Perhaps, in the end, Aileen's death was no more than an accident," Daniel said, but there was an edge to his voice that suggested he did not believe it either.

"Why did it all go away? Aileen. The money. Everything," Sean asked, sounding as much at a loss to understand as a too-tired child.

"I do not know," Daniel said, shaking his head, and Etta thought that at the moment he seemed more like a parent than a brother to Sean. "Perhaps you should have been firstborn?" he suggested with a wistful smile. "I daresay you could not have done worse than I—"

"Nonsense!" Etta said, surprising herself almost as much as she did the two of them. It was to Sean she looked, however, as she experienced a rising tide of ire. "You think you could have somehow done better than Daniel?" She gestured in her husband's direction. "Do you think you could have changed Aileen's health? Or made the estate more profitable? How? By drinking and idling your days away? No, Daniel," she interrupted whatever he had opened his mouth to say, "it is only the truth, and Sean should hear it."

Daniel pressed his lips together, and Sean released his brother's shirtfront, staring at Etta with open astonishment.

"Have you truly thought about what you should have had if somehow you had been the eldest? Do you think it a joy to have all these dependents relying on you, as Daniel has? There is not only family to clothe and feed, but the servants as well, not to mention their back wages to be paid. And what of the butcher, and the dairyman, and the farrier? What of the new well to be dug, and the larder roof that leaks? Do you have any notion how best to maintain the gardens so that the pantry might be as full as possible, or what choices might make best use of the barley fields that might one day restore our fortunes?"

"Etta," Daniel said gently, but she ignored him.

"I have no doubt it hurt you when Aileen died, but how much more would it have hurt had she been your wife? How much more would it have hurt you to think it possible you might never have a son to name as heir? How would you have felt to put every waking moment into a dream, only to have it all snatched away?"

"I know about snatched dreams," Sean said, but there was no fire in the statement.

"But you know little of responsibility!" Etta returned, her hands on her hips. "While you lost yourself in mourning, Daniel had to continue on, to do all that his position and his responsibilities required, regardless of his own heartbreak. You ought look to your own behavior, Sean, and stop seeking to blame others for the position in which you find yourself today! Fate played a part, but the choices were yours."

Etta broke off, feeling her face coloring under the twin stares of the two brothers, but not wishing back a single word of what she had said. Truth be told, for all she knew Daniel *had* played some heinous part in his first wife's demise, but she did not want to believe it, and decided with a sudden and crystal clarity that she would not tolerate its belief in any other person.

Sean turned to Daniel, the two staring into his each other's faces for a long while, until a reluctant smile pulled up one corner of Sean's mouth.

"I do not think I especially care for this new wife of yours," he told Daniel.

"I do," Daniel told him simply.

Sean gave a small, beleaguered snort, but then he shook his head, no longer meeting anyone's gaze directly. "Be a good fellow and fetch my crutch, brother. It seems to have slipped out of my grasp somehow."

As Daniel crossed to retrieve the crutch, Sean turned to Etta, still not quite looking at her. "I suppose I shall have to work on my temper," he said, passion replaced by a cool civility, though she thought there might be a small hint of repentance in the words as well. He looked up, and she knew she was not mistaken. "It is my dearest wish that you will, I pray, accept my apologies," he went on, perhaps doing his best to sound sincere, though not quite succeeding. "I would not want to initiate another lecture from my dear sister-in-law."

"I accept your apology," she assured him, putting her chin up. "And there will be no more lectures. But I do have an instruction for you."

"Indeed?" he asked, looking at her askance as he accepted his crutch from Daniel.

"Indeed, yes. I consider it your obligation to see that the plasterwork is repaired."

Sean gawked while Daniel smothered an impulsive smile.

"Dashed if I will!" Sean cried, settling his crutch in place.

"You will," she stated firmly.

Sean cocked his head and pressed his hand to his chest to

execute a half-bow in Etta's direction, saying nothing further before exiting the room via the door Daniel moved to hold open for him.

"I should have this door removed, for his sake," Daniel mused once Sean was gone. He turned to face Etta, the smile now having risen into his eyes.

"I think you should leave it. The man needs a challenge."

Daniel's lips quirked, but before he could reply he had to move out of the way of the opening door. Mrs. Lawton stood there.

"My lord! I beg your pardon. I had no idea you were right behind the door."

"It is quite all right, Mrs. Lawton. Did you require something?"

"Mr. Emmett has returned, sir."

"So late in the day?" Daniel frowned.

"He seems pleased, sir. He said something about a seed drill?"

"Ah! Mr. Damson means to sell, I trust. The fellow must have another offer pending, though, for Mr. Emmett to return so near to the dinner hour."

Daniel glanced at Etta, and she felt her heart dance at what she took to be a flash of regret in his gaze. "Will you excuse me?" he inquired.

"Of course," she answered, hoping her gaze was just as regretful that he must tend to business again this day.

"Very well," he said to Mrs. Lawton. "You have shown him to my study?"

"Yes, sir."

Daniel nodded, and Mrs. Lawton moved out of the doorway to let him pass.

"Is everything well, my lady? I heard shouting, I thought . . ." Mrs. Lawton inquired of Etta, who shifted her attention from the closing door.

"Mr. Rifkin was . . . vocal," Etta chose to say. "Men can be so . . . loud, but I am sure you know that of your own experience, Mrs. Lawton."

Mrs. Lawton stiffened. "Indeed, why should I? I have never been married, my lady."

"I beg your pardon," Etta said, well aware that the "Mrs." might only be an honorary title, one awarded to all housekeepers. "I only meant to refer to your years of service to this household. I am sure you know better than I how clamorous these two men might be."

"It is not my place to speak poorly of my betters, but Mr. Rifkin can be most vexing when he chooses! Has he upset you? You appear a trifle pale. Would you care for tea? I have chamomile, which is most soothing for the nerves."

"That would be delightful," Etta assured her on a grateful sigh.

"Do you require a shawl? The fire's going out, I see. Shall I have Roberta build it up again?"

"No, no, I am soon for bed."

"Very good, madam. Would you care for some whiskey in your tea?"

"Good heavens, no!" Etta cried, tempted to laugh in surprise at the suggestion.

"It was the other . . . that is to say, the former Lady Healey's habit to take a nip now and then, you see," Mrs. Lawton explained, looking sheepish.

"Well, it is not my habit," Etta assured her, thinking the day had certainly been full of revelations. Surely that could not have been healthful for Aileen to drink whiskey? But then, perhaps it might have relaxed the lungs, and that could have only been for the good. However, could Aileen have had too much whiskey one day—enough to forget to carry her oil of eucalyptus with her? Enough to accidentally lock a door behind herself, or to trip and fall and not be able to rise? Perhaps Daniel had the right of it, that it had all been an unfortunate accident. Perhaps the confused vision Etta had experienced had been of a drink-befuddled Aileen realizing too late that she was not prepared for the attack that had come upon her. . . .

Etta was sipping the tea Mrs. Lawton brought her and mulling over these comforting thoughts before the room's grate, when the parlor door swung open once more. She looked up with expectation, having chosen to remain in the parlor merely because it was the last place Daniel had seen her, and could be the first place he might look to find her . . . should he conclude his business and come looking for her, that is. At her eager call of "Enter!" however, it was only the man-of-all-work, Will, who pushed the door open.

"Ma'am," he said upon seeing her.

"Will?" She put a question in her response.

"I come to patch the plasterwork, if'n it won't disturb you, ma'am?" he said, lifting the wooden bucket at his side, which contained a milky-colored substance, presumably mixed plaster, and a trowel.

"Of course it will not. Please proceed," Etta said, reaching for her cup of tea. She sipped at the relaxing brew and grinned to herself, considering that she had won a battle—even if the other side's surrender had not proven, technically speaking, wholly complete.

Ten

Daniel did not return to the parlor, nor did Etta find him in his study once she had seen for herself that Mr. Emmett had gone. She hurried above stairs to their bedchamber, hoping to find Daniel there—only to discover it was equally as vacant.

She closed her eyes, trying to shut out painful disappointment, only to fail. What had suddenly come between her and Daniel? When he had turned from her the night before last, she could ascribe that action to exhaustion, the kind of numbing that followed a shock. But yesterday and last night? No servant had claimed to see yet another ghost. No barrier had stood between them—and yet Daniel had made himself absent from her presence, from her touch.

Tonight, when she had castigated Sean, she would have sworn Daniel had responded with a flash of appreciation, perhaps even approval. He had seemed reluctant to leave her company. She had thought the difficulty must be behind them—and yet now he did not seek her out. He was in fact nowhere to be found.

She turned to close the door with a heavy sigh, only to have her heart skip a beat when she spied Daniel at the opposite end of the hall, just coming from the drawing room. His coat was off and his cravat discarded, revealing the strong column of his throat. In his hand he held a glass of amber liquid, its presence explaining how he had chosen to occupy himself.

He looked agitated, even disheveled despite the conforming fit of his silver-shot waistcoat and buff pantaloons. There was something about his expression, and his hair was unruly, as though he had run his hands through the dark waves more than once. It flashed through her mind that a guilty conscience could put such a look to a man.

He started to move forward, but suddenly his gaze came up and met hers, and they both froze, staring across the space dividing them.

"Etta!" he called out after a very still moment had passed. He cleared his throat, stalling as he searched for words or some other response to her presence. "Etta, I wanted to thank you— for what you said to Sean." He blinked once, but the rest of his body remained poised as if at any moment he might move away.

Another silence fell, an uncomfortable one. Daniel cleared his throat again.

"You told him what he needed to hear," he went on, perhaps to break the awkward silence, "whether or not Sean is sensible enough to heed your words. Any such admonition from me would surely have fallen on deaf ears, so . . . I hope . . . Yes, well, the thing of it is, I do thank you."

"You are welcome," she said, unsure if her own voice had enough strength to reach his ears.

She watched him closely, unable to find more words, longing for words that would make him stay, would make him reveal all she wished to know, would make him walk to her side and take her in his arms. But all she could manage was a steady silence—for to speak would be to weep, and she would not cry. She would not ask for his comfort with the ancient trick of tears, not if he would not offer such comfort freely, of his own initiative.

"So then," he said, still not moving, staring.

She almost wished he would go, would leave her to attend her misery in solitude, but she could no more break off staring across the void that separated them than she could speak.

"About last night, and the night before . . ." he said, and still an invisible cord stretched between them, pulling at her, making her long to cross the space, to throw her arms about his neck. Its pull was so strong, so irresistible as to cause her to begin to shake, to ache with the need to give in to the impulse.

He fell silent again, and she could see that his breathing had become uneven. "Etta," he said hoarsely, perhaps reluctantly.

Even across the space dividing them she could see that he struggled with some emotion, that he fought to keep it hidden from her, but something as strong as doubt or guilt or fear found its way across his features. Too, there was a kind of hunger that radiated unmistakably from his being, a palpable need that surely could only add to his obvious anguish. Etta caught her breath, and dared to think that need reached out to her, sought *her* presence as a means of solace.

He swallowed thickly.

"Daniel," she said, her throat also thick with longing so acute, she could only expect he would see it written clearly on her face.

He moved at last, reaching out slowly to set his glass on a hall table, his gaze never leaving hers. Then he took a step, and another, and then he was running down the hall, and suddenly she was in his arms, and his mouth was kissing hers.

"Etta!" he whispered again, against her lips, her name sounding like the sweetest music as she kissed him back. "By God, I am a fool, Etta. I have been so afraid!"

"Afraid?" she echoed, her hands in his hair.

"Afraid of what I have brought you to, here, this house. What right do I have to bind you to this unhappy place . . . this unhappy man?" he told her, his kisses coming to a halt as he averted his gaze.

"Oh, Daniel, it is but a house!" she assured him, gently turning his head so that he must look down at her again. "A house with unhappy memories, it is true, but you must not despair that it will remain unhappy forever. Is that what you fear?"

He was silent for a moment, then he shook his head ever so slightly. "Not when I am in your arms."

"Then stay in my arms," she said, pulling his head down to hers, her lips brushing against his as she spoke.

Then there was no more room for words, only for holding on to each other, kissing and touching with a fever that came from a kind of desperate joy.

He put her from him just for a moment, just so he might scoop her into his arms, cradling her against his chest. He looked down into her face, silently asking for her agreement, her approval, which she gave him by slipping her arms around his neck.

He pushed at the bedchamber door with his shoulder, opening it wide enough to carry her within, and did not put her down as he kicked it shut again. He did not put her down then either, not until he had crossed the room to the bed, where he turned and sat, taking her with him. He kissed her hungrily as he reclined, pulling her down with him even as they rolled once, exchanging places so that he lay atop her.

He kissed her for several moments, and then lifted his head long enough to peer down into her face and to brush a tendril of her tumbling-down hair from her cheek. Whatever fears had turned him away, he was sorry for letting them rule his demeanor; she knew that with a certainty that outstripped whatever lingering questions she yet possessed for now. Now was for forgiving; later was for explaining fully, for forgetting.

He snaked one arm under her, the better to pull her close, and with his other hand ran a finger down the line of her cheek. Etta gazed up into his deep brown eyes, eyes filled with troubling experiences he might one day tell her of, and hopes, and dreams, and passion. She would never know all his secrets, just as he would never know all of hers; she could only hope that one day he might share the important ones with her. All the same, whether time proved this man to be good or wicked, loving or conniving, she could not pretend that he had failed to invade her heart.

She closed her eyes for just a moment, and when she looked up at him again, tenderness gave way to the mounting tumult he created not just in her heart, but also in her body. He lowered his mouth to hers and kissed her anew with all the appetite of a starving man, making her smile just a little into his kiss at the idea of being his banquet.

He used his weight to press her into the feather mattress of their bed, and she exulted in his weight, his length, the warmth of his mouth on hers. Perhaps she ought to care that there existed mysteries between them yet. She supposed she ought to push him away and demand he satisfy her questions before he ever sought the pleasures of lovemaking. But he had untied the tapes of her bodice, and his warm hand stroked the tip of first one breast and then the other, and it was more than gratifying, it was glorious. Daniel then reached for her skirts, bringing them up inch by tantalizing inch until they topped the garters of her stockings, and then Etta had no more thoughts of questions first, but only of wanting him as much as he obviously wanted her.

She arched up into his length, and was gratified to hear him draw in a sharp breath. He held her to him with the one arm beneath her, and she felt his other hand working now not with her own frustratingly multitudinous garments, but with the pinnings of his own clothing.

"Devil take it!" he lifted his mouth from hers to say on an exasperated half-laugh. "Only see the effect you have on me. I'm as green as a boy, for I cannot undo these deuced buttons of mine!"

Etta smiled at him, presumably a rather wicked and enticing smile, for he went suddenly quite still even as she reached for the buttons of his pantaloons. "Allow me," she suggested.

"My dear lady, I shall not only allow it, but thank you most heartily," he assured her, his voice shaking either from laughter or some even more fundamental emotion.

When Daniel sat down on the bed the next morning, Etta blinked herself awake to find her husband fully dressed, a note in one hand. He gazed down at her, smiling softly. "Good morning."

"Daniel. Good morning." She sat up, stretching.

His gaze fell to the gauzy fabric of her nightrail, and his lips and brows did a little dance of appreciation. Etta smiled at him even as she blushed. "I daresay you need not be thinking what you are thinking, my lord husband, for you are hardly dressed for cavorting."

"Undressed, rather," he corrected her, tapping her lightly on the nose with the paper in his hand. "We must not speak of such things, however, for I must not be kept from going out this morning."

She made a little moue of disappointment.

Daniel kissed where he had just tapped her nose with the paper. "Delicious minx! But, listen, Etta, I have had a letter from America. It seems there is a party interested in acquiring the inns I have established there. My overseer there thinks the offer a worthy one, in fact a generous one. But I cannot decide upon it without first speaking to our bank officers, and to Mr. Emmett as well.

"Etta," he said, gazing at her soberly, "if I could have the money from the sale of the inns available to me by May, I could put every field I own into use, and repair all my equipment as well. There will be no extra for repairing the house or for fripperies, but come harvest . . . well, that could be a different matter." His eyes glittered with satisfaction at what was surely the thought of a brighter, more prosperous future.

"Oh, Daniel, I hope it all turns about just as you wish!" Etta cried, throwing her arms around his neck and snuggling close to him, the covers bunching around her middle.

He slipped his arms around her and grumbled playfully, "Damn these covers. And damn my clothes."

"Such language!" Etta laughed.

He stroked her face with one finger, reminding her that he had done the same last night. She shivered against him.

"You do realize it was your dowry that allowed us to come

to this moment, do you not? I have been able to pay some of our creditors, and to afford the servants a portion of their back wages. Although we live yet in a hole of debt, at least the water is no longer rising about our knees."

"Excellent!" she said emphatically. "I cannot think of a better purpose for the money."

He pulled her closer still. "I have yet failed to fully explain my earlier, and appalling, behavior toward you, you realize."

"Tell me when you return."

"I may be quite late, well into the evening."

"I will wait up for you."

"I could offer a quip about the word 'up,' but I shall refrain—or else never leave. Etta," he murmured, then thought better of words and kissed her instead.

She could not help but laugh when he at last pulled away, called her a siren for tempting him so, and then immediately kissed her again before hastening from the room.

Etta lay back against the pillows and sighed happily as she reviewed the past night's tender moments—and those that she could not truthfully call tender but which had proved wholly as captivating. If she were sure of nothing else, she was sure of one thing: Daniel loved her. He might have secrets to hide, but this one truth was absolute fact.

She experienced a certain smug satisfaction that it was he, not she, who had brought up the unfinished matter of explanations. How could she believe he had aught to hide? In the past she had pondered that it would take an extraordinary actor to deceive her so thoroughly, and now she would have to also believe he was a prodigious liar as well, a liar who could tell mistruths with his body as well as his mouth. While it was true that her "sensitivities"—as Papa had preferred to label her fey nature—had been skewed and oddly unsettled ever since she had set foot in this house, she could not believe she could be so far mistaken in any man with whom she had been so intimate.

Wrapped in warm covers and warmer thoughts, Etta allowed

herself to drift into the kind of half-sleep that morning contentment sometimes allows. She tumbled into a dreamy vision, where she looked out of her eyes and saw Daniel. In her daydream he, too, was napping, slanted in his leather study chair, a book neglected on the nearby table. How had it got to be night, and so cold, like autumn?

Etta reached out a dream-guided hand to touch Daniel's cheek, only now she *was* Daniel, and he was no longer asleep, but nonchalantly mounting the stairs of their home . . . *their* home, somehow not her own, but, no, it was his and Aileen's. . . .

Now in her half-dream she was Daniel no longer, but another pair of eyes looking at him. Eyes that looked to him as he bent over and touched something on the floor, and then the eyes looked down to the floor. Daniel was touching a woman, a woman prostrate on the floor with her hair tangled about her face . . . a face gone quite blue. Daniel made a strange choked sound, but it was impossible to say if it was a stifled scream or laughter—a horrible sound. Or perhaps it was a scream after all, and it was Etta who screamed. It could not be the woman on the floor, not Aileen, for Aileen was dead and no longer able to cry out.

"Lady Healey!" The voice cut harshly into Etta's dream, bringing her instantly awake. She opened her eyes and saw Mrs. Lawton standing beside the bed, wide-eyed as she peered down upon her mistress. "Lady Healey?" the housekeeper repeated, looking relieved as Etta struggled up to balance on her elbows. "You were crying out and thrashing. I quite thought you had taken a fever!"

Etta reached up and smoothed a wisp of damp hair from her temple. The housekeeper moved forward, pressing her hand to Etta's forehead. "You've no fever, ma'am. But only look at you shiver!" She clucked her tongue.

"I was having a nightmare," Etta murmured, blinking, trying to chase the last of the vision's ghastly tendrils from her waking mind. But even the bright sunlight that spilled through the open drapes could not quite dispel the horror of the dream's images.

"Do you know, my uncle had terrible nightmares, ma'am. A vessel burst in his head one day, just like that! I daresay the one caused the other." Mrs. Lawton eyed Etta. "Shall I send for the doctor, ma'am?"

"No. Send Robbie to me. I wish to dress." Etta sat up, trying to look less shaky than she felt.

"Is it your stomach, ma'am?" Mrs. Lawton inquired, and it was impossible to miss the acute interest behind the question, and presumably the reason for it. It was only logical, of course, that the mistress of the house might be increasing. The servants would have to be either blind or stupid to miss the fact that the master and mistress spent more than a fleeting moment or two in their bedchamber together.

"No," Etta answered firmly. It had been but two weeks since her last menses, and she suspected that was scarce enough time for any morning sickness to beset her should she have become in a family way. No, it was the thought of that blue face under tangled light brown hair that had distressed her. And that other part of her horrible dream, the sight of Daniel bending over the prone body. . . .

She shivered anew. "Shall I ring for Robbie myself?" she fairly snapped at Mrs. Lawton, regretting the harshness as soon as she spoke.

"I will send her up," Mrs. Lawton said, looking offended by Etta's tone, as well she might. She curtsied and left the room without another word.

Etta stared after her, then huffed over to sit on the edge of the bed as she waited for the maid to come. "Oh, stuff!" she cursed aloud, gently rocking herself back and forth, trying to soothe her own ruffled nerves.

Despite a studied concentration, by the time Robbie scratched at the door, Etta had failed to decide if she wished Daniel were by her side at this very moment, or relieved that he was not. Perhaps the latter, for she considered that she required a space of time in which to consider why this house could be filled with such love but also with such dreadful mysteries.

Eleven

"Daniel, where *are* you?" Etta said aloud, her breath momentarily fogging the glass through which she peered.

It was half past nine, the sun had set hours before, and Etta had eaten her dinner an hour past, alone. Daniel had warned her that he might be late, but even possessing that knowledge, she could not keep from venturing past the parlor window that looked out toward the stables.

The day, which had started with that nightmare vision, had only grown worse. Etta had spent some time at a dozen tasks, but none of them had held her interest for long. She had gone from stitchery to reading periodicals to letter writing, never sticking to any one long enough to finish it. In the end, she spent a great deal of time walking about the gardens and even out to the fields, as a way to avoid any tendency to nap. She had no interest in discovering whether or not another nightmare vision might beset her.

Night had put an end to her walks, if one did not count the pacing that continually brought her back to the window.

She knew why she paced. Yes, part of it was an eagerness to see Daniel again, but in a larger sense she wanted him to explain the coolness he had demonstrated toward her for two whole days. She wanted to hear the words, and more. Tonight she would take Daniel aside, to a place where she could order away any servants or brothers-in-law, and he would talk, and she would understand. She needed to understand. They needed to be utterly open with each other. She must tell him of her visions, and he must confess his unspoken but undeniable dread whenever a ghostly presence was suggested. Sean claimed Daniel had experienced an apparition once, and although Daniel had refuted the possibility aloud, his actions since had spoken louder than any words he might utter. He had yet to admit it, but he believed in the ghost—and Etta could not fault him for the supposition.

Perhaps Daniel experienced odd dreams, even as she did?

Oh, yes, they needed to talk. If things went on as they were, something would have to give, and Etta vowed it would not be the marriage. Every servant might have to go to clear the house of old recollections and rumors, and perhaps even Sean must be found a new home. How could the wound that Aileen's death caused ever heal with the two men who had loved her living under the same roof? It could not, not if both Sean and Daniel failed to change the pattern of what had already been, and had already failed.

As soon as Daniel returned, she would quietly ask him to join her on the roof's terrace, where complete privacy could be theirs.

Because her ears were tuned to listen for Daniel's return, Etta heard a door close—only the door was not on her floor, but over her head. She started to look back to the window in disappointment at the thought it was just a servant moving about above stairs, but then she heard the creak of old, unused hinges. In fact, she heard it three times, unmistakably. She knew that creak, for just today she had asked Will for some oil, and had applied it herself to the rusting hinges of the door leading out onto the terrace built into the roofline.

Obviously she had not done a proper job of it, for the hinges creaked yet again, a long-drawn-out creak, as though someone were testing them. Will must be attempting to assist her efforts—so much for the servants not knowing where to look should the mistress and master not be in their chambers!

Etta shook her head and determined she would go up and thank Will, and let him know he could see to the matter in the morning. It was full dark now and the moon only a sliver in the sky—whatever strict privacy she had hoped to gain seemed lost for the day anyway.

As soon as she stepped up the last stair that rose to the narrow hallway leading out to the terrace, Etta wished she had fetched a shawl before coming up, for the cool of the evening breeze met her sharply.

"Will?" she called, hesitating, for the short hallway was steeped in murkiness, no lamp's glow evident to light her way. But that was odd! No lamp's glow or candle's flicker framed the open terrace door whose gray outline she could just pick out from the surrounding gloom—surely Will was not attempting to work in the dark?

"Will?" Etta called again, taking one cautious step forward.

There was only silence in response.

Bother! Etta thought to herself. She must have left the door off the latch earlier, and the wind had pushed it, causing it to squeak. That was it, of course. She did not realize she had been holding her breath until she heard the sound of her own relieved sigh.

Should she slip down the stairs to fetch a candle? Well, no, it would take but a moment to close the door, this time making sure it latched properly.

Running her fingers along the wall to help guide her down the dark hallway, Etta reached the open doorway. She issued a small mewl of exasperation, for her searching eyes and hands did not find the door, but a moment later she recalled that it opened outward.

She stepped out onto the terrace, clouds canceling any starlight except for where they parted to reveal a thin sliver of the moon. Still, it was just enough so that Etta did not even need to reach out with her hands to find the door, for she spied at once the dull gleam of the metal door-latch in the feeble moonlight. As she leaned forward to reach for it, a whooshing sound brushed past her ear, and she gave a small cry, her hand springing up instinctively to dash away whatever it was—a cobweb?

No, it had been more in the nature of a bird, for, too, there had been a slight rustling sound, like wings, or fabric. . . .

Something glimmered in the dim light, and Etta ducked without conscious thought. The rustling and the whooshing sounds came again, this time accompanied by a sudden movement of air right before her face. The movement was so close, it startled another gasp out of her, and she leapt back.

The moonlight was just enough assistance that she saw a silvery line that for a moment made no sense, until slowly the image sorted itself out in her mind, and she realized she gazed at the moonlit metal edge of a shovel's blade.

"Mr. O'Brien?" she asked, her voice high-pitched.

The silvery line leapt upward, and then arced down again, and Etta realized in swift and dawning horror that it was being brought down, aimed directly at her head. She cried out and stumbled back, throwing up her arms, and tripped over something bulky just as the heavy metal blade swished before her face again. "Stop!" she cried in a strangled tone.

"Who's there?" came a distant call from down in the yard, and Etta tried to call back, but only a wordless shriek made it past her fear-clogged throat. She searched the darkness for the silvery gleam that could warn her of another attack, but the gleam was gone, replaced by sounds only—sounds of a horse and rider below, and the same rustling sound, only now retreating. If there were footsteps, she could not hear them over the repeated calls of "Who's there?" from below.

"Will?" Etta tried to cry out, recognizing his voice if not the trembling and weak thing that was her own.

A sudden glow from the doorway lightened the darkness, and then a figure was there, stepping forward, holding aloft a candle. The man shielded the light with one hand, the better to peer beyond its small bright flame into the darkness, but the small light was enough for Etta to cry out jaggedly, "Daniel!"

"Etta!" he said, crossing to her at once. "You have fallen!" He stooped beside her, setting the candle on the terrace floor, his eyes raking over her.

"Did someone pass you just now?" Etta asked, latching her hands to Daniel's forearms, squeezing tightly.

"No," Daniel said, looking puzzled.

"Is there another door to this terrace?"

"Yes. At the other end," he began to explain, but then they were both distracted by Will calling up from the yard, "My lord, is everything well?"

Daniel looked to Etta for an answer. "Are you hurt? Should I get Will to help me?"

"No. No, I am fine," Etta said, although the trembling that was settling into her every muscle threatened to disprove her denial.

"Everything is fine, Will," Daniel shouted into the darkness. "It must have been Lady Healey's shadow you saw."

"Right, sir. I'll just see your horse to the stables then, shall I?"

"Right," Daniel called back in turn, and then gave his attention back to Etta. He turned his arms over, causing her hands to slide down his forearms until he held both her hands in his, an unspoken offer to help her to her feet. "Did your candle go out?"

"I did not bring a candle with me." She was grateful for his assistance as she rose on shaky legs.

He glanced up at the moon. "Hardly the night for it, my dear. Are you sure you are well? You could have been truly hurt out here."

Hurt indeed! Etta glanced down at the bulky item she had tripped over, the candlelight revealing it to be a metalwork terrace chair, now tipped on its side. She turned her head, meaning to explain that it was not herself who had almost brought harm down upon her head—but then her gaze traveled over Daniel's feet, feet clad in naught but stockings.

"Your boots!" she said, staring.

"I took them off. They were too muddied from traipsing about town all day to wear into the house," he said, then he leaned down closer toward her, peering into her face. "My dear, even in this light I can see you have gone all pale. You *are* hurt!"

Her assailant, Etta recalled with a sudden mounting despair, had moved away on soundless feet, as might a man without boots, a man whose feet were clothed only in stockings. She shrank back and tried to pull her hands from Daniel's, but his grip tightened and he frowned.

But . . . but! Her mind frantically raced away from the thought that her husband, this man she loved so much, could have stalked her and attacked her in that cold-blooded manner. It was impossible, it had to be impossible! There had to be some proof that would make any such conclusion absolutely untrue!

She shook her hands free of his, her breath abruptly coming in ragged gulps, but as soon as she was free from the grip of his hands, she lunged toward him again. She gathered the fabric of his clothes, his coat, his waistcoat, his shirt, in her shaking hands. She manipulated the fabric, kneading it with her fingers and listening for the small sounds fabric makes when it is rubbed against itself.

She gave a sound rather like a sob and changed it into a hiccough for his sake. This was not the fabric she had heard! She had heard the rustle of a satin or a silk, or perhaps a bombazine, not this fawn and light wool, nor even the brocade of his waistcoat.

And she would swear the attacker must have been dressed all in black, or some other very dark color, with not so little as a pale cuff or collar to catch the moon's light. All she had been able to make out was that tiny silver glimmer on the shovel's edge. Daniel was dressed all in dove gray, and his snowy white cravat would have caught the moon's inadequate light even without help from the candle that revealed the colors before her now.

Etta closed her eyes and swallowed the tears of relief that threatened to roll down her cheeks.

"Etta!" Daniel cried, sounding alarmed. He caught her hands once more in his. "By God, you are chilled as ice!"

He let go of her long enough to tug his well-fitted coat from his shoulders and settle it about hers. Then he scooped her into his arms and turned to the door leading into the house.

"Daniel," she said, clinging to him, half giddy with relief, "you have left the candle."

"I will come back for it in a moment, but first we must get you out of this night air. Whatever were you thinking, my girl, to go traipsing about on a cool night with no shawl and no candle to light your way?"

He did not allow her to answer until she was well settled under three thick counterpanes and sipping a second cup of steaming hot tea.

"I heard the hinges squeaking and went to secure the door," she explained.

"Ah! My dearest love, you must promise me that next time you'll take a candle so you might avoid any future collisions with the furniture," he teased, sitting atop the covers and smiling at her.

"I promise. But, Daniel . . ."

"Yes?"

"There will not be a next time. I mean to say, I would not dare venture up there again, not by myself. Something . . . happened. If it were not for Will calling out, and you arriving, I think . . . I am afraid that . . ." Etta bit her lip, frowning down into the tea.

Daniel's smile faded. "Afraid that . . ." he echoed.

She looked up at him, willing him to believe her, for she knew the retelling of what had occurred would sound peculiar at best. "Daniel, someone tried to harm me. I could even believe I was lured up there. Someone tried to strike me with a shovel, and it was only a happy accident that I tripped just before you came to my aid, or else I would be knocked senseless now . . . or even dead."

Daniel stared at her, his expression moving from shock to

alarm. "What happened? Tell me everything!" he said, his voice choked.

She told him what she knew, from the moment she had stepped onto the terrace to how she deduced that the assailant had to have worn all dark colors.

"And this person had a muffler over his face, and a hat pulled down over his eyes?" he asked, rising to begin pacing beside the bed. "How else could you have missed seeing his face, or even just the whites of his eyes?"

"It was very dark, and my eyes were not fully adjusted."

He spun suddenly toward the door, throwing it open. "Mrs. Lawton!" he bellowed. "Robbie! Will!" Apparently he had no patience to wait upon the bellpull.

It was Mrs. Lawton who first came at his call, wide-eyed. "Lord Healey?" she questioned, bobbing a curtsy. "Does Lady Healey require more tea?"

"You are to stay with Lady Healey," he ordered in a voice that brooked no arguments. "Stay by her side every moment until I return."

"Yes, sir." Mrs. Lawton looked from one to the other, but if she sought an explanation, Etta did not offer to give her one.

Daniel was back in ten minutes, shaking his head as he dismissed the housekeeper. "Thank you, Mrs. Lawton. I wished to be sure there was no more furniture over which someone might stumble."

"Oh, quite right, that, sir!" She looked to Etta. "Poor lamb! Shall I bring another pot of tea? I have laudanum, if you should require it?"

"No, thank you," Etta said, not sure whether she felt more like laughing or shouting at the housekeeper for her constant attempts to physic a problem away. "I was only startled, not truly injured."

As soon as the servant had closed the door behind herself, Daniel turned to Etta. "I found nothing. No cloak, no hat, no shovel."

"Whoever it was took it all away with them."

"Yes, of course." Daniel turned his back to her, and she saw his hands knot into fists at his sides. "Are you," he began, then half turned to face her, a grim uncertainty settling upon his features. "Are you positive it was a living being who attacked you?"

Etta sucked in her breath. "Could you mean . . . ?"

"Yes," he said, scowling severely. "I am asking if you believe it could have been a ghost." He lifted a hand as though to deny his own words, but then the hand fell to his side once more and he began to pace again. "I do not want to believe in such things, but . . . Sean told you about the time I thought perhaps my room was . . . I thought I felt a *presence* there shortly after Aileen died."

He shook his head, perhaps at what he perceived as folly, but when Etta said nothing, he went on. "You see, it was not unlike what you have described. I do not recall any sounds, however. In fact, it came and went so quickly, I am inclined to think it was a trick of the mind only."

"Sean said it was as though clothing brushed against you," Etta said, reaching out a hand toward him.

He hesitated, then crossed to take her hand, letting her pull him to sit once more on the bed beside her.

"Yes, it was like that—only less so. I cannot quite describe it. It was not quite . . . anything, rather like a remembered scent. Have you had that experience, where you think you smell something, but when you take a deep breath, the scent is gone? Still it brings forth a memory, and for a moment you are lost in the memory itself and it does not matter anymore whether the scent was there or not in the first place." He shook his head, not looking at her. "It was cold, abruptly cold, as though I had suddenly wandered into an ice well. I remember that most distinctly."

"Were you frightened?"

He thought for a moment, then reached up to cup her chin, his thumb caressing her cheek. "No, oddly enough. Mostly, I was saddened. Saddened enough that I made the mistake of mentioning the incident to Sean."

"Do you think someone killed Aileen?" Etta asked, meeting his gaze squarely.

"Yes," he answered, and shook his head again, though not in denial but something much more like weariness. "Or, rather, I think someone allowed her to die. You know what that means, do you not, Etta?"

"That someone who has allowed a death before might not scruple to bring about another?" she asked, her voice sounding hollow even to her own ears.

"Yes." He stood, pulling free his coat, cravat, and waistcoat. Still in shirt and breeches, he slid under the covers next to her. He gathered her in his arms and pulled her close, and for a moment they just clung to each other.

"Although," he said on a troubled sigh, "who would do such a thing? It *had* to be someone who had easy access to the house. I saw O'Brien in the yard just before I came looking for you, and Sean is either passed out or asleep on the front divan. We both know Will was below, and that leaves only Mrs. Lawton and Robbie, and I cannot see why either of them would attack you!"

Etta shivered in his arms, and not just from the chill he had brought in under the covers with him.

"There is the other possibility," she said.

Daniel was silent, but his arms tightened around her.

"Who could move so quietly and in such obscurity?" Etta asked with quiet reasoning.

Daniel closed his eyes, and even from the angle at which she lay tucked within his arms, she saw his expression was more than just uneasy.

"You say you do not want to believe it, Daniel," Etta said softly. "But you are already halfway to believing in the ghost. And if that belief makes you a fool, then I am one also, for I vow there is something amiss in this house. I think we would be bigger fools yet not to ask ourselves if it is possible that

Aileen remains in spirit, and if she might be loath to have another Lady Healey in the house."

He frowned and shook his head against the pillow. "But does a ghost need to wield a shovel?" he asked. "Could she?"

Etta half sat up, balancing her weight on her elbow, thinking it a very good question. "It does seem improbable," she declared. "But then, I am not the manner of woman who could be frightened to death. So how else would a ghost do anyone harm?"

"I do not know," Daniel said, shaking his head again, and pulling her yet a little closer. "Etta," he said, "I tell you I *do* half believe in Aileen's ghost, more than half believe. That time . . . in my room . . . Then, when Robbie claimed to have seen it, when I went in the parlor and found nothing that could have frightened her so . . . I asked myself, how could I have brought you to this place, this household of thievery and death and ghosts? It made me realize how selfish I had been in marrying you, in not giving you the time to learn of these things, to make a choice—"

Etta leaned over and kissed him into silence, and then forbade him to speak in such terms again. "I made my choice."

They lay wordlessly together for a long time, until Etta broke the silence with a gasp. "Oh, Daniel, I quite forgot to ask! Your business! You never had a chance to say. Are you going to sell the inns? Did Mr. Emmett think it advisable?"

Daniel gave a cocked smile. "Yes and yes. And the bank officers were pleased with the notion of our debts resting on a future of good old English corn, over what they consider pure speculation in America. I think it may all work to our advantage, Etta, God willing."

"I am so pleased."

"We are chasing some of the shadows from our lives," he said, the smile fading. He twirled a tendril of her chestnut hair around his finger and sighed. "I fear only that I may not be able to find a way to clear *all* the shadows away."

"We shall find a way."

"If it was a man who attacked you, I *will* catch him and he *will* be punished," Daniel said grimly.

"I do not care about punishment. I just want him gone so there can be peace here. This house needs some peace."

"We should not dismiss . . . that other possibility," he warned.

"Even if it is a ghost . . . Aileen, we shall find a way to go on, Daniel."

"Preachers and incense?" He raised an eyebrow at her, and she was happy to see the small glimmer of amusement in his eyes.

"If need be."

"How can you be so fey and yet so practical, my wife?" he asked, and she just shook her head for an answer.

When they finally whispered their good-nights to each other, he told her he would lie awake until she was asleep, and only then would he blow out the branch of candles on the bedside table.

Etta did not insist there was no need.

Twelve

The next morning Etta sat beside one of the vase tables in Daniel's study. Its small surface served, somewhat inadequately, as a writing table, for she was still loath to bring down the writing desk from Aileen's sitting room. That could come later; for now it was enough that she sat facing the portrait of Aileen. She did not sit so to dare the ghost, if ghost there was, but rather, it was something more in the nature of beginning to claim pieces of the household as her own. She would gaze anywhere she liked; at the portrait too, if she pleased.

Daniel glanced up from his list, having checked off every item. "I have found nothing," he told Etta. "There were no clues to be found! Nothing on the terrace. All the shovels were accounted for, and the other terrace door was locked."

"Of course, it would behoove the assailant to be tidy," Etta pointed out. "To not be caught out. But, my love, we have not considered that perhaps it was a beggar or a drunkard. Someone who was merely looking for a night's rest. Someone who was confused," Etta said.

"But why attack you?"

"I startled him?" she suggested.

Daniel sank back in his chair, looking doubtful. He tapped his foot, obviously thinking, then sighed. He sat forward and pointed to her sketch. "I see you are drawing again."

"Yes," Etta answered, casting him a somewhat absent smile, for she concentrated on the pattern she drew. "Drawing helps me think about things."

"Flowers," Daniel said approvingly, giving a nod toward the paper. "You have a talent, my love."

"Thank you." Etta smiled again in a quick thanks, but then she scowled briefly at her drawing, remembering she had meant to ask Daniel about one certain flower. "Daniel, why did you bring more lavender into our room? I should have thought you would have noticed I did not care to have it about."

"I did not bring any lavender in," he said, picking up and opening a newspaper from the chair next to his.

"You did not? Then, who did?"

"Mrs. Lawton likes to put flowers throughout the house," Daniel said, turning from the front page.

"But not in the middle of the night. Not while we are yet sleeping."

"Of course not." He looked up, perhaps meaning to question her allegation, but instead he said, "You like that pattern, I see. The X's."

Etta reviewed the sheet of paper, a little surprised to see that she had indeed covered the vase she had drawn with a series of connected X's, not unlike the pattern made by a trellis. And there were the same X's again, this time in tinier versions, in the way she had shaded the leaves and petals. There were some random X's, too, at the edges of the sheet, although a little effort could easily turn them into an attractive border.

"I cannot get this image out of my head," she explained, and then laughed at herself. "All these X's." She frowned, even though she was well used to unusual things turning up in her drawings. Had not Daniel's image been sketched by her pencil weeks before she ever saw his dear face? "It must be that I am developing some scheme of how to replant the little garden by the music room."

"It shan't include lavender, I presume."

Etta laughed. "Indeed not."

Mrs. Lawton entered through the open doorway. "My lord, Mr. Emmett is come to see you," she announced.

"Ah! It is time for the seed drill to be delivered from Mr.

Damson's." Daniel put his newspaper aside and glanced at Etta while Mrs. Lawton curtsied and left.

"You ought to go with him," Etta told him.

Daniel shook his head. "I cannot leave you alone."

"Would you be home before dark?"

He considered her words. "I would not be gone more than an hour or two. Only long enough to see that the drill is loaded on the cart properly, and to negotiate a lesser fee if we find it is in poorer condition than we think."

"Go, then. I shall be quite all right. I will find Mrs. Lawton and remain with her."

His face relaxed. "An excellent plan."

When he had gone, Etta looked down at her drawing and shook her head. Whatever had possessed her to draw all those X's? It was not a style she had ever employed before.

All at once a shiver of cold crept up the back of her neck, making the hair at her nape stand up. For a moment it felt as though she had walked into a winter's landscape, and just as abruptly the sensation was gone. She gasped and stared down at the drawing, and then slowly she raised her face to stare up at the portrait over Daniel's desk.

Had she put pencil to paper once again to visualize a coming event? Could it be . . . ? Was Aileen trying to tell her something? It certainly seemed the other woman's spirit was caught here, struggling to reveal unfinished business. Could that unfinished business be identifying her murderer?

Etta glanced back at the X's on her paper, and thought, no, this drawing was much more in the flavor of hidden pictures, such as favored in children's books. Look at the picture and see one thing, look closer and see another. These X's—could they be like the proverbial pirate's map, marking the location of a hidden treasure?

The jewels! The missing jewels—Aileen had hidden them. The hair on Etta's nape stood up again.

She began to walk, skirting the edges of the room, her gaze

intense and searching. X's—something had inspired her to
draw X's.

She would seek X's in a pattern. Perhaps she should go to
the garden, for were the X's not very like a trellis? But no,
Aileen would not have been very likely to dig in the dirt, to
risk the breath-stealing dust. She would have been far more
likely to find a place inside the house in which to hide the
jewels, a place not too difficult to reach, so as not to overexert
the limits of her body.

After half an hour Etta abandoned the study. It had always
been Daniel's domain anyway, and a more likely hiding spot
would be Aileen's sitting room. That is where Etta went next.

Two hours later she had searched every room in the house
except the servants' chambers, even including Sean's. The closest
she had come to finding an X pattern was on the hem of one of
her own dresses in her wardrobe, and a pattern in the frieze near
the ceiling of the front parlor—the latter of which was really two
crossed fronds that only vaguely resembled an X.

Daniel would be home soon—perhaps she should just wait
for his appearance? She would tell him what she thought, and
he could join in the search.

Ten minutes later, when Daniel had yet to make his return,
curiosity won the moment and Etta mounted the stairs, making
her way to the servants' quarters.

Everyone was busy at assorted tasks, but Etta knocked all
the same. It was her right to go where she liked in her own
home, but nonetheless she squirmed at the sense of invasion
that accompanied the opening of each subsequent door. Will's
room was the first on her left, but all she found within was a
mild disorder that Mrs. Lawton would hardly approve were she
to inspect it. As to Mrs. Lawton herself, her room was at the
end of the corridor, where it stood guard over the men's rooms
to the left, the female servants' to the right. That was one of
the things Daniel wished to change about the estate, should
there ever be money for it: He wanted to move the men's quarters to a separate building, as would be more fitting.

There were two more rooms, one each for Mr. O'Brien and Robbie, and another room next to the maid's, used for storage. Etta found nothing in them that resembled the X pattern, and so turned to the final room, Mrs. Lawton's, the presumably larger one at the end of the corridor. Etta knocked and reached for the handle, mildly surprised to find it locked. Now, why would Mrs. Lawton feel the need to lock her door? It was not as if the household were brimming with new hands—but then Etta remembered that Daniel had said they had once had a problem with items going missing.

She returned to her bedchamber, finding the ring of keys in Daniel's drawer, just as before.

She mounted the stairs once more, and after two false attempts fitted the proper key in the keyhole of Mrs. Lawton's door.

Etta swung open the door, finding the room dim, as the afternoon sun had already passed the windows by. She was instantly struck by the fact that the room was far more furnished than any of the other servants' rooms. There was a wider bed, complete with canopies that could be tied back on the posters. There were two lamp tables near the bed, each with a wide candelabrum atop it, and one of them also sporting an oil lamp. Good heavens, if the woman lighted the lamp and all the candles at once, she would have it like day in here even on the darkest night! Too, there was a vanity table replete with silver-backed brush and mirror, a profusion of ribbons and combs, and a half dozen bottles of scent.

Etta frowned at the extravagance—it seemed oddly misplaced in a housekeeper's room. But then, perhaps these were the collected valuables of a lifetime. Etta lifted her gaze to the walls, searching for the X pattern, finding instead a plethora of wall-mounted items. There were dried flowers hanging from hooks or small nails, long since wilted remnants of days past. There were paper valentines, faded with time, and small framed paintings of pastoral scenes—one of which was surely a painting of this house, only the trees were not so tall as they were now. There were pamphlets from lectures and balls presumably once attended, all neatly pinned about the walls, dust-free but still showing signs of aging. It would seem that Mrs. Lawton had once been a young woman of at least some social standing. What had gone amiss? Had there been no offer of marriage? Had her family lost its income, forcing Mrs. Lawton into a life of servitude? Something of that order had surely occurred. But how sad! The woman clung yet to what once might have been hers.

Directly above the housekeeper's bed hung a good-sized portrait of a man, and Etta could only guess the subject to be Daniel and Sean's father, for there was a strong family resemblance. She frowned. Ought it not be in the gallery? Arching above the portrait was a sword's scabbard complete with its sheathed blade, an ornate piece that ought to have been hung in a study or a library, but which seemed oddly out of place here.

Etta moved closer, finding pinned below the painting an article from a news sheet, old and yellowed, and tacked to the wall with a straight pin; a quick glance revealed it was a society column of old, and half an article apart but faintly underlined were two names: *Miss Georgia Lawton* and *Mr. Adam Rifkin.* Adam? That had been Daniel's father's Christian name, and reflected that this column must date from the days before he had inherited his title of baron from his own father, for there was no mention of the title.

Etta frowned and took half a step back. It would seem that Mrs. Lawton had, years earlier, known Daniel's father in a social sense. One might think she would avoid employment in his home, but Mrs. Lawton had in point of fact been the housekeeper since before Daniel's father had died. Extraordinary!

Etta's puzzled gaze traveled on to yet another table, one that served more to make the room crowded than it ever did to adorn it. She was struck by the arrangement of bibelots across its surface. There were china figures; and silver-gilt tea plates and spoons; delicate Oriental jade carvings; a small collection of timepieces, all wound and tick-tocking away; and one thing that made Etta gasp aloud. There, on Mrs. Lawton's table, lay a matched pair of simple little earbobs made of jet. They scarcely possessed any real value, Etta knew, not if they were the same pair she had presumed lost during the move to her new home. She crossed the room to pick them up, finding the tiny nick that had been made years ago when her own mama had accidentally dropped the one. The earrings were hers, undeniably.

Etta looked up, staring blindly in shock. Mrs. Lawton was the thief! The one who had prompted Daniel to ask Aileen to hide what remained of the family's disappearing jewels. Mrs. Lawton, of the graying hair and kindly manner!

Etta spun around to exit the room, for the walls suddenly seeming closer and dimmer. She jerked to a stop in surprise, for there, pinned to the wall next to the door, hung one of her own sketches of Daniel, one of the averted-face poses she had drawn before she had met him. "She stole my sketching!" Etta cried aloud. The woman had gone through her sketchbook! Somehow that infamy exceeded even the theft of the earrings.

The X-pattern drawing Etta still held rustled as she gathered up her skirts and fled the room.

She flew down the first flight of stairs, nearly colliding with Mrs. Lawton on the landing.

"My lady?" Mrs. Lawton said. Where only five minutes earlier Etta would have said the woman's gaze was filled with consideration, now it was suspicion Etta saw glimmering there. Did she imagine it?

Mrs. Lawton touched the ring of keys at her waist, and Etta's gaze followed Mrs. Lawton's down to where Etta clutched another set of keys.

"My lady?" Mrs. Lawton repeated, her expression flat.

Etta took a step back, but then she lifted her chin. "I have unlocked the sitting room that belonged to the former Lady Healey," she lied. "I mean to start using it myself."

This was neither the time nor the place to confront Mrs.

Lawton with what Etta had learned; that should wait until Daniel was present. He would know what manner of items had gone missing over the past year, and he would want to say how Mrs. Lawton was to be dealt with.

"I shall have Roberta begin to clean it tomorrow," Mrs. Lawton said calmly, and Etta wondered if the woman sounded perhaps just a little too calm. After all, Mrs. Lawton had just caught her coming down the stairs from the floor above, not from the direction of the suite of chambers containing Aileen's sitting room.

"Was there any disorder, or sign of beetles or mice perhaps?" Mrs. Lawton went on. "Anything I should see to personally?"

Etta looked away, striving to appear unconcerned. "No. A dusting and an airing will do nicely," she said, stepping around the housekeeper.

"Do you require luncheon at this time, my lady?" Mrs. Lawton asked, her voice floating over Etta's shoulder to touch her spine with a chill.

"No, thank you. I am not hungry," Etta answered, turning to face the housekeeper once more.

"Then might I bring you some tea?"

"No, thank you. In point of fact, I will be occupied for the next while and do not wish to be disturbed."

"Very good, my lady," Mrs. Lawton said, curtsying and moving away down the corridor toward Aileen's sitting room. *Blast!* Etta cursed—the woman would discover the room was not unlocked after all. She would have to realize that Etta had lied.

Etta gripped the banister as another thought struck her: She had neglected to relock Mrs. Lawton's door. The woman had only to go up to her room to confirm that her secret had been uncovered.

Etta took a deep breath and told herself that perhaps it was just as well to set the wheels of justice in motion. She was more than half convinced the housekeeper had some suspicion of what was to come. Surely Mrs Lawton had not expected that her thefts could go on, with herself never suspected? She might even have anticipated this day of reckoning's unavoidable arrival, for that would explain her notable air of calm. Still, would she remain calm once she knew conclusively that Etta had lied to her? All of this would be better handled if Daniel were home. Oh, how soon would he return?

Soon, please soon, Etta silently prayed as she walked slowly down the next flight of stairs, the motion completely at odds with her pounding heart. She gasped aloud when she saw another figure coming up from the ground floor toward her. But the gasp turned into a trembling sigh of relief when she saw it was Sean who slowly worked his way upward.

"Thank God!" he growled sourly, spotting her. "Now I shan't be required to climb all the way to the top floor."

"Sean!" Etta breathed. She came down the stairs to his side, intensely aware of the woman on the floor above her and the stolen earrings yet clutched in her hand.

"Your husband, on his way out, rang a peal over my head," Sean explained, "and said I was to keep my eyes and ears open while he was gone, on pain of death. Which, although odd, seemed odder yet when I suddenly looked about and found myself quite alone," he said dryly, but then a scowl slowly developed across his features as he gazed into her face. "And perhaps my brother's peculiar request was not so peculiar after all, Etta! You look as though you have seen our resident ghost."

Etta pressed her lips together, weighing whether or not to tell him of what she had found. What if Mrs. Lawton had a reasonable explanation—as if there could be one! Still, it was Daniel's place to deal with the issue, and to bring the rest of the household into it too soon might prove unfair, and certainly unsettling to all. She looked down at the ring of keys yet in her hand, and decided that, yes, it would be better all around to wait for Daniel to return before confronting the truth head-on.

She shook her head as if the action could erase the troubling thoughts there. She decided she would, even as she had told Mrs. Lawton, keep herself occupied for the time being.

"I have not seen a ghost, no, but I *am* looking for something. Perhaps you can assist me. I have been searching the house, attempting to find this pattern." She handed him the drawing.

"These X's?" he questioned, handing the picture back to her. "Makes me think of wine racks."

She stared, her eyes going wide. "Of course!" she cried. "Why, Sean, of *course!* Wine racks!"

"Oh, no, Etta. I can see by your expression that it is not enough that you have climbed to the top of the house. Now you mean to descend to its depths. How am I to keep you company if you will insist upon flitting about so?"

"I would not ask it of you," she said, pressing the drawing, the earrings, and the ring of keys on him. "Please keep these for me. These are not Mrs. Lawton's keys—I will explain all later! Go to the front parlor and . . . and order an afternoon repast, something suitable for a small celebration," she instructed him, starting down the stairs.

He turned to follow. "What exactly is it we are to celebrate, if I might be so bold as to ask?" he said, just barely managing to retain his sour tone.

"Why, either the finding of the hidden jewels or, wanting that, the fact you have decided I am to be your friend."

"Did I know about this so-called friendship?" he asked with a derisive snort.

"You began it when you called me Etta." She smiled at him. "I never did!"

"Just now. Not once, but twice. Too late, Sean, you have revealed your truer consideration of me. Tell Robbie that I would like to have some of the lemon cake at our little feast, will you please?"

She did not give him time to utter a denial beyond the sputtering sound he made, for she hurried down the stairs in the direction of the kitchen. She dashed through the room, startling Robbie and announcing, "Mr. Rifkin will be ringing shortly."

Etta sailed on through the room to the door that opened down to the wine cellar.

It was the work of a moment to put a rush to the ever-present kitchen fire and light a lamp, and then Etta worked her way down the cellar stairs, leaving the door to the kitchen open. After only ten steps the kitchen's light penetrated the cellar's darkness no farther, but her lamp showed her where next to step. She became aware that her heart was still pounding, presumably from a mix of dread of what the future confrontation with Mrs. Lawton must entail, and a growing conviction that she, Etta, would find the jewels Aileen had hidden.

She wavered for a moment in her determination when she stepped to the cellar floor. The dirt was cold beneath her feet, penetrating her slippers, and the air was an odd mixture, being both cool and stale at once. Its chilling touch reminded her of how the hair had stood up on the nape of her neck just a few minutes past, when she realized that her drawing could represent a way to find the missing jewels.

Too, she had forgot how many racks there were. The number of them that she could count was plentiful enough—and she knew her small light did not illuminate them all. Still, without doubt they formed neat rows of X's, and that realization was enough to spur her on. The family had no doubt searched there before, but perhaps they had concentrated on the hard-packed dirt floor and not on the racks themselves.

Etta chose the nearest one, set her lamp on the floor, and began running her hands over every piece of crossed wood, every side board, every dusty, cobwebby surface. She lifted the bottles when she came to them, shaking them and listening for the sound of something other than wine moving in the bottles, and peered at every label as if they might supply some vital clue as to where to look next.

She had completely searched every inch of the first wine rack, when the door leading from the kitchen above slammed shut.

Etta jumped and gasped, but then she held her breath, for there followed the unmistakable sound of a heavy crossbar being slid into place. The only way to bar the door was from the cellar; no one could bar, or open, the door from the kitchen side.

Which could mean only one thing, Etta realized with mounting alarm: Whoever had barred the door had done so quite deliberately.

There was only one way out, and that was to remove the wooden bar, which would be heavy but simple enough were it not for one vital fact: Etta was not alone.

Thirteen

There was the slight sibilant sound of fabric rubbing against itself, but other than that very little to indicate that the other occupant of the cellar was coming down the stairs, yet Etta sensed an approach as keenly as if she could see through the gloom. She stood up straight, slowly, stiff with alarm, knowing that particular shushing sound, the sound of a rustling fabric.

Dread filled her as she realized it would be pointless to attempt to hide. Where was there to go?

A figure came out of the shadows, at first just a dim outline, but then there was a gleam reflected from something metallic. Etta winced and remembered the shovel, and then the figure stepped into the circle of light cast by Etta's lamp.

"Mrs. Lawton," Etta said without any real surprise.

Perhaps because the limited light pooled at their feet, Etta noticed first that the woman wore no shoes, only dark stockings—the better to slip about quietly, no doubt. She was otherwise dressed all in black, in a bombazine gown that Etta faintly recalled having seen, although she had never noticed its lack of ornamentation before. Had the housekeeper paused to don a domino to cover her hair and face, Mrs. Lawton could have blended into any night. No, not quite, not as she was at the moment. There were about her person two exceptions to the cloak of invisibility: The first was that posed glinting in one hand was a sword—no doubt taken from the scabbard in the woman's room. The second was the jewels at her throat and ears, flashing red even in the dim lamplight.

"The rubies!" Etta gasped, her gaze rising to lock with that of the other woman. "Merciful heaven, you had to have taken them from—" she faltered, the thought too dreadful to say aloud.

"From that woman's dead body," Mrs. Lawton finished for her. She put up her chin, not deigning to call Aileen by name. "I did! I took them! I opened the casket and I took them back. It was foolishness to bury them with that worthless chit. They were never hers. They belong to me." She said the last flatly, as though it were an obvious truth. "I never told Daniel he could give them to that woman."

"But it is not your place to give or withhold permission," Etta cried, regretting the words at once as a flash of fury contorted the housekeeper's face.

"Not *my* place!" she roared. "Look who is talking! Who do you think you are? *I* am the Dowager Lady Healey. This is *my* house. I say who wears my jewels and who does not, even if my son never listens to me."

She is mad! Etta thought, pressing trembling hands to her mouth. "Your son?" she asked weakly.

"Daniel," Mrs. Lawton said. "He keeps bringing home wives." She wagged her head from side to side, her face contorting with disdain. "Why does he do that, tell me? I make a good home for him. Why does he need a wife?"

The point of the sword lowered as she stared straight ahead, lost to her own thoughts, her anger seemingly spent. Perhaps it might be possible to reason with the poor, confused creature, Etta thought.

"Daniel is not your son, Mrs. Lawton. His mother was Francine, Lady Healey. I have seen the portrait."

"No!" The cry, filled with pain, echoed in the dark chamber. Tears slipped down the woman's cheeks, but her face did not soften from sorrow, instead becoming a dreadful mask of denial. "No, no, no, no, no! *I* had that baby! Her husband was my lover. For years and years! *I* had that baby, not that stupid cow! He was mine, always mine. Haven't I tended him these years? He's my child! Adam was *my* husband," she ranted. She slashed the blade through the air as though she could cut the truth to pieces.

Etta looked toward where she knew the stairs to be, lost in darkness now, and back to the raging woman who blocked her access to them. Perhaps, if Mrs. Lawton ever lowered the sword again, Etta could fly at her and knock her over. Perhaps it might buy her enough time to climb the stairs and remove the heavy bar . . . in the dark. . . . Etta bit her lip, and remained very still, watching and hoping.

Mrs. Lawton pressed a hand to her forehead, her eyes momentarily closing. They snapped open almost at once, and she stated clearly, almost calmly, "She was breeding, you know."

Etta blinked, saying nothing.

"Daniel's woman, that Aileen chit. After two long years of proving barren, she was going to have a child." Mrs. Lawton looked directly into Etta's eyes, and Etta shivered at the coldness she saw there. "I couldn't let her do that, have a child. Everyone knows what happens to the dowager when there's a child. I would be out the door, stashed away in some little house they would have built for me."

Mrs. Lawton shook her head, disgusted. "So I let her die. I said I had steaming water ready for her. I had thrown dirt around her room, scattered it everywhere. She could not have avoided breathing its dust! She came into the room, and I took the oil from her, and then I—" She paused, laughing once, briefly, before resuming her terrible tale. "I locked her in the room and chased her about. With this very sword, you see. Adam's sword." She scowled. "Before he went into the army, he had meant to marry me, you know."

The woman's face lightened and calmed. "Instead, he married me later," she said, and Etta was convinced the housekeeper believed every word. Had Mrs. Lawton been one of the guests at Adam Rifkin's wedding? Had she long since refused to remember it was a woman named Francine who had married Adam, replacing the memory with one of her own making?

How long had this woman lived in a secret fantasy world, one that could not support the idea of interlopers, not wives, not babies.

"She thought I would cut her, silly creature!" Mrs. Lawton went on. "But no, her death must be natural, of course. There would be no fingers to point at me, not if her death could be made to seem an utterly natural one. So, once she was scarcely able to breathe, I unlocked the door and slipped out, locking it behind me once more, and the rest was left to happy fate. It took only a moment more to unlock the door before someone came to find her. A locked door would not have looked natural." Mrs. Lawton beamed at Etta.

"You know a lot about medicines and health, I think," Etta said, desperately wondering if flattery might subdue this woman's rages where reality never could.

"I know a lot about many things."

"And about flowers?"

"Of course!"

"Of course," Etta echoed to herself. That explained everything: The orangery full of flowers that represented love and affection—that was for the estate, for Daniel, for her "son." But the patch planted by the interloping Aileen—Mrs. Lawton had no doubt taken secret pleasure in recommending that the little garden be filled with flowers that represented doubts and stifled love. Poor Aileen had obviously known nothing of the botanicals' popular meanings. And it was surely Mrs. Lawton who had placed the lavender in their bedchamber, knowing full well that lavender stood for distrust. Daniel was to distrust his new wife; he was to attach himself to no woman but the housekeeper who had convinced herself she was his mother.

Dear God, Etta thought, this woman could persuade herself to believe any twisted notion she chose to form. Perhaps there was some inkling of truth in what Mrs. Lawton believed, as so often was true with those who felt they had been wronged or misplaced in life. Perhaps she had indeed once been Adam Rifkin's lover, until something had gone wrong. Or perhaps it had been something even more innocent than that: It was easy to believe that the previous Lord Healey might have once courted a girl who had seemingly had prospects. Perhaps the failing of her family's fortunes had turned him away, or perhaps he had witnessed one too many indications of the woman's unbalanced nature, but whatever had happened, Adam Rifkin had left her behind. He had joined the army, and then he had married another.

Georgia Lawton had invested too many hopes in being a part of the Rifkin family. Had it cost her in spirit to consent to be the man's housekeeper? She had come to serve on Adam Rifkin's staff shortly after his wife had died, Etta knew, so perhaps she had consented, hoping that Adam might renew—or begin—an affair with her? Perhaps he had made promises that were never kept, perhaps not when first they knew each other, nor later?

Etta gazed at Mrs. Lawton, saddened by the conclusion that some series of catastrophes must have conspired to result in this woman's fantasies. Somewhere along the line, hopes had turned into fears, and dreams had withered into delusions.

Mrs. Lawton sighed heavily. "I cannot allow it, you know."

"Allow what?" Etta asked, suspicion replacing sympathy.

"I cannot allow you to breed."

Etta caught her breath and let it out slowly. "I know you were pondering just yesterday whether or not I could be expecting a child, but I assure you—"

"I can tell."

"Truly, Mrs. Lawton, I feel you are mistaken—"

"And you unlocked my door. You know about my room, my things. You really ought not have pried." Mrs. Lawton raised the sword to about the same level she had raised the shovel just the night before, and Etta bit back a whimper of sheer panic.

"You cannot kill me," she cried, trying to sound firm, "and remain uncaught. There is no way to make my death seem natural."

"And no way to prove I did it. No way to prove anyone did it. They will say it was the ghost! The ghost, who was invented by me, and who was really terribly convenient. Even the young master began to believe it was the ghost of his woman who filled the halls with strange scents, or danced in sheets before the servants, or left flowers in odd places."

Etta stared. "It was you. You were the ghost." She shook her head, stunned. "But the drafts! How did you make such chilling drafts?" She shivered at just the memory of that brief, deadly-cold sensation.

Mrs. Lawton frowned. "The house is drafty," she said dismissively, then she chortled. "You should have seen Daniel the day after Roberta screamed at the ghost! Pale as a ghost himself, and all scowls. But you did not see him, did you, because he avoided you, did he not? Oh, yes, I saw. I daresay he was afraid he would bring the ghost's wrath down upon your head. And guess what, he has!" Mrs. Lawton smiled again, an awful, soulless smile.

"Nonsense! No one blames a bloody death on a ghost," Etta said from between lips drawn tight by dread.

"But how else to explain how the crossbar got in place and yet the room is found empty of all life?" Mrs. Lawton leaned forward as though confessing a secret to a friend. "There is a hidden passage, of course. The Papists who lived here had it put in. Everyone believes it inaccessible, for Adam had it bricked up after Sean hid there for most of one day to escape lessons as a boy. All I had to do over the years was chip the bricks loose, and when I restack them, no one is the wiser! I have used the passage these ten years past. All I have to do is listen to be sure no one is in the rear parlor, and out I come!"

"But . . . a death! They would search the house more thoroughly. They would find your loose bricks!" Etta argued, and although she sensed she ought not show fear, she could not help but step back a pace.

Mrs. Lawton's shook her head. *"If* they think to look here in the cellar after I assure them I saw you go out to stroll the gardens, and *if* they think to search the house before I can mix new mortar to cement the bricks securely."

"You are mad," Etta said in a choked whisper, because there was nothing left to be said. The woman could not be persuaded that her scheme was faulty, crazed, and her escape from suspicion surely doomed to failure. Etta reached out with shaking hands, closing them tightly around the first bottle she encountered. She hefted it. "I am going to go up those stairs—" she began to state, but her words were interrupted by a sudden loud banging.

Mrs. Lawton glanced over her shoulder. "The door!"

"Yes!" Etta cried out in overwhelming relief. "They know we are down here."

A muffled shout came down to their ears, the words unintelligible, but the voice wonderfully familiar.

"Daniel!" Etta shouted as loudly as she could, tears springing to her eyes. "Daniel!"

"Daniel!" Mrs. Lawton echoed.

Etta felt her mouth twist in distaste at the sound of that name on this woman's lips. "You would be caught out if you did anything to me now, surely you see that," Etta told her in scalding tones. "Daniel will see that it is all over."

Mrs. Lawton's face contorted as if two strong emotions battled for dominance there. She physically shook, but then her gaze fell to the floor, her shoulders slumping unexpectedly, and despite her apparent misery she seemed more like the Mrs. Lawton—the public facade—that Etta had known until that day. She seemed to have gathered a shred of her wits, to be aware that her conduct might be censured by others.

"Will he send me away?" the housekeeper asked, and her plaintive tone was almost pitiful to hear. "Will I have to live in a dower house by myself?"

The thudding from above stopped for a few moments, then resumed, now more forcefully. Was someone battering the door with some sort of ram, or perhaps taking an ax to it? Mrs.

Lawton did not seem to notice, sunk in deep thoughts, perhaps despair.

Etta took a step to the side, her eyes fixed on the woman, and then she took another. But she was not allowed a third, for of a sudden Mrs. Lawton's fury returned on a roar, and she hoisted the sword over her head as she screamed, "You want it all! Everything that is mine, you want it. You tell me lies! They still will not know who killed you, you she-devil, you succubus!"

"They can hear your voice," Etta tried to argue, but then the sword flashed downward, and it was only by thrusting up the bottle that she was saved from its cruel slice. The metal rang out in a loud clang, and the bottle shattered, pieces of glass flying and mixing with the liquid that streamed down Etta's arms and bodice. She felt one sharp tug at her jawline, just before her right ear, and then a sudden warmth there, but there was no time to consider that she must have been cut, for Mrs. Lawton raised the sword again.

Etta ran, dodging between the racks. Mrs. Lawton howled and gave chase, and howled again, leaving Etta to wonder if the woman had stepped on some of the broken glass in her stocking feet.

What was better, Etta thought frantically, to flee into the cellar's gloom-ridden corners and hope the darkness would hide her, or to dance around the lamp, that its limited glow might also illuminate her attacker?

The decision was taken from her, for she saw by the swinging arc of light that Mrs. Lawton had picked up the lamp and carried it with her. Now there was no place in which Etta could hope to hide.

The lamp's glow moved slowly but steadily toward the two racks between which Etta concealed herself. She prayed Mrs. Lawton would stop or turn before she came to this section, and knew it was a fool's wish.

She heard a small sound, amplified in this place and by her fear, and Etta knew that Mrs. Lawton had put down the full and awkward lamp even before she saw its light steady in the approximate center of the rows of racks. She imagined Mrs. Lawton wrapping both hands around the hilt of the sword, and trembled.

A metal gleam flashed at the corner of Etta's eye, just before Mrs. Lawton swept around the end of the rack. Etta leapt away, her heart in her throat, hearing the crunch of wood splintering where the blade bit into wood.

"Daniel!" she screamed, reaching with frantic hands for another bottle, only there was no time. Mrs. Lawton lunged again, and for a too-brief moment the blade tangled in the bottle supports of the rack behind Etta, only to be ripped free with a shattering of the carved wooden pieces.

Etta gave a small sound that might have been a scream had it not been so strangled by dread, and then she realized the only sounds she heard were her own ragged breathing and the sound of Mrs. Lawton's rampaging pursuit. There was no longer any pounding at the door. Etta threw a desperate glance in its direction, and her heart sank when she did not see the rectangle of light that would have meant the door had been opened. Had Daniel, then, in the end, left her to her fate?

"No!" she screamed, not able to believe it. Even if she had to die for it, even if it was folly to believe in him, she could no longer live with doubts, with distrust. He loved her. He would help her if he could. It had to be that he went to rouse others to help him assault the door.

She looked up, too late realizing that she had slowed her steps, had given Mrs. Lawton time to catch her up. Running half blind in the gloom, she had come between two racks, only belatedly realizing that they ended at a stone wall; she was cornered. There was no retreat, no way to get around the woman with the sword.

Etta spun, staring directly into Mrs. Lawton's gaze. For a moment she thought she saw a flicker of deference, but perhaps it was only a habit garnered from years of servitude, for Mrs. Lawton raised the sword once more.

"I am Daniel's wife," Etta said, pleased to hear the coolness of her tone, glad she did not cower now, at her last moments. She raised her chin and put back her shoulders, and hid her trembling hands in her skirts as she faced the unbalanced woman who trapped her. "*You* are naught but his housekeeper. You will never be anything more than his housekeeper, no matter how many lies you tell yourself."

Mrs. Lawton shook with fury, a shaking so profound that for a moment Etta thought the woman might drop the sword. But then Mrs. Lawton's hands tightened on the grip, and she cocked her arms back behind her head as far as her shoulders would allow, prepared to strike the fullest blow possible.

"Mrs. Lawton!" came an anguished cry, and both women twisted to see Daniel standing opposite the open end of the racks that had trapped Etta.

Mrs. Lawton hesitated, her attention caught by the sight of him. It was only when Robbie came up behind him, holding a candle, that it was possible for Etta to see where one wall overlapped another, and to understand that in the room's murky light the two walls would blend to seem as one. Robbie was weeping openly, the candle trembling in her hand. Sean hobbled in behind her, the apprehension in his rounded eyes clear even despite the uneven light.

"Daniel," Mrs. Lawton said, half turning to him, breathing heavily. "You will not ever make me live in a dower house, will you?"

He stared at the sword, and then at her face, and lastly he glanced at Etta. She saw the alarm in his gaze, and wondered what he must think of the red stains the wine had made on her dress, the sticky cut on her jaw.

"Are you all right?" he asked.

"Well enough for the moment," she answered, glancing between him and Mrs. Lawton.

"Son, I asked you a question," Mrs. Lawton said, sounding mildly impatient. "Will you ever make me live in a dower house?"

Daniel glanced at the sword, then at Mrs. Lawton's face. He frowned, obviously considering his words. "I cannot see why you would have to live in a dower house."

"When your woman breeds, of course, my darling boy. I *know* what happens! But I will not go to a dower house. I want to stay in *my* house."

Daniel glanced at Etta, bewilderment and alarm mixing equally across his features. "Etta?"

She shook her head, silently denying Mrs. Lawton's sanity as much as the suggestion that she was with child. "Tell her what she wants to hear," Etta said softly.

He looked back to Mrs. Lawton. "You will always live in *your* house, as you please."

An unsteady smile floated over Mrs. Lawton's mouth. "My dear boy, my good boy! I knew you would not turn your mother away."

"My mother?" he repeated, glancing at Etta again. She shook her head once more, a warning, but it was too late, for he was already saying, "My mother is dead."

"No," Mrs. Lawton said quietly, then repeated it, "No." She said it again louder. "No!" She turned toward him, the sword still poised to slash, and said between clenched teeth, *"I* am your mother. I am not *dead!* How can you say such a thing about your mother?" The last word rang out, echoing for a moment, and then she must have seen doubt or aggravation in his expression, for she howled in raw fury and sprang toward him.

"No!" Etta screamed, dashing forward, blind to any hope but that she might knock the sword from the woman's hands. The housekeeper half turned to meet the attack, and the two of them collided, stumbling over their own skirts, crashing into a wine rack. Bottles rattled in their slots.

Etta lurched back, dashing her falling hair from her eyes as Mrs. Lawton attempted to regain her footing. Instead, the woman stumbled again, rocking the wine rack once more. Now it slanted toward her, the old wood groaning in protest, the sound mingling with the startled scream Mrs. Lawton issued as the rack toppled on her, crushing the woman to the floor beneath its weight.

An abrupt silence fell, broken only by the sound of liquid running from broken bottles and a heart-wrenching cry from Robbie. The moment stretched out, all eyes exchanging glances, until suddenly Etta was running on unsteady legs, and Daniel scrambled over splintered wood and spilled wine to meet her. He crushed her to his chest, then thrust her away, running his hands over her body, plainly searching out wounds or broken bones.

"I am not hurt," Etta said on a half-laugh brought on by the delirium of release mingled with the joy of being alive, in his arms.

He pulled his kerchief from his coat pocket, dabbing it at the cut on her jawline. "Not hurt!"

"No, no, not really. Just a cut. And this red on my bodice is only from wine," she assured him, launching herself back into his arms, where he held her close. He ran his hands through her hair until it was completely free of its pins, and murmured her name.

"When Sean greeted me at the door, telling me you were locked in the cellar, I feared the worst," he said. "My God, Etta, what if— I brought you to this cursed house because I saw you were the kind of woman who could bring life back into these walls. I wanted you to push out any ghosts—it was so selfish of me to want your laughter, your love! To not take you from this place, to a new life, new hope! And look what happened!" he cried, his hands tight on her arms. "You were nearly killed." He stared at her, his eyes full of fear and love, and then he gave up any attempt to explain anything, simply kissing her with a passionate relief instead.

When he set her back, it was to remove his coat and pull it around her shoulders over her ruined gown.

As she rejoiced in his comforting touch, Etta became aware that Robbie had knelt next to the fallen wine rack, sobbing brokenly. Sean balanced on his good leg, bending over to reach through the ruined wood to the body below. "She is dead," he pronounced, and Robbie burst into fresh tears.

Etta closed her eyes, shaking her head. When she opened them again, Daniel was looking down at her. "What happened? Why all this madness?" he asked gently.

Etta explained about the X pattern, and how her search to find it led to discovering Mrs. Lawton had been the household's thief.

"She killed Aileen," Etta said to her husband, sorry for the flash of astonished pain that flitted across his face. "She confessed it to me. Perhaps it was even the guilt of it that led her to this today. She was quite, quite mad."

"She would have to be to do this to you," he said quietly but fiercely.

"Sweet heaven," Sean said, his voice little more than a whisper. He lifted his face to gaze at Etta and Daniel, and even in the dim light his eyes shone. "I did not do it. *I* did not kill Aileen!"

"I said as much all along," Daniel reminded him. "It is not in you to do such a thing."

Sean stared into his brother's eyes, and his mouth worked as though to keep back either a sob or a shout of joy as he gave an acknowledging nod.

Robbie's sobs had abated to silent tears, and now she leaned forward, reaching down through the shattered wood as Sean had done, touching the dead woman's sleeve.

"She were my mum," she said, her voice quavering.

The girl looked up at an astonished Etta, and she shook her head in grief. "She were my mum. A year ago, when I were old enough, she saw that I got hired on here, but she wouldn't let me say she were my mum."

"Good God, I never knew Mrs. Lawton had a daughter!" Daniel said.

"She made me live in Bristol most times, with my pa's sister, but she saw me every other Sunday. I never knew what she had

Teresa DesJardien

become, sir," she said, clearly searching his face for understanding or compassion. "I swear that at first I never knew she meant me to try and marry—" She hesitated, looking away from Daniel. "She ordered me, said as I was to marry you, sir. She called me Roberta—it ain't even my name, sir!

"I couldn't stand it," she said warmly, shaking her head fiercely. "And I knew it were impossible that the likes of me could ever marry your lordship, what with my pa having gone to America to flee debt afore he ever married my mum. But she insisted that I be this high and refined 'Roberta' person once I come here! And me a maid in the house! It ain't never made no sense, but she beat me when I said so. Roberta! It ain't even my name," she repeated, hanging her head. "My real name's Nelly." She began to cry again, looking at Etta through her tears. "Oh, ma'am, I'm that sorry, I am."

Etta stared at the girl. "Your mother—?" She put her hand to her forehead as though to spark comprehension there, and thought of all the things she had seen on Mrs. Lawton's walls, not least of which was the portrait of Adam Rifkin.

"It all begins to make sense!" she cried with dawning understanding. "Mrs. Lawton . . . your mother, she was Adam Rifkin's lover?"

Daniel whipped around to stare pointedly at the maid. "My God, can that mean you are my half sister . . . ?"

"Oh, no, sir," Nelly said, shaking her head and trying to sniff back the fresh flow of tears. "I'm no blood to you, sir! They were lovers, but not until years after I was born. It was nigh near Ma's greatest joy that she come to work for him, and that she and he at last . . ." The girl lowered her teary gaze, clearly if belatedly realizing how her words reflected on Daniel's father. "She loved him for years and years, you see. She never loved Pa, not even afore he left," she murmured in a low voice, as if to herself.

Perhaps, Etta thought but did not say aloud, even probably, Mrs. Lawton had hoped to marry her lover once Daniel's mother had passed away. Had that death been a natural one?

Etta shuddered at the question, wondering if it could ever be answered. But natural or not, Lady Healey's death had *not* led the old lord into marrying Georgia Lawton, had not brought the woman to what had surely been her most secret desire: to be his wife.

That dream forever dashed by the old lord's death, Mrs. Lawton had schemed to have her daughter marry the son. But something had shifted that design, too, and Mrs. Lawton must have decided it was not to be, for then she had decided she was *Daniel's mother.* Had she made up this new lie to satisfy her delusions, unable to accept that her daughter's unsuitability was caused by her birth and station in life, that Daniel could not be made to take the little maid as wife? Had Mrs. Lawton created a tolerable situation wherein Robbie—Nelly—could not be with Daniel because by then Nelly had evolved somehow, in Mrs. Lawton's twisted thinking, into his sister?

How many lives had Georgia Lawton's grasp destroyed, even beyond Aileen's death?

"My lord?" Will's voice, no doubt raised in a shout, was muffled by the heavy oak door at the top of the stairs.

Daniel went up the stairs to move the crossbar, letting in the cudgel-carrying Will and Mr. O'Brien, both men scowling even more darkly when they saw the destruction that had occurred.

Everyone pitched in as the events were explained to the two men. They worked to move the shattered remains of the rack so that Mrs. Lawton's body might be removed. Even Sean swept broken bottles aside with the tip of his crutch.

"I'll take her to my aunt's," Robbie said through fresh tears. "They'll see she's buried."

When the body was pulled free, the rubies at Mrs. Lawton's ears and throat shone red, and Etta turned her face away. "Do not think I ever wish to wear those," she told Daniel.

He shook his head. "Mrs. Lawton is welcome to them. For all the good they were, they make a perfect parable here. Those rubies are not real, they are paste. They are as fake as the life she led."

Sean stiffened. "Paste! You should have told me. I never knew."

"Aileen knew. She was the one who first suggested we ought to sell the family jewelry. The real rubies were the first to go."

"I should have known! Even at the time, I thought you gave in too easily to my demand that they be buried with Aileen." Sean's fist knotted, and he scowled, either at the memory of a funeral or, equally as likely, at the thought of Mrs. Lawton taking the jewels from their intended burying place.

Will and O'Brien, accompanied by Robbie, bore the body up the stairs.

"Let us leave this place as well," Sean suggested, but then suddenly he cocked his head to one side and said, "What is this? I think the necklace's string has broken." He nudged a glittering object among the debris with the tip of his crutch.

Daniel started to shake his head again, but then he hesitated. He stooped down, gathering up a handful of glittering items. "By Jove, Etta, Sean, these are not the paste rubies!" He dangled an item by a clasp, revealing a perfectly intact gemmed bracelet. "They are the missing jewels!"

Etta stooped at his side, and Sean leaned down, the closer to look.

"I recognize that brooch! Daniel, you are right!" Sean cried, reaching out to accept the two pieces Etta lifted toward him. "But where were they hidden all this time? We searched every inch of this cellar."

"Did we? Apparently not." Daniel held up two pieces of board, fitting them together. He turned the result to face Etta and Sean, and both of them said, "Oh!"

In his hands Daniel held part of a painted board. Painted upon it clearly in black and a variety of browns was part of a section that must have been painted to resemble the cross pieces of a wine rack. Even with Etta's lamp brought close, it was difficult to tell the painted section from the true open slots all around them.

"I speculate the panel was no more than four or five inches across—easy to miss in this light, in this far, dark corner."

"Aileen painted that?" Etta asked. Daniel nodded. "How clever of her!"

"Too clever, as it turns out," Sean said dryly.

Daniel gathered up the last pieces, and with those Sean held, Etta could see the collection was no more than two handfuls. She agreed with Daniel when he said, "These will not make us rich, but I think we might earn enough from their sale to afford the wages of the laborers we'll need come this harvest." He leaned down to plant a kiss along Etta's jawline, near her cut. "And all because of you, my dear wife. Thank you."

Etta beamed, and now it was her turn to ask questions, namely, how they had come to rescue her.

"I decided that with the exception of Will, no one knew the wine cellar better than myself," Sean explained with a new blitheness born, no doubt, of his exultation at finally knowing himself innocent in the matter of Aileen's death.

Etta grinned at him, and he almost grinned back, and she knew they had indeed become friends.

"Finding the door barred, he became alarmed," Daniel supplied.

Sean had gone to seek help, summoning Will and Mr. O'Brien, and that was when Daniel had returned. The four of them had assaulted the heavy cellar door, all to no avail, and that was when Sean recalled the secret passage down to the cellar—which they all believed to be bricked over. Still, it was more likely they could bring down a wall of old bricks than ever cleave their way through the thick cellar door.

"Robbie—that is, Nelly—insisted we could have the old brick wall down in a moment's time," Sean supplied, shaking his head in lingering amazement. "As we did, with a single blow from O'Brien's cudgel. We found a black domino, complete with mask, hanging on a peg behind the false wall. Rob—Nelly scarcely seemed surprised. Evidently, she knew more about her mama's peculiar habits than Mrs. Lawton ever imagined."

"Poor girl! She was used as badly as any of us."

"She means to settle in Bristol, to try and start anew," Sean said.

"I wish her well."

"And I wish you cleaned and in dry clothes, and that cut tended to," Daniel stated, taking Etta's arm firmly and leading her toward the stairs, toward that wonderful rectangle of light that spilled down to greet them.

Sean remained behind a moment longer, clucking his tongue at the mess. "All that wine, lost," he complained, loudly enough for the retreating pair to hear. He sighed. "I suppose it is a sign that I must give up drinking."

"Do that and I shall make you my overseer of the harvest," Daniel called over his shoulder.

"A *farmer?*" Sean spat out the word, but there was no real rancor in his tone, and he followed them up the stairs without further complaint.

Fourteen

The next morning Etta sat up abruptly in bed and stared at the vase of flowers on her dressing table.

Daniel, replete from the lovemaking they had just shared, glanced where she stared.

"Those flowers were not there last night," Etta said with emphasis.

"What are they? Do they bode ill?" Daniel asked, beginning to frown.

"They are called love-lies-bleeding."

"Oh, no."

"It is an unfortunate name, I agree, but they do not bode ill at all. Some kind soul decided they should represent undying love."

"So you do not mind that they are there? Unlike the unfortunate lavender?" His frown dissipated and he slid a hand up under her nightrail, momentarily diverting her attention.

"Daniel!" she pretended to scold. "Please think on this a moment: Will and O'Brien have ridden to Bristol, to precede Nelly's return with her mother's body. And Nelly has had no time for such niceties as arranging flowers while she attempts to sort her mama's things from those that the woman stole from the household! I awoke several times in the night, only to hear poor Nelly still hard at work packing. Daniel, desist from touching me there, and answer me as to who could have brought that vase of flowers here!"

He thought a moment, not bothering to cease the slow stroking up the length of her leg, but after a while he slanted a look up at her. "It was not me, my love, I swear it, and it is clear you did not, so that means *no one* could have had the opportunity to put them there."

"Daniel! You are suggesting that there is a ghost in this house after all! You know Mrs. Lawton was responsible for all of that, to scare away and reduce the staff, to have more of you to herself, so how can you think that yet?"

Daniel made a face.

"And stranger yet, Daniel, to the best of my knowledge we do not have any love-lies-bleeding growing about the grounds."

His brows rose in surprise, but he made no response.

"Well?" she demanded.

His stroking reached higher, moving to the inside of her leg. Etta gasped with pleasure, and tried to keep a stern set to her mouth. "Well?"

"Well, the flowers mean undying love," he said with a calm logic that defied the growing arousal in his body and in the depths of his deep brown eyes. "I choose to take that as a sign, from whomever you wish to call responsible, be it ghost or God or fate. I think that someone wishes us to understand that we, you and I, are to enjoy our lives together, and that our love is meant to be. They are only flowers, Etta, and very nice flowers at that. Do we need to worry about them, now or ever again?"

He gazed into her eyes, but she did not need to see again the love that was plainly written there to convince her it was real, that his love would keep her safe and cherished; she had been convinced last night, when there had been no more time left for doubts and fears. She could never doubt this man again.

She snuggled against his length, lifting her mouth to his. As he kissed her, she closed her eyes, only to throw them open as a chilled breeze stroked her skin. Daniel did not react, and just as Etta considered that exceptional fact, the scent of flowers encompassed the bed, heady and overwhelming.

"Daniel?" Etta pulled her mouth from his in surprise.

He lifted his eyebrows questioningly at her, and she felt her brow pucker in amazement that he did not seem to take note of the curious circumstances that engulfed them.

She parted her lips to point out what seemed abundantly obvious to her, but then the breeze shifted, becoming warmer, nearly pleasant.

With a sensation like a wave rolling away from the sand, the breeze drifted to one side, pulling away. Etta followed its invisible flow, her gaze drawn to and settling on the vase full of flowers.

"Etta?" Daniel asked, touching her face. "Is anything wrong?"

"No," she said, considering the strange event. She tilted her head to one side, and then gave him a slow smile. "In fact, I think from now on we have just been given permission for everything to be all right."

She did not give him a chance to question that curious statement, instead putting her arms around his neck and, pulling him down to her, to seal the start of their new life together with a happy kiss.

I enjoy hearing from readers!

You may write to me at: Teresa DesJardien, P. O. Box 33323, Seattle, WA 98133. Please include a self-addressed, stamped envelope for a reply.

Love's Magic

Cindy Holbrook

One

"Ma says there is trouble brewing," little Tommy Chant whispered. "She saw a crow walking backward this morn."

"Throuble," Jacob said with a lisp caused from losing his two front teeth. "Mr. Wolf thaid he thaw evil in the th-thtars last eve."

Leaning up against a barrel in front of Mr. Wolf's store, their bright, innocent eyes scanned the quiet streets of Chancellorville. Their gazes shied to the hill that rose majestically over the small village. The Castle Tor rode atop that hill, its turrets raking the bright October skies. Even in the newness of the morning, the castle held an aura of ancient strength and cloaked power.

"Ever since the fire," Tommy said. His reedy voice quivered.

"And Mr. Cranston's gone missing," Jacob said. He suddenly giggled. "Pa says he bets there is one more donkey wandering the woods."

"He was an ass," Tommy said. The boys looked conspiratorially to each other at the use of such a naughty term and giggled all the more.

Jacob's giggle turned into a hiccup, and he choked. Eyes widening, he pointed a finger. "There's the Goodfellow sisters coming out of Mrs. Randall's."

"So?" Tommy shrugged.

Jacob swung his finger to not a few yards away. "Dame Tureen."

"Jupiter!" Tommy gasped.

Both boys reached to their necks and grasped their talismans convulsively.

"I cannot believe it," Bathsheba said to her sister as she hustled out of Mrs. Randall's, her round, dimpled body quivering. "That woman is despicable."

" 'Tis evil," nodded Dorinda briskly, her tall, sparse body coiling anger. "Her plan is fell." Both ladies turned, then halted sharply. Dorinda's brown eyes narrowed at the sight of the woman who now stood before them. "Dame Tureen," she said curtly.

The woman smiled broadly. She well nigh smirked. "Why, Dorinda and Bathsheba. Good morn' to you."

" 'Tis not a good morn," Bathsheba said, her blue eyes snapping, her bountiful bosom puffing out like a pigeon whose tail feathers had been twitched " 'Tis not a good morn at all."

"Whyever not?" Dame Tureen's dark eyes glowed. She was a tall woman, as tall as Dorinda, but her body was full and voluptuous. "I think it a glorious day."

" 'Twill not be glorious," Dorinda said. "We've heard what you've planned for the poor duke. Burning his castle and causing his manager to disappear is one thing, but . . ."

"Why, whatever makes you think I had anything to do with that unfortunate accident?" Dame Tureen gasped, widening her eyes, and clearly failing to appear innocent. Her smugness would not allow it. "Everyone knows the cause for that fire has not been found."

"Of course not," Dorinda said. "I concede you have enough powers to succeed in that. But to burn the castle just to lure the duke back here is abominable. We heard he is soon to arrive. And for what? Just so you can try and make a match of it with your daughter, Gertrude? 'Tis wicked." Dorinda drew up her sparse body. "I assure you, we will do everything in our power to stop you."

Dame Tureen's black eyes quickly narrowed to slits. "You have nothing in your power able to stop me." She laughed. "You and your weakling 'white powers' cannot touch me. None in your coven can. Best you ladies return to your tatting, rather than deluding yourself in the belief you are actually witches."

Dorinda reared back. "Tatting! Merely because we choose the good of the universe and not the evil does not mean we do not have powers. 'Tis you who would be best advised to stop playing with the dark forces and save your soul."

"Cowards," Dame Tureen hissed, her eyes shooting shards of anger. "What does a soul matter when one controls the dark powers?"

"I doubt we'll have to use any powers." Bathsheba spoke up, her chin jutting out. "For even *your* powers will not be able to make the duke fall in love with your Gertrude and take her to wife."

"What?" Dame Tureen's voice scaled octaves.

"Your Gertrude is a want-wit, plain and simple," Dorinda said. "Pretty, I own, but she hasn't two thoughts to rub together in her brain box. 'Tis why she has no powers, witch's or otherwise. And the duke is known to be an intelligent man. He'll not be gulled."

"Gulled!" Dame Tureen's fingers turned into claws. "How dare you! I have foreseen it. He is destined to be my daughter's mate. Wizardry runs strong in his family, and it is only fitting he becomes my Gertrude's mate."

"But everyone knows the duke is mere human," Bathsheba said, frowning. "Which is no insult, of course."

"When he joins with my Gertrude," Dame Tureen said, her body beginning to shake as if in an apoplexy, "he will have the powers. He will be a great wizard and the dark powers will be unleashed."

"Oh, do cut line, Maudar," Dorinda said. "It has nothing to do with destiny. All you want is a husband for your daughter, and since no man hereabouts is fool enough to have her to wife, you've cooked up this wild, despicable scheme. You are air-dreaming."

" 'Tis not so!" Dame Tureen's voice came out in a low, almost inhuman growl. Her body rocked violently.

" 'Tis so," Bathsheba said "And is a totty-headed notion. Why, 'tis more likely the duke will fall in love with our darling Sarabeth before your bird-witted Gertrude."

"Never!" Dame Tureen's voice cracked. Thunder rumbled in the clear morning sky. "Never!"

"Too true, sister," Dorinda said, laughing. "Sarabeth is far more beautiful and will definitely catch the duke's eye before Gertrude ever will, anytime, day or night."

"Never!" Wisps of black smoke suddenly began seeping from Dame Tureen.

"And Sarabeth's charm and intelligence." Bathsheba nodded, blue eyes twinkling. " 'Tis well known. She's already had six proposals. And Gertrude . . ." She let the sentence fade. Then she grinned. "Dorinda, we should be grateful for Maudar's success in drawing the duke back here, for surely Sarabeth will catch his eye, and since no man here has attracted her, perhaps he will. Why, he might be just the right man for her."

"It shall not be!" Dame Tureen cried. Smoke whirled up, the acid smell of brimstone burning. "Sarabeth will never catch the eye of the duke. Never!" She raised her one hand high. "I swear it!"

Dorinda coughed and waved at the black smoke about her. "Come, sister. I mislike the air here excessively."

Bathsheba giggled. "Indeed, it has a foul stench."

The two Goodfellow sisters picked up their skirts and stepped past Dame Tureen, noses held high, leaving the woman enshrouded in the black cloud of her own making.

Sarabeth hummed as she knelt in the dirt, reaching to snatch out a weed she thought had replaced the sprig of rosemary she had planted. She leaned back to sit on her heels and surveyed the herb garden about her. Wiping a dirty hand across her face, she smiled and breathed deeply of the brisk, fragrant air about her.

"Sarabeth! Oh, Sarabeth," Aunt Bathsheba's voice called loudly. That good woman came around the cottage corner in a trot. "You'll never guess what just happened."

Aunt Dorinda stalked behind her at a much slower pace. " 'Twas a tempest in a teapot."

"We just had a dust-up with Dame Tureen," Bathsheba wheezed as her short legs brought her before Sarabeth. "A terrible row."

Dorinda grinned. "We left her belching black smoke."

"Huffing and puffing like a bellows, as she always does," Bathsheba said, giggling like a naughty child, "when she's in a temper."

"She has no control," Dorinda said, shaking her head.

Sarabeth's eyes widened. Then she sighed. "You know you shouldn't fight with Dame Tureen. Nothing good ever comes of it. And she is frightfully powerful."

Bathsheba's chin jutted out. "Well, powerful or not, we simply could not accept what she intends to do."

Sarabeth wiped off her hands. "What does she intend to do?"

"We found out why the Castle Tore had the fire," Dorinda said, her face taking on a stern cast.

"Yes," nodded Bathsheba, her blue eyes huge. "As we suspected, it was Dame Tureen. She did it in order that the duke would return here."

Sarabeth's heart leapt. Then she swallowed. "The duke? Return here?"

"Mrs. Randall told us," Dorinda said. "You know she is godmother to young Michalla, who has unfortunately joined Dame Tureen's black coven."

"She is young," Bathsheba said, shaking her head. "Perhaps she will learn in time."

"At least she knew enough to tell Mrs. Randall of Maudar's plan," Dorinda conceded. "There is hope there."

Sarabeth's heart began to drum unaccountably. "What plan is that?"

"She intends the duke to be Gertrude's husband," Bathsheba said.

"Her h-husband?" Sarabeth asked.

Dorinda snorted. "She's spouting some totty-headed notion that if he joins with Gertrude, he will gain great powers."

"But he is nonmagical," Sarabeth gasped. "A human just like—like I am."

"I know," Bathsheba said, "as does everyone else, except Maudar, it seems. There's not been a wizard or witch in the duke's family since his great-great-grandfather, but still Maudar has declared that he will be."

"Well, his grandfather did try," Dorinda admitted. "But Edwin was never up to snuff."

Sarabeth discovered she was clutching her hands tightly and that her fingers were cutting into her palms. "Then why does Dame Tureen—"

"She wants him for Gertrude's husband, 'tis why." Dorinda said. "The rest is just mere flourishing and hocus-pocus. Do you think she'll own outright she is desperate to find Gertrude a husband and cannot? This way it is not Gertrude's lack of anything resembling a brain that keeps her unwed, but destiny. And dark destiny at that. She's frightened everyone off with the claim." She snorted. "Not a soul wishes to stand in her path when she starts her talk of evil powers and foreseeings. They'll be clutching their talismans and saying chants for warding, rather."

"Do you think she'll succeed in—in getting the duke to marry Gertrude?" Sarabeth asked, her voice tightening.

"Not if we can help it!" Bathsheba said, her blue eyes firing.

A chill ran through Sarabeth. She forced a smile "Aunt Dorinda was right the first time, 'tis nothing but a tempest in a teapot. Even if the duke does come here it does not mean he will—will ever be attracted to—to Gertrude."

"So we told Maudar." Bathsheba nodded, her white curls bobbing. She smiled impishly. "We told her you'd be more likely to catch the duke's eye."

"Me!" Sarabeth stared. Her two aunts were gazing at her with loving pride. She laughed. "Now who's totty-headed? Or did you partake of the elderberry wine again?"

"Sarabeth," Dorinda said, frowning. "You know we never have but one glass of elderberry wine in the evening."

"I know." Sarabeth grinned, kindly not mentioning that her aunts' chant to make the wine's spirit strong and sweet was one of the few spells they performed with unfailing accuracy. She stood swiftly. "But for you to think that I would ever attract the duke's eye is sheer moon-gazing."

"Why not?" Bathsheba said. "You are far more beautiful with your blond hair and green eyes than that Gertrude. Why, with her black hair and black eyes she looks like a witch."

"And the duke does not hold with witchery," Dorinda said in satisfaction. " 'Tis why he never visits Chancellorville."

Sarabeth once again pinned a smile upon her face. "Well then, you have nothing to worry about. Dame Tureen's plan will fail upon its own." She held out a hand to each of her aunts. "I want you to give me your solemn promise you'll not attempt to cross spells with Dame Tureen. 'Tis dangerous, and you know that though your magic is tremendous—" She halted.

Bathsheba hung her head. "We—we don't always hit it upon the mark all the time, do we?"

"Not always." Sarabeth smiled. Then she laughed. "But when you turned the back meadow blue, I thought it a delightful color."

"We should not have used the word *blew*." Dorinda clicked her tongue in aggravation.

"No," Bathsheba said with a frown. "But the word just seemed to escape me."

"I know," Sarabeth said, smiling. "Don't let it worry you.

Magic is unpredictable after all, and if it were not, it would not be so interesting, now, would it?"

Bathsheba's eyes widened. "No, you are quite right, my dear."

"It would even become humdrum," Sarabeth said, her lips twitching. "If every spell worked every time. There must be some mystery to it after all." Both aunts' eyes lighted and they nodded. "Now, I know 'tis early, but the mention of elderberry wine sounded delightful."

Bathsheba's eyes sparkled. "Do you think we could?"

"Of course," Sarabeth laughed. "I'll join you in the nonce. Only let me finish here."

Dorinda and Bathsheba turned away and Sarabeth watched the two ladies as they all but raced to the house. They were the dearest and sweetest of aunts. A wind of fear crossed her heart. Unlike her aunts, Dame Tureen's magic held no mystery. Her spells were always dependable.

Rather than finishing her chores, Sarabeth wandered down to the large oak that stretched its aged branches out to the sky, its arms open in perpetual praise to the universe. She hugged the tree's trunk to draw from its life strength.

The Duke of Tor would be returning to Chancellorville. "Damian," she whispered. They had never talked, never met, the great scion of the castle and she, a lowly cottager within the town. Yet she had seen him and she whispered his name with a warm familiarity as she closed her eyes. The image of a laughing, dark-haired boy jumped vividly into her sight. She could not remember when she had not held that vision within her. Even as a child, only a babe, the vision had been there. As was the wrenching pain of a yearning love.

Sarabeth opened her eyes and stepped back from the tree. She patted its rough bark and smiled. "Moon-gazing again, aren't I?"

She turned and walked slowly back to the cottage.

* * *

"Dorinda! Bathsheba!" Sarabeth called out loudly. She halted, wrapping her black cloak tightly about her against the cold night air. Fog settled heavily over the land, beading cool droplets upon the strands of Sarabeth's hair that escaped the protection of her cloak's hood. "Dorinda! Bathsheba! Where are you? If you can hear me, come to me." She expelled an exasperated sigh. "They ought to hear me very well, I declare." Wolves had excellent hearing, if she was not mistaken, and that was what her two darling, aggravating aunts had changed themselves into this evening. *For better surveillance,* the note Sarabeth had discovered after returning home late had said.

Sarabeth shook her head wearily. Her aunts were far too determined. The Duke of Tor was to arrive sometime that night and they wanted to be the first to know he had returned. For what purpose, Sarabeth didn't want to know.

Muttering about stubborn, foolhardy witches, Sarabeth stepped into the road. There was no reason for her to ruin her shoes chasing after her aunts. Not that she hadn't ruined many of them over the years in such endeavors. She hated it when her aunts changed into animals. And wolves of all things! What if they met up with another wolf? A real one? Or a trapper?

Head down, Sarabeth trod along the road, deep in thought. Suddenly she heard a clattering, clashing noise behind her. She spun. A scream tore from her.

Four huge, snorting beasts charged down upon her from out of the fog. She stood, fear-frozen. The coachman holding to the reins of those charging beasts, hollered, his arms a flash in the night as he sawed upon the reins.

"Stop!" Sarabeth's mind screamed. "Stop! I love horses."

The lead horse, a gleaming black stallion, suddenly reared. Sarabeth saw his large, mighty rib cage before her, straining at its yoke, his hooves clawing the night. She smelled the sweat and lather. Neighing a challenge, the stallion suddenly twisted his large body and crashed down inches from her, slamming into the other horses. Trammeling bodies cavorted, and settled, quivering masses.

A calm entered Sarabeth. She was safe. The team of six now stood before her, apparently stunned and confused. "Thank you," she whispered.

"What the devil!" the coachman shouted.

Sarabeth, her mind steady, but her body shaking, slowly stepped to the side of the road.

"Huggins," a deep male voice said from within the shining carriage. "What in blazes is going on?"

The door swung open. A tall, broad-shouldered, dark-haired man alighted, brown eyes stern and flashing.

"Damian," Sarabeth whispered.

"Sorry, your grace, the woman was in the middle of the road," the coachman said. "Smack-dab in the middle of the road."

"What woman?" Damian swung his gaze to Sarabeth.

Lightning flashed through Sarabeth's soul. The boy had grown into a man. A tall, dark, saturnine man. His eyes weren't laughing and joyful. They were stern, enigmatic, and weary. Pain twisted in Sarabeth. "Damian."

"Yes?" he said quietly. Slowly he walked up to her. Their gazes twined. Magic swirled about them. No witchery, just magic. "Yes?"

"I am sorry," Sarabeth said softly. He was close enough for her to see the lines about his eyes. Close enough to see his chiseled, aristocratic face, with clefts of control and severity. "I am sorry."

Something flashed in his dark eyes. "Who are you?"

"I am Sarabeth"

"You could have been killed, Sarabeth."

"I know." Sarabeth nodded slowly. "But I was not. I . . ."

Suddenly Damian stiffened, his eyes widened, and then went blank.

"Bejeezus, bejeezus," the coachman cried.

"What?" Sarabeth asked quickly to Damian. His eyes were blank, as if looking through her. "What is the matter?"

"Gawd!" Huggins cried. "Where'd she go? Gawd!" He crossed himself swiftly.

"Where'd who go?" Sarabeth cried, spinning about and looking in confusion. She turned to look back at Damian. "Damian, what is it?"

"Chancellorville," Damian muttered so softly, it was a dark breath. He looked past and through her. "Chancellorville." Slowly, almost drunkenly, he turned away.

Sarabeth reached her hand out. "Damian, don't go!"

"Where'd she go, your grace?" Fear caused Huggins's voice to rise in a wail. "Gawd almighty."

"Never mind!" Damian's voice cracked out. He stalked toward the carriage.

Heart pounding, Sarabeth stepped slowly after him. "Damian?" She reached out a hand. "Damian, I am here!"

Damian, without a look back, climbed into the coach. His face was bleak, unforgiving, as he gazed out the window. "Drive on, Huggins," he ordered, his voice a loud whiplash in the night, cutting through the fog, cutting through Sarabeth's heart. "Drive on!"

"But, Yer Grace?" Huggins cried, his gaze flicking hurriedly about, scanning past the numb Sarabeth, whose blood was freezing in her body. "B-but. . the woman . . ."

"Drive on, dammit!" Damian shouted.

"Damian, I am here," Sarabeth choked out, stretching out her arms pleadingly.

"Sweet Mary," Huggins muttered. "Sweet Mother Mary." He cracked the reins. The coach tore off as if demons chased it.

"Damian," Sarabeth cried softly. She lowered her arms. A tear slipped down her face. "I am here. I am here."

Two

"Chancellorville," Damian said, forcing his body to ease back into the seat. It was strung tightly, as if every muscle, tendon, and particle had been shot through with electricity. He closed his eyes and breathed in deeply. Damn the wild, freakish village with its belief in witches and magic and fairies.

The vision stood relentlessly before him. That woman. That woman in the swirling fog, a cloak enshrouding her, only her white face, a hauntingly beautiful face, visible, and damp, soft golden curls slipping out beneath a dark hood. And her eyes. Green, deep green with fear. And something else, something that had called to him, called to him like a forgotten dream. She had known his name.

"Damian," her voice said softly once more in his mind. "I am sorry." Her voice had been so sad. Yet when she spoke, he had felt as if a balm had assuaged his heart. Stepping close, he had almost believed in the magic of his forefathers. Something living and glowing had wrapped about them.

Then she had disappeared before his very eyes! Vanished! A jolting pain overwhelmed him, inexplicable and unreasonable in its intensity. Gone! When for a moment his heart had leapt and felt as if he had at last discovered its lost part.

"You're drunk," Damian muttered. "Damn-fool drunk."

It did not matter that Huggins had seen the hallucination as well. Huggins was known to take a dram or two in his time. Damian thought back. He knew he had drunk more ale at the last posting house than he generally did. He had quaffed a few extra to fortify his return to the Castle Tor, that brooding entity with its turrets and stone walls that always called to him, no matter how many miles and years he had remained away. And remained away he had, and always would. Like his father and mother before him, he'd not fall prey to the superstitions of magic and wizardry that the Castle Tor, and the village below, wore like an invisible mantle.

"No," Damian said starkly, coldly. "Never."

Something strong and joyful had flared up in him when the message had arrived that the Castle Tor had suffered a fire and he must return. Finally to return! Yet he had shut it out, slammed the door of his emotions and extinguished those feelings with the strength of his resolve, a resolve he had forged into iron over the years.

And just as he had closed the door upon the Castle Tor, he would close the door upon the vision of the woman on the road.

"Sarabeth!" Her name escaped his lips in a soft whisper. He clamped his mouth shut, the cord along his jaw popping. Never would he speak it again. He would cast out the vision. It had been one brought on by too much ale and nothing else.

Sarabeth stood, shocked. Tears streamed down her face. He had left her. She had heard her name upon his lips only once, and then he had left her, as if she were nothing.

"Sarabeth, dear," a sweet, sympathetic voice called.

Sarabeth turned slowly. A silver wolf stood before her, a blue bow gracing its right ear, a pair of spectacles perched upon its thin, canine nose. Bathsheba always needed spectacles in dim light.

"Auntie," Sarabeth choked out.

"I am so sorry," Bathsheba said, her blue wolf eyes tearing.

"Well, I am not," Aunt Dorinda's voice said. A brindled wolf padded up, a mobcap askew upon its head. "I am furious. 'Tis infamous."

"What happened?" Sarabeth asked, a numbness quilting her pain.

"Why, dear, you disappeared from the men's eyes," Bathsheba said. "We were just answering your call, and saw the whole thing."

"D-disappeared?" Sarabeth asked.

"Yes, disappeared," Dorinda said, and gave out an angry yap. "Sorry, but it makes me just want to howl."

"But how could I just disappear?" Sarabeth asked. She stretched out her hand and looked at it. "I can see myself."

"I know, dear," nodded Bathsheba. "But no one else can. You have a spell upon you."

"We saw you disappear," Dorinda said, and clicked her canines a few times. "It took us a moment to remember the correct verse to be able to see you ourselves."

"But why?" Sarabeth asked. "Why would . . . ?"

"Dame Tureen," Bathsheba said. A low growl rumbled from her. "Oh, forgive me, dear."

The brindled wolf shook her head. "I knew Maudar swore you would never catch the eye of the duke, but this is the outside of enough." She suddenly lifted her snout to the sky and keened a long howl. Her body trembled and her fur ruffled. "My, but that felt good."

"Dame Tureen cast a spell upon me?" Sarabeth asked. Her numbness incinerated in the anger that shot through her. She felt like howling herself. "How dare she. How dare she!" Sarabeth put her hands to her hips and glared at her wolf-aunts. "Well, remove the spell. She is not going to get away with this."

Bathsheba lowered herself to the ground and rested her head upon her outstretched paws, looking up at Sarabeth sorrowfully. " 'Tis a puissant spell, I fear."

"I do not care," Sarabeth said, shaking with rage. "You said you would stop her, and you shall." Her eyes narrowed. "And I shall, too."

Dorinda shook her head, her mobcap slipping farther over

her long, pointed ear. "The spell is very strong. You disappeared from both men's sight, not just the duke's. Maudar really did it up fine."

Sarabeth's eyes widened. "Are you saying I must remain invisible, and let—let that witch and her daughter capture Damian?"

"Oh, no, dear." Bathsheba wiggled her body, her plumy tail waving in a pacifying overture.

" 'Tis merely that we must think," Dorinda said. She sat back upon her haunches and scratched at her head with her back paw. "We must think."

"Yes," Sarabeth said. "Think. For you are going to lift this spell. Then I am going after Damian myself. Gertrude Tureen shall not have him!" Her heart swelled with a rage and a yearning. She saw Damian's dark eyes again. Felt the one brief moment of magic when he had stepped close. "She shall not have him! With or without witchcraft, that I swear!"

"Y-Your Grace," Thomas, the footman, said after making a stumbling entrance into the breakfast room. "Y-you have visitors." His uniform was rumpled, and he swayed like a sapling in the breeze.

Faith 'twas not even ten o'clock and the man was castaway, Damian noted as he lowered the paper he was reading and placed it beside his unfinished congealing eggs and burnt bacon. Perhaps if Cook had borrowed some of Thomas's liquor and applied it to the breakfast, *it* would have been more palatable.

"Visitors?" Damian asked. "I doubt I know anyone in Chancellorville after all these years."

" 'Tis Dame Tureen and her daughter, Gertrude," Thomas hiccuped. "D-Dame Tureen is . . ." His bloodshot eyes widened. "Er—er powerful in-fl-uential rounds here." A silly grin crossed his lips. "And her daughter, she be as pr-pretty as a picture." Thomas winked broadly. "Ifn you knows what I mean."

"I rather think I might," Damian said calmly, not blinking a lash at his drunken, winking footman. He was fortunate to have any servants left. Apparently after the fire and disappearance of his estate manager, his butler, two maids, and the housekeeper had all taken French leave. As did Huggins', his own coachman, after delivering him to the castle and crossing himself five times. His staff, he discovered, now consisted of Thomas, his drunken footman, Millicent, the cook, who was as stalwart and tough as her culinary efforts, and one scullery maid. "Where have you put the ladies?"

"In the drawing room," Thomas said, stiffening and attempting a dignified manner.

"Very well," Damian said, sighing. "I shall meet this powerfully influential dame and her pretty-as-a-picture daughter." He rose. "And if you would be so kind as to see if you can commandeer more help from the town, I would appreciate it."

"Yer Grace?" Thomas's brown eyes widened.

"Hire," Damian said gently. "See if you can hire more help."

Thomas's face turned a blue color and his body twitched. "Yer Grace, ain't no one going to wants to come. Not after old Cranston's disappearance. Mean, bet he's a blooming toad by now . . . or a phooka . . . or . . ."

"That will be enough," Damian said, gritting his teeth. "Just try to find some help and offer them better wages."

"Yes, Yer Grace," Thomas said. "But I don't think . . ."

"Good, continue to refrain from doing so," Damian said. "And try what you can."

"I tell you, no one will come." Thomas swung his head to and fro. He stumbled back from his own self-inflicted dizziness. "Th-they know. Someone wanted old Cranston gone, and turned him into G-God knows what."

"And they couldn't have just thought of murder?" Damian asked. He strolled from the room, leaving a frowning, befuddled Thomas behind. "A phooka," Damian muttered as he crossed the large gray-stoned hall with its large tapestries of unicorns in battle with other mythical creatures. He entered the parlor. Thankfully this room had been done over by his mother, and was decorated in light gold and blue, a modern, normal mecca in the Castle Tor's domain.

He halted at the sight of the two ladies awaiting him. The older lady was a handsome, regal woman. As for her daughter, the sot Thomas was indeed correct. She was pretty as a picture, with a voluptuous build, glossy black ringlets, and wide black eyes. Damian smiled in pleasure. "Ladies." He bowed. "It was kind of you to come and greet me."

"Indeed, Your Grace," the older woman said, smiling and rising. "We heard of your arrival and thought to come and welcome you back to dear, dear Chancellorville. I am Dame Tureen"—she performed a quick curtsy and looked to her daughter, who still sat, wide eyes upon Damian—"and this is my daughter, Gertrude. Dear, do make your curtsy to His Grace."

"Oh, yes, Mama," the girl said in a husky voice, and rose. She performed a quick, less graceful curtsy. "Pleased to meet you, Your Grace."

Damian bowed. "And I you, Gertrude." He waved a hand. "Please, do be seated." He crossed and sat down across from the ladies. "I own it is rare for me to visit Chancellorville." He smiled to the beautiful girl and said, "My mistake, I fear."

Gertrude flushed. "Your Grace."

Dame Tureen laughed merrily. "Ah, you naughty man." Then she shook her head with sympathy in her own black eyes. " 'Tis such a shame that your return was because of such an unfortunate incident."

Damian frowned. "Yes. I have not seen it as yet, but I heard that the whole left wing of the castle was burned."

"Dreadful," sighed Dame Tureen. "Just dreadful. The castle is such a magnificent structure. And for the estate manager to disappear as well. So odd."

Damian lifted a quizzing brow. "And what animal do you think he was turned into?"

Dame Tureen's eyes narrowed and she studied him. "I beg your pardon?"

He shrugged, unable to hide his impatience. "Everyone thinks him to have been turned into some sort of creature. They have him as a veritable menagerie, in fact."

"I see," Dame Tureen said. She laughed lightly. "You must forgive me, but I do not hold with such superstitious notions."

"Mama?" Her daughter looked wide-eyed.

"Neither does Gertrude," Dame Tureen said. She smiled to her daughter. "Do you, dearest?"

Gertrude blinked her big, dark eyes. "No?" she asked, a hesitancy in her voice. Dame Tureen smiled and Gertrude looked to Damian with a brilliant, sizzling smile "No, Your Grace."

Damian returned the smile. She truly was a fetching girl . . . and gratefully not laden with superstitions. "A rare treat in Chancellorville."

Dame Tureen leaned forward. "But what do you think happened to Mr. Cranston, Your Grace?"

"I do not know," Damian said, and shrugged. "But I am sure there is a logical explanation. Perhaps he went off on a drunken spree, or else he did not wish to deal with the strenuous repairs the castle will now require from the fire."

"Ah, yes, the fire." Dame Tureen sighed. "There will be much work to be done."

"Yes, I fear so," Damian said, frowning.

"It shall take weeks, I would hazard," Dame Tureen said, clear sympathy in her eyes.

"Yes," Damian said.

"Well," Dame Tureen said, smiling. "We'll not let you suffer by yourself. You can depend upon our staunch support." She laughed gaily. "You may even find that you enjoy yourself. Chancellorville is not bereft of social functions. Of course, not as grand as those in London, but simple pleasures." She clasped her hands together. "And if you are still here in three weeks, it will be All Hallows' Eve. Chancellorville's celebration of that day is grand."

"I have no doubt," Damian returned, his voice dry.

"For shame." Dame Tureen laughed. "Indeed, despite all the silly notions of witchery and magic that the townsfolk hold, it is still quite a festive event."

Damian smiled and said, "Then I believe I shall attend, since I have no doubt I shall be here, whether I wish it or not."

"Excellent." Dame Tureen rose. "Well, we do not wish to overstay our welcome."

"Impossible," Damian said politely, and rose. He looked at the beautiful Gertrude. "When I have my house more in order, perhaps you ladies would care to dine with me."

"We would love to," Dame Tureen said swiftly. "In fact, why not tonight?"

"Tonight?" Damian blinked. "Well, I—I fear that everything is at sixes and sevens. Half of the staff has left. And I fear that Cook is not very er—proficient."

"Oh, we know well of Millicent's cooking," Dame Tureen chuckled, waving a negligent hand. " 'Twould not bother us. After all, 'tis the company that counts and not the food."

"So it is," Damian said. He smiled. He'd be a fool to turn down the offer of sane company. "Perhaps tomorrow night, then. I have no doubt the company will be fine, but perhaps we should give Millicent some warning, in hopes that she will rise to the occasion. Besides," he said, chuckling, "with such a dearth of staff, no matter her inabilities, I'd not want her to give notice at this juncture."

"Very well," Dame Tureen said, smiling. "You are right. 'Twill be better. I have some . . . cooking to do myself. Unlike Millicent, I am an excellent cook, almost magical, you would say."

Damian lifted a brow, but then laughed. "Very well. Let us say tomorrow at eight?"

"We would like it above all things, I assure you," Dame

Tureen said in liquid tones. She turned to her daughter. "Come, Gertrude."

"Yes, Mama," Gertrude nodded. She looked to Damian and curtsied. "Your Grace."

Damian bowed, grinning. Perhaps Chancellorville would have its pleasures after all. "Gertrude, until tomorrow night."

"I don't think I'll ever be seen again," Sarabeth sighed, and plopped down in the kitchen chair.

"Now, dearest," Bathsheba said. "Don't lose heart."

"I haven't lost heart." Sarabeth grinned "Only visibility."

"Magic takes time," Dorinda said, hugging a book close to her. "And the white magic even more. For we do not change the laws of the universe, merely use their powers. Nor do we ask for help from 'other sources,' " she said darkly. Her ire was marred by a smudge of white upon her cheek. 'Twas not flour, but powdered arrowroot.

"And the spells are very tricky," said Bathsheba, rifling through the stack of books that piled over the table, one toppling to the floor with a thud.

"Very tricky," Sarabeth agreed, casting a wry eye about the kitchen. It was in shambles.

The ivy in the pot upon the kitchen window was a virulent purple and gold—Bathsheba and Dorinda's first attempt to change her back to visible form. Bathsheba admitted she should perhaps not have used the term "full and vibrant color" in the spell.

The chair that sat to Sarabeth's side and now vaunted six legs was her aunties' second attempt. Sarabeth winced. If they had succeeded in making her visible that time, would she have had two extra limbs herself?

As for their third attempt, a miniature but fully grown apple tree sprouted from the bowl in which it had once held a simple core. That tree, popping up in all its leafy glory, had caused their cat Tomolina to howl and dart for refuge under the kitchen bench. "Perhaps the words 'human' and 'Sarabeth' need be employed," Sarabeth murmured. Her aunts' magic seemed to do well with plants.

"I think I have it," Bathsheba said, jabbing her finger at the book she held. "Do look, Dorinda"

Dorinda leaned over and studied the book Bathsheba held out to her. "Hmm, yes. Yes, I think that is it!"

"Stand up, Sarabeth," Bathsheba said, her voice breathless.

"Does it have the word *human* in it?" Sarabeth asked, dutifully standing.

"Human? Hmm . . ." Dorinda's mouth worked as she read over the spell. "No."

"But it says *living form*," Bathsheba cried eagerly. "That should do the trick."

"I hope so," Sarabeth said a little nervously, for both aunts gazed at her with bright eyes and fervid intent.

"We'll use Latin for this one," Dorinda said in decisive tones.

"Oh, yes," Bathsheba said, nodding. "That should help. Now, stand very still, Sarabeth."

"All right," Sarabeth said weakly.

Both aunts' heads dipped over the book once more. Then they gazed at each other.

"Do you have it, Bathsheba?"

"I have it, Dorinda."

"Very well."

Her aunts looked at her. They began to chant in Latin, which caused Sarabeth no small amount of unease. She could not understand their words. She only prayed that they did. Then she experienced even more unease. She felt strange. Her sight began to dim, her world to whirl. She thought she heard a whooshing sound in her ears, but it felt like it was in her very soul. Suddenly everything went dark.

When she could see again, Sarabeth cried out. Or she thought she cried out, but she could hear only a cat's howl. She saw her aunts, but it was from a totally different level, a very low level. A wooden cover was above her.

"Sarabeth!" cried Bathsheba, blinking like an owl and peering about her. "Heavens, where are you?"

"Oh, dear," Dorinda exclaimed. "Where have you gone?"

"I am here," Sarabeth said. "D-down here." She moved. She saw black furry paws as she crawled forward. She felt totally different muscles flexing and working as she padded out. "Oh, Lord!" she exclaimed, stopping and raising a clawed paw in astonishment.

"Sarabeth?" Dorinda stared down at her.

"Oh, Sarabeth!" Bathsheba gasped and her hands flew to her mouth. "You are Tomolina."

"S-so it seems," Sarabeth said, studying her black-furred body.

Dorinda and Bathsheba rushed over and bent down to peer at her.

"Oh, dear," Bathsheba murmured.

"Yes, oh, dear," Sarabeth said.

Dorinda frowned. "Where is Tomolina? Is she in there with you?"

"In here with me?" Sarabeth asked, stunned. Her eye caught sight of a little bug scurrying across the floor a goodly distance from her. Hmm. Playtime. Wait until she patted that bug about some. Maybe she'd eat it for good measure. Sarabeth shook herself firmly. "Yes, I believe Tomolina is in here with me."

"Oh, dear," Bathsheba said. "I wonder who is in control."

Sarabeth wanted that bug terribly. "I—I think Tomolina is."

"Don't be silly," Dorinda said firmly. "You are in control."

Sarabeth tore her gaze from the bug and asked, "What makes you think so?"

"Why, your eyes are green," Dorinda said. "Tomolina's are yellow. When two share the same body, whoever's eyes you are seeing through shows which one is in control."

"Oh, yes." Bathsheba nodded, sighing in relief "How silly of me. I didn't notice at first."

"Thank heaven," Sarabeth said, sighing herself. Eating bugs wouldn't be her cup of tea, even if it were Tomolina's.

"Well," Dorinda said, standing, a pleased smile upon her face. "We are a step in the right direction. Sarabeth is visible and in living form."

"Yes," Bathsheba said, though dubiously. She stood. "But how is it going to help her?"

A strange surge of excitement coursed through Sarabeth. What an unusual experience, being a cat. "I agree with Dorinda," Sarabeth said. "I at least can be seen." She purred all of a sudden. "I believe I shall go to the Castle Tor and do some p-p-prowling." She stalked across the floor with a feline grace. "I mean surveillance."

"But, Sarabeth!" Bathsheba cried.

Sarabeth stopped at the door, her tail whipping, a new appendage to show emotion. "I'm not leaving Damian to Maudar's fell ministrations for a minute, and if I have to go to him as a cat, I will. Tell me, will Dame Tureen know that I am me and not Tomolina?"

Dorinda snorted. "Not unless she knows Tomolina's eyes are yellow."

"Excellent," purred Sarabeth.

"And you keep your mouth shut," Dorinda warned. "Witches can understand if you speak in human."

"Oh, I'll be mum," Sarabeth said. "I'm just a stray cat after all." She licked her whiskers. "Just a poor stray cat."

Three

Sarabeth's heart pounded. She stretched her legs and dug her claws into the ground as she leapt and leapt. The beast! He bayed ferociously behind her. She could hear the snapping of his fangs.

She chased across the Castle Tor's neglected lawn, bounding over high grass and weeds. She saw a man. Salvation! Sarabeth pelted at the man, sprang up his leg with no consideration to modesty, and scaled farther, to cling desperately to his chest with all her nails.

"The devil!" the man cursed. It was Damian! Sarabeth clung on all the harder. She mewed a plea.

The ravaging, foul dog, not inches behind her, leapt, his teeth snapping. He growled obscenities Sarabeth never knew a dog could until then. Damian's hand shot out and promptly cuffed the foul-mouthed animal. The dog yelped in surprise.

"Down, sir," Damian said.

The dog plopped back, falling to his haunches. He whined profuse apologies, all the while glaring at Sarabeth. She glared back and meowed, "Toad eater."

"Now, be gone with you, sir," Damian said sternly to the dog. The dog lolled his tongue. He sat a moment, staring longingly at Sarabeth. "I said, be gone with you."

The dog whined in his throat. Vanquished, he stood and trotted off. Sarabeth watched, amazed. Apparently Damian had a way with animals.

"Now, puss," Damian's voice said softly, soothingly. "Please remove your claws from me." He reached up and plucked Sarabeth from his shirt. She released her claws in embarrassment. He held her out in front of him, she dangling but feeling secure in his grasp.

"Where did you come from, sir?" Damian asked. Sarabeth meowed a welcome. Damian's eyes lowered upon her and he smiled. "Forgive me . . . madam."

Sarabeth cringed in mortification. Being a cat with nary a garment to cover oneself was quite embarrassing. Never again would she check an animal's gender so cavalierly. She glanced at Damian, grateful that cats could not blush.

Damian's eyes widened as he looked into her eyes. Sarabeth's own heart jumped, and she felt the jolt of electricity she had when she had seen him upon the road. Recognition glimmered in his dark gaze for a moment. Sarabeth's breath caught.

"Faith," he muttered. He promptly dropped her to the ground. "You are safe. But beware of the dogs."

Sarabeth meowed lowly. She would have none of that. She fully intended to remain with Damian, and unlike the dog, she would not be dismissed. She circled his legs, rubbing up against them.

"Very well." Damian chuckled and knelt. He ran his large hand across her fur, and Sarabeth purred in pleasure. It was truly indescribable, to have one's fur rubbed, every hair feeling it.

Unfortunately Damian desisted and stood. "That's enough, Kit. I have work to do."

Sarabeth looked up at him with longing. She meowed for more.

"No," Damian said firmly. "I have work to do."

He turned from her and walked away. Sarabeth, eyes narrowing, bounded after him.

Damian stood in the charred ruins of the west wing. He sucked in his breath. The acrid smell of smoke and cinders burned his lungs.

The gray stone walls, laden in dark soot, still stood, as they had always stood. Yet everything within those strong, unyielding walls was burned. Objects, unrecognizable, scattered the room in dark shapes. The large tapestries hung in blackened tatters upon the walls.

A rage built within Damian, demanding, protective. Tor! How dare anything, even the elements, dare think to destroy it. The rage within him was alien, for he had denied this home of his ever since he had left it upon his parents' deaths. Still, the rage built with a strange, pulsing power beneath it. He closed his eyes tightly and lifted his head. "Tor!" The word was ripped from his throat. The rage consumed him.

Suddenly a slight sound from behind distracted him. The driving power evaporated. Damian opened his eyes and turned. The black cat he had saved from the dog was teetering over a charred rafter. Its glossy fur was no longer glossy, but dulled by soot.

"Meow," the cat said, and daintily picked its way across the ruins. It came to sit before him, looking up at him with incredible green eyes. A deep, drawing sadness glowed within them, as if the cat were human and grieving.

"You should not have followed me," Damian said.

"Meow."

" 'Tis no fit place for cat or human."

The cat's green eyes were steady upon him. "Meow."

Damian smiled despite himself. "Is that an agreement or a negative?"

It seemed as if the feline smiled. "Meow."

"Very well." Damian nodded. "But I've warned you. I have work to do." He gazed about the desecrated room. "We'll clear this clutter and I'll have workmen if I have to pay them to come from London."

Sarabeth padded behind Damian as he walked into his bedroom. Her muscles ached. The stench of smoke clung to her fur, burning her nostrils. She glanced about the bedroom with avid curiosity. It was huge, done in wine-red and gold. Dark mahogany furniture, large and masculine, was parceled about it, clearly arranged for comfort and pleasure. A warm fire crackled, welcoming, in the cavernous fireplace to the side.

Sarabeth plopped down upon the plush Aubusson carpet in contentment.

"Faith, Kit, I am tired," Damian said, striding across the room to sit down upon the large mahogany four-poster.

Sarabeth meowed agreement. Damian had worked like a demon the whole day long, pulling and clearing the burnt rubble from out of the west wing. Certainly a London aristocrat should not have even soiled his hands, but Damian had worked with a single-minded intentness, his chiseled face stern, his dark eyes filled with a banked anger.

Damian's gaze roved to the fire and his eyes lighted. "Drunk or not, Thomas is a charm."

That was when Sarabeth noticed a large bathing tub, steam rising from it, set before the fire. A knock sounded at the door, and a footman entered, weaving slightly, and carrying a stack of towels.

"Ah, Thomas," Damian said. "I thank you."

"Well nigh broke me back, Your Grace," the footman slurred, and trod slowly over to Damian, thumping the towels upon the bed. He straightened. " 'Tis far too cold a night for bathing, ifn you ask me, Your Grace."

" 'Twould be a worse night if I remain in this filth," Damian said, his hand going to his lawn shirt.

"I imagine so, Your Grace," Thomas said, little conviction in his voice.

"That will be all," Damian said, unloosing the first button.

Thomas turned. He jumped as he spotted Sarabeth, who lay watching the procedures with wide eyes.

"Bedamn," Thomas said. "How did *that* get in here?"

Damian's gaze turned to Sarabeth. "She's been my staunch supporter all day. It appears she has adopted me."

"It's a cat," Thomas said, his voice dark with condemnation.

"Why, so it is," Damian said.

"Shoo," Thomas cried, and with maniacal energy flapped his hands wildly in Sarabeth's direction. "Be gone! Be gone!"

Sarabeth's fur ruffled and she meowed lowly.

"Leave her be," Damian said. "She does not bother me."

"But she's a cat!" Thomas said. He crossed himself quickly. "She could be a familiar to a witch, Yer Grace."

"A familiar?" Damian cracked a laugh. "I do not believe in such." He frowned suddenly. "Though I own she seems human sometimes."

"You must not let her stay here," Thomas said, clearly agitated.

"She has been my companion, she stays." Damian smiled at Sarabeth "She does not do well at protecting herself from dogs, you see. And you yourself said 'twas a cold night. Surely you would not throw her out into it."

"That I would," Thomas said. "Cats are evil creatures, v-vassals fer witches."

"Oh, be gone with you," Damian said, laughing. "I wish to take my bath."

"Ye don't know what you are doing," Thomas muttered. He circumvented Sarabeth, gazing at her as if she were two-headed. She glared back at him and hissed. For good measure, she sprang up and bounced toward him.

"Gawd!" Thomas stumbled back. He spun and ran. He missed the door's opening and crashed into its frame instead. He fell back, his body jerking. "E-vil, e-vil!" He sidled a step over and successfully lurched through the door. His loud cry of witches and familiars trailed back to them.

"For shame, puss," Damian said, chuckling. " 'Tis not kind to tease the locals. You'll find yourself in a burlap bag and thrown in the river if you don't watch out."

Sarabeth sat back, raised a paw, and licked it with a loud, satisfied purr. "Meow!"

Damian laughed and stood. "You have no conscience." He

undid the next button of his shirt. "Perhaps you are a witch's familiar after all."

Sarabeth blinked her eyes rapidly at him, hoping to appear innocent. "Meow."

Damian stopped and his brows arched down. "If you were any witch's familiar, it would be the woman with the green eyes upon the road. Sara—" He did not finish the word. His face darkened. "Fool!" With a stunning, angry movement, he tore at the buttons on his shirt and stripped it from his shoulders.

Sarabeth's breath expelled so rapidly, she bleated. Damian stood before her, his broad shoulders bare, his chest covered with a dark mat of curling black hair, the muscles of his torso molded and defined. A shocking volt of desire coursed through her. She let out a yowl of embarrassed surprise and swiftly spun, turning her back to Damian.

"What in heaven's name?" Damian said. Sarabeth heard his tread from behind, and then he hunkered down in front of her. "What is it, you silly cat? Did Thomas spook you with all his wild, superstitious talk?"

Sarabeth gazed at Damian's face, attempting to steer her glance away from his bared torso. He reached out and ran a finger under her chin. Sarabeth purred and shivered at the same time.

Damian pulled his finger back. It was black with soot. His brow rose. "I am not the only one in need of a bath." Sarabeth stared at him, confused by the emotions coursing through her. " 'Tis a filthy familiar you are, if familiar you be," Damian said, grinning. Sarabeth lost her heart to him all the more. "Come," he said, and swiftly grabbed her up around her neck's ruff.

"Meow," Sarabeth yowled, stunned.

He held her out, dangling from his arm. She swatted at the air ineffectively. "I know you cats do not like water, but this cannot be helped. I'll not tolerate a filthy feline in my presence."

"Yowwl!" Sarabeth's eyes widened as they approached the tub. Tomolina's outrage and hers rose up. Neither of them wanted a bath at Damian's hands. "Grr meow!"

"Don't you dare scratch me, Kit," Damian's voice commanded.

Then Sarabeth was falling. She splashed into the water. She had always liked water, but as she sank, a fear overtook her. She didn't know how to swim as a cat! She began windmilling her four legs and surfaced with a yowl.

Damian's firm hand caught the scruff of her neck as she circled in the bathing tub, which seemed a large ocean to her at the moment. "Don't worry, I won't let you drown."

Sarabeth fought down her fear, feeling that large, supportive hand upon her. After the tenth wild, splashing revolution, Damian suddenly pulled her from the tub. Sarabeth sputtered and hissed, employing Tomolina's language as best she could.

"There now," Damian said, and scooped her up against his broad chest. Sarabeth's wet fur rubbed up against his skin. The scent of male invaded her nostrils. She calmed down amazingly. Her thoughts were definitely not cat as she cuddled into his arms and he carried her to the bed and sat. Feline perhaps, but not cat.

He leaned over and drew a towel from the stack beside him. He dropped it over her and rubbed her thoroughly. Sarabeth set up a contented purr.

"There you go, only clean felines here." Damian chuckled and set her down. Sarabeth gazed up at him. Desire coursed through her. She belied his words, for her thoughts were not at all clean. She balled up comfortably upon the bed and watched Damian as he stood and stretched. She adored the play of muscles upon his rib cage and shoulders. When he reached for the band of his unmentionables, however, she ruthlessly closed her eyes. 'Twas not fair to gaze at him so, even as a cat.

Sarabeth heard splashing and then a deep sigh. She was unable to resist. She opened her eyes. Damian sat in the tub, his muscled arms stretched upon its rims, his dark head resting against its back, his stern profile relaxed in repose.

She thought of the boy she had seen as a child and had always yearned to know. Now he was a man. As she silently watched the reposed figure before her, her heart twisted. "Oh, Damian." The words whispered through her soul. "You are still my love."

Damian stood at the site of Castle Tor. No castle rose before him. The grounds were empty. Trees and brush grew where there should have been stone and turret. A cold night wind moaned about him, lonely and chilling. It blew a fog up, enshrouding him.

A man stepped out of the fog. He looked similar to Damian, but was dressed in clothes of another time. He stood a moment. Then the man lifted his hands and said, "Rise, be of me and mine."

A blue-white pillar of light funneled up to the skies. Slowly the outline of Castle Tor appeared. Damian blinked as the fog rolled back, and the castle lay clearly before him, glowing with the blue light that had created it.

The other man seemed to slump. Then he lifted his right arm high, his palm outstretched to the castle. "O Ancient of Days, may this be a stronghold of light. Ward it against the evil powers."

The man disappeared, becoming just another mist. Damian turned to the blue-glowing Castle Tor. Suddenly the left wing tindered up, blazing with fire. Numb, he watched as other figures chased about, trying to put the fire out. He wanted to run and join those figures, but could not. He was bound, unable to move. Helplessly he watched.

Behind him, he suddenly heard the strains of a waltz and laughter. Enraged, he turned. Lady Seffington's ballroom, the one he had been in just a week earlier, lay before him in all its splendor and glittering candlelight. He saw himself there, dancing and laughing down at the woman who had intrigued him at the moment. Choking, he spun back. The Castle Tor burned, flames roaring high. He turned again. He danced with the woman in his arms.

It was that night. The night of the fire.

Trembling in agony, he turned back to the burning Castle Tor. No longer did it burn. The west wing rested, cold and burnt out. It looked as it had when he had first arrived, nothing but a dark shell. Then a small, eerie red point lit within its center. It grew and grew. Damian cried out, but the red glow suffused the wing. Before his pained eyes it evasively crept to encompass the entire castle. The red turned deeper and darker to the color of blood.

"Forsaken," a voice cried.

"Damian, I am sorry," another voice said to his right. He turned.

It was the woman upon the road who stood beside him. Mist swirled about her. Her deep green eyes gazed at him, pools of sadness. He reached out to her, as he had wished to do that night. She raised her hand and took his. Blue-white light flared about them. It shot pure white for a brief moment.

Then she disappeared.

"No!" Damian cried. "No!"

He jerked awake. Panting, he sat up in bed, staring into the darkness. An iron hand clenched itself about his chest. Sweat beaded his face.

"Meow," Damian heard. Blinking, he looked down. In the glimmer of moonlight a black cat lay tumbled before him. It sat up and blinked green eyes in confusion.

"I am sorry, Kit," Damian said. His voice came out hoarse. "It was—was a nightmare."

The green eyes of the cat deepened, deepened to the green eyes of the woman of his dreams. "Meow." Slowly it rose and padded to stand upon him. It reached out a paw, its claws retracted, and Damian felt a velvet pat upon his cheek. "Meow."

He sighed and his arms went about the warm, living creature. "Yes," he said shakily. "Meow." He lay back, holding the cat to him, its furry body nestled upon his chest. Its purring rumbled into his skin, soothing, warm.

Damian closed his eyes. "Only a nightmare," he whispered, and drifted off to the cat's soft purring.

Faith, but Damian was a gentleman, Sarabeth thought, and squelched a yawn. She sat beneath the table, hidden by the linen tablecloth while Damian and Gertrude dined. Her fur had stood on end when she discovered who was dining with them that evening. Gratefully, Maudar had not attended, claiming to have fallen sick, and sending only Gertrude with a chaperone, a woman Sarabeth new to be an inept witch of Maudar's coven.

Well, Maudar had shot herself in the foot, Sarabeth thought wryly as she lifted her paw and licked it. Maudar had most likely thought to have arranged a romantic evening for Damian and Gertrude, since the chaperone had said not a word throughout the meal. Yet Gertrude was bumbling it frightfully. The girl had no conversation skills. Her major words were "Yes, your grace," and "No, your grace."

Damian had just set out upon another foray of conversation about the politics of the day. What a gallant fighter he was, Sarabeth thought with a purr. He had already covered the conversation of his travels abroad, weaving stories of distant lands and customs that had enthralled Sarabeth and made her quiver. It took all her strength not to have crawled out from beneath the table and demand of him an explanation of the custom of Indian women to throw themselves upon the funeral pyre of their dead husbands. Amazing. Damian did not believe in magic or witchcraft, but the custom of the Indian women reeked of a dark ritual and incantation to Sarabeth. He accepted *that* as reality, but denied magic?

Then Damian had proceeded to inquire about Gertrude's life. Sarabeth would have liked to think that Gertrude had merely been wise not to discuss her life, since it included a black witch for a mama, but she seriously doubted it had anything to do with wisdom. Gertrude was merely a widgeon. And even worse, when prompted to talk about her life, Gertrude had missed the opportunity to turn the tables and ask Damian about his own.

Why, oh, why could Gertrude not ask the right questions? When Damian had left the Castle Tor at the age of nine, after his parents had died in a boating accident, what had he done? What had he felt? Why had he never returned to the Castle Tor in all these years? Sarabeth willed the dolt to ask Damian these questions. But no. Gertrude "your-graced" Damian to death, with an occasional giggle thrown in to be passed off as conversation.

Now they were upon politics. Damian would draw a blank at that one, Sarabeth knew. Yet he was espousing a Tory opinion that Sarabeth thought quite ridiculous. Did not Gertrude know enough to refute Damian in regards to the corn laws? Damian was an intelligent man and should be called to task for his shortsightedness and unfeeling belief in regard to the farmers. Granted, Sarabeth was but a country girl, but even she knew better! And to think, she had slept in the man's bed the night before! Granted, it was as a cat, but still, she had slept beside him and allowed him to hold her close when he had awakened from that nightmare. A feline growl rose in her throat and she muffled it quickly.

Sarabeth heard a commotion from the entrance to the large dining hall. Quickly she padded over to the draping tablecloth and peeked out.

Thomas, at the moment, lurched and weaved his way into the room with a large, laden tray. Apparently that was the man's perpetual mode of transportation, for it could not be called walking. "Yer Grace," he pronounced with a silly grin, his bloodshot gaze clearly focused upon Gertrude with drunken desire. "Here is the des-sert."

"Ah, yes." Damian's voice said, a tinge of gratefulness clearly definable. "I believe Dame Tureen sent this along and 'tis not Millicent's cooking?"

"That be right," nodded Thomas, wagging his head up and

down. He lurched another step forward. "You be in fer a real treat."

"You must thank your mother, Gertrude," Damian said, his voice sounding eager, "for being so kind as to send this, even if she could not attend. I am sure she is an excellent cook and I look forward to the dessert. Faith, I doubt I've had one morsel of food here that was not burned, lumpy, or soggy."

"Yes, Your Grace," Gertrude said for the one hundredth time.

Sarabeth's eyes narrowed and her fur rose. Anything brewed in Maudar Tureen's kitchen could only be fell. Sarabeth thought hastily back. No, last night was but a half moon. If it had been a full moon and Maudar had cooked whatever was upon the tray, it could very well be lethal.

Well, Damian would just have to suffer burned, lumpy, soggy food, for the delicacies upon the tray would not pass his lips or she wasn't Sarabeth Goodfellow! With an ear-splitting opening yowl, she pelted out from underneath the table.

"Wh-what the . . . !" Thomas cried, his face one of utter shock as she rocketed at him.

"Gr-howl," Sarabeth flew at Thomas's leg, attaching herself to him with all claws extended.

"Ouch, ouch," Thomas cried. "Get orf, creature of dark."

Thomas spun about, performing a frantic hopping dance in an attempt to shake Sarabeth from him. Tartlets flew from the tray at high velocity on each revolution.

"Kit!" Damian roared over Thomas's curse and the women's shrieks. "Down!"

Sarabeth ignored him. She scaled higher and sunk a paw into Thomas's thigh. He cried out, but obstinately protected the tray with its remaining fell cookery. The alcohol must have numbed him to pain. Sarabeth hated to fight dirty, but fight she would. She lifted one paw up in a deliberate display, threatening a higher, ignoble purchase.

"God, Kit, no!" Damian cried.

Thomas's innate self-preservation must have finally surfaced in his drunken blood, or it may have been the horrified shock in Damian's voice that tipped him off, but release the tray he did. It crashed to the floor.

He looked down to the clinging Sarabeth, defined her intended, sensitive target, let out a roar, and grabbed for her. She swiftly released her hold and dropped to her four feet. "Unman me, would you, you devil's spawn!" Thomas shouted. He lurched forward and reached to swat her. Sarabeth sprang from his reach. He overbalanced and toppled forward.

"Thomas!" Damian shouted. "Enough!"

Thomas crawled to all fours. Rage showed in his bloodshot eyes. He snatched at Sarabeth. She merely bounced away. She landed unerringly upon a tartlet, and with a fine back kick sent it flying directly into Thomas's face. It splattered blue jam upon his nose as it hit.

Quickly, with obsessive determination, Sarabeth hopscotched over every tart she saw, placing a firm cat's paw in each one of them. Thomas bellowed and crawled behind her, ineffectively swinging at her.

"No! No!" Gertrude's voice cried up. "You are ruining my mother's spe—"

"Dessert!" the chaperone cried.

Sarabeth growled and ground into another tartlet with refueled vigor.

"Come here," Thomas cried. "Ye puissant witch, you phooka, ye bleeding—"

"Enough, I said," Damian roared. His chair toppled and he stalked over to Sarabeth. Much quicker than Thomas, he snatched Sarabeth up by the scruff before she could say meow.

"Wh-what c-creature is it?" Gertrude stammered, wide-eyed and pale as she stood up from the table. She was a vision in a soft pink dress, the darkness of her glossy curls set to advantage against its pale sheen. Her neckline plunged indecently low. Sarabeth noticed. She growled.

"My cat," Damian gritted, shaking the dangling Sarabeth slightly. His dark face was angry granite, his eyes blazing fury. "At least, I thought it was my cat."

"I told you, Yer Grace," Thomas cried, stumbling to his feet. " 'Tis no cat. 'Tis—"

"Do not say another word," Damian barked, his gaze still upon Sarabeth. She stared back. She could feel the force of his anger against her, but she would not back down. The fur on her stood straight out, but still she would not withdraw her battling gaze. " 'Tis fortunate you are a cat," Damian said lowly. "I do not know what craziness has entered your head, but I'll have none of it, do you hear?" He bent and dropped her. In clear, cold dismissal, he turned to the two women who stood, gaping. "Forgive this interruption. Kit is a stray. I had no notion her manners were so abominable." He turned to Thomas. "You may put Kit outside until she learns better social etiquette." He did not even look to Sarabeth upon the floor. "And then be pleased to bring us our after-dinner drinks in the parlor." He bowed to the two women. "Ladies. Let us forget this unfortunate incident. Please, follow me."

The women nodded. Gertrude murmured, "Yes, Your Grace" and they moved to file obediently behind Damian. They left the room. Silence fell within it. Sarabeth turned a wary gaze upon Thomas. He glared at her, his anger clear, even through the blue jam smeared on his face.

"Come here, you blighter," Thomas growled. "I knows you're a familiar."

Predictably, he dived for her. One would have thought he had learned his lesson before, Sarabeth thought in disdain as she swiftly leapt away. 'Twas fortunate she did, for Thomas hit the marble floor full front and surfed, body length, along it. He effectively cleaned up the smashed tartlets within his path.

Sarabeth hesitated not a moment, but scampered out the door, leaving a cursing Thomas behind. She padded softly down the great hall, searching for the room where Damian and the ladies would be. Dismiss her, would he? Have her thrown out by the drunken Thomas, would he?

Hearing murmurs in one of the rooms, she tread up to it. The door was shut. She meowed a pithy curse and glanced around. She spied a side table along the wall and darted beneath it. Interminable minutes passed. Sarabeth controlled her growls of disgruntlement. While she waited the thought that she just might like to go and scare up a nice juicy mouse for a snack surfaced in her mind. "No, Tomolina," she said repressively. She was after larger quarry than that.

She was rewarded, alas, when she saw Thomas's stumbling approach down the hall. His uniform was rent and jam-smirched. He carried a silver tray with decanters upon it, all the while glancing about him in fright.

Sarabeth ducked back under the table. When Thomas stopped before the door and opened it, muttering dark words about black magic and blacker cats, Sarabeth waited a second more. Then she slipped out and stealthily followed behind him into the room. She darted immediately for the safety of a large wing chair. No exclamations arose, and she deemed herself secure.

Everyone sat comfortably around the large fireplace upon brocade settees and gilt chairs. How Sarabeth wished she were visible and human and could be sitting there in the social company of Damian.

"Thank you, Thomas, that will be all," Damian said briskly. Perhaps it was not such social company after all. Damian's face portrayed thunderclouds. He nodded curtly to Thomas and then turned to the fire, his back to the group.

"Yes, Yer Grace," Thomas muttered. He set the tray down with a thunk and beat a hasty, limping retreat.

The room fell quiet a moment. An unjovial host, Damian stared down at the fire, his whole attitude one of brooding. Sarabeth saw Gertrude's chaperone jab her in the ribs. Gertrude jumped and cried out.

"Gertrude, pour the sherry," the chaperone ordered, nodding and performing odd, gesturing motions.

"What?" Gertrude's eyes widened. "Oh, yes. I forgot." She stood and crossed over to lift the decanter and pour the sherry. Her hand shook noticeably. Fumbling, she then pulled out a small vial from the cuff of her dress. Sarabeth rolled her eyes. Faith, certainly she wasn't going to use that old trick? But yes, she was. Dark green liquid oozed out of the vial into one of the sherry glasses. Sarabeth all but raked the carpet bare in exasperation. If Damian weren't so engrossed in his dark musings, he would have seen such an obvious stunt.

"H-here you are, Your Grace," Gertrude spoke up in a squeak. She held the glass out.

Damian turned, his gaze dark. It was obvious he forced himself, for a stiff smile crossed his face. "Thank you, my dear." He walked over to take the glass.

"Here we go again," Sarabeth thought. She bounded across the room. She sprang into the air, using all the feline litheness at her command. Her body knocked the glass on the way up. She swiped out and clawed Gertrude's hand on the way down.

Gertrude screeched as the sherry flew, splattering her perfect pink dress. She screeched again as she experienced Sarabeth's claws.

"Kit!" roared Damian, standing frozen as Sarabeth plopped to the floor, winded and stunned. That leap had been phenomenal, and she blessed Tomolina for being the superb cat she was. "Damn you!"

Sarabeth blinked a moment. Damian pounced upon her with a speed no less lightning than what she had just performed. His large hand clamped her neck and jerked her high into the air. "Have you not done enough for the night?" Sarabeth spat and hissed. Evidently she hadn't. She was suddenly furious at his obtuseness, fear of what the potion might do, goading her to another feral growl. It was not a very wise response, for Damian growled himself and shook her ruthlessly.

"Oh, oh, oh," keened Gertrude, her face red, her large, dark eyes swelling with tears. "My beautiful dress. That cat spilled mama's love p—"

"Yes, that cat spilled the sherry on the dress your mama loved so much," the chaperone said swiftly.

Sarabeth, her head rattling from Damian's shaking, hissed.

The "beautiful pink dress" showed not only the red of the sherry, but a green stain as well. Even as a human, Sarabeth could notice an odd steam rising from it. She swung her paw out, since she could not point, and meowed, since she could not speak it aloud.

"Be quiet!" Damian roared. Gertrude stopped wailing abruptly. She hiccuped, and peeked at Damian with wide, frightened eyes. "I did not mean you," he said curtly. "I meant this infernal cat." He shook Sarabeth for emphasis, making her feel as if she were a furry rag. "But please, do stop crying." Big tears rolled from Gertrude's eyes nevertheless, and a sob escaped her. "I am sorry the evening was ruined," Damian said more gently. "Perhaps—perhaps we could go riding tomorrow morning?" He lifted Sarabeth high. "Where this one can't bother us."

Gertrude's brown eyes lighted and her tears disappeared magically. "I would like that."

"That's a good girl," Damian said, his tone approving. "Now, if you will excuse me, I personally shall get rid of this cat."

He stalked from the room. Sarabeth remained prudently silent as Damian strode through the large hall. With his free hand he opened the large oak door. He flung her out. Luckily, Sarabeth landed upon her feet with Tomolina's nimbleness.

"Now, stay out there," Damian said. "Cat or not, familiar or not, you behaved abominably. Go find some other unfortunate victim to adopt." His face dark and raging, Damian slammed the door shut in Sarabeth's face.

The October cold sliced through Sarabeth's fur. She looked up to the moon that was even fuller tonight. She shivered. A lonely moan rose from her throat. Desolate, she turned to make her way home.

Four

"Hmm—purrr," Sarabeth said. Drowsily she opened her eyes and blinked. "Yowl!" she howled, shooting straight up. The cottage was filled with morning light, dreaded morning light.

"Spo-what?" Bathsheba murmured. She sat, slumped in the kitchen chair, her silver hair shooting out at odd angles, her nightgown rumpled and bespotted by different potions.

"It's morning," Sarabeth cried.

"Morning?" Bathsheba blinked her eyes opened. They widened in dismay. "Oh, no, it's morning already."

She reached over and shook Dorinda, who slept in the other kitchen chair, her upper half sprawled over the table, one book for a headrest, another, opened, and curved possessively in her arm. "Dorinda, Dorinda, do wake up."

"G-r-rr," Dorinda said. Her sleepy brown eyes cracked open. "Wh-at?" Her tone was decidedly cranky.

"It's morning!" Bathsheba cried.

"Morning?" Dorinda closed her eyes. They immediately shuttered open. "Morning!" She shoved herself up from the table. Books and scraps of paper flew. Her thin face took on a look of horror. "Morning, already?"

"It crept up," Bathsheba moaned.

"And I'm still a cat," Sarabeth said. "Damian must be out riding with Gertrude by now."

"Oh, dear," Bathsheba said. "Heaven only knows what she'll try and do."

"You mean hell only knows," Dorinda said.

"Yes," nodded Bathsheba, her blue eyes darkening. "To use a love potion, 'tis evil. Love is the gift and fate of the Great Creator himself, and to try to control it and change it with magic . . ." She shivered. "Nothing ever good comes of it. Maudar must be stopped."

"Tsk." Dorinda clicked her tongue and stood abruptly, her thin body enshrouded in a voluminous white nightgown. "And we no closer to the right spell."

The cottage kitchen held new and various objects. The pots and pans hanging upon the fire now wore healthy coats of cat fur. The broom to the side of the door had the curves of a woman, all in wood, of course. And the walls themselves were covered in a plush foliage of ivy. It was the plant motif again.

"No, I fear not," Bathsheba sighed, sadly looking about the room.

"But you've tried," Sarabeth said bracingly. Her aunts were indeed game as pebbles. She had arrived late that night, begging them to turn her back into her true and visible form. And they had tried—all night, in fact.

"We must try again," Dorinda said, lifting her chin. "We shall not be defeated." The peach pit that now rested beside her, the size of a footstool, belied her statement. "Stand up, Bathsheba."

"Oh, yes." Bathsheba dutifully stood.

"And you too, Sarabeth!"

"C-certainly," Sarabeth said, rising from her crouch.

" 'Tis time for a new spell," Dorinda said. "We shall make it from scratch. Bathsheba, your hand."

"Yes, we must not tarry," Bathsheba nodded, her sleepy blue eyes lighting. She promptly clasped her sister's hands.

"Shall I do the honors?" Dorinda asked, her face set and determined.

"Do, sister dear."

"Very well," Dorinda nodded shortly.

"Oh, no," Sarabeth murmured. She closed her eyes tightly.

When the sisters digressed from well-worn spells to try their hand at new ones cut from whole cloth, things had a tendency to go awry. "Oh, Damian," sighed Sarabeth.

Dorinda heaved in a deep breath. "Spirit of the Universe . . ."

"Spirit of the universe," Bathsheba repeated.

"Spirit of souls and bodies . . ."

"Spirit of souls and bodies . . ."

"Separate woman and cat . . ."

"Separate woman and cat . . ."

"Leave cat within her form . . ."

"Leave cat within her form . . ."

"And transform the woman back . . ."

"And transform the woman back . . ." Dorinda halted a long while.

"What next?" whispered Bathsheba.

"I'm thinking," Dorinda hissed. She drew in another breath. "Here it goes. . . . Transform the woman back to living, visible form, that she may fly to her love and speak the truth."

"Transform the woman back to living, visible form . . ." Bathsheba's voice repeated. The words faded from Sarabeth's hearing. She felt her spirit twirling. "That she may fly . . ." Suddenly Sarabeth felt disembodied, floating in a dark void. "To her love . . ." She had no hands or legs, or body. "And speak the truth!"

"Squawk," Sarabeth cried out as she felt suddenly compressed, molded, and confined. "Squawk." She opened her eyes, and jumped. Her vision was quite odd.

"Oh, dear," Bathsheba sighed, shaking her head.

"Oh, dear," Dorinda murmured.

"Squawk. What? What?" Sarabeth discovered 'twas all she could say. Her mouth wouldn't finish or form anything else. She lifted her hand. She saw a feathered wing instead.

"You are a bird, dear," Bathsheba said, looking slightly shamefaced.

"A parrot, to be exact," Dorinda said, her mouth pursing.

"A pretty parrot though," Bathsheba said consolingly. "You are a blond parrot." She smiled. "We at least got the hair color correct this time."

"And green eyes," nodded Dorinda, after peering at her. " 'Tis your eyes."

"Squawk" Sarabeth said, and ruffled her feathers.

"I like the mornings," Gertrude said as she rode a gentle mount beside Damian.

Damian blinked. It appeared Gertrude was verbose in the mornings. It was the first non "Your Grace," she had offered to him. "Do you?"

"Yes, it is light," Gertrude said simply.

"Too blasted light," muttered Thomas, who was enacting their groom, from behind. 'Twas clear Thomas was not a horseman, for he clung to his mount in a lopsided manner.

"Yes, that it is," Damian nodded kindly. He gazed at the girl. She was a delight in an emerald-green riding habit. She held the horse's reins tightly. Another poor equestrian, he thought wryly. Without thought, Damian glanced about the open field they meandered through. There was not a sight of a living creature anywhere about. His conscience pricked him. Where had Kit gone? Indeed, he had been furious last night, but to know the cat had been left out in the cold due to his temper bothered him. It was a mere animal, and he a human. Surely no animal should suffer because of his lack of control. "What do you like to do in the mornings?" he asked Gertrude, forcing his attention back to hand. He must forget the cat.

Gertrude's eyes widened. "Why, I sit and watch the light."

"A worthy occupation," Damian said, controlling a twitching smile. No one could say that Gertrude was not a restful girl. She certainly did not chatter like the London debutantes, or demand constant gallantry as did his London flirts. "And what else do you do?"

"I help Mama," Gertrude said.

Damian heard Thomas snort from behind. "It is good to be a dutiful daughter," Damian said solemnly.

"Yes," nodded Gertrude. "One should always be dutiful."

She would clearly never set herself up against her husband, Damian mused. He heard a loud squawk all of a sudden. Confused, Damian looked up from whence the cry had come. A bird was descending from the clear morning sky, its wings flapping in an ungainly manner.

Stunningly, it alighted upon Damian's shoulder. He swiveled his head and found himself staring into the green eyes of a parrot, a blond parrot. "Faith."

"Craw, hello," the parrot rasped. "Hello, hello."

"It's a birdie," Gertrude exclaimed in delight.

The bird twisted its head. "Pretty Polly. Pretty Polly."

"Hello, Pretty Polly," Damian chuckled. "Where did you come from?"

The bird reached over and rubbed its beak against his cheek. "Love! Love!"

"Stop that," Damian said, laughing.

The parrot ruffled its feathers and then slid over and nibbled upon his ear. It was light and soft. "Pretty Polly, love."

"Gore," Thomas muttered from behind.

"Pretty Polly," Gertrude giggled.

The bird nibbled Damian's lobe once more. "Love."

"Behave yourself," Damian chuckled. "That tickles."

"It's cute," Gertrude giggled. "Cute."

The bird turned its head and squawked. Damian's cheek was slapped by a blond wing as the bird flew from his shoulder. "Witch," the parrot suddenly cawed, and flapped directly at Gertrude. "Witch!"

"Oh!" Gertrude cried. The bird winged madly about Gertrude, darting and diving at her dark head. Gertrude raised her hands up in fright.

"Witch, witch," the parrot squawked, and clamped its talons into Gertrude's hair.

"Ouch!" Gertrude waved her hands wildly, flapping as much as the bird did.

The parrot, a firm grasp on a hank of Gertrude's hair, soared upward. Damian stifled a laugh, unable to help himself. It looked as if all Gertrude's hair was standing on end.

"Here now!" Thomas cried. "Stop that!"

The bird dropped Gertrude's hair. The strands toppled in her face. Pretty Polly abruptly shot toward Thomas. "Drunk, drunk!" it squawked. Thomas shouted as it dived at him. He let loose his clutch upon his horse to fend off the frenzied bird.

"Drunk, drunk," it cawed.

"Be gone!" Thomas shouted, and swatted at the bird. His swing unbalanced him and he rolled right off his mount. The horse, neighing in fright, kicked up its heels and galloped off.

"Bad bird," Gertrude cried. "Bad bird." It was but a puff from beneath the mass of hair mopping her face.

"Love," the bird cooed as it winged lightly past Damian.

"Witch," it then cawed. Circling around the blinded Gertrude, it swooped down and applied a sharp beak to the rump of Gertrude's horse. The beast shrieked in anger. Gertrude shrieked in fright.

"Witch," the bird cried raucously, and beaked the horse again. It reared, Gertrude clinging desperately to it. Thudding down, the horse tore off.

"Witch, witch," the bird cried, and flew after the galloping horse, bedeviling it each time it dared to slow down.

Damian, holding firm rein upon his own cavorting horse, watched, stupefied. Gertrude, horse, and parrot disappeared down the meadow, a noisy, squawking trio.

"Witch," drifted back to him upon the morning wind.

Sarabeth winged merrily back toward the Castle Tor, having triumphantly left Gertrude's horse pelting straight into Dame Tureen's stables. She felt like whistling, but had learned that speaking as a parrot, she could perform only certain linguistic feats. It seemed only when she truly wanted to say something would a word pop out of her beak, and then she could not even stop herself from speaking it.

Sarabeth caught an air current and played with it, practicing the lift it gave her. Learning to employ her wings had come naturally, but she knew she wasn't the most proficient of the species in the sky. Indeed, she noticed a sparrow flying higher than she and circling with an ease that showed her own flapping as unsightly and amateurish. Braggart, she thought.

Then she looked down and spied the figure she desired. Damian was just then walking toward the large doors of the Castle Tor. Thomas, his footman, was limping behind him.

Best hurry, Sarabeth thought, and dived.

"Hello, hello," she said happily as she landed upon Damian's shoulder with a decent grace. Let that sparrow take note. "Hello, hello."

"Gawd!" Thomas cried. He looked the worse for wear, his livery grass-stained and rent. His limp was even more pronounced close-up. "Damn near killed me, that bird did."

Damian turned his head toward her, and Sarabeth shifted, cocking her own head to be able to see him. His dark eyes were enigmatic, but just a trace of a smile touched his lips. "I thought I would see you again."

"Craw! Pretty Polly!"

"Pretty Polly!" Thomas said. "The devil's bird, that's what it is!"

"To you every animal is the devil, Thomas, or its familiar," Damian said mildly, and opened the large entrance door, Sarabeth clinging to his shoulder.

"And I'm right," muttered the footman.

Damian laughed as they entered the hall. "Go find yourself another bottle of wine, Thomas, and you shall soon be set to rights."

"Need more than a bottle," Thomas mumbled, glaring at Sarabeth.

"Beg pardon," a timid voice said. The company turned to

the voice. An unfamiliar maid stood before them, holding a feather duster in one hand, a missive in the other.

"Hello," Damian said, smiling. "You are new, are you not?"

The maid dipped a curtsy. "Yes, milord, er, your honor . . . er."

"It's 'His Grace,' " Thomas hissed.

"Er, His Grace," the girl said, and dipped another curtsy.

"No, no," Thomas said. *"Yer* Grace!"

"My Grace?" the girl asked, wide-eyed. She turned to Damian and dipped another curtsy. "Yes, My Grace."

"Yer Grace," Thomas repeated.

"I's said that," the girl said, her face darkening.

"That is fine," Damian said. "And who are you, my dear?"

The girl's face broke into a relieved smile. "Me name's Tilly. I'm from Landinton, but Murtle be a cousin of mine and said you was needing more servants."

"An understatement," Damian said. "I am pleased to see you."

"I be new at being a maid, but I cans learn. Ma says I be a fast learner."

"I am sure," Damian said.

"Oh, I forgots," the girl said. "Ye have a letter from London town, My Grace." She scurried forward and handed a letter to Damian, then backed up, performing three obsequious curtsies.

Damian frowned down at the missive. "Thank you." Sarabeth cocked her head. The missive was upon the finest of pink paper, with a ruby-red seal. She misliked the looks of it and the way Damian studied it.

"Sh—should I d-dust now, My Grace?"

"Yes, Tilly," Damian murmured, his voice sounding distracted. "That will be fine."

"Yes, My Grace," Tilly said. She brandished her feather duster high and scampered down the great hall, making toward a door.

"Tilly!" Damian suddenly roared. Sarabeth squawked in surprise. His roar nearly split her eardrums. "What are you do-ing?"

Tilly froze, her hand upon the doorknob, her eyes wide. "You—you told me I c-could dust, Me Grace."

"Not in that room," Damian said. Sarabeth could feel his muscles beneath her talons cording. "Leave it. That room is never to be entered, do you understand?"

"Y-yes, Me Grace," Tilly stammered. "I—I'm sorry, Me Grace." Her face crumpling, she spun and dashed away.

"Damn," Damian murmured.

"Perhaps Yer Grace could use a nip yourself," Thomas said.

Damian was silent a moment. "Yes, I believe I could. Bring me brandy. I'll be in the parlor."

Damian turned so abruptly, Sarabeth was forced to hang on for dear life. He strode to the parlor and entered. He stretched out his arm and said commandingly, "Come down, Polly, I have no doubt you have ruined my jacket." Sarabeth walked precari-ously down his arm. "Not to mention my morning ride with the fair Gertrude."

Sarabeth squawked in indignation and flew to alight upon a wing chair. She cocked her head back and forth. "Pretty Polly."

"Pretty Polly perhaps," Damian said, "but certainly not nice Polly." He strode to the sofa and lowered himself down upon it. His gaze narrowed upon her. "Odd, all the animals about here seem bent upon ruining my chance at romance." He frowned. "Cats that well nigh unman a footman, and for what, I wonder?" He lifted a considering brow toward Sarabeth. "You haven't perchance seen a black cat . . . with green eyes, have you?"

Sarabeth shifted from one claw to another. "Squawk, hello, hello."

Thomas, at that moment, entered with a silver tray and de-canter upon it. He stopped, arrested. "You be talking to the bird, Yer Grace?"

Damian blinked. "Why, so I am, Thomas."

"Ye shouldn't," Thomas said, and limped forward, all but

dropping the tray upon the accompanying table beside Damian. "That bird could be—"

"I know, the devil's own," Damian said, sighing. He reached for the decanter. "In Chancellorville, everyone can be the devil's own." He poured a glass and lifted it. "And probably is, Thomas."

"Yes, Yer Grace," Thomas said. He glared at the bird and limped out of the room. "Wise man, Thomas," Damian murmured. "He stays drunk." He quaffed the entire glass swiftly. Sarabeth watched him in surprise. "I'm not a drinking man, Pretty Polly," he said, pouring another glass. "For I get odd notions . . . see things, visions, as it were." Then he laughed. "But what man does not?" He quirked his brow. "And since I'm talking to a parrot, I might as well indulge myself" Fortunately he sipped from this glass. His dark eyes studied her. "A blond parrot with green eyes."

Sarabeth decided it was time for a distraction. She promptly flew over to Damian, landing beside him upon the sofa. She reached to peck at the pink envelope that Damian had thrown to the cushion.

"Hmm, yes," Damian said, setting his drink down and picking up the missive. He lifted it to his nose. "Her favorite scent. I should have known she would write me."

Sarabeth's feathers fluffed out in displeasure. Damian broke the seal upon the missive and opened it. Unable to wait, Sarabeth flapped up to Damian's shoulder. She peered at the letter.

My darling Damian,
    How could you have left town without telling me? I am bereft of your company and await your return anxiously.
                                                        Melissa

"Witch, witch," Sarabeth crawed, unable to help herself. She was seeing green.

"Bitch, bitch, t'would be better." Damian chuckled softly. "Milady dallies with every man in Christendom, but let one dismiss himself from her court and she will do anything to bring him back to heel." He tossed the envelope to the sofa and picked up his glass. "A close escape, Pretty Polly, a close escape. Lord, I must be getting old, I don't normally skirt so close to parson's mousetrap."

Sarabeth dove upon the letter. She grabbed it up into her beak and flew over to the small fire that was set against the chill. She promptly dropped it into the flames. "Witch, witch," she cawed, and flapped her wings, remaining to watch it burn.

"Huzzah," Damian said. Sarabeth turned and winged her way back to settle beside Damian. His glass was held out to her, a smile upon his lips. "A toast."

"Love," Sarabeth said, pleased to see his smile.

"Love," Damian said, shaking his head. "No, I shan't toast to that, for I don't believe in it. I shall toast to—to freedom."

"Love," Sarabeth cawed again.

"No, no," Damian said. "I shall not drink to it."

"Love."

"You must be a young parrot," Damian said, a sudden twist to his lips. "Just a chick, indeed, for there is no such thing as love." His eyes darkened. "I have known many women . . ."

"Squawk, squawk, squawk!"

"More than that" Damian said, taking a deep drink from his glass. "But I shan't sully your young parrot ears with how many." His eyes darkened. "And always I think, there is a woman . . . and then they become unfaithful, liars, deceivers . . . or I become unfaithful, liar, and deceiver . . ." He chuckled. It was not a pleasant sound. "Else they disappear into thin air. How fitting. That is what love does."

"Love," squawked Sarabeth.

"Find another word, Pretty Polly," Damian said, his words curt.

"Sorry, sorry," Sarabeth said.

"You're sorry? Faith, 'tis I that am sorry. I'm arguing with a bird." He suddenly leaned over and lowered the glass of brandy. "A drink of forgiveness?"

Sarabeth cocked her head and looked at the glass. Why not? Damian did not believe in love. Now she knew why his face was the dark, weary one that it was. He did not believe in love. Swiftly she nipped her beak into the glass.

"S'death," Damian said, "I really had not expected you to—"

Sarabeth, the brandy a pungent trickle flowing down her throat, gurgled. 'Twas stronger than the aunties' elderberry wine. Her eyes goggled. "Cr-raw!"

"Hmm, yes," Damian said, his eye lighting in amusement.

It was rather tasty. Sarabeth pecked her beak into it once more for a hearty draft.

"Enough," Damian laughed, pulling the glass away. "Far be it from me to put your foot . . . excuse me, talon . . . upon the path of ruination."

"Brr-clk, clk, clk," Sarabeth said. "Br-rease."

Damian glanced at her consideringly. "Just one more beakful, then." He lowered it and Sarabeth quickly took her beakful. She settled back and trilled happily.

Damian shook his head. "A blond parrot with green eyes that likes brandy." He quaffed the rest of the drink. "Bedamn." He promptly leaned over and poured another glass. The decanter was now only half full.

The brandy went to Sarabeth's bird's brain like a straight arrow. She felt dizzy, light as a feather. She spread her wings and flew merrily about the room. Suddenly a chandelier loomed before her eyes. She squawked and dived down, skimming onto a table that held a chessboard, talons spread out for braking. Kings, queens, and pawns flew in the air.

"No, no," laughed Damian. "That's not the way to play chess." He heaved himself up and grabbed the decanter with his free hand. He carried it over, plunking it and his glass down upon the table. "Let me show you." He knelt down and reached for the pieces.

His unattended brandy glass tempted Sarabeth mightily. She dived her beak into it. Damian's head popped up and he cast her a quelling look. "Polly. That is enough."

"Brrr," Sarabeth called dulcetly, and blinked her eyes.

"Don't try to bamboozle me," he said, crawling to sit in his chair. "I saw you." He moved the glass away from Sarabeth. "You'll be a squiffed parrot if you don't watch it." Mechanically he replaced the chess pieces upon the board. He took the glass and drank from it. "Just as I will be a castaway human. But . . ." he said, frowning and aligning the pieces up in form to play. "Drink is a human folly. 'Tis not meant for your bird brain."

"Squawk," Sarabeth said indignantly.

"Oh, sorry," Damian said, his smile lopsided, even as his eyes remained upon the board. "Did not mean to insult you so." Sarabeth crooned her forgiveness. "Now, attend." He moved the pawn into king four position. " 'Tis the opening. Though, and no insult again, I do not expect you to catch on very quickly."

Sarabeth ruffled her feathers in ire. Parrot she may be, but she was no want-wit. She was far too drunk to consider that a parrot should not engage in a game of chess. Sarabeth, her eye upon her choice, scrabbled onto the board.

"Watch it, you are knocking over . . ."

She clamped the pawn in her beak and plopped it onto the king four position as well.

A strangled sound came from Damian "The king's gambit!" He snatched up his glass and drank swiftly Then he gazed at her, his brown eyes blurry. "Very well." His glass plunked to the table. He grabbed up the decanter and splashed his glass full. "But you must stay off the board. Point of order, you know."

"Brrr," Sarabeth said, and walked jerkily from the board.

"And now, dear Polly." Damian grinned rather evilly. "Let's see."

He sat a moment. "Pawn to king bishop four." He shoved his piece over. "Rudimentary, but we'll keep it that way for now."

Sarabeth crawed, flapped her wings, and jerked her head

back and forth, gazing at her own pawn. "Yes, yes," Damian said, and moved her pawn to bishop four. "All right, we know the rudiments."

He gazed at the board in concentration. Deeming he was distracted, Sarabeth hopped over to his brandy and dipped for a sip. She scrabbled fast when Damian's hand went to the glass to lift it and drink of it himself. He moved his piece with decision then. "Your turn, Polly."

Sarabeth chortled her glee and wobbled over to consider her next choice. She squawked and gyrated to designate her final decision. Damian moved it without mistake.

Man and parrot played, both drinking from the same glass. When Damian wasn't noticing, that was. However, Sarabeth's game began to wane, since she was beginning to see four. Damian laughed all the more as her moves became reckless. "I'll have you checked soon, Pretty Polly," he crowed ignobly.

Aggravation shot through every feather tip, and Sarabeth promptly hopped upon the board, spread her wings wide, and swatted the pieces from the board.

"Foul, foul," Damian laughed. He lurched up from the table. "End of game." He stumbled over to the sofa and fell upon it. "I win b-by default." He turned his head. "You knew I had you." Sarabeth squawked her displeasure, feeling embarrassed at her tantrum. Strange, as a human she would never have behaved so badly, squiffed or not. Damian's smile was long and wide. "But no matter, you play well." It widened and he teased, "For a parrot." He raised his hand to his forehead, his tall body ranged in relaxation upon the sofa. "Faith, I am castaway."

Even seeing four of him, Sarabeth thought her tiny heart would burst out of her breast. "Love," she crooned.

"Hmm, yes?" Damian murmured.

Negligent or not, his response shot heat through the already warm Sarabeth. She crowed loudly, and with the ebulation of a drunk, she flapped up her wings and soared. She darted crazily about the chandelier, whizzed low over a wing chair, and pulled up again to circle madly. Damian's loud, deep laughter filled the room. It spurred her on. She all but did tailspins to gain more of his wonderful laughter.

She twirled one too many times, became dizzy, and flapped shakily up to the valance of the curtains. She tipped over, but managed to hang on to the fabric with one talon. It did not matter that she hung upside down, she felt delightful. Suddenly she sang out, " 'Drink to me . . . drink to me . . .' " 'Twas all she could warble out. " 'Drink to me . . .' "

" 'Only with thine eyes,' " Damian continued for her with a deep baritone.

" 'Thine eyes,' " warbled Sarabeth.

Damian swiveled his head to gaze at her. "Thine eyes . . . green eyes . . ." His own closed. A look of pain crossed his features. "Green eyes."

" 'Drink to me . . .' " Sarabeth warbled again. " ' . . . With thine eyes.' "

" 'And I shall pledge with mine,' " Damian murmured softly.

"Love," Sarabeth crooned.

Damian did not answer. He lay quietly, his expression one of sleep, but still with weary pain upon it. Sarabeth cocked her head and gazed at him. Her eyes bleared with tears.

" 'Drink to me . . .' " she squawked, and untangling herself from the curtains, flew from the room. She flapped through the large hall. " 'With thine eyes.' " The new maid was dusting there and the girl dropped her duster with a gasp as Sarabeth whizzed past her. " 'Drink to me . . .' " Sarabeth cried, and flew through the meandering corridors to the back labyrinths of the castle. She winged into the large kitchen and spied an open door. " 'With thine eyes . . .' " She flapped past the cook's face just as the woman leaned over a plucked chicken upon the table. Cook shrieked. " 'Drink to me . . .' " Sarabeth sang, and darted for the doorway. Thomas just then appeared in it and Sarabeth's talons ruffled his hair as she flew over him and into the bright outside. His curses sounded after her.

" 'And I shall pledge with mine!' " She soared up into the clear sky, allowing the wind to whip her tears away.

Five

Bathsheba and Dorinda sat comfortably ensconced in their tiny parlor. A fire crackled cozily. A glass of elderberry wine rested beside each of the aunties. Books lay stacked at the ladies' feet.

"Dorinda," Bathsheba cried. "You really must read this spell. However have we missed it? 'Tis a far simpler one for the healing of gout than the one we use."

Dorinda looked up from the book she perused, her face stern. "Bathsheba, we are not looking for a spell for gout."

Bathsheba blushed. "I am sorry, but it caught my eye."

"Well, let it cease to catch your eye, and focus upon finding a spell to help Sarabeth."

"Yes, sister." Bathsheba sighed heavily. "Poor Sarabeth." Her blue eyes became watery. "And the poor duke. 'Tis all our fault. If only we hadn't brangled with Maudar, she'd never have thought to turn Sarabeth invisible."

"It cannot be helped now," Dorinda said. "What is done is done. All we can do is try to discover a way to bring Sarabeth back."

"Poor Sarabeth," Bathsheba murmured again. "And poor Damian." She shivered. "How terrible it would be if Maudar succeeds, he would have that ninny, Gertrude, for wife, and Maudar for a mother-in-law."

"And he a mortal with no defenses," Dorinda said, clicking her tongue. "He does not even like magic."

Bathsheba frowned. "I do not understand his dislike of it.

Indeed, his mother and father spurned the art, but they were not so—so strong and loud in their dislike as Sarabeth says he is." A sudden clatter interrupted Bathsheba. She jumped slightly. "What was that?"

"I don't know," Dorinda said, frowning. "But 'tis in the house."

" 'Drink to me . . .' " A voice drifted to them. Bathsheba and Dorinda both gasped as a blond missile whizzed into the room. " ' . . . With thine eyes . . .' "

"Sarabeth!" Bathsheba exclaimed as her eyes focused upon the parrot that flapped jauntily in a zigzag about the small parlor.

" 'I will pledge . . .' " Sarabeth sang, " ' . . . With mine.' "

"Heavens," Bathsheba exclaimed as Sarabeth abruptly thudded to the floor between the two women.

"No love," Sarabeth crawed sadly. "No love." She wobbled upon her two thin legs. "No love." She promptly capsized, her two wings spread wide to the side of her, her two talons cocked up, stiff and straight.

Silence fell in the room as the two aunties gaped.

"Sarabeth?" Dorinda said. She crawled from her chair and knelt beside the motionless bird. She poked at a wing.

"Oh, dear," Bathsheba cried, and rose swiftly from her chair to kneel upon the other side. "Sarabeth?" She jabbed a finger at the parrot herself. Her gaze rose, stricken, to look at her sister. "Is she dead?"

"I—I hope not," Dorinda said. She leaned down, placing her ear to Sarabeth's little chest. Her head snapped up and she expelled a breath. "Heavens!"

"She is dead, isn't she?" Bathsheba whimpered.

"Dead drunk," Dorinda said, her eyes narrowing. "She reeks of brandy."

"Brandy?" Bathsheba gasped.

"Brandy," nodded Dorinda.

"Oh, dear," Bathsheba said. "And as a parrot! She shall feel frightful tomorrow morning."

"I have no doubt of that." Dorinda stood swiftly and stalked toward the door.

Bathsheba cast a worried look to the sprawled, still parrot. "Whatever are we to do? And where are you going?"

"I'm going to brew up a potion for a hangover," Dorinda said tartly.

"Oh, yes," Bathsheba cried, springing up. She scurried after her sister. "A fine notion."

The two ladies departed while Sarabeth lay frozen upon the parlor floor. A small snore arose from her.

Damian knocked upon the large oak door before him, a bouquet of flowers in his other hand.

"Are ye sure you wants to do this, Yer Grace?" Thomas asked from behind him. His voice held a nervous quality.

"I am sure," Damian said. He winced. Even the sound of his own voice hurt. It seemed as if large drums were pounding within his skull. " 'Twas unconscionable of me to not check upon Gertrude and see if she returned safely yesterday."

"But . . . but . . . I's don't think you wants to go into—"

The door opened wide. Dame Tureen stood upon the threshold. Her dark eyes flashed in what appeared triumph, but the look disappeared before Damian could be certain. "Why, Your Grace. What a pleasant surprise."

Damian bowed low. He gritted his teeth as he straightened. His head swam alarmingly. "I do hope you do not mean to cast me from your doorstep, madam," he said in what he hoped was a charming voice rather than a pained one. He tried for a broad smile. "Or, worse, slam the door in my face."

Maudar laughed. "And why should I do that, Your Grace?"

He smiled this time in relief. "Perhaps because Gertrude returned here without my escort yesterday."

"Ah, that . . ."

Damian suddenly frowned. "She did return safely, did she not?"

"Yes, she did," Maudar said, smiling. She stepped aside. "Do come in. There is no reason to stand upon the stoop."

"Er, I'll watch the horses," Thomas muttered. His eyes were strangely cast down.

Damian nodded, smiled at Maudar, and entered the hall. He looked about. Dame Tureen's manor was not overly large, but well situated. He noted the decor to be of the finest. "You have a lovely home."

"Thank you," Maudar said, and gracefully turned, her voluptuous figure stately as she led him into the parlor and sat. "Do have a seat. I shall ring for tea."

"Thank you," Damian said, sitting. He looked at the bouquet of flowers forgotten in his hand. "These are for Gertrude." He held them out.

"Why, thank you," Maudar said, and rose to take them. A maid entered at that moment and Maudar said, "Please put these in water and bring us some tea."

Unlike Thomas, the maid said nothing other than "Yes, mum," and left with proper decorum.

"Is Gertrude at home?" Damian asked. "I wish to offer my profoundest apologies."

Maudar shook her head. "I am afraid she is not here. The child is already out and about. She enjoys the mornings."

"So she told me." Damian frowned. "And I profusely apologize that hers was ruined yesterday. Was she terribly upset?"

"No, not at all," Maudar said. She laughed, waving a negligent hand. "I assure you, Gertrude is not such a widgeon as to be cast in the fidgets over something as humorous as what transpired yesterday."

"I assure you, I would have followed her directly, but Thomas's horse bolted and he had injured his leg, so I felt it necessary to take him back to the castle."

"How kind you are," purred Maudar.

"And then I was detained," Damian said, his jaw clenching. "Upon . . . urgent business." He couldn't very well say he became drunk and played chess with a parrot. He clamped the door shut upon the thought. He had been bosky. He clearly had only imagined he had played chess with the bird.

"Was it in regard to the restoration of the west wing?" Maudar asked.

Damian smiled. "The workmen from London should arrive tomorrow to begin its restoration."

Maudar's smile turned sympathetic. "You could not find any local craftsmen?"

Damian laughed. "No, madam, I could not."

She shook her head ruefully. "They are such a superstitious people. Believing in witches and whatnot."

Damian laughed himself. "Even their birds know the name."

"Yes," Maudar said with a slight frown. "Gertrude said the parrot flew at her, crying out 'witch.' "

Damian shrugged. "In Chancellorville 'tis not unreasonable that the bird learned it from his master."

"Strange," Maudar said. "I do not know of anyone who owns a parrot."

"Perhaps it escaped from a traveling troop of players," Damian said, shrugging.

The maid entered, carrying a tea tray. He and Maudar fell silent as the girl set it down upon the table, curtsied, and left.

" 'Twould explain its acrobatic feats," Maudar continued as if there had been no interruption. She reached to pour the tea. "Gertrude was slightly confused," she murmured as she handed Damian his tea, "but she said she thought the parrot was white."

Damian stiffened as he held his cup and saucer. What did it matter what the parrot looked like? He merely wished to forget it. "Yes, so it was, I believe." He smiled. "Like Gertrude, I did not have time to take full notice."

Maudar's gaze narrowed upon him. "You did not perchance see the color of its eyes?"

A vision of green eyes arose before Damian. " 'Drink to me only with thine eyes.' " He glanced at Maudar. She seemed tense of a sudden. An odd feeling overtook Damian. He shook it off and forced a smile. Yet he discovered himself saying, "No, I did not notice. But parrots' eyes are commonly green, so I wouldn't be surprised if that was their color."

"Neither would I," Maudar said lowly. She sipped her tea. "And the cat from the prior night also had green eyes, did it not?"

"Ah, that pesky cat." Damian laughed. The feeling was swelling within him, unsettling, demanding. He used his iron control to quell it. "A stray that had adopted me. An ill-mannered stray, I fear."

"It seems you have been beset by animals."

"I have always attracted them," Damian, said with a laugh.

Maudar's brows rose. "Have you? How interesting."

"Interesting? I would say it is more of a nuisance," Damian said. "My town house in London always has a stray cur or two loitering about it."

"Here in Chancellorville it is believed that 'tis a power if a man can attract animals and control them."

Damian stared levelly at Maudar. "Here in Chancellorville they would." Then he laughed. "And I certainly seem to have very little control over them, or else, I assure you, I would not have permitted Gertrude to suffer such accidents as she has."

"I can believe that," Maudar said. Then she smiled and laughed. "Well, enough talk of such ridiculous superstitions."

"Indeed." Damian nodded gratefully. "Let us rather talk of when I may have the honor of your ladies' company for dinner. A dinner, I promise, which I'll allow no animals to interrupt."

Dame Tureen smiled. "Why, anytime, Your Grace."

"Perhaps two days hence?" Damian asked, setting his tea down untouched. He doubted he would wish to drink anything for the rest of the day. "I fear I must make preparations for tomorrow and set the workmen upon their task, but surely in two days I shall have everything in progress."

"Certainly."

Damian stood. "Then I shall not detain you, but look forward to your company."

"And we yours." Dame Tureen rose and led him out of the parlor and into the hall. "I know Gertrude shall be so disappointed that she missed you." She smiled playfully. "And I shall tell her you promise to control any animals that might be about."

Damian chuckled and bowed. "Madame, I vow I shall show the door to any animal that seeks to put paw or claw within my sphere."

"Die, I shall die," Sarabeth crowed weakly as she rested upon the kitchen table, where Bathsheba and Dorinda had placed her.

"No, you shall not," Dorinda said. "You are merely suffering from a hangover."

"Die," Sarabeth crowed again. 'Twas not only that she felt dreadful, as if every feather upon her body were a pin sticking into her, but she now knew Damian did not believe in love. And he had had so many women! "Die!"

"You'll feel better after drinking this," Bathsheba soothed, and placed a thimble full of liquid before Sarabeth's beak. "Now, take a sip. The potion does not taste bad . . . or so I've heard."

Sarabeth sipped the liquid dutifully, but without interest.

"Sarabeth," Bathsheba said, her voice sounding breathless. Sarabeth lifted hazy eyes to peer at her aunt who stood before her. "Dorinda and I believe we have found the spell."

"Craw," Sarabeth said morosely. At the moment she did not care whether or not she remained a parrot forever. All was hopeless. And her tiny bird brain hurt so very much.

"Yes," Dorinda said from the other side of the table. "We've been studying all night. We have found it at last."

"Craw," Sarabeth said, since Bathsheba looked at her with bright expectation.

"Shall we try it now, dear?" Bathsheba asked.

"Craw."

"Very well," said Dorinda, nodding. "Place your hands upon her, Bathsheba," she instructed, moving to stand close to her sister. Both aunties' hands came to rest upon Sarabeth. She cringed. Could parrots become nauseated like humans did, she wondered desperately.

"Now, you must concentrate, Bathsheba," Dorinda said in a stern tone. " 'Tis of dire importance."

"I know," Bathsheba said rather indignantly. "And you must do so also."

"I will," Dorinda returned. Sarabeth closed her eyes and permitted her aunts to squabble over and above her.

"All right, here we go." Dorinda drew in a deep breath. "Envision Sarabeth in your mind's eye as she has always looked. 'Twas our mistake last time. We ourselves were not focusing upon the image of what she should be."

"I'm focusing," Bathsheba said.

"Silence," Dorinda said. They all remained frozen for a moment. Sarabeth was grateful for the rest. "Oh, spirit of the universe . . ."

"Oh, spirit of the universe . . ."

Her aunts' hands upon her began to grow hot. Sarabeth's eyes snapped open.

"Spirit of souls and bodies . . ."

"Spirit of souls and bodies . . ."

She blinked. Blue-white light shimmered before her and around her. She could not see her aunts, so blinded by the light was she. She could only feel the burning of their hands upon her.

"Return this woman to her true form . . ."

"Return this woman to her true form . . ."

She felt a trembling in her body. Heard a roaring in the kitchen. It was the sound of a great wind rushing and swirling about, but nothing was being overturned by it.

"Living and visible . . ."

"Living and visible . . ."

She felt her body expanding, changing.

"To the image that lives in our mind's eye . . ."

"To the image that lives in our mind's eye . . ."

She was growing. Faith, she was growing!

"Sarabeth, return to us . . ."

"Sarabeth, return to us . . ."

Sarabeth cried out loudly in astonishment. Her aunts' hands fell away from her and both stumbled away, as if drunk or dazed. They dropped into the kitchen chairs.

Silence reigned. Sarabeth slowly lifted her hand to her eyes. It was a human hand with nary a feather or fur upon it! She cautiously looked down. Yes! Yes! She was human, and with the proper number of limbs at that. Thank the good Lord! Suddenly, however, she frowned.

"Bathsheba!" Dorinda's voice shouted. "How could you."

Sarabeth looked up, stunned. Dorinda was staring at her, a look of pure exasperation upon her face.

"I am sorry," Bathsheba said, large tears swelling in her eyes. "You should not have used 'the vision that lives in my mind's eye.' " She broke into sobs. "I always remember Sarabeth as that darling child that came to us at ten."

"Child!" Sarabeth cried. Her voice came out high and young. She nimbly scrambled up and jumped down from the table. She wasn't very tall at all.

"Child," Sarabeth expelled her breath upon a sigh.

"You . . . you were such a beautiful child," Bathsheba wailed.

"And now she looks just like that child," Dorinda said with disdain.

Sarabeth looked to her two aunts. Dorinda's face was angry and exhausted. Bathsheba's streamed tears. "How do you see me?"

"We told you . . ." Dorinda said.

"Just like when you were ten," Bathsheba cried, bursting into fresh tears.

"No," Sarabeth said urgently. It didn't bother her that she was a child. Indeed, she was more at home in her body than she had been for days. "How do you see me? Are you looking at me through witches' eyes?"

"Of course not," Dorinda said, raising her hand wearily to her eyes. "We are drained. I have not an ounce of magic left, I fear."

"Bathsheba, what about you?"

"I have no more magic," sobbed Bathsheba. "I am so sorry."

Sarabeth suddenly gave out a loud whoop and jumped up and down. She felt young and alive . . . and visible. "You've done it, Aunties, you've done it. Child I might be, but I am human and visible!"

Both women stared at her, their eyes dazed. She rushed over and kissed Bathsheba's wet cheek. "You've done it. We'll worry about my age later, but for now I am just so glad to be human and visible that I could expire from the joy of it."

"Oh," sobbed Bathsheba. "My little Sarabeth."

"Little or no," Sarabeth grinned, and chased to smack Dorinda upon the cheek. "I can be seen and can talk to Damian!" She hugged her aunt close. Dorinda was limp. "Now, promise me, you must rest. You've both been overtaxing yourselves."

"Yes, dear," Dorinda sighed, and patted her almost absently. "Now do go outside and play."

Sarabeth laughed merrily. "I intend to, Auntie, I intend to!"

Damian lay supine underneath a tree in the meadow. Dusk was falling and he watched the sun mellow to pink through half-lidded eyes. He closed them for a moment. It did not matter that the air was cold and biting. 'Twas easier to sleep out here. He'd not been able to rest within the Castle Tor. Always the dreams came of the Castle Tor turning to bloodred. It seemed as if the very walls were calling and demanding something from him.

And the vision of the green-eyed woman with blond hair upon the road was always there as well. Calling to him. Demanding something from him. He frowned. Green cat's eyes stared at him from the dark behind his lids. Those eyes meta-morphized into the parrot's. " 'Drink to me only with thine eyes.' "

Suddenly he heard a giggle. Damian opened his eyes and scanned the scenery before him. The grass blew in the cool air. The sun still set. He saw no one. He closed his eyes again.

Then he heard another giggle. He snapped his eyes open. Still he saw nothing. Condemning himself as a fool, Damian closed his eyes. A moment passed and Damian began to drift off

"Hello," a merry voice said.

Damian snapped his eyes open once more. They widened. A little girl sat cross-legged next to him. She wore a woman's wool dress, pinned up and belted. Her hair was of shimmering blond and her eyes were green . . . laughing, impish green. Damian sat up swiftly.

"Were you sleeping?" the child asked solemnly, though her lips twitched.

"Where did you come from?" Damian asked, his eyes nar-rowing.

"Oh, here and about." The child waved her hand in a wide arc.

"I did not hear you come."

She giggled and her fine brows rose. "Did you not?"

He grinned. "Imp. I did. But I did not hear you sit down here."

"You were dozing perhaps." Her eyes twinkled.

"Perhaps."

"I know who you are," she said, and pointed a little finger at him. "You are the duke of the Castle Tor." She frowned. "Must I call you Your Grace?"

"No," Damian laughed.

She grinned. "My Grace?"

He stared at her. "No."

She shook her head. "But I am a child. I cannot call you Damian."

His name upon the child's lips made Damian breathe in sharply. Something inside leapt. He studied the child. The last rays of the sun glinted pink about her, setting her in a soft glow. Her eyes turned a dark, verdant green as she gazed at him. "You may call me Damian."

"Damian," the child said in pleasure. "Damian, Damian, Damian," she caroled as if exploring the name in all its angles. Her joy seemed to fill Damian each time she pronounced his name. "I like it," she giggled. She looked at him and her eyes widened. "You do hear me saying Damian, do you not?"

He laughed. "I hear you saying it. I am not old and deaf."

"No," she said, and she cocked her head to one side. "You are not old . . . Damian."

Once again a frisson ran through Damian. The blond-haired, green-eyed girl reminded him of the woman upon the road. "Who is your mother, child?"

"I do not have a mother," the little girl said, her face turning serious. "Nor a father. I am an orphan."

"I see." He nodded. "I know how it is. I lost my father and mother when I was about your age as well."

"Did you miss them?" Her eyes were intent.

"Yes, I did." Damian thought of his agony as a boy, when the parents he loved had died in a boating accident. Memories crowded into his mind of the cold, lonely times in the boys' school in which his uncle had deposited him, his last instruction being for Damian to "be a man about it." Well, he had become a man about it. He had learned to dismiss the loss of his parents just like he had learned to dismiss the thought of his home.

"Don't," the little girl said quickly.

Damian's gaze snapped to her. "What?"

She reached over and ran a small finger down the bridge of his nose. "You scrunge there."

Her light touch soothed away his frown. He laughed. "I am sorry."

"We shall not talk of our parents," the little girl decreed.

"Very well," he said. "Let us talk of who takes care of you, then."

The little girl sprang up suddenly. "No, we shall not."

"But if you do not tell me," Damian said, "I shall think you have sprung from nowhere. Perhaps you are a fairy or a pixie."

The little girl looked at him and cocked her head. He immediately thought of the blond parrot. "Do you believe in them?"

Damian's smile was erased. "No, I do not."

"You do not believe in magic?"

"No, I do not."

"I think the world without magic would be sad," the girl said. She danced away from him. She turned her back to him and looked out across the meadow. Suddenly she jumped up and down, pointing her finger. "Look!" Damian narrowed his eyes. A man's figure was walking across the meadow in the distance. " 'Tis the hermit Tarrel."

"The hermit?"

"Yes." She turned back to him, nodding her head vigorously. Damian smiled. "I suppose he lives in a cave."

"Yes, he does," she said, her eyes widening. "How did you know?"

"Just a fortunate guess," Damian said. Leave it to Chancellorville to have the prerequisite hermit in a cave. "And does he eat bad little children?"

The child giggled, and skipped back to him. "No, of course not, silly. He is not a troll or giant." She plopped down and sat cross-legged again. "But he hates all humans. Especially women. The people in the village say that when he was born, the moment he was weaned, he crawled away from his own mother and would have naught to do with her."

"At so young of age?" Damian asked, laughing.

"Even then." She frowned. "We are born what we are."

"Yes," Damian said softly.

Her eyes watched him carefully. "We cannot help what we are born as, or not born as."

"Yes." Damian nodded, confused to know what the child was thinking.

Her mouth pursed. "Do you hate women?"

Damian started and then chuckled. "No, I have never been known to eschew women."

"But do you hate them?" she repeated, her gaze solemn.

"No," Damian said. "In fact, I seem to be overly attracted to them." He smiled. "The world without women would be sad."

"Like magic," the girl said. "And love."

"I do not believe in love."

"Love is magic," she said simply.

"No wonder I do not believe in it."

"You do not love anyone . . . a woman right now?"

The haunting image of the woman upon the road crossed through Damian's mind. He pushed it away and said, "No, I do not."

The child grinned impishly and her green eyes grew mischievous. "Would you marry me, then . . . when I grow up?"

Damian looked at the beautiful fairy child and smiled. "Ah, a proposal. I accept, Madame, that is, if you still want me after you have grown up."

The girl giggled and sprang to her legs. "I will." She reached over and her finger just tipped the corner of his smile. "You promise me you will wait until I grow up?"

It was an odd gesture from a child, but Damian nodded. "Certainly."

"I warn you, I shall grow up very fast," she said with a twinkle. "I must be going now. Good-bye." She turned and dashed away.

"But . . ." Damian called. He saw only the gleam of her hair as the child disappeared into the gloaming dusk. He laughed. "Proposed to, and I don't even know her name." He stood swiftly. He would return to the Castle Tor. He had not slept, but he felt rested, amazingly so.

Six

Damian frowned, watching the men at work. They seemed a good crew. They should be, since they were from London and being highly paid, even for London standards. They moved proficiently, but still they did not move fast enough. The Castle Tor must be repaired. He once again saw the vision in his dream, the red glow starting within the fire-ravaged wing and slowly suffusing the castle.

"Superstitious fool," Damian muttered under his breath. 'Twas but a dream. It made no sense. Yet still, there was an overwhelming desire within him to repair the wing, to erase all the signs of damage and the foul scent of fire.

"Look lively there, Fulsham," he called to the foreman who was just then ripping down a burned frame.

"Yes, Yer Grace," Fulsham said. Damian heard him mumble something under his breath.

"Hello," a young voice said from behind.

Damian turned. It was the little girl from the night before, grinning up at him. She carried a huge basket in front of her. It was well nigh as large as she.

"Well, hello," Damian said, slightly surprised. "I did not think to see you here."

The child grinned. "Why not?"

Damian smiled. "I thought you just a little sprite from the meadows."

"No," the girl laughed. She rattled her basket. "I've brought a picnic lunch."

Damian stared. "Have you?"

"Yes." The child nodded with solemn eyes. "I thought we could eat it."

"I fear I have much work to do here," Damian said in a gentle voice.

She cocked her head. "How long have you been working?"

"Since dawn."

"Then it is time to eat," the child said with a stern, definitive voice. A laugh escaped Damian, so very grown-up and serious did the child appear. Her bright green gaze roved over the various men at work. "Which is the foreman?"

"Mr. Fulsham over there," Damian said, pointing a finger.

"Mr. Fulsham," the little girl said, walking directly up to that burly man. "Could not you spare Damian, I mean the duke, for a short while?"

"Could I!" Mr. Fulsham said, mopping his brow. His features reddened. "I mean, er, certainly, lass."

The child leaned over to the large man and whispered, "Getting in the way, isn't he?"

The large man stared down at the child and suddenly grinned. The other crew members had paused to listen, and a ripple of covert laughter went up among them.

Damian frowned. "That's enough, young lady."

The child swung around and smiled innocently. "Mr. Fulsham says he can live without you for a while. And I do have a very g-g-good luncheon. There's tarts, and cakes, very good cakes!"

Damian's stomach growled. Nevertheless, he frowned. "Perhaps after a while."

The little girl set her basket down and stomped up to him. She put her hands upon her hips and glared up at him with sparking eyes. "Is this how it is going to be when we are married, Your Grace? Shall you ignore a luncheon I pack?"

"Married?" Mr. Fulsham asked loudly. He flushed then, looking swiftly away from the two. His men were not as polite; they gaped in open consternation.

"We are not getting married, young lady," Damian said. He felt a ridiculous flush rising to his face. What a confounded situation to be in. It was clear every man in the room thought him a bluebeard or worse.

"But you promised," the little girl said. "Yesterday."

"I said when you grew up," Damian gritted. He cast her a quelling frown. "And you are not grown-up. You are still at the age when young ladies are spanked for impertinence."

"Ye can't spank the child," Mr. Fulsham said. "Not if ye proposed to her."

Damian stared at the man. His face was quite serious. Was the world gone mad? "I did not propose to her."

"But you accepted," the child said in reasonable tones. "I asked and you said you would."

"He accepted," one of the men murmured. All of them shook their heads at Damian with expressions of severe disapproval.

"Ye shouldn'a be toying with the child's heart, Yer Grace," Mr. Fulsham said. The atmosphere in the room was turning cold and ugly. Faith, Damian thought. He'd probably be the only duke lynched by his workers for not conceding to a ten-year-old who claimed to be his fiancée.

The child grinned up at him. "Lunch?"

"Lunch," Damian said curtly.

"Good!" The little girl dashed over and grabbed up the basket. She looked up to the burly Mr. Fulsham. "Thank you."

"That's a good lass," Mr. Fulsham said, and then grinned. " 'Tis a pity I'm married already." She giggled. He lowered his voice. "But ye best think about this here marriage of yours. Looks like yer gent wishes to play fast and loose with ye."

"I'll think about it," the little girl whispered back. "If he keeps this up, I'll change my mind. A lady always can change her mind, can she not?"

Mr. Fulsham nodded his head, his eyes suddenly twinkling. "That she can."

"Lady?" Damian muttered. "Imp, rather." He straightened.

"Very well, I am going for a picnic, Mr. Fulsham. I believe you will be capable in my absence."

The men laughed and one even forgot himself so far as to applaud.

" 'Tis a beautiful place," Damian said, gazing about to the cove of trees surrounding them. "I did not even know this was part of the castle's land."

"I love it here," Sarabeth said, gazing about. "I always come here to think—" She stopped. She always came here to think about Damian, to dream about the lord of the castle.

"To think about what?"

"Oh, everything," Sarabeth said quickly. "Tell me more about France!"

"Enough," Damian laughed. "You have asked me everything I've ever known, Elizabeth."

It was the name Sarabeth had finally given to Damian. She would have liked to use Sara or Beth, but feared it was too close to her own. She gazed at the lounging man upon the quilt who was just finishing off another of Bathsheba's strawberry tarts. She loved the way his eyes were alight with pleasure. And she hated the way he called her by a name not her own.

"I am sorry," she said, flushing. Indeed, she had plied Damian with food and a barrage of questions, entertained and intrigued by his stories, enthralled by the very timbre of his voice.

His face gentled. "Don't be. It shows you have an inquiring mind."

"Then I have not . . . bored you?"

Damian shook his head, his eyes turning suddenly surprised. "No, indeed. You carry on conversation far better than most London debutantes. If I have to hear one more, 'Yes, Your Grace,' or 'Fie, Your Grace,' I am sure I'll commit justifiable murder."

"Yes, Your Grace," Sarabeth said, her lips twitching. Damian cast her a suspicious look. Sarabeth looked down quickly and traced the design upon the quilt with her finger. "And is Gertrude Tureen's conversation . . . interesting?"

"Gertrude? Her conversation is—" Damian halted. He laughed and said, "A gentleman does not speak of one lady to another. I assure you, 'tis the quickest path to an early grave." He frowned. "And just how do you know about Gertrude Tureen anyway, young lady?"

Sarabeth looked at him and grinned. "There is not much in Chancellorville I do not know."

"Faith, I hope that is not so," Damian said. He shook his head. " 'Tis no healthy atmosphere for a child, with all its belief in superstitions."

"Not everything is superstition," Sarabeth said softly.

Damian's eyes grew dark. "Who has the care of you, child?"

Sarabeth breathed in deeply. "Ah . . . my—my uncle." Surely that would be safe enough.

"Does he believe in all this magic and whatnot?"

"Perhaps," Sarabeth said. She schooled her expression. "But he changes his opinions very often. Some days he says he's a man of reason and will have none if it. Then some days he looks for every spell and sign of magic he can find. And some days he believes in good, and other days he believes in bad. But aren't all adults that way?"

"Good Lord!"

"Do you believe in bad?"

Damian paused a moment. "There are certainly bad things in this world. And people do bad things."

"No," Sarabeth shook her head. "I mean evil. Dark magic."

"Evil?" Damian's eyes narrowed. "Does your uncle talk of such rot?"

Sarabeth stood up quickly. She could not meet his eyes. She had thought it was heaven simply to be able to be seen and talk to Damian, but it was becoming more like hell. She feared for him. The need to tell him the truth overwhelmed her. Yet he did not believe in magic and she appeared but a child to him. He would never believe her if she told him Dame Tureen was a black witch and wished to not only make him marry Gertrude, but also intended to turn him to the dark powers.

It seemed the sky suddenly grew darker, the air colder. Sarabeth shivered. She turned and said, "You think my world strange, but the stories you tell me of all these other places, they seem strange to me."

Damian frowned. "What do you mean, Elizabeth?"

"What you tell me you know to be real. Then why cannot the things I tell you, no matter how strange, be real as well?" Damian stared at her. It seemed as if he could see into her very depths. Yet, she had too much to hide. Sarabeth forced a smile and a childish laugh. "Let's go play hide-and-seek. You're it." She tore off without waiting for an answer, running into the woods.

"Elizabeth!" Damian said, standing quickly. The child was gone before he could stop her. He saw her disappearing into the woods. He looked up to the sky. It was darkening, and the suddenly chilling air promised rain. Faith, it was much later than he had noticed. He had sat spinning tales of his journeys to the child, her eager questions making him see all his travels in a different light, a clearer, more innocent one. It must be because he had seen it through a child's eyes. "Elizabeth!"

He took off at a lope into the woods. In the middle of the foliage he stopped, glancing about. Suddenly he heard a giggle. He saw the flash of a pink dress and a blond girl dashing from one tree to another. Even in the darkening woods the child's hair was shining like a golden halo. His lips curved into a smile. "I'm going to find you!"

He saw the figure dash to another tree, an elusive sprite. Suddenly Damian halted. He felt strangely disoriented. It was as if the little girl flitting through the trees were his own. He felt oddly out of place and time. It did not feel as if he were in the present, or even the past. All he knew was that the blond-haired girl who slipped behind the tree made him think of a child who might be his someday. He saw it clearly and distinctly, as if he stood in the future and the blond child he played hide-and-seek with were his in that future.

Damian shook his head to clear it. Never had he considered having children. Never did he want them. He didn't even want a wife, let alone a child. Yet this Elizabeth caused something to stir within him. Time, reality, and his heart all blended and changed when she was about, as if in a prism refracting unknown pictures from different angles and lights.

"You'll never find me," her merry voice called out.

"Yes, I will," Damian called. He ran forward and spun around a tree. He stopped quickly.

Elizabeth stood frozen, her eyes staring at the ground. He noticed a circle upon it, drawn in sticks and stones, or what he thought were sticks. He did not care. The stiff, still child before him mattered more.

She lifted huge green eyes to him. The fright in them made it seem as if she were not a child. " 'Tis black witchery. Never before has it been in this forest. Never . . . never this close to the castle."

Damian knelt. He wanted to reach out to her, but it seemed as if he dared not. "There is no such thing as witchery, black or otherwise."

"She is strong . . . she is stronger than I imagined."

"Who is strong?"

Damian saw a shiver rack the child. She looked at him then, eyes so very dark. "Damian, I am afraid."

"Don't be," he said softly, forcefully. "You are believing in myths and fantasies. 'Tis not real."

" 'Tis all too real. 'Tis evil."

"Then I will protect you," Damian said. "I'll not let it harm you."

She shook her head. "You cannot. And we . . . I cannot protect you, but I will try."

Large, frigid drops of rain began to fall upon them. It infiltrated through the cover of the trees and branches, coming down stronger and heavier, staining them both. It matted the shimmer of Elizabeth's hair.

Damian stood. He reached out his hand. "Come, Elizabeth, we must find shelter. Let us return to the castle."

"Yes." She nodded, her words but a whisper. "Let us find shelter."

Sarabeth watched covertly as Damian talked to Mr. Fulsham the next day. She hugged her knees to her as she sat upon a small stool Damian had found for her. It was as if she lived in both a dream and a nightmare. The dream was every time she was with Damian. The nightmare came when she was away from him and knew she could not break Maudar's spell or go to Damian as her real self.

Even when they had returned to the Castle Tor the night before, and she had stayed until the storm cleared, she had not found the words to tell him who she really was. He had been oddly gentle, going out of his way to entertain her over an early dinner. He had even offered to read her fairy tales and stories. His eyes, though, had shown a deep contemplation when he gazed at her. It was as if he were waiting for her to speak to him of the truth she hid. She found she could not, so she had acted the carefree child and drawn every moment's pleasure she could from being with him.

It was already late afternoon the next day, and still she watched Damian in silence. She could see his workmen had been taxed to their last degree. Even in the coolness of the room Damian's shirt was wet and plastered to his large body. The men's were no better.

Sarabeth pursed her lips. It was past time for Damian to rest. His face was weary, the lines about his eyes pronounced. She uncurled herself and stood. She remembered to skip over to Damian.

"Damian," she said, grabbing up his hand and interrupting

him as he spoke to Mr. Fulsham. Being a child had its advantages. "Let's go play."

Damian frowned down at her. "Not now, Elizabeth."

Sarabeth swung his hand and pulled a child's pout. "But it is late. 'Tis close to five."

"Five!" he exclaimed. "Faith, I did not realize."

Sarabeth grinned. "I know."

He turned to the foreman. "I am sorry, Fulsham, have the men quit."

Fulsham smiled. "Yes, Yer Grace." He cast a sparkling glance to Sarabeth. "Ye shouldn't have kept yer fiancée waiting so long. Though she was a good child today."

Sarabeth smiled back at him and giggled. "I'm still making up my mind about him, Mr. Fulsham. But you are married and he is not." She tugged at Damian's hand. "Let's go play."

Damian laughed. "Very well, imp."

She pulled him from the room. "What do you want to play?"

"I do not know," Damian said. He frowned. "It *is* late. Won't it be time for dinner at your home?"

Sarabeth shook her head. "No, not yet."

He slowed, forcing her to stop. "Does not your uncle worry?"

"No," Sarabeth said quickly. "No, he doesn't."

"But you were here all yesterday, and here again today."

Sarabeth nodded. "I like being here."

"But surely your uncle—"

"He doesn't care," Sarabeth said. "Honest."

Damian's eyes darkened. "I would care."

"Would you?" Sarabeth's heart raced. How deeply she wished it were true. She forced a giggle. "Would you be a stern old meanie, telling me when I'd have to be home for dinner, and when I'd have to go to bed?"

"Yes, I would," Damian said. He smiled. "I'd be the sternest old meanie around. You'd not be staying up so late like last evening. I'd have you in bed at an early hour, I assure you."

Sarabeth wheezed slightly and a flush rose to her cheeks.

His words were innocent to him, but not to her. The thought of him "having her in bed" at any time did strange things to her. "Then I'm glad you are not my uncle," Sarabeth said, looking down and hiding her eyes. "For he does not care at all."

"He should," Damian said softly. "He should."

Sarabeth's breath caught as she glanced up, for Damian gazed at her intently. "You hide," she said swiftly. "You hide and I'll find you."

Damian laughed. "We played that yesterday."

"I know," Sarabeth said. "But I like the game."

"Very well." Damian cast her a stern look. "But you must count to twenty, and no peeking."

Sarabeth slapped both hands over her eyes. "I won't," she said, and promptly peeked through the cracks of her hands to watch Damian's lithe body stride down the hall. "One, two, three . . ." she said slowly. "Six, nine, thirteen, fifteen, eighteen . . . twenty." She'd been seeking Damian all her life and didn't plan to stick to the count at that moment. She skipped down the hall. "I'm coming to find you!"

Sarabeth entered the main portion of the house and peered into each room, determining more by the feel of the room if Damian was present or not. A witch she wasn't, and never could be, but she had discovered she was finely attuned to Damian. Strange, it was a child's game they played, but it was fun nevertheless. What a shame such simple pleasures were forgotten.

She tiptoed into a large, vacant bedroom and halted. She paused a moment. Damian was in the room. She could feel it. She thought she heard the slightest of swishing sounds, but she could not decide from whence they came. Out of the corner of her eye she glimpsed a large armoire against the wall, sitting upon dragon-clawed feet, an expensive beveled glass upon it. Its door stood slightly ajar.

"Damian?" Sarabeth called softly. "Oh, Damian? Where are you?"

She giggled like the child she appeared and tread stealthily over to the armoire. Her fingertips lightly grasped the door and with a triumphant cry she pulled it open. Old clothes hung within it, nothing else.

"Boo!" a voice boomed from behind. Sarabeth squealed and jumped into the air. She spun, her heart racing. A dark-caped figure loomed over her.

"Ahh!" it cried, and lifted its cape up in a swirl.

Sarabeth scuttled instinctively from the overpowering dark shape and dashed away. The room's bed lay within her path, and she jumped upon it in her escape from the caped figure.

"Elizabeth, 'tis I, Damian!" the voice shouted.

Sarabeth halted and turned, a little wobbly since her feet sank into the plushness of the feathertick. Her eyes widened. It was indeed Damian, dressed in a large black cape. "Damian?" Her eyes widened. " 'Tis you?" He was magnificent, his tall body cloaked in the dark silk.

"Yes," he laughed, and spread his arms out impressively. "You, child, did not count to twenty, did you?"

Sarabeth stood, her mouth agape. "N-no . . ." He appeared a different man.

"Let that be a lesson," Damian laughed. "Even in a game, Elizabeth, one must have honor. One should not cheat."

"You—you look like a wizard," Sarabeth stammered.

Damian eyes darkened. "I am no wizard." His hand reached for the cape. "I do not believe in such."

"No." Sarabeth bounced upon the bed. "Do leave it on. You look . . . mysterious."

"Not like a wizard?"

"No," Sarabeth lied even while her heart soared. Damian, dressed as such, was a man to bring home to meet one's mother or aunts . . . if they were witches. "No, no!" She sprang on the bed, bouncing up and down. "Whee, this is fun."

"Yes," Damian said. "But do get down. Young ladies should not bounce upon beds."

Sarabeth soared high. "And do grown ladies?"

"Not in that particular manner," Damian said, his eyes secretly laughing.

At least he thought it was secret. Sarabeth's breath caught. "But then, in what manner do they . . . bounce?"

Damian started. He frowned sternly. " 'Tis not something I intend to tell you, imp, so forget it."

Sarabeth grinned and flapped her hands for extra leverage. "But you will tell me when we are married? And show me?"

Damian laughed. "I told you, you'll not want me when you've grown up."

"Perhaps," Sarabeth gurgled. "Not if you're going to be an old meanie about everything. Telling me I have to stay off the beds . . ." She boinged. "When I have to behave . . ." She bounced.

"Do get down," Damian laughed, and reached out a hand. "You are making me dizzy just watching."

Sarabeth grinned wickedly. "Catch me!"

She leapt at him.

"Elizabeth!" Damian cried, but catch her he did. His arms went swiftly about her and he cradled her diminutive body to him. "You are a naughty child!"

Sarabeth gazed raptly into Damian's eyes. No, she was an unwise woman. His arms about her set her to trembling. The air about them crackled with a full-grown passion. Damian's eyes darkened, turning confused and questioning. Sarabeth tore her gaze from his, lest he see the woman within her. "Let me down. It is your turn to find me!"

"Find you?" Damian's voice was stunned. He slowly let her down. "Find you?"

Sarabeth stepped back. She ached at leaving his arms. "Yes." She nodded. "Hide-and-seek, remember?"

Damian's hand clasped her chin and he lifted it, forcing her to gaze at him. His eyes were searching. "Yes," he said softly. "I remember. You like the game well, do you not?"

Sarabeth pulled back quickly. She dashed to the door. "It's your turn to find me!"

"Hasn't it always been my turn?" he called out sharply.

"Remember, count to twenty . . ." Sarabeth called, never stopping. She dared not. Damian's last words were too dangerous. She chased down the hall and took the old winding stairs two at a time. She reached the first floor. "Fifteen, sixteen . . ." She reached the main hall. "Seventeen . . . uh-oh." She skidded to a halt. "Drat." She ducked low, taking prompt refuge behind a large side table.

Dame Tureen and Gertrude stood within the entrance, the new maid Tilly dipping and curtsying before them.

"His Grace is expecting us," Maudar was saying in a haughty tone.

Gertrude was resplendent in a feminine dress of teal and cream. "Yes, he is."

Sarabeth darted for the cubbyhole beneath the table.

Maudar suddenly stiffened. Her dark gaze narrowed and roamed about the large entrance hall. Sarabeth held her breath. Finally Maudar's gaze returned to the maid. "He is expecting us. I am Dame Tureen and this is my daughter, Gertrude. We are to dine with the duke."

"Elizabeth," Damian called as he loped down the hall, a frown upon his face. Something had happened in that bedroom. He had to find the child, to look into her eyes and prove he had been insane, that she was but a child and his strange thoughts mere imagination. He entered the main hall, his senses telling him he was about to achieve success. Elizabeth was there.

He skidded to a halt. "Oh, my God."

Dame Tureen and Gertrude stood before him. Gertrude gazed at him with mouth agape. Dame Tureen, however, turned to him, and when her gaze fell upon him, it flared. "Your Grace!"

Damian choked slightly, and he flushed. "Er, I am sorry." His hand flew to the ties of the silk cape he wore, which clearly was the focus of the women's attention. He felt ultimately foolish. Between working with the men, and then Elizabeth distracting him, he had completely forgotten that he would be host to Dame Tureen and Gertrude.

Dame Tureen's eyes glowed. "You . . . look as you should."

Damian laughed as he ripped the cape from him. "And how is that? I hope it is not as a wizard."

The glow in Dame Tureen's eyes became banked fires. She laughed lightly. "A wizard? Of course not, neither you nor I believe in them."

Damian bowed deeply, the cape now safely upon his arm. "I thank you, Madame. Elizabeth saw me in the cape and said I looked like a wizard."

"Who is Elizabeth?" Dame Tureen asked, her eyes narrowing.

Damian forced a smile. "No one but a neighbor's child."

"A child?" Dame Tureen laughed, her face clearing. "Is that all? Children do have such fantasies."

Damian grinned. "Especially those reared in Chancellorville."

"True." Dame Tureen's eyes glinted. "But no, I did not think you a wizard yet, 'tis only you look so dashing," Her brow arched. "And rakish."

Damian laughed. "Thank you, Madame." He lifted a quizzing brow to Gertrude, who still stared. "And what do you think, Gertrude?"

"You look like—" Gertrude halted abruptly, for Dame Tureen, taking off her own cloak, knocked into her. "You look nice, Your Grace."

"Thank you," Damian said. He glanced quickly about the hall. Where was Elizabeth? Instinct told him the child was near. "I—" He clamped his mouth shut. He certainly was not about to say he had been interrupted playing hide-and-seek with a neighboring child, and worse that he had harbored strange, unfounded notions about that child. "Let us go into the parlor," he said. He cast another covert look about the great hall. Where was Elizabeth? He forced a smile. Bowing, he led them into the parlor.

As the two women sat, Damian excused himself. "Permit me to check upon Cook." He smiled wryly. "I wish to ascertain she is preparing what I hope to be an adequate meal." Dame Tureen laughed and Gertrude smiled.

As he made his way to the kitchens, Damian peeked into corners, bending to look under each chair and peer into every crevice. "Elizabeth?" he whispered. No little girl.

He entered the kitchen to discover Millicent, a stern, frowning woman, bustling about. Thomas sat, sprawled on a rickety bench, supervising her movements, a bottle lovingly clutched to his chest.

"Did you remember we have guests?" Damian asked without preamble.

Millicent stopped. "Of course, Your Grace." Her eyes fell. "D-Dame Tureen and her daughter dine with us tonight."

"Thank heaven," Damian said. Millicent remembered he had said they would have guests, even though he had not. "We shall dine within an hour?"

"But of course," Millicent said quickly.

"Knows better than to fail with Dame T-Tureen," Thomas said from his corner. He hiccuped and said, "Y-you enter-taining in them clothes?"

Damian started. He looked down. "Good Lord!" He just realized then that he was in his work clothes. "Blast it, I have no time to change and they've already seen me this way." He cast a quick glance about the kitchen. "Did you see Elizabeth come through here?"

"No, Your Grace," Millicent said, wide-eyed.

"Elizabeth?" Thomas asked, frowning with drunk confusion.

"The little girl," Damian said curtly, his eyes still seeking out the kitchen's recesses.

"No, Your Grace," Millicent answered.

"The one with the green eyes?" Thomas crossed himself with a wavering hand. "No, Yer Grace. Haven't seen her."

* * *

"Millicent outdid herself, it seems," Dame Tureen said, setting her fork and knife down.

"Yes, Your Grace," Gertrude said, nodding and following suit.

"Indeed," Damian murmured. His gaze, despite his best efforts, flickered to the door. Twice during the meal he had heard a giggle and saw a flash of a blond child traipsing across the dining room's portal. "If you will excuse me." He smiled perfunctorily and stood. He heeded not the looks upon his guests' faces, but strode to the door and out it.

"Elizabeth?" he hissed. His mind was relieved, however. She was clearly only a child. An imp of a child who was still determined to play hide-and-seek, no matter the hour. Surely she should be at home and asleep at this time. No matter if her uncle was lax and uncaring, the child should not be here. "Elizabeth, show yourself!"

He narrowed his eyes to see into the hall's shadows, lit by torches in the sconces. There was no answer. "Damn!" He had no time to look for her, but when he did find her he'd ring a peal over the child's head. Damian spun on his heel, purpose set, and strode back into the dining room. His two guests looked up at him with strong curiosity upon their faces. He fabricated a smile. "Are you finished with your dessert?"

"Y-Your G-Grace?" Gertrude stammered.

"Excellent." Damian nodded. Where was the little minx?

"But we did not have the—" Dame Tureen began.

"Let us adjourn to the parlor for after-dinner drinks, then," Damian said.

"Yes, Your Grace." Gertrude obediently stood.

"But we have not . . . oh, very well," Dame Tureen said, throwing up her hands.

"This way." Damian bowed and turned without waiting for his guests. He needed to find Elizabeth and send her home.

His guests followed him and Damian hid his frown of aggravation. As they sat, the women upon the settee closest to the fire and he in a wing chair across from them, he donned a polite smile. "Yes, Millicent outdid herself," he said, remembering the thread of conversation from before, though he did not remember the taste of the food. "Did she not?"

Gertrude frowned. "Yes, my lord."

"As I said," Maudar spoke, her eyes wary and narrowed. "She seems to have—"

A flash of white appeared at the darkened window behind the ladies. "Blast!" Damian sprung up. A child's pale face pressed against the window's pane and he distinctly saw a small white hand wave. She was outside now! It was far too cold out there tonight.

"My lord?" Maudar's face was indignant.

"Er, a thousand apologies," Damian said, flushing. "Please excuse me a moment . . . I—I wish to see what is keeping Thomas with the after-dinner drinks."

Damian beat a hasty retreat and all but knocked Thomas over as he pelted out the door. Thomas stumbled back, none too steady at any time. "Me lord!"

"Thomas, where are the after-dinner drinks?" Damian said loudly to prove his excuse to the woman in the room behind him.

Thomas's eyes widened. He shook his head in honest befuddlement. "Ye wants after-dinner drinks now? But you ain't had dessert yet. And this times I think old Millicent did it up right proper."

Damian halted, stunned. He frowned and lowered his voice. "What do you mean we did not have dessert? Surely we did?"

"No, Yer Grace." Thomas shook his head vehemently. "I swears it."

"Thomas," Damian growled. "You are bosky, we had dessert."

"No, Your Grace." Thomas said, frowning in confusion.

"Damn," Damian said, attempting to think back. He shook his head. He couldn't remember, so worried was he over Elizabeth and her games. " 'Tis of no significance," he said curtly. He had to find the child. He took one more moment to say, "Serve the after-dinner drinks to the ladies. I shall be there in a moment."

He whisked past Thomas, who gurgled in an odd way, and strode out of the large castle doors. "Elizabeth?" he called, and tramped into the darkness. He waded through the prickly bushes that masked the window to the parlor. She was not there. "Fiend, seize it!" He peered into the lighted window from the cold dark. "Blast and damn!" He could see Dame Tureen's and Gertrude's backs as they sat in the cozy scene. "This is asinine, I'll kill her," he muttered, and disentangled himself from the bushes, scratching his hand and snagging his clothes as he went.

Chasing back, he let himself into the castle, all the while looking about for a blond-haired green-eyed child. Seeing and hearing nothing, he strode back into the parlor.

He noticed he must have been absent a goodly amount of minutes, for a tray with sherry was set before the ladies as he entered. Thomas must have put it there while he was tramping back. Both ladies looked up, odd expressions upon their faces.

"Well," Damian said jovially as he strolled over with as much aplomb as he could. He quickly picked a pernicious twig from his sleeve as he sat down. "Our after-dinner drinks, how nice."

"Neighboring child," seethed Dame Tureen as they climbed into the ancient coach and she rapped sharply upon the roof for it to start. "I swear the child was Sarabeth Goodfellow."

Gertrude frowned in the darkness. "But he said her name was Elizabeth."

"It does not matter," snapped Maudar, staring off into the darkness. "It must be Sarabeth. I knew she was there the moment I entered the house."

"But—"

"Be still," Dame Tureen cried. Gertrude fell silent, for even in the dim, moonlit carriage, she could see a darker smoke rising from her mother. " 'Tis no coincidence the cat and parrot both had green eyes. The eyes will always tell." Her own narrowed into slits. "It is Sarabeth, and she has ruined all our plans. The duke did not even notice us, so damned intrigued was he in finding *the child*." Her voice dripped acid. "How dare he! He does not know with whom he plays!"

"But, Mama, how can you be sure? Perhaps it was just a child—"

"Be still," Maudar screeched, puffs of smoke now billowing from her and filling the confines of the carriage.

Gertrude coughed and waved a hand. Her brow lowered. "But if it is Sarabeth, why do you not kill her, or turn her into—"

Gertrude was slapped so sharply across her face, she reeled.

"I did what I could." Maudar's voice came out in a steaming slither. "She has a warding about her."

'Wh-what?" Gertrude asked, never bright, and only all too human.

"They all do," Maudar said lowly. "No matter how incompetent the Goodfellow sisters are, they have a warding about them."

" 'But—"

"It is not of their making," seethed Maudar. "Never could their powers be that great. Never. But there is a warding about them. My spells I can cast, but to destroy them . . . this I cannot. There is a power . . . a power I dare not touch." She fell silent. Gertrude prudently did so as well. Then Maudar crooned, "They have the warding as white witches, but the duke does not. He was meant for the dark powers. He shall be great, and you—you shall be his mate."

Sarabeth stood silently, her eyes wide as she lifted the candle she had stolen from the great hall. It was just a library. The

room no one in the Castle Tor was permitted to enter was nothing more than a library. A huge one, granted, with long walls
filled with books, but that was it. Moonlight glowed in from
tall mullioned windows at the far end of the room, casting a
peaceful, quiet atmosphere about it. Large, deep wing chairs
cluttered the otherwise clear room. One, large oblong table
rested in the center.

"Only a library," Sarabeth murmured in confusion. Deciding
she had irritated Damian enough, she had thought only to hide
safely for a while. Then her curiosity had gotten the better of
her and she had slipped through the door which Damian had
declared none must enter.

She treaded softly over to the book-lined wall, her candle
lifted high. She peered at a title upon the shelf. *A Book of the
Ancient,* she read. Her eyes quickly flashed to the one beside
it. She gasped. Heart pounding, Sarabeth dashed down the
length of the wall, scanning each title.

She spun and raced across to the other side of the room.
Speeding down the length of that book-lined wall, her breath
came in short gulps. Phookas, co-walkers, demon binding,
druidic lore, necromancy, wardings, wizardry, and witchcraft—
all of it was there. Sarabeth halted and she gazed about the
room in sudden awe. There must be a thousand books, all of
them about magic.

Oddly, her heart silenced to a calm. She turned again to the
shelves. She walked more slowly, reading the titles once more.
She stopped and pulled out one of the smaller books. Hope
flared within her as her fingers clasped the thin volume.

"What are you doing in here?" a voice cracked. Sarabeth
gasped and spun. A dark, looming figure fell upon her. It was
Damian, his eyes blackened to midnight. He grabbed her shoulders. "I've been looking everywhere for you." He shook her,
the anger in his touch searing into her skin. "You should not
be here!"

The book Sarabeth held fell from her nerveless fingers. She
clutched the candle lest she drop it also. Hot wax splattered

upon her hand, a stinging pain. Yet it was the only light she had against the dark, swirling rage of Damian. "I—I . . ." She could not speak. "I—I . . ."

"God!" Suddenly Damian's hands released her, shooting to his sides, fists clenched. Reason seemed to return to his face. "Did I hurt you?" The candle shook violently in Sarabeth's hand. He reached swiftly for it and she relinquished it from her trembling fingers. "Did I hurt you, Elizabeth?"

"N-no," Sarabeth breathed, her eyes wide upon him. "I am sorry. I came here to hide and—"

She saw Damian breathe in deeply. "This room is forbidden."

"It's only a library," Sarabeth said.

"Is it?" He looked quietly about the room. His eyes became distant. She had lost him to another place. "I have not been here since I was a child." Like a sleepwalker, Damian moved slowly about the room.

Sarabeth watched him. "Wh-what happened here?"

" 'Tis not as strong," Damian said softly, and set the candle down upon the large oak table. His hand reached to smooth its surface, almost as if he were just discovering it. " 'Tis not like when . . ." His voice faded away.

"What happened here, Damian?" Sarabeth whispered. He was a man of moonglow and flickering candlelight.

Damian turned to her, his eyes dark shadows. "Cannot you feel it?"

"N-no," Sarabeth said. Damian's head was cocked to one side, as if listening for something. "N-no, I cannot."

"I came here as a child," he said, and tread softly toward her. "I entered when Mother and Father had forbade me. And I saw, I heard—"

"What?" He was silent. "What did you see? What did you hear?"

"Figures, creatures, voices, chants in many languages. It was as if the whole room cried out to me." Damian halted and gazed solemnly about. "I wanted to open every book and read them . . . and I could not read." He came and knelt down before Sarabeth. "Mother found me here, frozen, unable to move or leave. She carried me from the room." The slightest ghost of a smile touched his lips. "She never had to fear I would enter again, never had to lock this door."

"Magic," Sarabeth said softly.

"Magic," Damian said, his eyes deadening.

"Why didn't you . . . didn't you . . . ?"

"Burn the books?" Damian asked as if reading her mind. " 'Twas in all our thoughts. Yet it is our heritage, Elizabeth. I might as well burn the Castle Tor down as burn these books . . . if one could."

"Magic is from all the universe," Sarabeth said quietly. "It breathes in the life of every plant, every animal, all the creatures of the earth. It is our choice to draw from the spirit of good, or from evil. But the choice must always be made."

"I'll have none of it," Damian said in a rasping voice. His eyes glittered. His face sculpted into rigid lines. "I'll have none if it, do you hear?"

"I hear," Sarabeth said softly, her heart wrenching with pain for him. He looked away from her, then he stirred and slowly reached down to pick up the book Sarabeth had dropped.

The Lifting of Dark Spells." Damian's gaze shot to her. Sarabeth flinched. His face was wary, his eyes piercing. "Is that it, Elizabeth?"

"Wh-what?" Sarabeth asked.

"Are you spellbound?"

"No, of course not." She stepped hastily back. "No!"

Damian dropped the book, staring at her as if she were alien. "Who are you?"

"I—I am E-Elizabeth," Sarabeth whispered, the look on his face destroying her. Burning tears formed at the corner of her eyes.

"It's hide-and-seek," he said softly. "And it's my turn to find you." His hands shot out and gripped her small shoulders. "Who are you? Your eyes . . . I have seen them. Ever since I came here. The cat. The bird. The woman upon the—" He bit off his words. His grip tightened. "Why do you, a child, choose a book on the lifting of dark spells? Are you spellbound? Is that it? Are you spellbound?"

Sarabeth swallowed. "You—you do not believe in magic. You said so yourself." She could not tell him. Not having seen the rage and loathing in his eyes. Her tears escaped, and stung a hot path down her cheek. "I am . . . I am just Elizabeth."

"God," Damian cried, and pulled her to him, enveloping her in a trembling hold. Sarabeth sobbed, vulnerable and quaking. "Don't cry, child. I didn't mean to make you cry." He shook his head. "I don't know why I said all that. It must be this damn room. It must be. And for a moment, only for a moment, I thought . . . wanted you to be . . ." He halted. "Don't cry."

He scooped Sarabeth up, cradling her. Swiftly he strode from the room and carried her into the hall. He set her down. Sarabeth remained silent.

Damian knelt in front of her, his eyes solemn. "You will not go into that room ever again."

Sarabeth gazed at him, her very soul bleeding. He did not believe in magic, yet only magic could release her. "No," she said softly. "I shall not. I—I shall not if you do not want me to."

"I do not want you to," Damian said, the cord along his jaw leaping. "Never shall I want you to."

"I am sorry!" Sarabeth rasped. "Sorry for—" She killed the very words upon her lips. She could not say she was sorry for lying to him, for being spellbound, for loving him and being helpless. "I am sorry for going into the room."

Damian smiled slightly and lifted his hand toward her cheek. It halted just a touch away. He pulled it back sharply. "No, 'tis I who am sorry," he said. His eyes filled with disgust. "I do not know what came over me." He shook his head. "I no longer even know the man I am. Always looking for phantoms, seeing in every creature one I do not know." His lips twisted bitterly.

"Ranting and raving, accusing you, a child, of things I do not even believe."

Sarabeth's own hand reached out to him. She wanted to touch him, to confess that she was indeed his phantom, but not of her own choosing, never of her own choosing. It was no game to her. She pulled her hand back. "I should be going."

Damian nodded. "Yes, 'tis far too late. Your uncle shall be worried about you."

"Yes," Sarabeth said, not meeting his eyes. She stepped past him quickly.

"Elizabeth?" Damian asked.

Sarabeth turned. He had stood and was watching her. "I frightened you." It was not a question. It was a statement.

Yes, he had frightened her, frightened her deeply. She needed him, loved him. She was more spellbound by him than by Maudar's curse. "No," she whispered. Then she asked, unable to stop herself "May I come and visit again?"

Damian smiled. "Of course, imp. We should be finishing the first room in the west wing tomorrow."

She smiled tremulously. "I will see you tomorrow."

Sarabeth turned and dashed toward the door. Her heart sang. He had not banished her. Tomorrow she would see him again!

Seven

Fathomless clouds moved stealthily through the night sky, blackening the stars' brightness, grasping the waxing moon with dark fingers.

"He shall be ours," a voice cried out, stilling the land. The night birds cut off their singing. The creatures ceased their restless passage in the underbrush. "He shall join us! It is his destiny."

Maudar held her arms outstretched to the pressing, deadening night. Before her upon the ground lay a circle, a precise configuration within it. It was drawn with bones, and bodies of small animals, some still twitching their last life's breath.

Her voice rose in a chant. At first low and keening. Then growing relentlessly to demonic frenzy. A wind whipped up, but only about her, swirling and howling.

The clouds choked the last of the moon's glow.

Sarabeth wandered out into the late morning's brightness. She had just left the men hard at work. Where was he? Already hours had passed and still Damian had not appeared to work with them. No one in the house knew where he had gone. He had said she may visit him. He was no longer angry with her. Where was he?

Uneasiness gripped Sarabeth. "Don't be silly," she said to herself. Still, the uneasiness plucked at her heart. "Ninny!"

She lifted her hand to shield the sun from her eyes and

scanned the yard before the Castle Tor. A horse and man appeared in the distance. Sarabeth stood waiting, her heart pounding.

"Damian!" she shouted. He was safe! She took off at a skip and a run. Breathlessly she met him. "Hello."

"Hello, imp," Damian said, grinning down at her from atop his large black stallion. He was dressed in the finest of tailored clothes, the resplendent aristocrat. Gone was the dark, haunted man from the night before. Sunlight glinted about him, and so did his eyes. They were light and alive, alive like she had not seen them, except in her memory of him as a boy.

Sarabeth's smile answered his, as did her heart. "Where have you been?"

"Where have I been?" Damian grinned and dismounted from his horse. He knelt down before her to be upon her level and took up her hands. "You must congratulate me, Elizabeth. I am an engaged man."

Ice froze Sarabeth's blood. Her hands jumped in his. "Wh-what?"

"I am an engaged man," Damian repeated, holding firm to her hands even as she tugged. "Meaning that I proposed and the lovely lady accepted."

"But . . . how?" Sarabeth shook her head. "Why?"

"I woke up this morning and instantly knew," Damian said softly. "Knew that I loved Gertrude Tureen. I thought I was mad and that she would never accept me. But she did, Elizabeth. She did!"

"No!" Sarabeth tore her hands from Damian. He spoke such evil words, yet his face was innocent, happy. "No!"

"Yes," Damian said, frowning slightly. " 'Tis sudden, I know, but it is right."

Sarabeth stepped back slowly, gazing at him as if he were a serpent. "No!"

"What is it, child?" Damian asked, his face showing concern. Sarabeth swallowed hard, unable to speak. Suddenly his eyes gentled. "Forgive me, Elizabeth. I had forgotten your kind proposal of marriage. You wanted me to wait for you to grow up?"

"Yes," Sarabeth cried. "You were supposed to wait! Wait until I grew—"

" 'Twould have been a long time," Damian said softly, reaching out a hand. "I know I promised you—"

"Yes, you did!" Sarabeth cried, a sudden anger flushing through her, thawing her frozen heart. "You made a promise and you broke it!"

"Elizabeth," Damian said with a sigh. "You are but a child. I did not think you took our make-believe so seriously." His smile was whimsical. "I assure you, you will grow up and discover you never wanted me."

"I have always wanted you," Sarabeth cried, the words ripped from her. "Always!"

Damian started back, blinking. Their eyes met. Something stirred within his gaze. Sarabeth could not help herself, her heart was in her eyes as she reached out her hand. "Damian?"

He looked swiftly away and said, " 'Tis but a child's love, Elizabeth."

" 'Tis not a child's love," Sarabeth said, lowering her hand, her fingers clenched, the bite of her nails against her palm soothing compared to the pain lashing her soul. " 'Tis a true love."

"No." Damian's gaze flashed back to her. "You are but a child. I am sorry if I have hurt you, 'twas a mistake. But I am in love with Gertrude."

"No, 'tis a spell," Sarabeth said fiercely. The Damian she loved was disappearing before her very eyes as effectively as she had before his the first night they met. "You are spellbound."

"No!" He shook his head firmly. Again the light was back in his eyes. "I am in love."

Sarabeth's breath caught. "You said you did not believe in love."

Surprise crossed his face. "I did, didn't I?" He shook his

head as if to clear it. Then he laughed. "But now I know differently. I believe in love and it is wonderful."

"No!" Sarabeth shook her head in a daze. Emotion was strong in his eyes, in the very breath he spoke to her. God help them. Spellbound! Both he and she. "No!" She spun and ran, ran from the dark cruelty.

"Elizabeth! Come back!"

Sarabeth did not stop. Damian had finally come to love, but it was for Gertrude and only under the command of magic. She ran faster, harder, leaving his calls far behind her.

"And where should the wedding be?" Maudar's voice asked.

Damian stood, looking out of the parlor window. A small smile twitched at his lips. He had actually been rustling through those bushes one night, chasing after the child Elizabeth. His smile disappeared. He had not seen the child for three days. Surely she would soon overcome her anger and return. That he had hurt her he regretted deeply. He had never thought she was serious in her make-believe games. 'Twas because he had no understanding of children, he thought. Yet then he saw Elizabeth's green eyes, heard her voice as she said she had always loved him. An odd tremor coursed through him. How could a child have always loved him?

"Should it be here in Chancellorville, or in London, Your Grace?"

"What?" Damian turned, shaking off the feeling.

"Should the wedding be here or in London?" Maudar asked again.

"Whichever," Damian said quickly. His gaze went to Gertrude, who sat quietly upon the settee. A jolt of desire, almost painful, shot through him. He smiled at her, lost to her beauty. "What would you like, my love? Should it be a large London wedding?"

"That would be fine, Your Grace," Gertrude said quietly.

He frowned. "Or perhaps a quiet one here in Chancellorville, since it is your home."

"Yes, Your Grace," Gertrude said.

Sudden irritation shot through Damian. He wished to please Gertrude, but she gave no sign at how he was to do so. It was always "Yes, Your Grace," and "No, Your Grace." He loved her. When would her obsequience turn into something more? When would he see her true desire and spirit? He forced back his aggravation. He must be patient. He should cherish her obedience and bending spirit, not strive against it. "Choose, my dear."

"Let us have it in Chancellorville," Maudar said swiftly. "To plan a London wedding would take so long and I have no doubt you would grow impatient, Your Grace, with such a delay."

Damian's spirit leapt. Maudar spoke the truth. He could not wait. "Then let us most definitely have it here in Chancellorville."

Maudar's eyes lit with triumph. "Everyone should attend. The entire village shall see—er, celebrate in the marriage of you and Gertrude."

"Very well." Damian nodded and turned to look out the window once more, smiling. Soon Gertrude would be his wife. It would be a fine celebration. "Do not forget to invite Elizabeth and her uncle," he said over his shoulder in sudden inspiration. Perhaps if he met the child's guardian, they could have a talk and he could warn her uncle to have a care for her.

"Elizabeth!" Maudar's voice cracked like a whip, a loud one.

Damian turned from the window in surprise. Maudar's eyes were dark and unaccountably fulminating as she looked at him. "Why, yes, the neighboring child I've told you about. Do you not remember?"

"I remember," Maudar said, her lips tightening. "I very well know which *child* you mean."

Damian stepped quickly toward the women. "Do you know where her uncle lives?"

"Uncle?" Gertrude frowned. "She does not have an uncle."

"What?" Damian crossed and took up the seat beside Gertrude. "What do you mean, my dear?"

"She has an uncle," Maudar said swiftly. Damian caught her glaring at Gertrude. "What Gertrude means is that we do not know where he lives."

"You do not?" Damian asked. An undercurrent flowed within the room.

"No," Maudar said, and shook her head. Her face showed sympathy as she sighed. "He—he moves around so very much, I am afraid. He is not . . . a stable person, you see."

Damian frowned. "From what Elizabeth said, I had gathered that. He does not sound a fit guardian for a little girl."

"No," Maudar said. She suddenly smiled. It sent a chill down Damian's spine for some reason. "But I assure you. Your 'Elizabeth' will definitely receive an invitation to the wedding. And so will her—" She halted. "Her uncle."

"Good," Damian said. He must be satisfied, yet an unrest was growing within him.

"But, Mother," Gertrude said, her brown eyes wide and nervous. "I do not want her there. She will . . ." Her face clouded. "She might . . ."

"Might what?" Damian asked, his eyes narrowing. "Do you not like the child?"

"She does not know the child, in truth," Dame Tureen said, her own eyes narrowing. "Do you, Gertrude?"

Gertrude bit her lip. "No, Mother."

Damian looked to the woman he loved, trying to understand. "Do you not like children, dear?"

"Oh, no!" Gertrude exclaimed. "I like children very much. But she is not—"

"She is not someone who should concern us," Maudar said, her chin lifting. "We are discussing Gertrude and your wedding plans, what does it matter about this Elizabeth?"

"Yes." Damian clenched his jaw. "Forgive me. You are quite right. Let us discuss something else."

Maudar's eyes studied him a narrow, challenging moment.

He met her gaze steadily. "Let us discuss—" She halted and then smiled. "All Hallows' Eve, since it will be within the week. Do not you think it would be a marvelous time for the wedding?"

Damian drew back. Revulsion curled through his veins. He forced a laugh and shook his head. "No, I must confess that I do not."

"You are superstitious, then? For shame, Your Grace."

"Perhaps Chancellorville is affecting me after all," Damian admitted. "But the thought of holding a wedding upon that night, especially here in this town, seems morbid."

"Morbid? Nonsense," Dame Tureen said. "It is a fantastic night. The finest in the world."

"For witches perhaps," Damian retorted. Gertrude gasped loudly. Dame Tureen's eyes darkened. "I am sorry," Damian said swiftly, looking to Gertrude. "Would you truly wish to be married upon All Hallows' Eve?"

"Of course she would," Dame Tureen said.

Gertrude's gaze shied away from his. "Yes, Your Grace."

Damian stared. He should not be selfish. He should give all to this woman who was to be his bride. He needed her so very much. Yet to wed upon All Hallows' Eve in Chancellorville, when the night meant so much to the inhabitants? "You are spellbound," a child's voice cried within his mind. He gritted his teeth. "Let me think about it. I own I do not care for the notion, but I shall consider it."

"Yes, Your Grace," Gertrude murmured.

"Excellent," Dame Tureen said. "I am sure you will come to agree with us." She rose. "Come, Gertrude. If you are to wed upon All Hallows' Eve, we must see to your wedding dress."

Gertrude dutifully rose and followed her mother. Damian walked them to the door. "I have not said yes yet," he said, the revulsion rising within him again.

"But you shall," Dame Tureen laughed, her tone confident.

She departed down the steps with Gertrude, and Damian closed the door slowly.

He turned to discover Thomas meandering across the hall. "Thomas," he said. "Where are you going?"

"Millicent s-says I m-must get her some lamb in town."

"For a sacrifice?" Damian asked, laughing.

Thomas stiffened. "For dinner, Yer Grace."

"Tell me, Thomas," Damian asked, slowly walking away from the door. "What do you think of me being married upon All Hallows' Eve?"

Thomas started. His hand flashed to make the sign of the cross. That motion poured swiftly into pulling out his ever-present flask. "All Hallows' Eve? Gawd!" He uncapped it and drank a hearty swig. He closed his eyes, shivered, and then opened them to look at Damian. "You are bamming me."

"Dame Tureen wishes it."

"She would," Thomas muttered, and gulped quickly once more.

"So what do you think?"

"I think . . ." Thomas tottered over to him. "You should have a drink." He jabbed his flask toward Damian. "C-can understand you wanting to have Gertrude. Is pr-retty as a picture, but her ma?"

"You do not like her?"

Thomas's face showed a sheen of sweat. "I cannot say more, Yer Grace." He shook his head. "They still haven't found old Cranston. But—" It seemed as if he struggled. "All Hallows' Eve, Yer Grace? Every witch, ghost, and demon walks. Their powers are at th-their g-g-greatest."

"So you do not think I should wed upon the night?" Damian asked in a dry tone.

" 'Twill be a full moon this year as well." Thomas rattled the flask before Damian. "Have a drink, Yer Grace."

Damian looked at the flask. " 'Drink to me only with thine eyes,' " he murmured softly.

"Your Grace?"

Damian frowned, his gaze still upon the flask. "Have you seen the child Elizabeth, Thomas?"

The flask trembled within his footman's hand. "Th-the one with the green eyes?"

"Yes, the one with the green eyes." Damian lifted his gaze to study Thomas. "Have you ever seen her before this?"

Thomas's normally red complexion paled to gray. "N-no, Your Grace, and I don't want to. Don't want to see any damn cat or bird either. Don't want to see anything with g-green eyes."

"Do you know of her uncle?"

Thomas's face screwed up. "She gots an uncle? Wouldn't know if she had. I's told you, I never saw the child afore . . . not till you came."

"I see," Damian said. "And you've lived around here for quite some time?"

"All me life."

Damian pushed the outheld flask away from him. "No, Thomas, I do not need a drink." His gaze turned to the door at the end of the hall. He straightened. "I need something else."

"Please, Sarabeth," Bathsheba said, book in hand as she stood over Sarabeth in the garden. "Let us try."

"Yes," Dorinda said. "We are sure we have found the right spell."

"Only read it and see if you do not think so." Bathsheba held out the book.

"Read it?" Sarabeth clenched the weed in her hand as she knelt among her herbs. She restrained herself from reaching out and swatting the book away. "What does it matter? I am not a witch. I am powerless."

"But we are not," Dorinda said.

"Against this you are," Sarabeth said, and slowly unclenched the weed, dropping it to the dirt. "Damian now loves Gertrude and is going to marry her."

"He is spellbound," Bathsheba said. " 'Tis Maudar's wicked doing."

"Yes," Sarabeth said softly, gazing off into the distance and seeing nothing but the vision of Damian's face that last time she saw him. "He is spellbound. But for once he is in love. And he has never been in love before . . . never believed in it."

"But in love with Gertrude?" Dorinda retorted. "He would not be if Maudar hadn't used a spell. 'Tis as plain as the nose upon my face." Since Dorinda's nose was rather hawkish and unmistakable, it had to be very obvious indeed.

"Yes," Sarabeth said, dragging her gaze back to her two aunts. "But if he were not in love with Gertrude, spell or not, do you think he would be in love with me?"

" 'Of course he would," Bathsheba said.

"I know he would," Dorinda nodded.

Sarabeth smiled sadly. "I do not know that he would."

"But, dearest, he has never seen you in your true form," Bathsheba said in reasonable tones.

"But he knows me," Sarabeth said almost fiercely. "I know he does. Deny it he does, but he knows I was the cat and the bird. He knows. But that was magic and he'll have none of it." She sprang up swiftly. "He does not believe in magic. He does not believe in love."

"But now he says he loves Gertrude," Dorinda said. "You know 'tis not possible without Maudar's spell."

"Yes!" Sarabeth said, and swallowed hard. "Perhaps he will never love unless he is under a spell. And for him to never love . . ." She clenched her hands. "Which would be worse?"

"Maudar will destroy him," Dorinda said briskly, coldly. "What if he does marry Gertrude? And then Maudar discovers he does not turn into the great wizard she dreams of, or he does not turn to evil, but defies her. She will destroy him."

"Destroy him, dear," Bathsheba said softly.

"Stop!" Sarabeth cried. "Say no more."

"Let us try this spell," Dorinda said. "Dame Tureen shall not win."

"Will she not?" Sarabeth laughed, a dry, rasping laugh. "I think she has already won." She rose and walked away from her aunts.

"Elizabeth." Sarabeth's eyes snapped open. She sat up in her bed, blinking into the darkness about her. She thought she had heard Damian's voice. It had called her.

She looked around in confusion. Moonlight shadowed her room. Everything was in its ordinary place. She was alone. She had been dreaming.

"Damian," she sighed softly.

"Elizabeth." She heard his voice in her head. She shivered. The feeling swelled within her, overwhelming her. She must go to him.

Her feet swung to the floor. Fool that she was, she must go to him. She must see him one more time.

Sarabeth walked quietly into the great hall of the Castle Tor. The large oak doors had been unlocked, as if they expected her. She did not hesitate. She did not need to, for the feeling that drove her led her directly to the door of the library, the one she had promised Damian never to enter. She silently opened it.

A lone candle burned upon the table. Damian, tall and stern, sat behind it. His gaze lifted and he looked directly at her as she stood, silent, within the entrance.

Sarabeth felt no surprise. "Hello."

"Hello," he said. "I knew you would come."

"You did?" Sarabeth asked. She laughed a little. "I did not. I thought I heard you calling me."

"I did not call you," Damian said, his eyes darkening. "But I knew you would come."

Sarabeth hesitated. "May I enter?"

"Yes." He nodded. "Do. For I doubt this room frightens you like it did me when I was a child."

Sarabeth tread softly into the library. Damian's voice was odd, his eyes enigmatic. "You are not afraid of the room now?"

His gaze turned from her and moved slowly over the book-lined shelves. "No, I have spent the day in here." The books that lay strewn around him testified to that. "It almost seems safe in here now."

"You hear nothing? See nothing?"

"No," Damian said, turning a piercing look back upon her. "I am not a child anymore. But then again, you are not a child either."

Sarabeth froze. "Yes, I am."

"You lie!" He shot up from the chair, standing tall and taut. "You lie."

"No, I do not." Sarabeth trembled. "When I am around you, I feel like a child."

"And you speak of loving me."

Sarabeth swallowed hard. At least that much she must be able to confess. "I have loved you since I was a child."

"And how long could that be, if you truly are a child?" Damian slammed his fist upon the table. "How long, Elizabeth? It could be only a few short days if you are but a child." Sarabeth tried to tear her gaze from his. Yet she could not. His blazing eyes demanded her to look at him. Demanded the truth. "When I told you I loved Gertrude, you said I was spellbound." He lifted a book from the table. " 'Tis not I who am spellbound, but you. *The Lifting of Evil Spells*. I have read it, Elizabeth." A moment's silence entered the room as they stared at each other. "I asked before, and you lied. I ask again. Who are you?"

Sarabeth's heart cried out. Could she tell him the truth? Show him her true desire and spirit? "I—I . . ."

"What kind of creature are you?" Damian tossed the book back to the table. His voice was laden with disgust. "Phooka, co-walker, changeling?"

Sarabeth stiffened as if he had slapped her. "I am no creature. I am an ordinary mortal."

"No, you are not," he growled, and spun, striding away from her to the far end of the library, as if he could not be even that close to her. "You were the cat, were you not? The one that destroyed my dinner with Gertrude. And you were Pretty Polly, the bird who flew at poor Gertrude and sent her racing home." From across the great expanse Damian looked at her, his eyes challenging. "You cannot lie. I know you now."

"Yes," Sarabeth said softly, and walked farther into the room. "You know me now. And yet you call me creature."

"What else can I call you?" His voice was a rasp.

"You can call me—" She choked back the words. He could call her Sarabeth. He could call her his love. A tear slid down her cheek. "It does not matter. To you I am a creature." She lifted her head. "A poor, miserable spellbound creature. And I am. I have come to you in every form I could. I—I could not stay away from you."

His own head lifted, his eyes dangerous. "I am telling you to stay away from me now."

Another tear slipped down Sarabeth's cheek. "I came because I . . ."

"Because you love me?" His hand made a slashing movement. "Do not speak to me of love."

"No, I shan't," Sarabeth cried sharply, her wound deep and bleeding. "Never again." She stiffened. "But I at least can say I loved when I was not under a spell. But you, you did not love until magic forced you."

"Be quiet!" Damian roared. "Do not try your witchery with me. 'Tis you who are spellbound. I am free."

"But your love for Gertrude is—"

"Do not speak of Gertrude!" he shouted. "Do not speak of my love for her and of magic in the same breath. I am going to marry her three days hence and—

"Three days?" Sarabeth gasped. "On All Hallows' Eve?"

"Yes." Damian's face turned to granite. "It would please her and I shall do so."

Sarabeth froze. It was evil. For him to marry upon All Hallows' Eve would be unholy. Maudar's powers would be complete. "No," Sarabeth cried, and ran to Damian. "No!" She reached out a desperate hand. He stepped back. "Please no. I—I will do anything if you promise not to marry upon that night."

"You will promise never to come to me," Damian said, looking down at her with cold eyes. "Be it in any form."

Sarabeth swallowed hard. He must not marry upon All Hallows' Eve. She would never say she loved him again, but she did. "Yes," Sarabeth promised. Her hand remained outstretched in entreaty. "I promise. You shall never see me again, in any form. If only you will not marry upon . . . upon that night."

"Then I vow I will not," Damian said. He stepped forward and clasped her hand to bind the oath. Magic swirled about them. The moonlight about them seemed to flare to blue-white.

Damian jerked his hand away. "Leave."

The glow was still about them. The white light of love. Yet he denied her. Still he ordered her to go. Sarabeth silently turned and walked to the door, head held high. She turned to gaze at Damian. The expanse of the library and all its wealth of magic lay between them.

"You said you read the lifting of dark spells. There is no spell darker than what you have just done."

She turned and walked from the room.

Eight

"The fool!" Maudar screeched, and paced the parlor with swirling skirts. Her hands flexed out into talons. "He still fights me. He says he shall not marry upon All Hallows' Eve. And you," she cried, turning to Gertrude, who pushed back into the sofa's cushion with frightened eyes. "You are no help. I cast a spell upon him in the very domains of the Castle Tor and with a well nigh full moon, and still you cannot attract him."

"I am sorry, Mama," Gertrude said, her hand raising to her breast. "I try. But . . . but I do not understand. He talks of things I do not know. I never know what to say."

"Say! Say!" Maudar's arms flapped up like an angry hawk's. "Do not say, you fool girl. Do! Flirt with him. Kiss him! My spell is of the body, his spirit I cannot yet control. Bind him physically, and 'twill be enough."

A dark red color flushed Gertrude's face. "He does not love me."

Maudar swooped down upon her and slapped her sharply. "Do not speak of love, imbecile. We talk of power. Power that will be unleashed and ours. He will be a great wizard and you shall be his consort." She snorted. "And you go on about love. It is weak. It destroys our powers. Look at the Goodfellow sisters and their puny efforts." She leaned into Gertrude. " 'Tis the dark forces that have the power. Bind him now, and I soon shall have his soul."

"H-how?" Gertrude asked with a stammer.

Maudar jackknifed up. "How?" Her eyes narrowed. "He will not wed you tonight, but he shall bed you."

"Mama!"

Maudar's eyes snapped to Gertrude. "He fights my spell. He is stronger than most. Which is only fitting, for when he comes into his powers, all the greater shall he be. It will be All Hallows' Eve tonight, and what I have cast will only be strengthened. All the dark powers will descend. Mate with him upon the witching hour and the spell will be cast forever. Not only will his body be bound, but so shall his spirit."

"Oh, dear," Bathsheba said, staring disconsolately at the dinner before her. "I have this dreadful feeling."

" 'Tis All Hallows' Eve," Dorinda said, putting down her fork. "Maudar shall most definitely try something."

"Damian will not wed Gertrude tonight," Sarabeth said lowly, her hands clasped in her lap. "He has promised me."

"Then Maudar will try something else," Dorinda said.

"Let us try to turn you back one more time," Bathsheba pleaded. "We shall have stronger powers tonight than before."

"To what purpose?" Sarabeth asked, strengthening her own resolve. How she yearned to see Damian again, but she had promised. "He wishes not to see me in any form."

"He is spellbound," Bathsheba said. "He does not speak as himself."

"Good gracious," Dorinda said, gasping. Her eyes widened and her face paled. "Maudar has cast her spell. She need not have Damian wed Gertrude tonight, only that he—" She halted with a flinching glance to Sarabeth. "Only that he . . . consummate with Gertrude."

Bathsheba's face turned a rosy hue. "Consummate?"

Sarabeth did not react the same. "Consummate!" Her child's hand slammed to the table. "If he and Gertrude—" She ground to a halt. "They shall not!" She sprang from her chair. "I swore to him never to appear again if he did not marry Gertrude tonight, but if he . . . he beds Gertrude, it will be the same as if he weds her."

"Yes, dear," Bathsheba nodded. " 'Tis what marriage is all about."

Sarabeth shook. She felt betrayed in some fashion. "He is a man of honor, surely he would not—"

"He is a man spellbound," Dorinda said. "He is engaged to Gertrude. Do you honestly think if Gertrude and Maudar set the trap, he will not fall?"

Sarabeth paled. "I promised him, promised him I would never appear before him again."

"Well then," Bathsheba said, standing. "You shall not appear before him. But you did not promise to desert him, did you?"

"He wishes it," Sarabeth said, hurt.

"And do you wish it?" Dorinda asked, eyes narrowed.

Sarabeth slowly shook her head. "No, I do not, cannot."

"And you did not promise him that, did you?"

"No," Sarabeth said softly. Deny her he had. Yet she had told him he had cast the darkest spell in turning her love away. Would she permit herself to suffer the same spell? She looked to her aunts. "He must not see me, but we must help him."

"Yes, dear," Bathsheba said, nodding. "We have failed you and him before, but we shall not tonight."

Dorinda rose, smiling. " 'Tis all Hallows' Eve. We must prepare."

Damian dined in lone splendor. His food sat before him, untouched. His glass of wine also sat untouched. He reached for it, and then withdrew his hand. Already too many visions swirled and mingled within his head. He needed no new ones from wine's fumes. He saw Gertrude in his mind's eye. The instantaneous jolt of desire coursed through him. How he needed her beside him. When she was not there, his body ached and tensed, never soothed unless she was close.

"This could have been my wedding night," he murmured.

Visions of taking Gertrude to him flooded his mind. He was kissing her, molding her full and naked body to his. She was responding, passion in her eyes. Then suddenly her eyes turned green.

"Damn you!" His hand slammed against the table. What kind of creature haunted him? Damian once again saw the woman upon the road, her eyes welcoming, but sad even as she vanished. He remembered waking from a nightmare and a cat with green eyes patting his cheek. He saw a bird, hanging from a curtain, singing, "Drink to me only with thine eyes." He saw a child with tears in her eyes, and a bright white light about them as he clasped her hand. "No!"

He lurched from the table. Words, chants, and spells resounded in his head. All the things he had read in the library clamored in his ears. "No! I tell you, no!" Then it seemed as if a mist swirled up about him, cloaking the dining room. The Castle Tor rose before him, glowing crimson. "No!"

"You called, Your Grace?"

Damian blinked. All was gone. He looked about. The dining room was sound reality again. Thomas stood swaying within the door, drunker than usual, if that were possible. Thomas looked more like an African savage than an English footman, for about his neck he wore every kind of amulet and necklace imaginable, and some indefinable. The crucifix intertwined with wolfbane, tangled with a string of garlic, and all weaved through various small pouches holding only God knew what contents. The chain of garlic, though, made him a rather strong man to be about.

"No, I did not," Damian said, coughing. "I believe I shall retire."

"Thash the t-ticket." Thomas wagged his head up and down. "Sh-tay s-safe h-here. All c-creatures w-walk thish night." His blurred eyes turned owlish. "A-and d-don't o-open any doors." He shook his head back and forth. "L-let no one e-enter. N-no one. Y-you may be—be inv-iting evil."

"Indeed," Damian said, studying the footman. "Why don't you retire as well, Thomas? Before you fall down."

Thomas gasped. "R-retire? N-no, Y-Your Grace, I—I c-could not sleep thish n-night. A suc-cubus m-might c-come and s-seduce m-me."

"Very well," Damian said. "Do what you wish. I am retiring."

Three small mice scurried over the lawn toward the Castle Tor.

"Hurry," one squeaked. "Hurry!" Her body was brindled and her nose was exceptionally pointed.

"I am," the one behind her squeaked, the tiniest of glasses perched upon her twitching nose. "Oh, I hate being so small. A cat or bird could get us."

"I feared Tomolina might," the third squeaked, its eyes a bright green.

"Well, we could not help it," the leader squeaked. "This will be the best way to go unnoticed and spy upon Damian."

"I am so sorry, Sarabeth," squeaked the second.

" 'Tis far better than being a fly, I would say," Sarabeth squeaked back with a tiny chuckle.

"May the powers be with us," Dorinda squeaked as she led them toward the castle walls. "For I have a very bad feeling."

"So do I," Bathsheba squeaked.

"No matter," Sarabeth squeaked back as they scampered along the stone wall, all searching for a hole. "As long as Damian does not know we are here, all will be well."

Damian threw the book down beside him in bed. He rubbed his eyes. Faith, he was tired. The candle beside him burned low. The clock had already chimed the half hour minutes before. 'Twould be midnight shortly. He shook his head ruefully.

He had no care for the book he read, but still he did not wish to sleep. He'd have less care for his dreams, he was certain.

He heard a soft movement at the closed door. He stared at it, tensing. Thomas's superstitions crawled into his mind. *Let no one in, lest you invite evil* . . .

The door opened slowly. Damian sucked in his breath. 'Twas no fell creature. Gertrude, his beloved, stood within the door.

Damian was stunned. It was not only her appearance at his bedroom door that surprised Damian, but what she wore, or, rather, did not wear. She was dressed in a thin sheath of ruby gauze, cut low in the front and clasped at her shoulders by two brooches. Her naked body shone through the sheath, every full curve and line.

Hot desire thrummed through Damian. "Gertrude!"

She stood gazing at him, hesitancy in her eyes and body. "M-may I e-enter?"

"Yes, do, please," Damian said, swallowing hard. "Do come in."

"I—I have come, Your Grace," Gertrude whispered as she walked slowly toward him. "B-because I—I wish to be with you."

"And I you." His voice came out in a rasp. His breathing paced faster. *Control yourself,* Damian's mind demanded from somewhere in the maelstrom of hot desire swirling within him. *You are a gentleman.*

"But we are not wed yet," Damian forced out. It was as if the words were the hardest thing to say. "We should not." Suddenly he heard squeaking sounds, displaced but clear. He glanced swiftly about, then shook his head. "Gertrude?"

She, too, looked nervously around, but then turned back to him. "But I want to b-be with you. A-and now!" Her eyes, however, were wide and frightened.

Take her, a voice suddenly shrilled within Damian. His loins were taut, his body aching to close against Gertrude's.

"You are sure?" Damian asked. Still there was that damn squeaking noise.

"Yes, yes." Gertrude nodded. Her hands were clasped tightly before her. "And we must do it now!"

God, he wanted her.

Take her, the voice echoed once more, far louder than the squeaks that persisted in the room.

Damian forced himself to breathe in deeply. "I would not . . . not wish to do something you—you would regret later."

"I—I will not regret it," Gertrude said. "We must bed now." Her tone was odd, her words hurried. She lifted her hand to the one brooch at her shoulder. The squeaks turned rapid and furious. Mice, Damian thought suddenly, inconsequentially, even as his eyes remained hypnotically upon Gertrude and his body tensed with excitement. There were damn mice in the room.

Take her, the voice whipped through his thoughts.

"I want you," Gertrude said. Her words sounded unnatural, rehearsed. "I want you." She began tugging and twisting at the brooch. The infernal mice were squeaking loudly. The large clock in the hall added its clamor, chiming the midnight hour.

Damian, enthralled, ignored it all as he gazed at Gertrude. He slowly pushed back the covers and put his hand to the space beside him. "Come to me, my love. Come to me."

A swirling sound of wind suddenly filled the room. A bright white light flared, blinding in its intensity. Gertrude screamed. Damian lifted his hands to shield his face. He felt a sudden weight join him upon the bed.

The light and wind disappeared. Damian brought his hand down. Gertrude screeched once more. Damian stared. "You!"

The woman from the road lay beside him, just as he had seen her that night. Her dark hood was fallen back, long blond hair fanned out against the pillow. Her green, green eyes stared up at him in undisguised shock. "Damian?"

"You!" Damian shook. His emotions turned wild within him.

"Wh-what? H-how?" She sat up slowly. She stretched out her hand and gazed at it. Her gaze flew to him. "You can see me?"

"I see you!" Damian said.

"No, no!" Gertrude cried. "You should not! You should not!" She hopped up and down. Her eyes were saucers.

The blond woman's face lit and she gazed at him in excitement. "I don't look like a child, do I? I look like me."

"Yes," Damian said, knowing full well what she meant.

"I am free!" she cried. "I am free. Damian, you can see me!"

"I see you," he said through a clenched jaw. He was being torn apart inside. When he looked at the woman beside him in his bed, a feeling like magic swelled within him, strong and frightening. Yet then he looked to Gertrude, his beloved, now sobbing loudly, tears streaming down her face.

Take her! the voice cried in his mind.

Damian turned his gaze back to the woman in his bed and the words came on their own accord. "Get out."

The woman reared back. Her cheeks flushed red as if his hand had slapped her there. "Damian, please, no."

"You promised never to return." Rage swelled within him. He would have no part of her witchery. "You promised."

"I had not meant to appear," she said, bewilderment crossing her face. "Truly." She turned her head and looked over to the bureau behind Gertrude, her eyes upon the floor. "You were supposed to turn Gertrude into something, not me."

Two small mice scurried suddenly out from beneath the bureau into the center of the room. Amazingly, one had on tiny spectacles.

"No, no!" Gertrude sobbed, dancing back from the two. "No!"

The mice let up a symphony of squeaks and chirps. Oddly, those squeaks began to sound like human voices. "We didn't, we didn't," it sounded like they were saying.

"Be quiet!" roared Damian. The mice silenced. Gertrude choked on a sob. The woman beside him slowly turned her gaze back to him. Her eyes were green pools of yearning. "I did not mean to appear. I only came to—to save you."

"Save me!"

"Yes, you are under a spell. . . ."

"The only spell I am under is yours," Damian said. He could feel it, drawing him to her. Magic. "You are a witch, aren't you?"

"No," she said softly. "I am mere human. I have no powers. One is born with them or not. But Gertrude . . ."

"Ah, you will claim her the witch," Damian said.

"No, she is like me. She has no powers. 'Tis Dame Tureen who has them. She is a black witch and has cast a love spell upon you."

Damian turned to look at Gertrude. A jolt of need rocked him.

"She lies," Gertrude said, her face full of fright. "You must believe me, she lies."

Damian turned his gaze back to the woman in his bed. "I believe Gertrude."

The woman's green eyes turned sad, so deeply sad. "I—" She halted and shook her head. "I told you I would never say it again. 'Tis one promise I can keep."

Quietly, with dignity, she rose from the bed. "Come," she said to the mice. They squeaked softly. She walked across the room. Gertrude moved back as the woman stopped before her. "If you have any love for him, any kindness," she said lowly, "you will not let your mother have him."

"I . . ." Gertrude's face turned pale and she shook her head. "I must."

The woman turned, standing proud. She was the vision that had haunted Damian for so very long. "Good-bye, my—" She halted. She gazed at Damian mutely, a shimmer of tears submerging the brightness of her eyes. She turned away from him and grasped the doorknob.

"My love," Damian whispered, finishing the words she would not speak. Something tore through him. He wanted to hear those words upon her lips once more. He must.

"Sarabeth!" he cried out. She spun. "Wait!"

"No!" Gertrude screeched. "Tell her to go. She must go."

"Say it," Damian said.

Pain flashed in her green eyes. "What?" But she knew. He knew she did.

"Don't! Don't!" Gertrude cried, her hands flapping in the air. "Leave."

"Say it one more time," Damian said. A force was building in him. It was a force he had fought all his life. Now he welcomed it. "Say it, Sarabeth!"

He saw her swallow. The slightest tear slipped down her face.

"My love," she whispered. The force flooded through him, white and beautiful.

"Be quiet!" Gertrude yelled. "Don't say that!"

Damian swung his gaze toward Gertrude, eyes narrowed. "I . . ." He struggled. A war of opposite powers battled within him, he merely the ground in which they fought. "I—I do not love you, Gertrude."

"No." Gertrude shook her head, her expression aghast. "You must! You must! Mother has cast her spell upon you."

A calm entered Damian. "I do not love you, Gertrude. Please leave."

"You can't!" Gertrude cried. "Mother will kill you if you do not do what she wants."

"Do not threaten me," Damian roared with a new strength. "Be gone! Do you hear me!"

Gertrude's hand flew to her lips. She cried out and stumbled past Sarabeth and through the door.

Damian looked to Sarabeth. She stood frozen. He had done so much against her. "Sarabeth?" he asked. He stretched his arms out in a question, a plea. She choked slightly, and then she flew across the room, throwing herself into his arms. Damian closed them tightly, holding her close, feeling for once the woman he had thought just a vision in his mind. He closed his eyes tightly, overwhelmed with sudden new sensations.

"My God," he whispered. "That I might have never known you. That I—"

"Hush," Sarabeth said, drawing back. "We are both free of Maudar and Gertrude."

"Yes, we are free." Damian shook his head, a fierce anger pulsing through him. "But what evil. If I had the power, I would wish that they would suffer the same spell they put on me."

Sarabeth grinned. "Then you believe in magic?"

Damian gazed at her a moment, amazed at her every feature. He smiled. "You are in my arms, how can I not?"

" 'Tis not magic," Sarabeth said, shaking her head. " 'Tis merely love."

"As I said," Damian murmured. " 'Tis magic."

He leaned over and kissed her. It was magic!

Gertrude ran down the stairs, tears streaming down her face. They blinded her eyes so that she did not see Thomas at the foot of the stairs. She collided with him like a thunderclap. They both yelled and capsized.

"Bejeezus!" Thomas cried.

Gertrude looked at the footman sprawled on the floor next to her. Her world rocked. An explosion cracked her heart.

"I love you," she breathed. "I love you."

Thomas yelped and stumbled up, swaying madly.

Gertrude gazed at him. He was the most magnificent man. He was a god. She sprang up. "I love you!"

Thomas stared at her. "Gawd!" He backed away, though his drunken eyes were riveted upon Gertrude's exposed charms. His hand scrabbled to his neck, rattling the many necklaces there until he gripped an amulet. He jerked it forward so swiftly, it ripped from his neck. He brandished it at her. "Stay away!"

"I love you," Gertrude cried loudly.

Thomas choked, gurgled, and coughed. Swiftly he turned and ran.

"Come back, I love you! I love you!"

Gertrude caught Thomas in the dining room when he tripped over his own feet. He hit the floor with a loud wail. She flung herself down upon him, kissing him with passionate abandonment.

"Grrr," Thomas mumbled. His one hand still gripped the amulet. Gertrude kissed him wildly, worming her body against his. Slowly, his hand unclenched the amulet. It was lost between their two striving bodies. He reached out and enfolded her charms.

Maudar stood in the meadow, laughing before a roaring fire. 'Twas her night! All Hallows' Eve. Soon, soon, the duke would be Gertrude's and hers. He would come into his great powers and she would be in control of them.

Suddenly, an alien, unknown force struck her. She stiffened. Her eyes widened.

"No! No! It cannot be!" She let out a feral growl, spun, and ran. She tore into the woods, trying to escape the feeling upon her, the weak, draining power. "No, no," she cried. "Never!"

She crashed through the thickets. Branches tore at her cloak. She heard a noise behind her. Instinctively she turned. A bolt like lightning hit her as she gazed upon a man who stood in the woods, his hand grasping up a snared rabbit.

"My love!" Maudar suddenly cried, stretching out her arms. "Come to me!"

The hermit Tarrel dropped his rabbit without a word and ran.

"My love," Maudar cried. She immediately thought of a spell to hold him. No! She could not. He was her love! She chased after him, back through the brush. She cried out his name and her love. She'd follow him anywhere, be it over hill and dale. He was her love!

Sarabeth gasped in sheer delight. She was in Damian's arms and his kisses were turning her to melting desire. She returned them fervently. At last to be able to do so! Damian's hands threaded through her hair, cupping her head.

"Sarabeth, Sarabeth, Sarabeth!" His lips traced to her ear, and the whisper of her name with his lips upon her skin sent shivers coursing through her.

Suddenly, swiftly, Damian rolled her over, following atop her.

"Damian," she gasped, but held him closely, reveling in his weight upon her. She closed her eyes, awash with the passion.

"Excuse me," a voice said.

"Oh, dear, yes," another said. "Sarabeth, I—I really believe you should stop."

"What the devil!" Damian's head lifted from Sarabeth's. "Oh, Lord!" He rolled from her to sit up.

Sarabeth groaned and sat up as well. Her two aunts stood at the foot of the bed in their human forms, their eyes wide.

"Who are you?" Damian's eyes were equally wide.

Sarabeth giggled. His voice sounded terribly irritated. She herself did not care for the interruption "They are my aunts."

"Your aunts!" Damian stared at her. Then he smiled. "You have no uncle?"

Sarabeth shook her head. "No, only aunts."

"We were the mice," Dorinda said.

"And we're sorry to interrupt," Bathsheba said, shifting from foot to foot. "But you two seemed to be carried away."

"And you really don't know each other well enough for that," Dorinda said.

Damian's gaze flashed to Sarabeth. "No, we know each other."

"Yes," Sarabeth said, smiling softly. "We do."

He laughed. "But I like you best in this form." He reached out his hand and laid it to her cheek. "I thought you were a dream." She felt the tremble in his hand. "That night on the road, when I first saw you, I felt as if I had finally discovered a lost part of me. I think even then that I loved you."

"And I—I loved you before that," Sarabeth said, rubbing her cheek against his hand.

"Since you were a child," he murmured, his voice tender.

Then he frowned and his gaze grew tortured. "But when you disappeared before my eyes, I—I could not accept it, so I denied it . . . and you."

"I could not help it, Damian," Sarabeth said. She raised her hand to his and drew it from her cheek, holding it tightly. "Dame Tureen cast a spell."

"Yes." Bathsheba nodded. "Maudar had sworn that Sarabeth would never catch your eye."

"But why?" Damian asked.

"Well, you see, we—er, had a slight tiff with Maudar," Bathsheba said, looking shamefaced. She dashed around the bed to sit beside Damian, touching him lightly upon the shoulder. "We truly did not mean to cause such trouble."

"Yes," Dorinda said, walking over to sit upon the other side near Sarabeth. " 'Tis only that when we heard how Maudar had contrived to draw you back here and her plans for you . . . well, we were slightly miffed."

"It was Maudar who caused the fire, Damian," Sarabeth said. "And made Cranston disappear."

"Faith!" Damian appeared stunned. "Then he really was turned into something. All the villagers said so, only I could not believe."

Bathsheba sighed. "He really wasn't a very good manager, but Maudar really shouldn't have turned him into something. It was unconscionable."

"I personally believe he is that mule Farmer Jenkins found wandering," Dorinda said, tapping her finger to her cheek.

"Yes, yes." Bathsheba nodded. "He has the same features as Cranston. And is just as lazy as he was in human form."

"Good Lord," Damian said, staring. He shook his head. "And Maudar did all this just to draw me back here? Just so I might marry Gertrude?"

"Well, there was a little more than th-that," Bathsheba said, her eyes flickering to the other two women with a question.

"What?" Damian asked. His grasp upon Sarabeth's hand tightened. "Tell me, Sarabeth."

"Maudar believes you have latent powers," Sarabeth said. "Powers as a wizard. She believed if you mated with her daughter you would come into the dark powers and that she would be the one to control you."

Damian ripped his hand from hers. "My God!"

"Totty-headed," Dorinda said.

"Cast one too many spells." Bathsheba nodded.

"And what do you believe?" Damian asked, his gaze intent upon Sarabeth.

She laughed softly. "I believe you have great powers, Damian, over me, that is." Then she frowned. "But the thought of what Maudar planned, I could not—not tolerate it either. Not after I saw you again."

"So you came to me," Damian said gently.

"I could not stay away." Sarabeth looked down, flushing. "I never meant to lie to you, or to—to play games, yet I knew not how else to reach you or—or protect you."

"Thank you," Damian said softly. Suddenly his eyes darkened, and it seemed he had left them for another place. "Now I understand the dream."

"What dream?" Bathsheba asked.

"I saw the Castle Tor burning," Damian said. "And then it turned to bloodred."

"Oh, dear," Bathsheba cried, her hand flying to her mouth.

"Gracious," Dorinda said, clicking her tongue. " 'Twas a close thing, then. You were being warned. It's what would have happened if Maudar had claimed you."

Damian's gaze returned to Sarabeth. "And you were there beside me. I knew not who or what you were, but you were there."

"As I wished to be in true life," Sarabeth said, her heart in her eyes.

"It was our fault, I fear," Bathsheba sighed, shaking her head. "We were unable to lift Maudar's spell. Every time we tried, well, things went awry. We only managed to turn her into—"

"A cat," Damian grinned. "Or a parrot, or a little girl."

"Er, yes," Dorinda said, grimacing. She shook her head. "Magic is tricky."

"I'm sorry, Sarabeth," Damian said lowly. "The dream tried to tell me. You tried to tell me. But I could not believe in magic or love."

Sarabeth held her breath. "And what do you believe now?"

"That I will need you beside me for life," Damian said, his eyes turning dark and questing. He leaned over and kissed her gently upon the lips. Sarabeth's eyelids fluttered shut as feelings of love and desire coursed through her, shortening her breath.

"Oh, dear," Bathsheba gasped. "Perhaps we should leave."

"Not now," Dorinda said sharply. All eyes turned toward her in astonishment. "It is All Hallows' Eve. There is no spell upon them, yet from what we saw before, if they should . . . er, well, become carried away, heaven only knows what will happen."

"Gracious!" Bathsheba cried. "I was not thinking. That is why Gertrude came here. If you had mated with her, Your Grace, Maudar's spell would have been cast forever. You would have been bound to Gertrude for life."

Damian's eyes widened. Then his gaze turned to Sarabeth intently. "And would you care to be bound to me for life, Sarabeth?"

"I'm already bound to you," Sarabeth whispered.

"Then you would marry me?" Damian asked.

Sarabeth held her breath. "Are you proposing?"

He smiled slightly. "I promised Elizabeth I would, didn't I?" His dark eyes studied her. A slow, heart-catching smile crossed his face. "And you are definitely grown now."

Sarabeth laughed. "I told you I would grow up fast."

Damian reached out and cupped her face in both his hands. "I need you, Sarabeth. I need to see you every day, have you by my side, and not only in my dreams. Say you will marry me."

Sarabeth gazed into Damian's eyes. Love shone in them, and it was for her! "I will marry you. I love you."

"And I you," Damian said, softly capturing her lips.

"Oh, how wonderful," Bathsheba sighed. "They are finally together."

Damian pulled back from Sarabeth and laughed. "Finally! I must be the only man who has fallen in love with a vision, a cat, a parrot, and a child. I thought I was mad, a stark, raving bedlamite."

"When do you intend to marry her?" Dorinda asked.

Damian looked at Sarabeth, his eyes warm and laughing. "Post haste, Madame, lest she disappear on me again. But not, I think, upon All Hallows' Eve. We'll not need the powers of this night to keep us together forever."

"No," Sarabeth smiled, her heart flooding with the joy of that knowledge. Suddenly she frowned and bit her lip. "But you do not mind the magic?"

Damian laughed. "No, this kind of magic is wonderful."

"No," Sarabeth said, shaking her head. "I mean Bathsheba and Dorinda, they are both witches."

"Yes," Bathsheba said. "We hate to disappoint you, but we are."

"We are of the white coven." Dorinda nodded. "But we are witches nevertheless."

Damian grinned. "Then I guess I will have to get used to having witches in the family. After all, if you two had not made Sarabeth appear before me in my bed, I might very well be bound to Gertrude by now."

Bathsheba gasped. "Oh, but we didn't!"

Dorinda shook her head. "I know I did not do it."

"Neither did I," Bathsheba said. "I swear it."

"I am mortal," Sarabeth said. "You know I could not!"

Everyone stared at one another one moment. Then the three women turned to stare at Damian.

He jerked up stiffly, his brown eyes appalled. "No!"

Sarabeth laughed and leaned over to kiss him lightly. "Love and magic, Damian, 'tis all the same. You may very well be the master of the Castle Tor after all. But no matter who *you* are, I will always love you!"

"And we would have accepted you as just a mere mortal," Bathsheba said, patting him kindly upon the shoulder. "A wizard in the family was too much to hope for."

Damian shook his head. "Impossible."

"I wondered," Dorinda said, eyes narrowing. "How you were able to throw off Maudar's spell, for it was a strong one, and upon All Hallows' Eve at that!"

Sarabeth's lips twitched. "And with a full moon even!"

Suddenly Bathsheba gasped. Then she giggled. All eyes turned to her. Her giggle broke into a merry laugh. "Oh, my!" Her hand pattered upon her chest rapidly. "Oh, my!"

"What?" Damian asked. "What are you laughing at?"

Bathsheba's blue eyes twinkled. "Do you remember what your very last words were, Your Grace, before Sarabeth appeared in your bed?"

Damian frowned and thought a moment. Then his eyes widened. "They were, 'come to me, my love.' "

Sarabeth laughed, leaned forward, and entwined her arms around his neck. "And I appeared, did I not?"

Damian's arms pulled her close against his hard body. Suddenly he smiled, a crooked, wicked smile. "Hmmm, perhaps I'm not going to mind this magic after all . . . not if I can call you to my bed anytime I so wish."

A thrill shot through Sarabeth at the delicious thought. She lowered her eyes, however, and performed a pout. "But are you going to be an old meany and not let me bounce upon it?"

"Oh, no, my dear," Damian said, his eyes alight with devilish fire. "You can 'bounce' on it all you want. Anytime, day or night, in fact. And I assure you, I shall strongly encourage you to do so."

"W-will you?"

"Very strongly," he said, nodding. Then his lips twitched. "But I warn you, bedtime will be early for you, my girl. Unlike your imaginary uncle, I'm not going to let you run wild."

Sarabeth laughed. "Oh, no?" She reached up and kissed him fervently, demandingly.

"All right," Damian murmured as she drew back. "Maybe sometimes."

"Only sometimes?" Sarabeth just lightly brushed his lips this time.

"All right," Damian growled, though his eyes were tender. "You can run wild anytime you so desire!"

"And I do so desire," Sarabeth whispered. She kissed him once more. Joy and passion mingled within her. Their kiss held the taste of forever in it.

"See, sister." Bathsheba's voice drifted through Sarabeth's passion-filled conscience. "We were right all along"

"We were?" Dorinda's voice asked.

"Sarabeth did catch the duke's eye!"

Dorinda clicked her tongue. "I'd say she caught more than that, sister. Much more than that!"

About the Author

Cindy Holbrook lives with her family in Fort Walton Beach, Florida. She is the author of six Zebra Regency romances, including *Lord Sayer's Ghost, A Rake's Reform, Covington's Folly, A Daring Deception, Lady Megan's Masquerade* and *A Suitable Connection.* Cindy's newest Regency romance, *The Actress and the Marquis,* will be published in March 1997. Cindy loves hearing from her readers, and you may write to her c/o Zebra Books. Please include a self-addressed stamped envelope if you wish a response.

The Vampire Rogue

Valerie King

One

Emma could not see Lord Chace clearly even though she
was standing close to him, her hands held tightly in his clasp.
The darkness of the fog-shrouded night and the heavy limbs
of the Spanish chestnut tree overhanging the lawn prevented
her from actually seeing his face. Lights from the well-lit ballroom on the second floor of the dilapidated castle glimmered
ineffectively into the mist. Still, she knew what he looked like
as he whispered into her ear, his breath warm on her cheek.

"Come with me to the Continent—a fortnight, a month, a
sennight. I should be content with just a sennight. Only say
you will come with me." In turn, he drew each of her hands
to his lips and placed gentle kisses on her fingers.

His conduct was scandalous and reprehensible. She knew as
much. Why, then, had she deserted her guests and allowed one
of the beau monde's most notorious rogues to entice her into
the eerie, secluded garden? She didn't know. Well, perhaps she
knew very well, but she thought it wise not to think about that.
Instead, she responded to his invitation.

"What a simpleton you are, Chace, to think that I could be
persuaded to join you in Europe simply because you have me
alone under this tree."

He chuckled, but did not pay heed to her rebuff. Instead, he released her hands quite suddenly, took her in his arms, and drew her roughly against him—swift movements that quite robbed her of breath and sent a shiver of excitement rolling through her. Heaven help her! She liked Lord Chace ever so much! He seemed to know instinctively what pleased her.

As a wealthy heiress, most of her beaus danced about her slippers as though she were a delicate succession house flower. But not Lord Chace. He treated her like—well, like a woman.

Heaven help her! She liked him very much!

He placed a series of light, flirtatious kisses on her cheek. She knew precisely what he meant to do and that he had planned his assault with care.

For one thing, he had already removed her black mask as well as his own intricate, heavy mask of a buck's head made of felt, antlers and all. Both masks were now sitting in quiet, stately dignity on the gray stones of the terrace some thirty feet away. For another, he had taken her away from the curious scandal-seekers who were presently dancing the waltz in her ballroom.

"You know you want to come with me," he whispered, commencing a second volley of fire. "You're of an age to do whatever you please and no one would fault you."

"You are being absurd," she returned, taking forbidden delight in the strength of his arms about her, in the sound of his resonant voice, in the sheer enjoyment of doing something against the order of the day.

She was used to his seductive advances, for from the first, when she had met him at her come-out ball some three years earlier, he had been intent on stealing her heart and, by all indications, her maidenly virtue as well.

Until tonight, however, she had never even let him kiss her. She shouldn't do so now, but the mist swirling all about the skirts of her white silk gown was having a strange effect on her. She should push him away. She should not be letting him drift his lips down her cheek as he was.

She drew back and for some reason looked up at the balcony

attached to the ballroom. Through the white fog she saw the dim outline of a man. An odd dizziness began to assail her and her thoughts were drawn back quite suddenly to the curious estate documents she had been reviewing, for the hundredth time, only that morning—documents that spoke of the living dead, of flying creatures, of vampires. Of course there were no such things as beings who drank the blood of the living in order to survive. These were myths only. Yet this particular myth had woven a constant thread into the papers belonging to several past owners of Castle Breage. And now the castle belonged to her. Several times the documents had warned against filling in the moat of the castle, for in doing so—according to legend— she would be inviting the return of the vampires.

The dizziness in her mind increased. She felt as though her mind were being touched and probed by the man on the balcony. But that was impossible.

She turned back to Chace and her senses became fixed quite suddenly on how strong his hand was as he pulled her even more closely to him. His muscular thighs were pressed against her legs and she parted her lips, releasing a sigh of pleasure so profound, she felt Lord Chace become very still.

"Kiss me," she murmured. All she wanted was a kiss. More than anything, a kiss.

She felt his lips softly on her cheek. She could hardly breathe. Again she begged him to kiss her.

In the depths of her mind, Emma knew that something was not right, but on the surface of her mind so much pleasure had begun to move languidly over her that she didn't care if the whole world had suddenly gone to the devil. She wanted only one thing, for Chace's lips to be on hers.

"Emma," came his deep-throated whisper.

"Chace," she murmured. The next moment he was kissing her deeply and passionately, tasting of her, searching her roughly, sweetly, seductively.

She was falling into the center of the earth in a swift, complete movement. Or was she floating, was the mist lifting them both high in the air? Had she moved into another world? She slipped her arms about his neck, he moaned her name, she whispered his in return.

She wanted him to ask her again to come to the Continent with him. She would say yes this time. She would.

A voice intruded from afar. "Emma!" She heard her aunt calling to her as though from outside a dream. She tried to draw back from Chace, but he held her imprisoned within his arms.

"I must—" she muttered lethargically. She didn't want to leave him, she didn't want to respond to her aunt's voice. She kissed Chace hard again. She felt herself being pressed to the mossy earth. Her foot slid on the grass, Chace lost his balance. He slipped. The spell broke as a rock dug into her leg.

"Emma, where are you?"

Emma opened her eyes, her senses clearing abruptly. She wasn't certain where she was, or what had just happened.

"Ow!" she cried, the rock biting her thigh. "Chace, whatever are you doing? Get off me."

"I slipped. I'm sorry. But why are you miffed? I thought you wanted me to kiss you." He rolled onto his side, freeing her legs.

She still couldn't see his face and she was cold from having been in the mist for so long without even her shawl to protect her.

"You've tricked me somehow!" she cried. "Chace, how could you!" She rose to her feet, and as she did so she heard the white silk of her ball gown rip, as her foot got caught in the hem. "Oh, dear! Look what I've done!" She began brushing out her skirts and felt for the rip, which she discovered to be the smallest tear at her high waistline. Chace was still sitting on the damp ground, staring up at her. His face, dimly lit by the light from the ballroom, held an expression of bewilderment.

"You are such a rogue!" she cried at last, then turned on her heel and headed back to the terrace.

"Where have you been?" her aunt called to her as she stepped from the mist into the light. "Your butler has been searching for you everywhere. Supper has been ready these twenty minutes and more and why are there leaves and dirt on your gown?"

"You might as well know—Chace kissed me, and I don't know why I let him!" She mounted the steps of the terrace and took her mask, which her aunt held out to her.

"I could tell you why, but you'd only think the worse of me, so I won't. All I know is that if I was twenty—well, thirty—years younger, I'd set my cap for that fellow as quick as the cat could lick her ear. My word! The best-turned leg I've seen in over a decade! And such stunning eyes—the most brilliant green!" She clicked her tongue and began brushing at the debris on Emma's skirts and afterward plucking leaves out of her hair.

"He's a very bad man," Emma said.

When her aunt sighed lustily in response, Emma rolled her eyes and tied her mask about her head.

When Chace emerged from the mist, Emma turned to look at him and shook her head impatiently. Why must he be so handsome, she thought distractedly. She had been half in love with him forever, or perhaps three-quarters in love with him, or, dash it all, maybe she had been fully in love with him since the day she met him nearly three years ago. For three years he had driven her to distraction.

She looked at the crooked, shameless smile on his face and recalled the moment she had first laid eyes on him. He had come up to her at her presentation ball, taken her hand in his, and even with Aunt Powler staring at him in astonishment, he had kissed her wrist rakishly, then turned to wink at her poor aunt. He had then moved on, his head high, his expression if not arrogant then thoroughly confident, his gait provokingly self-possessed.

She had watched him closely after that, observing that all eyes were upon him when he entered a room, when he spoke, when he singled a lady out. Who could not help but watch Lord Chace, or admire his broad shoulders, narrow waist, and perfectly proportioned physique. He was godlike, a Grecian athlete, a Roman gladiator, one of Arthur's knights.

She had had only one thought at her come-out ball, that she wanted to marry Lord Chace. But there was an incredibly poor chance of that ever happening. Her wish to become Lady Chace had been neither unique nor original. A dozen of her friends had expressed the very same notion, time and again. Lord Chace, Lord Chace, Lord Chace.

They had tried. And she tried. At least for a month.

But when he showed no sign of his heart becoming engaged, she had given up her silly schoolgirl dream and began to ignore the handsome viscount. Not viciously, of course. Hers was not a cold, vengeful heart. Still, she had no use for a man who liked to keep a dozen ladies dangling after him.

Yet, how odd to think that within a sennight of her disinterest he had come around to begin his haunting of her. The more cool and reserved she became, the more she insisted on rational conversation with him; the more she pressed him not to ply her with his absurd, rakish attentions, the more he began moving restlessly about the edges of her life like a hungry wolf.

So it had been for the past three years.

And tonight she had let him kiss her, but she couldn't understand why. Suddenly, she recalled the man in the mist and glanced up at the balcony overhead. But he was not there. The balcony was empty. She also recalled how his presence had put her oddly in mind of the vampirish legacy, absurd as it was, belonging to Castle Breage.

She gave herself a mental shake, and smiled. How silly of her to be thinking of vampires and how truly absurd to blaming a vampire for her sudden and overpowering desire to be kissed by Lord Chace. But then, she was giving a Halloween ball, so what else could she expect but a little mystery and mayhem. Besides, the grounds were covered with mist and she was being hunted, though not by a vampire, but by a wolf.

Turning back to Chace, she thought he rather looked like a wolf with his strange, beautiful green eyes slanted beneath strongly arched brows. He was certainly a handsome man, or wolf, or whatever he was. He mounted the steps and donned his costume, which included the fabricated head of a stag—quite lifelike in design—and a long cape billowing out from the base of the stag's head to cover his evening dress.

"My lord," Aunt Powler said to him, shocked. "You ought at least to brush yourself off before you enter the ballroom, or everyone will know you have been attempting to seduce my niece—again!"

"Of course, Mrs. Powler. How stupid of me!" He then set to holding his long cape away from his black coat and pantaloons and slapping at the elegant superfine fabric.

Aunt Powler was a plump lady of fifty-five, or though she said. By her own calculations, Emma knew her aunt to be nearer to a decade beyond her professed age. She had graying blond hair, light blue eyes, and a disposition mingling the raucous, less restrained attitudes of the previous generation and a sweetness of temperament that made her a favorite in Mayfair's most prominent ballrooms and drawing rooms, especially with the men.

"I wouldn't tease your niece at all," he said, smiling at her wickedly as he brushed away the leaves from his pantaloons. "If *you* would agree to part with a kiss or two yourself."

Aunt Powler pursed her lips and attempted to appear severe, but she succeeded only in looking adorable, which caused Lord Chace to smile. "There, you see! You know what I am saying is true!"

"I won't listen to such humbug!" she cried, trying to restrain a chuckle but failing. "You owe an apology to my niece, and I insist you beg her for a waltz as your atonement."

"Aunt!" Emma cried. "You are giving him the very thing he wants! Don't you see as much?"

"Nonsense!" Aunt Powler cried.

Lord Chace shifted his gaze to Emma, and winked. "I must

atone for my wretched conduct, Miss Keverne, your aunt has made her pronouncement. And now that I think on it, a waltz with you will do as well as any other punishment. What do you say?"

Emma saw that his green eyes were dancing with amusement. "I say that you are the most odious man of my acquaintance."

He turned instantly to Aunt Powler. "See how graciously she has acquiesced? Do you think she loves me?"

"I think you are self-indulgent and rather shameless, but I like you. If you have any sense at all, you'll marry my niece and be quick about it. Now, the pair of you, come! We've guests to feed!" When Chace bowed to her and caught her cheek with one of his soft felt antlers, Aunt Powler chuckled, pushed the antler aside, and led the way back into the castle.

Chace held Emma back, and when her aunt had passed into the castle, he whispered, "We could steal a few more minutes under the chestnut trees, if you are of a mind."

She drew in her breath sharply. "Odious, odious man!" she cried, picking up her skirts at the same time and turning to walk briskly away from him.

After supper, the revelers' costumes and masks were set aside in favor of enjoying the last hours of the Halloween ball in comfort. Chace drew Emma out for his waltz of atonement, and when the orchestra struck its first note, he began guiding her expertly about the room.

He whirled her around and around, up and back, the length of the polished planked floor. A single, massive chandelier lit the ancient ballroom in a quiet glow that lent a romantic, warm atmosphere to the otherwise scarred and dilapidated chamber. A large stone fireplace glowed with the dull red embers of what had begun as a large wood fire. Bursts of laughter erupted now and again among the dancers, the sliding of feet a constant rhythm against the music of the orchestra. The musicians were settled in an alcove adjacent to the fireplace.

Chace was an uncommonly good dancer, especially for a man who enjoyed sport as much as he did. In many ways, Emma thought as she looked up into his green eyes, he was a remarkable specimen of a man. He was undeniably handsome. His brows were dark brown, like his hair, which was brushed forward at his temples like a Roman senator's. His cheekbones were high and pronounced, his jaw was firm, his nose straight, and his lips were so very soft and, yes, she admitted, quite sensual. But it wasn't just his physical attributes that so appealed to her. When pressed—through any number of devious means—she had been able to force him to reveal several unsuspecting qualities.

He had a kind heart, for one thing. He was solicitous and sympathetic with those who were ill, and he helped to support an East London orphanage through quarterly donations.

He was generous with his servants, concerned for their well-being and comfort, and never spoke harshly to any of his staff. He was an excellent master and he had a good mind which had been trained at Oxford and not just superficially. Again, when pressed, he could argue any position of a given debate, which for her meant that his thoughts could be flexible—a most critical quality in a husband, surely.

Lastly, she had had an opportunity to witness him with his sister's children last February. He was a devoted, considerate uncle who enjoyed teaching his nieces and nephews to ride, to play at spillikens, and to master the intricacies of fencing, which he taught patiently even to the girls—though quite against his sister's wishes and knowledge.

"What are you thinking?" he asked.

She gave her head a shake. "Of having learned last spring that you have been teaching Annabelle and Horatia to fence."

He smiled wickedly. "Sophia was mad as fire."

"And you enjoyed watching her eyes spark and smoke, didn't you!"

He sighed contentedly. "Yes," he admitted. "I did. Very much so."

"You are a wretched, wretched man!" she cried playfully. She had long since forgiven his conduct beneath the Spanish chestnut trees. "And how very glad I am that you are not my brother."

He opened his eyes wide. "I must confess, I am grateful as well that we are not related, especially since I have just kissed you."

She gasped at his audacity at actually alluding to such a thing. But then, she frequently gasped in his presence, which she suspected was the reason he continued to make his scandalous observations and speeches.

Her gaze fell to his lips, and her thoughts were again drawn to the kiss they had shared so recently.

Why had she allowed him to assault her, and that so thoroughly?

She felt a blush rise on her cheeks as she remembered how fully he had bruised her mouth and how much the sensation had given her a pleasure she had never dreamed possible.

"You will love Paris," he whispered, pulling her suddenly toward him during a turn of the dance.

"I will not go to Paris with you," she whispered in response, wondering if he had somehow divined her thoughts. "I don't know why I let you kiss me as I did, but I don't intend to let you do so again. So, you can forgot about anything so ridiculous as a tryst in Paris."

"You enjoyed being kissed," he returned, leaning scandalously close to her ear as he again whirled her about.

She drew back from him and eyed him piercingly. "No more nonsense," she stated. "Or I shall leave you standing alone on this ballroom floor."

A crooked smile overtook his face. "You wouldn't do that," he said, daring her.

"Wouldn't I just," she snapped in response.

She began to quickly draw her hand from his, and he was

equally as quick to respond, exclaiming, "All right! No more nonsense. At least for the present."

She relented at once and allowed him to continue partnering her about the floor. It wouldn't do to cause tongues to wag by leaving him alone during a waltz, she told herself. But even as the words formed themselves in her brain, she knew that this wasn't the real reason she continued to dance with him. The truth was, she couldn't help herself. When she was with Chace she felt as though her heart were on fire. Something about him made her feel so fully and completely alive. She thoroughly enjoyed his flirtations, and so long as he did not very frequently pass the bounds of propriety, she would give herself over to the pleasure of his company.

She frowned as he guided her around and around, up and back. But what of the kiss, she wondered. She had felt so strange beneath the chestnut tree and she had behaved in a manner at odds with her usual sensible self. But why?

At that moment her gaze was drawn quite suddenly to a man standing by the fireplace, a man she did not know. What was a stranger doing at her ball? It was possible, of course, that her aunt had invited him, yet how unlike Aunt Powler not to have informed her of the addition to the guest list.

Whatever the case, he was an attractive man. He wore exquisite black evening dress and his neckcloth was tied with great precision and care. He wore his glossy black hair cut à la Brutus and his eyes glittered in the dim candlelight like black volcanic glass. He was watching her, and for some reason she couldn't quite take her gaze from him.

His expression was familiar, rakelike, similar to the arrogant, self-assured smile and piercing stare Chace wore when he was readying himself to pursue a female.

Another rogue, she marveled absently.

"Who are you staring at?" he asked. As he turned her within the movements of the waltz, he, too, caught sight of the man. "Who is he? I can't say that I've ever seen him before, and I thought I knew all your guests."

"I don't know him either," Emma murmured. "Yet, he is so familiar to me—I know I've seen him before somewhere. But I just don't quite remember."

"A friend of your aunt's, then?"

"Perhaps," Emma said. "That must be it. She has a very large acquaintance and a certain type of man has always appealed to her." She smiled wickedly as she glanced back at Chace.

Chace chuckled, but then fell silent as they progressed down the length of the ballroom. When they had reached the large windows overlooking the terrace and the Spanish chestnut trees, Chace said, "Why do you keep looking at him? I don't think I care for how he stares at you. Emma?"

Emma heard him but only faintly. She felt odd again, just as she had earlier, outside in the mist, moments before Chace had kissed her so scandalously.

She shifted her gaze from the stranger to Chace. She looked into his eyes, she squeezed his fingers, she moved into him. She saw him blink at her in surprise.

"Kiss me," she said. Was this her voice? Was she speaking? Oh, she wanted Chace to kiss her again so very much!

For the first time in his life, Chace was utterly astounded.

Emma Keverne had asked him to kiss her!

He should have been exultant at the expression on her face, an expression he had been hoping to achieve for the past three years. But something about the situation did not seem right to him.

For three years he had been flirting outrageously with the lovely heiress, in part because he wondered whether or not he could actually seduce such a strong-willed innocent and in part because it was so much devilish fun. What a wondrous conquest it would be, too, if he could one day win her heart and her body and make her his mistress. If he felt a trifle guilty at having made an innocent the object of his pursuit, he somehow managed to overcome such useless thoughts and sensations. He wanted Emma, and whether she was innocent or not, he would have her. He had made it clear to her that he was a rogue, he had never pretended to be anything else. So if she was hoping for a tidy wedding breakfast, then she was not the sensible female he believed her to be.

No, if Emma agreed to go to Paris with him, he knew quite well she would understand the implications of such a journey.

So here she was, begging to be kissed in both her words and in her demeanor. Here he was, ready to oblige her, except . . .

Except, the devil take it, something wasn't right. Emma would never oblige him like this. Never. He knew her too well, her character, her diffidence toward his advances, the boundaries of her flirtations. And now that he thought about it—damme, even the kiss he had stolen from her beneath the chestnut tree had a deuced funny feel to it. Not that he hadn't enjoyed taking the object of his flirtations in his arms and kissing beautiful Emma so thoroughly, but why had she so suddenly acquiesced, falling into his arms as though she had done so a thousand times before?

Still, as he turned her about the ballroom, he thought never had she been so pretty as she was now, looking up at him with her face full of promises. She was a diamond of the first stare—a great beauty. Her black hair was luxuriantly thick, and she had refused to crop it as many of the ladies of his acquaintance had, following Caroline Lamb's lead. No, Emma Keverne had kept her tresses, and more than once he had wished he could see what she would look like with her thick black mane cascading about her creamy white shoulders. Her complexion was entirely edible, milky and tinged with roses. Her eyes were an unusual hazel color, flecked with gold and brown and green hues. Her nose was charmingly retroussé, her lips, just as he had imagined a hundred times before and finally discovered tonight, were delightfully kissable.

He recalled her come-out ball and how he had stunned her by placing a kiss on her wrist—and that in full view of her aunt! He liked that she hadn't flinched a bit and he had liked even more that her gaze had followed him everywhere that night and for a month afterward.

Then she had done the unthinkable—she had scorned him. Oh, not as many damsels before her had done, by lifting her nose to him. She had merely turned her attention elsewhere even though he had been so carefully nurturing her obsession for him—an obsession that proved not to be an obsession at all.

For a few days he had been confused as to why the many dances he had previously cast her, the several conversations he had deigned to conduct with her, the strong glances he had bestowed on her from across a ballroom floor had not been sufficient to bind her obsessively to him. But so they hadn't. In fact, she had become utterly disinterested.

At first he had suspected she was employing artifice, that she had been trying to gain his attention by ignoring him. But in the end, after a week of living with her lack of attentions, he had had to accept she was disinterested and nothing more.

Then he had begun his campaign in full. He watched her respond, yet it seemed somehow that she had gained the upper hand, always taking him to a delightful point of flirtation and flirtatious tension, then she would draw back behind a professed screen of maidenly virtue. She was certainly unique and had sustained his interest for three years now—three years! It seemed incomprehensible, and of late, the betting at White's had begun to proliferate on just how soon he would offer for Miss Keverne.

Which, of course, he never meant to. He had no intention of marrying, now or ever. He had three nephews in line to succeed him as heir to his viscountcy and he would rather die a rake and a rogue than leg-shackle himself to the insipidity of the married state.

No, he knew precisely what he wanted of Emma Keverne, be it so utterly wicked and ignoble. He wanted to conquer her, to take her to Europe, to possess her completely, innocent though she was. Which was why he ought to be gratified now as he looked down into her hazel eyes, glittering with desire. But he knew something was not right, not by half.

Full of doubts about what was happening to her, he proceeded carefully. "I'd love to kiss you, Emma, but here?"

"You're right," she breathed, her clasp about his hand growing tighter and more tense. "Not here. Take me—take me anywhere, into the hallways, the stairwell, into the shadows. Only take me—now."

Her voice was a trail of murmurings and breathless longings.

"Emma," he said sharply. "You are speaking fustian! Stop it at once!"

She shook her head, blinked several times, and her hazel eyes suddenly came into focus. "Dear God," she cried. "Did I? Oh, Chace, I didn't ask you to kiss me again, did I?"

"Is something wrong, Emma? I don't like to mention it, but you are behaving as though you've become addled—quite unlike yourself."

She glanced quickly back to the fireplace and at the same time the waltz drew to a close. "He's gone," she said. "That man—that strange man. I wonder—" She did not complete her thought, but added quickly, "I think I know who he is. But it seems so impossible! Yet it must be him!"

Chace turned to the fireplace as well, then let his gaze drift quickly about the ballroom. The stranger was indeed gone.

"Emma, what are you talking about?" he asked.

"Never mind that," she said. The usual rise of conversations replaced the lilting music. She slipped her arm about his and slowly began guiding him toward the ballroom doors. "Only answer my question—did I again ask you to kiss me?"

"Yes—you did," he responded, a frown between his brows. He smiled crookedly. "And ordinarily I would be immensely pleased and hopeful that you'd come round at last, but I begin to fear something is amiss. Am I right?"

"Yes," she responded simply. "Only, come with me to the gallery. I've something to show you."

Two

Emma held Chace's arm tightly as she led him from the ballroom, through an antechamber, and into the hallway leading to the staircase. Her chest felt constricted as she reached the landing at the top of the stairs which led to the gallery that connected the receiving room to the west tower. Her mouth felt dry and her heart was now pounding in her chest.

Crossing the landing at the top of the stairs, she glanced down into the massive stone entrance hall below. What a strange house this is, she thought.

Castle Breage was a curious edifice that was more manor house than castle. An ambitious ancestor, a Norman knight by the name of St. Austell, had built the castle in the twelfth century. In its day, the stone structure had been a complete working castle, fit with moat, bridge, and iron portcullis. Twin towers rose some five stories in height, each bearing a functioning parapet and slitted with apertures for the bowmen. A wall-walk had surrounded the castle, patrolled by the knight's army and protecting the castle keep. How odd to think of so much history having come to belong exclusively to her.

Yet the castle was not much of a bargain. All that remained today of the original structure were the twin gray stone towers that had been incorporated into an Elizabethan house of three stories surrounding a weed-ridden courtyard. The entrance hall, leading through a doorway over which was hung the iron portcullis, was a lofty chamber, icy cold year-round and constructed of stone, including the wide staircase that rose to the first floor.

Magnificent armor—polished for the occasion of Emma's Halloween ball—stood in stately dignity about the perimeter of the hall.

She shuddered as she let her gaze quickly take in so many implements of war—the suits of armor, shields, lances, and cruel, barbed maces, the latter designed to rip through heavy armor.

"What is it?" Chace asked. "Why are you staring down at the entrance hall? Did you see that man again?"

Emma shook her head. "No, but I have a terrible feeling," she returned as they finally crossed the landing, then rounded the corner of the hall that brought them into the gallery. "A sense of dread that I cannot escape."

Chace chuckled. "Almost, you frighten me."

"I think you ought to be frightened a little," she said. They passed several portraits, many of which had suffered from the effects of mildew, until they came upon the portrait of a family—a mother holding her newborn child lovingly in her arms, a sweet smile on her face. Behind her stood Emma's relative, a distant cousin by the name of Edward St. Austell. "Edward, Mary, and young Benedict."

Chace frowned down at her. "Does this mean something to you?" She looked up at him as a faint ringing began to sound in her ears. His face was dimly lit by the glow of candles arrayed in several wall sconces opposite the portraits. Fear began to slide through her veins. Her heart was pounding in her chest. Chace took hold of her arm. "Who are they?" he asked. "Why have you grown so pale?"

"Chace, something is going to happen, but I don't know what. Something having to do with this family. I feel so peculiar. I read about the family in the estate documents. Edward, his wife, and his son disappeared when Benedict was eight years old in circumstances so mysterious as to be macabre. Blood was found on each of their pillows and their coach was missing. But a search of the estate and the moors beyond, a questioning at various inns in a several-mile radius, even in

Falmouth, proved fruitless. They simply disappeared. They were never found after that night."

She watched Chace look up the hall, then down the hall. "You have me so jittery that I vow I just heard laughter," he said. "A man's laughter, deep and jeering." He gave himself a shake and laughed aloud himself. "You are very good at teasing me, Emma Keverne. Now, why don't we return to the ball, or better yet, since we are now in the shadows, why don't I—" He took a step toward her as if to continue his earlier advances, but she placed a trembling hand on his chest.

"Chace," she whispered. "I'm not finished. There is something you must see."

"Emma, you have tears in your eyes!" he cried.

She covered her mouth, fear having taken strong hold of her. She understood—or at least thought she understood now—what was happening. Her knees were weak. She brushed past him and ignored the next three portraits, moving to stand in front of the painting of a gentleman sporting a long, curling black wig. He stood with a hand on his hip in the attitude of a man who controlled his world. His eyes were black, his complexion pale, his lips curved in an arrogant, knowing smile.

She heard Chace draw in his breath sharply. "But—I don't understand? There must be some mistake. Who is this man?"

"Count Lansallos. He arrived at Castle Breage in the sixteen hundreds with a claim to the property, since he was descended from the St. Austells on the female side. He later adopted the St. Austell name, but in all the papers I could find, he was always referred to as Lansallos. He married, bore three children, and one day vanished, just as Edward St. Austell and his family vanished."

"What are you suggesting?" Chace whispered, taking a step closer to the portrait. "That man—in the ballroom, by the fireplace—he looked so much like your count. He must be a relative, then."

Emma shook her head. "No. He *is* Count Lansallos. I shouldn't have had the moat filled in this summer. I found papers among the estate warning me against it, but I thought it all humbug. Now I know I have behaved foolishly."

A movement at the far end of the gallery, where the hallway joined the tower, tore Emma's gaze from the portrait. She caught her breath as a child emerged from a secret door.

"Come!" the boy cried, gesturing frantically toward them.

On instinct, Emma began moving quickly to him, breaking into a run. The child held the secret door open for them both. "He's coming," he whispered, his young face twisted with concern. His eyes were a bright blue, a child's eyes, yet Emma thought they were oddly intelligent, beyond his years.

Chace, however, refused to pass into the passageway beyond the door and prevented Emma from immediately doing so as well. "Who are you?" he asked sharply. "Why should we follow you? A child's prank, if I'm not mistaken."

"Benedict," he responded. "I am Benedict St. Austell. Emma knows. She understands. If you want to live, you must come with me. You must come now."

Emma looked up at Chace, took sudden and strong hold of the lapel of his coat of black superfine, and pulled him into the passageway. He did not resist her.

Benedict then took command, squeezing by them both and with a lantern in his hand led them down another long hall, then a twisting of stairs. He paused at what appeared to be a wall, felt for a lever up and to the right, and a narrow door swung inward.

The next moment Emma was standing in the library on the ground floor, blinking at the several branches of candles that illuminated the chamber.

The boy, if he was a boy, moved quickly to the door and closed it. "We will be safe here, for a time."

"We are running from Lansallos, aren't we?" Emma queried.

Benedict nodded. "Of course, and you are very right to think you made a mistake in filling in the moat. Why didn't you heed Papa's warning? He was very clear in his instructions."

Emma shook her head. She felt weak and dizzy. "I thought

it all a passel of nonsense!" she cried. "The dead still living and sustaining their existence by taking the lifeblood of their victims—how could I believe this?"

"You have proof enough now," Benedict stated in a boy's voice, but with the logic of a man full grown.

An old man, Emma realized suddenly. The St. Austells disappeared in 1741. He ought to be six and seventy by now, she thought, staring distractedly at Benedict. "Yes, I have proof now," she murmured.

She looked back at Chace. He stood by the fireplace and stared into the bank of red glowing coals, a thoughtful yet horrified expression on his face. "I don't believe any of this," he stated at last, turning toward the child. "Who are you really and why are you so intent on disturbing Miss Keverne's peace of mind?"

Benedict did not try to argue with Chace as a child would have. Instead, he moved to sit on the edge of the library's ancient sofa, a worn, intricately carved relic covered in a faded moss-green velvet rubbed thin in spots from use and age. He clasped his hands lightly between his knees and responded. "You have every right to be skeptical, Lord Chace. It all seems preposterous in the extreme. I don't blame you for doubting the evidence you have witnessed thus far. I can't convince you of what is happening here—now—tonight. My only fear is that you will become convinced when it is too late." Benedict turned to look at him and held his gaze squarely for a moment.

"This *is* preposterous," Chace declared, an expression of stupefaction on his face.

Benedict rose from the sofa. "You must do as I say," he said, his voice and expression pleading. "Lansallos is very powerful—more powerful than either of you can imagine."

Emma moved to stand very near Chace and took his hand in hers. The fire was warm on her white skirts as she looked up into his face and squeezed his hand. "There can be no harm in doing as Benedict tells us if we are not in any danger. But set aside your reason for just a moment, set aside all that you know to be normal and true, and listen." She then revealed all that Edward St. Austell's papers had indicated, that Lansallos was a creature who had been born in the natural way but who had never died, and who lived by drinking the lifeblood of any unfortunate person who happened by him at the wrong moment. He had left Castle Breage, and his family, because he feared he would one day make them like himself. He told his wife to again refill the moat which had not been used for over a century. The water in the moat had then prevented him from living at the castle and he had quit Cornwall to live in the darkest, most backward places of Europe.

After many decades, however, his loneliness became acute, and when Edward St. Austell filled in the moat—also against prior warnings—he returned and because of his loneliness transformed the St. Austell family into his kind.

"You are speaking of vampires," Chace said, shaking his head in bewilderment. "A myth only—a story made up to frighten young children into better conduct."

"It is not a myth," Benedict stated.

Emma and Chace turned to look at him, and Emma's heart suddenly went out to the child who was not a child. She went to him and took his hand. "You are very sad," she said softly. "Your childhood—your life—was robbed from you. I can feel it."

An expression of acute suffering passed over his young features. He was a handsome boy, with curling blond hair, a straight nose, and a proud chin. "You can have no idea, the pain I—we—have suffered—Mama, Papa, and I. Immortality is always such an attractive notion, but the reality of this manner of existence, of always being the hunter, is beyond fatiguing. There is no rest when one must hunt and pursue and conquer. The drive is unbearable and leaves little rest for the soul. One feels compelled to always seek a victim and to entrap the victim through cunning and wiles and powers of which you cannot begin to conceive."

Chace drew close to the child and looked down at him with

a curious expression. "You have no choice," he said. Chace looked at Emma. He had such a strange look in his eye, one of understanding.

Emma thought that Benedict's description of his life was not far different from Chace's existence. She sensed he felt in some way like the poor boy. When he drew in his breath and slowly returned to the fireplace, she was sure of it.

Emma wished more than anything that she could speak with Chace about the thoughts that were now tormenting him, but there was something far more critical at stake—their lives, their precious mortality, if Emma did not mistake the matter.

"Are my guests and my servants in danger?" she asked.

Benedict shook his head. "Only you."

"I'm not certain I understand why," Emma said. Though she was reassured that her friends, her aunt, and Lord Chace were not threatened, she had read nothing in St. Austell's papers that would indicate otherwise, or why *she* in particular was in danger.

"Lansallos has taken a vow. He intends to give immortality to his nearest relative before taking the drink of life again."

Emma drew in her breath sharply. "You mean me?" she cried.

"Yes, but you mustn't worry," Benedict said hurriedly. "We have come to help you. I came ahead, as quickly as I could. Mama and Papa do not travel so easily as I. They are awaiting your arrival in Falmouth aboard a ship called *Victory*."

"Should we go now and bring them to Castle Breage?" she asked, her heart again beginning to pound in her chest.

Benedict shook his head. "It is too late. The hour is past three o'clock and soon the dawn will be upon us." Benedict's gaze drifted to her throat, and she felt a strange sensation sweep over her.

"How odd I feel—almost as if—"

Benedict released her hand and moved swiftly away from her, toward the secret passage. "I'm sorry," he murmured.

Emma's senses cleared quickly. "Oh, my!" she cried. "Then you—"

"I may be here to help," he offered by way of explanation. "But you must never forget that I am what I am. I must go. I haven't—taken some nourishment—for some time. I'll be back as soon as I can—"

"My guests?" Emma asked, startled. "You mean to attack them?"

Benedict broke into a smile. "My family drinks only the blood of lesser creatures. Now, listen sharply—collect as much garlic as you can find, silver crosses, and some Brussels lace. These will protect you."

When Chace joined Emma beside the sofa, Benedict looked longingly from one to the other. He then laughed bitterly and disappeared back into the secret passageway.

"Good God!" Chace cried. "I felt as though his mind was overpowering me just then, for a moment."

"So did I," Emma answered. She shifted her gaze from the closed, secret door to Chace. "I can't remember being more frightened," she whispered.

He slipped his arms gently about her. "We'll be all right—you'll be all right. I'll see to that, I promise."

She leaned her head against his shoulder. "When I read St. Austell's warnings, I thought it was some sort of absurd joke. I never credited any of it for a moment. My uncle was a recluse, you see. I never saw him above once in my entire life. Upon his death, I inherited the castle and Aunt Powler agreed that I could dispose of it as I wished. I thought it might be amusing to have an ancient relic in Cornwall to go to once or twice a year—for a Halloween ball. But I never supposed, never imagined—" She broke off, her own disbelief rising. She thought back, trying to determine when the whole situation began to rise. "The Spanish chestnut tree."

"What?"

"It all began there," she said, pulling back from him and looking into his green eyes. "You were flirting with me and the next moment I couldn't resist you. I was under a spell even then."

She saw an odd light enter his eye. "My spell," he said, a half-smile playing at the edges of his lips. "You were under my spell."

She smiled in return, grateful that the moment had taken a lighter turn. "I have been under your spell since my come-out ball three years ago."

"You have not," he stated, his arms still fully wrapped about her, disbelief on his face.

She didn't try to argue with him, but remained in the circle of his arms, intensely grateful that he was with her. "I'm glad you're here," she told him. Her fears having receded slightly, she became acutely aware of how intimate their embrace was. She could smell his shaving soap, a scent that brought a heady sensation flowing over her. She felt safe in his arms, impervious to anything. How odd to think that the presence of an immortal being would thrust her into Chace's arms, a position she had resisted for so many months and years. But now that she was there, she found her first schoolgirlish daydreams returning to her, of what it would be like to be loved by Chace, to become his wife, to share his bed.

Something of her thoughts must have communicated themselves to the viscount, since he suddenly leaned toward her and placed a warm kiss on her lips. She slipped a welcoming arm about his neck and kissed him in return. The teasing, the odd friendship, the seduction of the last three years began to flow through her. She allowed him to assault her deeply and passionately, as before yet not as before. This kiss was different from the one shared beneath the chestnut tree. She was under no spell except his this time.

"Emma," he said, drifting a trail of kisses over her cheek. His breath was warm on her neck as he began tracing the curves of her ear. She caught her breath. A spattering of gooseflesh rippled down her neck, her shoulder, her side. Then he was kissing her again, maddeningly, wondrously. Her mind drifted away from the library at Castle Breage. A wind began to move through her mind and her body. She felt caught up, enraptured by being in his arms. The wind roared through her.

"I loved you, Chace," she breathed between kisses. "From the first."

He looked as though he wanted to say something, but Benedict's voice intruded.

"Emma!" he cried sharply.

The intensity of his tone broke Chace's spell. Emma drew back slightly from him and turned to see the young boy emerge hastily from the secret door, then run toward the library doors.

"You must hurry!" he cried. "Why have you been dawdling in here? Lansallos is almost upon you! Leave at once and collect the items about which I told you!"

Chace whirled Emma instantly toward the door, and a moment later they were in the cold stone entrance hall. Benedict disappeared into the tower opposite the library. A chill at the shift in temperature shot through Emma. She shivered, wishing she had at least a shawl to cover her bare arms. From up the stairs she could hear the orchestra playing another waltz. From opposite the ballroom, on the west side of the mansion, giggling, along with a hum of conversation, drifted down from the drawing room.

They quickly climbed the stairs to the first floor, then the second floor, and went directly to Emma's bedchamber. The room was cold, the fire waiting to be lit when she retired for the night, but an oil lamp illuminated dimly the neatly dressed chamber.

Emma had refurbished her bedchamber upon coming to reside at Castle Breage in midsummer, decorating the whole of it en suite in a royal blue velvet trimmed with gold. Three arched windows in the gray stone wall to the right of her bed, presently covered with blue velvet draperies against an encroaching autumnal chill, gave the chamber a medieval cast.

Attached to her bedchamber and also to the right of her bed was a large dressing room in which her gowns, a fine dressing table, a chest of drawers, and a looking glass were kept. She passed the bed, whisking the lamp from the table next to her bed, and entered the dressing room.

She hunted through her jewel box for the three silver crosses she possessed, and having found them, she gave one to Chace. Removing her pearls, Chace helped her don the second cross, the third she kept clutched in her hand. She was about to quit the dressing room, when he said, "What of the Brussels lace? Do you own a shawl or a fichu or something?"

"Yes, of course," she cried, retracing her steps. Opening the bottom drawer of the chest of drawers she drew out a beautiful lace shawl.

She returned the lamp to its station beside her bed and a few moments more saw her running beside Chace toward the back stairs heading to the kitchens. Three flights more and she was in the nether regions, startling Cook by requesting, in as calm a manner as possible, several clusters of garlic.

"Whatevuh fer?" Cook asked, her eyes wide. "I mean, of course, Miss Reverne. But I do be that surprised by yer request!"

Emma laughed lightly. "A prank for my guests," she said with a bright smile. Cook relaxed instantly, though a frown of concern did not quite leave her eye as she procured the garlic.

Having it in hand, Emma left the kitchen and moved toward the back stairs again, but stopped before climbing the steps. She looked at Chace, who was holding the shawl. She lifted the large clusters of garlic with one hand and stared at them in bewilderment. "What on earth are we supposed to do now?" she cried frantically.

Chace laughed suddenly and Emma joined him. "Have we gone mad?" he queried.

Emma's laughter faded. "Oh, I wish we had, then I'm certain I wouldn't be nearly as frightened as I am at the moment."

"You'll do," he said, holding her gaze steadily.

Emma squared her shoulders. "Let's return to the antechamber behind the ballroom and line up our defenses there. What can Lansallos do with seventy people nearby?" She picked up a branch of candles from a table near the bottom of the stairs and moved as swiftly as she could up the stairwell toward the first floor without putting the flames out.

Since both the kitchens and the antechamber were at the back of the manor house, Emma reached the dilapidated antechamber in good order and without having seen even once the smallest sign of Lansallos. The room, decorated in the faded brocades of a half-century prior, smelled musty. For the Halloween ball Emma had closed the chamber off by boarding up the doorway and placing an ancient tapestry over the boards on the ballroom side. In the center of the chamber was a round table, scarred but at least free of dust, since Emma's primary housekeeping object had from the first been to maintain a clean if not perfectly decorated home.

She set the branch of candles and the lace shawl on the table. Chace settled the garlic next to the candles.

When these tasks were complete, he drew her opposite the door but behind the table. He held his arm tightly about her waist.

A man's low laughter rippled through the chamber.

"He is near," Emma whispered.

"His laughter again," Chace returned.

"I'm frightened," Emma said, taking in a gulp of air, her heart pounding in her ears.

He held her waist more tightly still.

"I can feel that he is close by," Emma said.

"I know. So can I."

Behind them came the muffled sounds of a country dance.

The door opened slowly. The blackness of the hall beyond was a tangible thing. Lansallos emerged, strolling into the antechamber as though he hadn't a care in the world.

He was remarkably handsome, and except for the unusual pallor of his complexion appeared as every other man of her acquaintance might have appeared—a little bored, a little amused, ready to be entertained at a ball.

"I've found you at last," he remarked easily, his dark eyes becoming fixed on Emma's face.

Already she felt faintly dizzy. Already feelings of longing were settling within her.

"How do you do, Count?" she offered politely.

He smiled. "Very, very well. Imagine my pleasure, my joy, when I realized you were having the moat filled in. You invited me here, you know, by doing so." His gaze drifted over her face, her hair, her gown. "And I must say, a prettier invitation I have not had in centuries. But you wear the wrong jewelry, my dear. Take it off."

Emma shook her head, knowing he was referring to the silver cross about her neck. At the same time, she felt his mind moving into hers and her resistance in quick stages began to weaken. He moved slowly toward the table. Not once did he even look at Chace, as though the viscount didn't exist.

From the corner of her eye she watched Chace take the cross from his pocket and hold it up to Lansallos. Lansallos closed his eyes, but paused in his steps.

"Leave her alone," Chace commanded.

Lansallos took a step backward and recovered his composure. Emma felt his hold on her mind relax as the count shifted his attention to Chace. "So you think you can protect her," he said. "You are a foolish man and I would suggest if you cherish your life, you will leave as quickly as you can."

Chace struggled to speak as he straightened his shoulders. "I won't . . . be . . . intimidated," Chace returned haltingly. Emma heard the pauses in his speech, so unlike him, and felt her fears return to her.

She held the lace up to Lansallos, who snatched the shawl from her and threw it over his shoulder. The lace had no effect on him at all!

Lansallos laughed, throwing his head back slightly. For the first time Emma caught sight of the points of his teeth, sharp, purposeful points. She grew instantly sick with dread.

Lansallos explained. "Benedict's little joke, I see. Did you think the lace would stop me? Benny knew I had been in love once with a capricious wench who favored Brussels lace. I tired of her, however, and in the end I took her life."

Very briefly the count's gaze drifted to the garlic. Emma instinctively picked up several cloves, rounded the table, and walked toward him. An expression of revulsion came over his face as he took several steps backward.

She felt his mind worming its way into her own. "Go away!" she cried, pausing in her steps.

Chace moved to stand next to her again.

Lansallos's lip curled as he met her gaze. Gone was all pretense to civility and courtesy. "Your defenses are paltry," he said evenly. "This is far from over. You've sampled only the smallest of my abilities and before the night is through, you'll know the heavier part of my hand."

He turned on his heel and left the antechamber.

Emma released a sigh she had not known was trapped in her throat. Still holding the garlic, she bid Chace come with her. She moved into the hallway that overlooked the courtyard in the center of the manor and said, "I intend to develop the headache. I think my guests ought to leave. You should leave too, Chace. In fact, I insist on it. I won't have your blood on my hands." She looked up at him and saw an expression on his face she had never seen before.

He lifted his chin. "If you think for even one moment that I would leave at a time like this, then you've never known the smallest part of my character. I should be offended, but I know your heart and that your intention is all honor and sacrifice. But don't ever suggest anything so dimwitted to me again."

Emma smiled, a warm sensation encompassing her heart. She knew she hadn't misjudged Chace. From the first, from that first moment at her come-out ball when her eyes had met his, she had known him. He was a gentleman in every sense of the word—except, of course, in his silly pursuit of females for sport. "Come then," she said. "Help me convince my guests that I am unwell."

Three

An hour before dawn, the house was quiet. Emma had been able to convince her aunt and her guests that she was suffering from a terrible headache, a whisker that had quite easily drawn the Halloween masquerade ball to a swift conclusion. Within a relatively short time she had seen the last of her guests depart for Trevisgate, a nearby village, or for Falmouth, where most of her friends and acquaintances would spend the remainder of the night before traveling home the following day. Aunt Powler had soon afterward sought the comfort of her bed, and Chace had emerged from his hiding place in the library.

Emma met him in the hall, holding high a branch of candles. "They are all gone," she stated, taking her skirts in hand as she prepared to mount the gray stone steps. "Will you come with me to my bedchamber? I think we will be safe there."

He smiled crookedly as he took the branch of candles from her and at the same time offered her his arm. "I have been waiting for this invitation for some time now, though I feel in good conscience I ought to remind you that though I will undoubtedly be perfectly secure in your bedchamber, you will not!"

She did not mistake his meaning. "I should reprimand you," she returned, trying for a light note she did not feel. "But our present circumstances prevent me from saying anything to you other than that I am glad you are willing to accept this particular invitation and I am perfectly happy to risk your incorrigible presence in my room."

He only chuckled as he supported her up the stairs.

Once within the safety of her bedchamber, Chace locked the door and placed a chair beneath the knob in hopes of deterring Lansallos. Emma crossed the room and lifted back one of the royal blue velvet drapes, wanting more than anything to see a glimmer of dawn breaking through the mist. She groaned as only blackness greeted her eye, the blackness of a thick white mist that obscured even the Spanish chestnuts from view.

Turning around to glance at the chamber, she wondered if she had done all she could to protect herself and Chace. She still wore one of the silver crosses about her neck, Chace had one, and she settled the third one on the table beside her bed. But where had she put the garlic?

Realizing she had left the clusters on the chest of drawers in her dressing room, she quickly gathered them up, then returned to her bedchamber door. She placed all of them in a line at the base of the door, hoping that they might serve to keep the count from entering her room.

She stared down at the garlic and touched the silver cross at her neck. Lansallos had said their defenses were paltry. Were they, she wondered anxiously.

She glanced over her shoulder and saw that Chace was lighting the fire. Only then, as the flames began to dance, did Emma realize she was cold. She had been so occupied by seeing to her guests and by worrying about Count Lansallos that she had not considered her own comfort.

Sighing with an encroaching fatigue, she returned to the dressing room to retrieve a shawl of soft gray wool from her wardrobe. "Why don't we play at cards for a time until the dawn comes and we can be easy again?" she called to Chace as she emerged from the dressing room.

Chace settled the poker on the hearth and rose to his full height. "An excellent notion," he said. "I'll set up the table."

Emma searched the nightstand on the far wall beside her bed and found in its drawer a deck of playing cards. She was feeling tired and worn, the earlier preparation for the ball and the later trauma of confronting Lansallos having left her bones dull and aching. She moved lethargically across the room back to the fireplace.

Chace had drawn forward a small table which he settled in front of the fire. A blue velvet wing chair for Emma and a small black-lacquered chair for himself soon saw them seated and engaged in a brisk game of piquet.

After losing a round, Chace threw down his cards somewhat distractedly and glanced all about her bedroom. "A very pretty chamber," he remarked. "Blue suits you, I think. A lovely contrast to your black hair."

Emma sighed, shuffled the cards, and summoned a smile. "Thank you, Chace," she said. "You've a charming ability to help me relax, even now, when I'm nearly frightened out of my wits."

He reached across the table and touched her hand in a reassuring gesture. "We'll keep playing," he said. "The dawn cannot be far away now."

The card play that followed did little, however, to allay Emma's sense that Lansallos could appear at any moment. For one thing, ever since Benedict had first appeared at the end of the gallery earlier in the evening, she feared that more secret entrances and passageways existed with which the count might be familiar and of which she might be ignorant.

She glanced at the clock on the mantel and saw that the hour was closing on six o'clock. At what hour did dawn arrive in late October—no, early November? She wasn't sure. From the documents left to the estate she had become aware of some of the idiosyncrasies of the vampirish state and that the dawn, that is, *light,* was deadly to the nocturnal creatures. She and Chace, therefore, had only to make it through the remaining hour or so and their lives would be spared for at least another day.

"You are not attending to your cards," Chace said lightly. "You've just laid down your queen."

"Oh, how silly. But I fear I can scarcely concentrate."

"I know something we could do that would most certainly relieve your mind of its present concerns," he suggested ignobly.

Emma's cards slipped from her fingers and she gasped. "Chace!" she cried, knowing him far too well to have misunderstood him. "How can you say such a thing?" In spite of wishing it otherwise, she felt a blush creep up her cheeks. She gathered up her cards and continued the round.

"There, that's better," he said. "Admit that at least for a moment you forgot all about your fears."

Emma laughed. "What a rogue you are!"

"What else would you expect of me, given our present seclusion?" He glanced about the bedchamber, then looked back at her and smiled. "Have you ever done anything so very bad as this? To all intents and purposes—once this silly business regarding Count Lansallos is laid to rest—I will be able to boast of having spent the night in your bedroom."

In spite of herself, Emma felt better. Chace was being absurd, of course, but a little absurdity seemed to be just what she needed for the present. "You are being idiotish," she retorted. "Besides, no one would believe you anyway, and I certainly would have no intention of owning the truth."

He grimaced playfully. "You may be right. Perhaps I ought to take a souvenir before I go—as proof of my conquest—something you couldn't deny."

"What would you take?" she asked. Having lost the round, she gathered up the cards and began shuffling again. The minutes began ticking by and the light, teasing conversation that ensued convinced Emma that very soon they would be out of the woods. He named several articles within the chamber he thought might be proof of his visit—a hairpin, a shoe, a bottle of rosewater—but she countered that these items were no proof at all, since they would be indistinguishable from similar fripperies found in any other lady's boudoir.

When she won the next round, he stated he had grown fatigued with piquet and needed a different sort of diversion altogether. He rose from his Empire chair and rounded the table to drop to his knees beside her. "There is one thing you could give me that I would promise never to reveal," he whispered, laying his hand on her arm, a familiar, crooked smile on his lips.

Emma looked down at him and shook her black curls. "I can't give that to you, my lord," she murmured, smiling. "You know as much. So do stop pestering me."

"Will you give me a kiss, then?" he asked.

Again she shook her head.

"Please," he begged, leaning toward her. His breath was on her cheek and against her ear as he drew very close to her. "Just one," he whispered, sending gooseflesh rushing down her neck and side. "I promise to be very good."

Emma's mind became suddenly consumed with how very much she wanted Chace to kiss her. "No," she said softly yet firmly, her gaze sliding to his lips as she struggled within herself. "You know you shouldn't even be asking me such a thing."

"I know I *shouldn't*," he returned easily. How warm his breath was, how deeply resonant his voice. Emma closed her eyes and tried to still the flutterings of her heart. He continued. "But, then, I wasn't asking you whether or not I *should* ask for a kiss. I was merely making a gentle query—will you give me a kiss?"

Emma sighed. Of the moment, the thought of kissing Lord Chace seemed pleasant in the extreme. "No," she responded sadly. "Not now. It wouldn't be in the least sensible."

"Of course it's not sensible," he responded. "But I can see that you are not to be dissuaded from your refusal." He rose from his kneeling position, took her hands gently in his, and drew her to her feet. "I do have one request, however, which you might not find so impossible to fulfill."

She eyed him warily. "And what would that be?" she asked.

"I've always wondered how long your hair is. Would you let it down for me?"

Emma was a little surprised, but since his request was relatively harmless, she saw no reason not to oblige him. She smiled and without further argument began removing the several pins and ribbons that had kept her locks secured into a knot of cascading curls at the crown of her head. Before long her black mane was dancing past her shoulders.

He voiced his appreciation and began gently tugging on her curls. "You've beautiful tresses," he said softly. "What an exquisite woman you are. Oh, Emma, what am I going to do with you?"

She was looking into his green eyes and found that a riot of butterflies had begun to sweep about her stomach in an odd manner. "Chace," she answered quietly. "Whatever am I going to do with you?" She leaned into him and placed a hand on his chest, lifting her face to him.

When he took her in his arms, she didn't demur in the slightest. He kissed her, assaulting her sweetly. His tongue became a gentle search to which she submitted with a growing weakness in her knees. He held her tightly against him, a sensation she was beginning to enjoy almost as much as the manner in which he would play his lips against hers. "You are not an 'Ice Maiden,' " he said. "Emma, I think I'm falling—"

But his words drifted away as he suddenly slumped down to her feet.

"Chace!" she cried, trying to catch him. At the same time, she became painfully aware of the reason for his sudden faint. *Lansallos.*

The count was before her, having appeared as if from nowhere. He carried no weapon, so she could only presume that he had struck him brutally with his own fist. "How easy the pair of you have made this for me," he whispered, a hateful smile on his face.

She glanced past him and saw that the chair and the garlic were unmoved. Then he had not entered by way of the door. How had he come into her bedchamber? Was there a secret entrance of which she was unaware? There must have been.

Backing away from Lansallos, she returned her gaze to his

face. He seemed altered somehow. A vein showed at his temple and another pulsed along his right jaw. Was he tired, she wondered. Or just hungry?

Emma did not wait to converse with him, but ran to the table by the bed to retrieve her silver cross. Lansallos caught her from behind, apparently unaware of what she was doing. He took her into a rough embrace and kissed her once, hard on the mouth. "You will know more of that, my dear," he said.

A familiar dizziness began to overtake her as his mind began to work its powers within her own. Hoping that the silver cross would have an effect, she lifted her hand and pressed the cross into his cheek. He released her suddenly, crying out and brushing the cross away from him. The force of his release flung her onto the bed. He looked down at her, rage in his black eyes.

Emma held the cross toward him. She watched him take a step backward, then another. Hope began to rise in her heart. The mark of the cross on his cheek was a red flag against the white of his skin. She heard Chace groan. Lansallos paid him no heed.

"Chace!" Emma cried, but she received no response from him.

When she looked back at Lansallos, she realized she had made a mistake, for the moment her gaze met his, she began to feel dizzy again and wretchedly disoriented. Power emanated from the vampire, a power that began moving steadily through her mind. She dropped the cross, only faintly aware she had done so. Her eyes, her mind, her soul, were all for Lansallos. She slowly removed the cross from about her neck, then let it fall to the floor. All the while her gaze was fixed upon Lansallos.

What a handsome man he is, she thought, wondering why she had ever feared so exquisite a creature.

She slipped her legs over the side of the bed and rose to face him. Her fear of him was entirely gone. Only desire remained within her mind. He held his arms out to her. Languidly he moved toward her. She walked into his embrace and felt his strong arms surround her. She rolled her head to the side and felt the sharp points of his teeth on the tender flesh of her neck. She waited. Desire for him rolled through her in wave after wave.

Again she was thrown backward, this time to the floor, but why? Why would Lansallos want to be rid of her?

She glanced toward the count and saw that he was struggling with a man. What man? She gave her head a strong shake. Desire and dizziness began floating away. She looked back at Lansallos, and the horrible nature of her situation returned to her as she recalled precisely who he was and what he wanted of her.

"Chace!" she called to the viscount.

But he was no match for Lansallos. The count tossed him easily away from him. He crashed into the table on the far side of the bed, opposite the windows. She watched him fall unconscious to the floor. Lansallos moved toward him. Emma could see in his countenance his intent to kill the man she loved.

She glanced toward the draperies and the windows then to the clock on the mantel. Dawn must be near, she thought, wild with desperation. Perhaps near enough. She moved close to the center window, then called to Lansallos.

"Come to me!" she cried. "I can't bear being separated from you!" Would he respond to her? Would he believe her? Was she enticing enough to distract him from Chace?

She swept her long black curls around her neck, exposing her throat, knowing full well she was offering food to a starving man.

How quickly Lansallos forgot about Chace. She watched the vein at his temple and the one along his jawline pulse in anticipation. She felt behind her, catching the drapery firmly in her hand. She couldn't let his mind rule her entirely, or she would be lost indeed. She pretended, therefore, to already be within the clutches of his mesmerizing powers. She closed her eyes and moaned pathetically.

She heard his steps, she felt his nearness. When she opened

her eyes, he was frighteningly upon her. She flipped back the drapes. Only darkness rewarded her effort. Even so, Lansallos threw up an arm to protect himself.

"Confound it!" he cried, whirling away from her. "I've lost the hour! But I've not done with you yet! I will come back for you! Make no mistake!"

He ran to the door and cast aside the chair that Chace had earlier placed beneath the knob. The garlic had no effect on his flight. A moment more and he disappeared into the cold hallway beyond.

Emma remained by the window, holding the drapery back just in case he should decide for some reason to return and try again. The cooler air beyond the bedchamber flowed in from the hallway and she began to shiver. Her woolen shawl had been lost in the struggle.

She heard Chace moaning again. "Emma," he whispered.

She glanced back at the window, and after staring into the misty darkness for a moment, she finally saw what had frightened Lansallos away—a faint grayish glow heralding the dawn. Only then was she able to release her strong hold on the royal blue velvet drape.

Moving to the far side of the bed, she found Chace curled up on the floor, trying to right himself. He had a hand to his head, holding it as if he were in great pain. Dropping to her knees beside him, she touched his face, his arms, his hands.

He rolled onto his back and opened his eyes. "Are you all right?" he asked, wincing badly.

"Yes. He's gone. We made it through the night."

For a moment he said nothing, but finally smiled ruefully. "I guess I proved who is master, eh?"

"You were brilliant," she responded, refusing to allow him to think ill of himself.

He looked at her again. "And you are an excellent woman," he said. "I take it you saved my life."

"Nonsense. Let me help you gain your feet. You can rest on my bed. We are safe until nightfall."

Chace rose unsteadily and Emma helped him slide onto the bed. She covered him with blankets she retrieved from the chest of drawers in the dressing room. She would have removed his coat, but he was asleep before she could even offer to do so.

She felt suddenly drained and in great need of rest. She thought that for propriety's sake she ought to seek another bedchamber, but the fear of what had just transpired was too heavily upon her. She would remain with Chace.

After crossing the room, closing the door, and locking it, she crawled into bed beside him. When she drew near him, and placed her hand on his arm, he awoke sufficiently to pull her against him. Yet there was nothing roguish about this gesture which she found wondrously comforting, and before she could even form the thought that what they were doing was unthinkable, she fell into a deep sleep.

Emma felt something brush against her cheek. She was in the midst of a strange dream in which she was standing beneath one of the Spanish chestnut trees and leaves were falling all around her. She was frightened, but she didn't know why. A leaf brushed against her cheek, then another. She tried to brush the leaves away, but one of them caught her hand and held it firmly. Another and another began to come alive and attach themselves to her. She battled with sleep and the fear the nightmare was bringing to her.

She awoke suddenly, remembering Count Lansallos in a wrenching wave of terror.

"Gently," Chace whispered. "You've been tossing for some time now."

He was holding her hand.

"Oh," she breathed. "It's you. I thought—I didn't know. For a moment I feared Lansallos had returned. Is it—?" She looked toward the blue velvet drapes which were drawn tightly across the windows. But the glow of light in a pattern fitting the arched windows beyond told its own tale. "Thank God," she muttered.

"It's only three o'clock in the afternoon," Chace said. "We've time to spare, time to be safe."

Emma closed her eyes and ordered her heart to slow down. After a time she turned to look at Chace, who was leaning up on his elbow and looking down at her. He still held her hand, a gesture that soothed her immensely. "You saved my life," she said.

"And you saved mine," he returned. "The last thing I recall before regaining consciousness was a shadow hovering over me. I knew I was going to die. You are a very brave woman, Emma Keverne."

She squeezed his hand but could think of nothing to say. She had not been brave at all. She had done only what seemed sensible, given the particulars of the moment. "What do we do now?" she asked.

"Benedict spoke of retrieving his parents from a ship at Falmouth. I expect we ought to do so the moment night falls. Perhaps then we can forestall another of Lansallos's attacks."

She nodded. "We need help, that's for certain." She glanced down at her rumpled, white silk ball gown, "I long for a bath and a change of clothes." She then glanced at Chace. "But what of you? All you have is evening dress."

"I could send to Trevisgate for my portmanteaus." He was silent apace, his brow furrowed. "Only what to do about my valet? I don't want him to know what is going forward here. He is very protective of me and would probably suffer injury trying to be of service if he thought I was in danger. I think I shall dispatch him on an errand to Truro."

"That might be wise," she said. "And somehow I shall see that my servants are dismissed for the night. As for Aunt Powler, she will not leave me, nor will she like knowing you have been here all night."

Lord Chace kissed the back of her hand. "Unless I much mistake the matter, she will consider the event an act of God."

Emma laughed outright. "Well, yes, I suppose she will. I hope she does not offend you with her schemes to see the pair of us wed?"

"Aunt Powler could never offend me," he responded, placing yet another kiss on the back of her hand.

Emma gave him a sidelong glance. "Has the daylight returned your roguish ways to you?" she asked.

He lifted a brow. "If you recall, I kissed you more than once last night, or did you think my actions less roguish a few hours ago?"

Emma withdrew her hand from his. "You forget that I know you far too well, my lord Chace. Last night, when you kissed me, you were wearing an entirely different expression from what I see now."

"And what do you see?" he asked playfully.

"You look like the cat who ate the mouse."

He merely laughed in response.

If she knew the faintest disappointment, she refused to let the viscount know of it. Last night he had behaved differently toward her. For one thing, he had almost said he was falling in love with her. But now she saw only a familiar roguishness that would never embrace the married state.

She slipped from the bed and went into her wardrobe to fetch her brush. From long habit, she began smoothing out her tousled black locks and at the same time paced the long stone chamber. "I think we ought to tell my aunt that you got yourself monstrously foxed and that you fell asleep behind the sofa in the library."

He sat up, wincing as he did so. His right cheek was bruised from having battled Count Lansallos and there were bloodstains on his neckcloth from where his head had struck the table.

"What a delightful whisker," he remarked. "Though I don't hesitate to tell you, I take offense at the very notion of telling anyone I was so deeply in my cups, I actually lost consciousness. I've never done so, you know."

"Yes, yes, I know you are quite proud of your ability to hold your wine, but this way we can explain your rather battered appearance. Have you looked in a mirror yet?"

He shook his head. "I've been afraid to," he said, grimacing. "Between my unkempt appearance and my bruises, I fear I am disgracing my gender."

"You could never do that," Emma returned, offering her compliment in such a genuine and offhand manner that she could see she had caught Chace quite off his guard. Continuing to brush her hair in short jerks, she decided to elaborate. "You are always dressed immaculately," she said, enjoying the surprised lift of his brows. "And besides, you are so handsome that even with a stubble over your chin you are still uncommonly attractive. But of course you already know as much."

His smile became crooked. "Are you trying to flirt with me, Miss Keverne?"

"Not at all," she reassured him. "I am only saying what any woman of sense would say."

He leaned against the headboard of the beautifully carved cherrywood bed frame and crossed his legs at the ankles. "You never cease to surprise me," he said, giving his head a shake. "Just when I think I know you—"

"The trouble with you is that you believe everyone must have a motive because a motive for your conduct is all you've ever known, or allowed yourself to know."

He grew thoughtful for a moment. "Perhaps you are right. I have been thinking of Benedict and how he described his existence as a hunter."

"Does the shoe fit a bit too snugly?"

He would have answered, but a scratching sounded at her door. Chace immediately rolled off the bed on the side near the windows and stole quickly into the attached dressing room.

Emma crossed the room to open the door and found that her maid had become concerned for her. "Ye didna call fer me last night, miss—and 'tis so late in the day. Are ye feeling well? Yer aunt was wishful of knowing whether t'doctor ought t'be summoned."

Emma shook her head. "I've not felt entirely well," she said slowly, not allowing her maid to advance too far into the chamber. "But I don't think I'm ill—my headache is all but gone. I am, however, famished and in dire need of a bath. Would you see to a hearty tray of food and several buckets of hot water?"

Her gaze fell to Emma's gown.

Emma felt her cheeks grow a little warm. "I was so tired from dancing last night that I vow I fell asleep before I could ring for you. But pray see that a bath is brought immediately to my chamber. For the present, I need nothing more."

"Very good, miss," the maid said, dropping a slight curtsy.

When Emma closed the door, only then did she dare to call for Chace, but there was no answer. She went hurriedly into her dressing room, only to find it deserted. She glanced around the small chamber and concluded that Chace must have discovered the secret door and passageway leading from her bedchamber, the passageway Lansallos would have used just a few hours earlier. Slowly, she began scrutinizing the walls of the dressing room.

A moment later, to the left and back of the chamber, a narrow panel of oak opened and Chace peeked through. "This is how Lansallos came to your room unheeded," he said.

"Charming," Emma returned, grimacing. "Where does it lead?"

"To the library. I can get there without being seen."

"Go, then," Emma said anxiously. "I've already given my abigail more fodder for gossip than I could wish for—her eyes were bulging at the sight of my rumpled gown. I told her I fell asleep before ringing for her. So do go at once."

Chace blew her a kiss, then disappeared into the secret passageway.

An hour and a half later, Aunt Powler sat in a tall wing chair covered in ivory silk-damask. She stared with pursed lips at Lord Chace. "And you expect me to believe this humbug?" she queried. Aunt Powler was a lively woman for her age and her blue eyes twinkled with excitement. "I think the truth is more at that you've compromised my niece and you ought now to offer for her. Were I a man, I would demand it of you!"

Chace had bathed and shaved and now wore afternoon dress of buff pantaloons, Hessians, a dark blue coat of superfine, a buff and white striped waistcoat, and an exquisitely tied neck-cloth. Ignoring the implications of Aunt Powler's speech, he closed the three feet between them, took up one of her pudgy hands in his, and placed a gallant kiss on her fingers.

"Now, don't start your antics with me, young cub! Only tell me what really happened. I've never known you to be in your altitudes before."

Chace took on a sheepish expression and shrugged his shoulders. "There is always a first time," he said sadly. "I was never more mortified than when I awakened in the library."

"How do you explain that none of the servants found you?"

He looked up at the ceiling appearing quite embarrassed. "I don't like to reveal everything to you, but when I came to my senses I was behind the sofa, which must in some extraordinary way explain this strange bruise on my cheek."

Aunt Powler leaned forward in her seat, narrowing her eyes as she watched him closely. "There is something mysterious about all of this—yet, I see nothing unreasonable in your explanations."

Emma decided to make use of her aunt's wish to see her become the next Lady Chace. "The fog has already begun creeping about the shrubs and trees," she began innocently. "I don't like to think of Chace tooling about the countryside in such wretched conditions. Don't you think he ought to remain with us for another night?"

Aunt Powler's eyes glittered, and the truth of her hopes was clearly written in every satisfied line of her face. Her words however, indicated her sense of propriety. "I suppose we ought to try to accommodate him—I daresay I could never live with myself were an accident to ensue. On the other hand, it would create a very odd appearance were I to agree to such a scheme, as though, well"—she looked piercingly at Chace—"as though you had certain intentions where my niece was concerned."

"But, Mrs. Powler, you have not considered. You are of a marriageable age and I daresay if there was to be gossip, our names could be linked just as easily as Emma's and mine."

"Don't pitch that gammon to me!" Aunt Powler cried, laughing. "I suppose, then, you are not to be bullied into marrying Emma."

"Aunt Powler!" Emma cried.

But Chace laughed, and only then did he release Aunt Powler's hand.

An hour later dinner was announced. Dusk approached through the November mist surely and steadily, a gloomy fact that kept Emma's gaze fixed more often than not on one or the other of three arched, diamond-paned windows in the dining room. Little could be seen because of the fog, however, a fact that did not disturb her so much as the knowledge that the light was quickly deserting Castle Breage. Once night fully descended on Cornwall, Count Lansallos would be free again to roam at will.

Benedict could come from his place of seclusion as well, she thought, slicing a broccoli floweret in half. But this was poor consolation. Benedict was only a child.

"You've grown oddly quiet, Emma," Aunt Powler said kindly, scrutinizing her niece over a forkful of sliced roast beef.

Emma, startled from her unhappy reveries about the encroaching night, smiled and speared one of the halved flowerets with her fork. "I fear I am merely fatigued from our delightful Halloween ball."

"Are you still suffering from the headache as you were last night?"

"Yes, a little," Emma replied untruthfully. She glanced at her aunt and wondered, not for the first time, just how she was to keep her out of danger. There was only one way, she thought ruefully. She would have to make certain Aunt Powler slept deeply and soundly the moment her head hit the pillow, and the earlier in the evening, the better. "I was wondering if perhaps you brought your laudanum with you from London. I daresay were I to take a few drops, I would sleep well tonight."

"You know I never travel without it," Aunt Powler responded helpfully. "And I know you would awaken tomorrow much refreshed."

Emma determined that the moment dinner ended, she would have the laudanum brought to the drawing room. Lacing Aunt Powler's tea surely would not prove overly difficult, particularly if Chace was commissioned to entertain her while she performed the nefarious but necessary deed.

"Do you know," Chace said quite suddenly, his gaze fixed to the doorway leading into the antechamber that connected to the drawing room. "I think I heard cats fighting. Are many kept in the castle?"

"Cook has one or two she employs in the kitchens," Mrs. Powler said. "To keep the usual vermin at bay."

"I know it is dreadfully uncivil of me," he said, "but I'm sure I heard the sound coming from the direction of the gallery. Will you excuse me? It won't do to have wild beasts roaming the halls."

He smiled as he rose from his chair and was gone before Aunt Powler could protest that one of the servants could attend to it.

"Upon my soul," Aunt Powler cried, staring in astonishment at the empty doorway. "I've never known Chace to desert his hostess in the middle of a meal, and what is this nonsense about cats?" She turned to look inquiringly at Emma.

Emma shrugged slightly. "I don't know. But, Aunt, have you noticed what a strange place the castle is? I've never seen so much mist and fog in my life. Somehow I wouldn't be surprised if Chace is right and that wild animals have got past the towers."

Mrs. Powler looked all about her and shivered. "I know one thing for certain—there isn't a chamber I've been in that doesn't have a terrible draft along the floors. I don't think I care to reside here through the winter. Cornwall is supposed to be noted for its temperate climate, but so far I've seen nothing of it."

Emma took a bite of potato and sighed. Her thoughts had reverted to the laudanum scheme. Was any of this real? Was she indeed going to put the sleeping potion in her aunt's tea? Was she actually in danger of succumbing to a vampire? "Will we be enjoying our tea in the drawing room as usual?" she queried.

"Of course," Mrs. Powler responded.

Emma nodded and sipped her glass of Madeira. "I think we ought to have the footman build up a roaring fire for us. What do you think? I, too, have grown to dislike this chilly house."

At that, Mrs. Powler smiled and lifted her own glass of Madeira in an enthusiastic toast to her niece's idea. "An excellent notion," she said.

A few minutes later Chace returned. To Emma, he seemed rather pale, but he smiled and made a hearty meal all the while assuring the ladies that he had been quite mistaken—there had been no cats to be found anywhere in or near the gallery.

Not much above an hour later, Emma led an extremely drowsy Aunt Powler to her bedchamber, where she helped her maid dress her for bed. Mrs. Powler couldn't understand what had come over her, but ever since she had taken her second cup of tea, a terrible fatigue had simply driven the life from her body. She wanted sleep, nothing but sleep.

When she was settled between the sheets, her mobcap down low on her forehead, Emma took her aunt's hand and pressed it. "Don't think I don't know what you are about, Aunt," she said teasingly. "You want me to spend the evening alone with Lord Chace. You are shameless, you know."

Mrs. Powler, experiencing the happy effects of several drops of her own soothing laudanum, smiled at Emma's words. "A good scheme. I only wonder that I didn't think of it myself. I must be getting old." A gentle snoring soon followed, and Emma released her aunt's hand. She stood up straight, tears suddenly stinging her eyes. Would she even see her aunt in the morning, would she be alive, or, worse, would her life as she knew it be altered forever?

She dismissed the maid and upon returning to the drawing room learned the particulars of Chace's search for brawling cats. He had left the dining hall abruptly earlier in the evening because he had heard a faint, high-pitched call—Benedict's summons, as it turned out to be.

The young son of Edward and Mary St. Austell had provided him with information as to where his mother and father could be found in Falmouth and also that Lansallos was not yet abroad. Therefore, the sooner they left Castle Breage to fetch his parents, the better.

Emma nodded. "And now I must somehow get rid of my servants."

Asking Chace to leave her for a few moments, she summoned her butler to the drawing room and explained that she wished for all the servants, including all but one of the stable hands, to leave Castle Breage as soon as possible and not to return until noon on the following day.

"Are ye certain, Miss Keverne?" the butler asked, clearly astonished.

Emma stared coolly at her servant. "If you wish to remain in my employ, I beg you will do as you are bid. I wish for all the servants, including yourself, to leave the castle tonight. No one is to return until tomorrow afternoon. If my aunt has need of anything, I shall tend to her myself. If any servant finds the order inconvenient, I shall happily pay for a room at the inn at Trevisgate. Please see it to it, immediately."

He looked stunned and did not at first move to obey her.

Emma rose from the ivory silk-damask sofa where she was seated and said calmly, "Have I not always shown great good sense in the past?"

"Well, yes, but—"

"I understand that my orders may seem a trifle out of the ordinary, but I promise you, all will be well." The butler bowed to her, turned on his heel, and strode in a dignified manner from the drawing room.

An hour later Emma, seated beside Chace in his traveling chariot, clutched his hand tightly as the carriage bowled across the drawbridge heading for Falmouth. The last remaining stableboy rode postillion, guiding the horses slowly through the swirling mist.

Four

Falmouth at night presented a pretty picture as the traveling chariot descended into the streets that surrounded the wide-mouthed natural harbor. Numerous sailing craft were anchored in the harbor, and lanterns, suspended from the mast beams of the ships, twinkled in the fogless, rainless night.

Emma had been right in thinking that the fog was peculiar to Castle Breage. Once the traveling chariot had left the lanes near the castle, the mist disappeared entirely. Had Lansallos created the mist? Did he possess such powers?

She shivered as the coach rumbled along the narrow seafront lanes. The smell of salt was thick in the air and pleasant to her as the traveling chariot arrived at the wharf Benedict specified. According to the boy, Emma's arrival was all that was necessary to bring the undead to her.

She stepped down from the coach and stood for a moment, looking all about her. She was struck by the lapping of waves against the damp wooden pilings and by the creaks and groans of the huge sailing ships as the gentle tides rocked them asleep. In front of her, the *Victory*—a merchant ship—sat majestically in dock.

Dim lanterns lit the length of the wharves. Sea chanties, laughter, and an occasional shout could be heard all along the waterfront.

Chace joined Emma, informing the stable boy that they were meeting relatives of hers, who would be along shortly. She dug her hands deeply into her fur muff and was grateful for her warm poke bonnet of burgundy velvet. November was not a balmy time of year. Overhead, stars peeked through a thin layer of wispy high clouds and a sudden breeze ruffled the skirts of her gray wool pelisse.

She was beginning to wonder if they ought to inquire of the ship's captain about Mary and Edward St. Austell, when an ethereal couple, pale-faced and solemn, began slowly descending the gangplank to the wharf below. The man, clearly a gentleman, carefully guided his lady's steps, and Emma was struck to the core of her heart by the sight of them. An air of terrible sadness hung upon their shoulders, evidenced by their markedly slow steps. She felt their pain as though it were a tangible thing.

Once they were on the wharf, Emma could not seem to resist moving toward them by way of greeting. She paused beside a lantern and waited for them to complete the remaining few feet. When they appeared within the circle of the lantern's light, Emma wanted to cry, for a prettier couple had never existed than Mary and Edward St. Austell.

Mary smiled faintly at Emma, and the warmth on her face, even though her complexion was bluish-white in hue, prompted Emma to move forward and to embrace the tall, thin, and quite beautiful woman. Mary returned her embrace, but Emma felt her shudder and her own mind grew dizzy. She recalled Benedict's words. *Never forget what I am.*

She drew back. "I'm sorry," she said. "Benedict told me of your plight."

"Nonsense, child," Mary said softly. "Your tender, affectionate greeting has warmed my poor heart. May I present my husband and your cousin, Edward St. Austell."

Emma turned to the handsome man beside Mary and looked into eyes that tore at her heartstrings. His suffering over the years had been acute, that much was clear. He had written in his letters to his descendants that he blamed himself for the evil that had befallen his family, and it was clear to Emma that he had never forgiven himself for permitting Lansallos to turn them all.

Her sympathies were with him and she offered Edward the same affectionate greeting she had given Mary. He received her equally as warmly, holding her fast and promising that he would do all he could to prevent Lansallos from succeeding in his wicked schemes.

"But who is this?" Edward asked, spying Chace at the end of the wharf, where he had remained politely in order that Emma could greet her cousin privately.

"A most excellent friend who saved me from Lansallos's assaults last night. Please, let me introduce you."

"What is his name?" Edward asked as the three of them moved back toward the viscount.

"Lord Chace," Emma said.

"Ah," Edward said. "I thought he looked familiar—something in his carriage, I think."

When Emma made the introductions, Edward explained his impressions. "I knew your grandfather quite well, my lord," he said politely. "A good man, honorable, and quite involved with the East India Company, as I recall."

Lord Chace smiled. "Indeed. Our family's fortunes were much revived through his efforts on that score."

"As were many, but I must thank you for taking care of our little Emma. We have watched her progress over the years, knowing that this day might come."

Lord Chace helped Mary into the carriage, then Emma. Once Edward was seated beside his wife, Emma could not help but ask, "Are you saying, then, that you have a power to see me, to see into the future?"

"Only a very little," he said, "though our foresight was strengthened by our desire to protect our kindred from Lansallos's foolishness and depravity." Emma watched Edward take his wife's hand in his, then kiss her fingers tenderly. She was again struck by a depth of sadness between husband and wife, and it bothered her immensely. Something more was transpiring, Emma thought, than appeared on the surface, of that she was convinced.

The journey from Falmouth back to Castle Breage was spent in hearing the details of Edward and Mary's life on the Continent and of things Emma would have never believed possible, in particular of the number of vampires in the world.

At one point Mary laughed. "Why do you think that such an absurd medical treatment was created involving the draining of blood from the human body? How can health ever be assured by the lessening of a man's or woman's lifeblood! Vampires, of course."

"There are wars too," Edward said, his eyes taking on a faraway appearance. "The undead claiming predatorial territories and killing one another with stakes through the heart, with fire, with crosses burned into the brain, with sunlight—the most painful of all." He shuddered, then drew himself out of the macabre portrait he had painted. "But enough of this. You must tell me all you have seen of Lansallos—the various powers he used on you last night. I must know all if I am to succeed in protecting you and in vanquishing Lansallos at last."

Emma saw the passion in his face and understood that he lived to see his cousin destroyed. She glanced at Mary and wondered why she was looking out the window, almost as though she were disinterested in what her husband said.

Once arrived at Castle Breage, Emma led her cousin and his wife to the drawing room. Benedict, somehow divining their arrival, soon joined them in the drawing room. Both mother and father embraced their son.

Chace took the moment to draw Emma apart. "Something is amiss," he said quietly. "I can feel it, especially in Mary."

"I know what you mean," she said, observing Mary beyond Chace's shoulder. "She is so sad."

"More than that," Chace returned. "I believe she despairs of victory here tonight."

"What do you mean?" Emma queried, looking up at Chace.

In a whisper he responded, "Edward is not strong enough to prevail. Mary knows as much. I can see it too."

Emma felt her heart quail in her breast. Ever since she

greeted her cousin and his wife, she had felt calmer and more certain of safety. "You are mistaken," she breathed.

Chace looked down at her, a serious expression in his green eyes. "You'll know it to be true yourself if you'll search your heart. You've strong instincts, Emma. Use them now."

Emma placed her hand over her mouth. "I don't want it to be true," she murmured, tears biting at her eyes. "What are we going to do?"

"I'm here," he said, lifting her chin with his fingers. "We survived last night—we can survive again tonight."

Emma looked deeply into his eyes and felt some of her confidence return to her. Chace was a strong man, physically and within the fibers of his being. In the few years she had known him—in spite of his flirtatious nature—he had exhibited several admirable abilities. He could command without becoming dictatorial. She had watched him bring about more than one uncomfortable situation quite effortlessly. He seemed able to turn aside a potential conflict with a few well-chosen soft words. In short, if anyone was capable of meeting Lansallos on his own terms, Chace was that man.

She smiled up at him, dimly aware that her relatives were in quiet conference among themselves.

"Emma," he whispered, his gaze drifting over her face. "There is something I would say to you, but not here." He released her chin and turned toward the St. Austells. "Would you excuse us for a moment," he called to them. "I—that is, Emma and I need to collect our few weapons."

"Of course," Edward said, his deep-set brown eyes appearing pained as he nodded to Chace and waved him toward the door. "But don't be gone long. Lansallos could come at any moment."

"We won't," Chace promised. He offered his arm to Emma and she took it, eyeing him curiously.

"Weapons?" she asked once they were in the cold hallway outside the drawing room. "I lost one of my crosses in the struggle last night, but the other is in the pocket of my gown and the garlic has disappeared. I suppose one of the servants returned it to the kitchens. Other than that, I begin to believe our only weapons now are our combined wits."

"You are right," he said. "But I was only making excuses to Edward when I spoke of our going in search of weapons. I wanted to be alone with you for a few minutes, before—well, before anything happened. There is something I want—I need—to say to you."

Emma wore a lavender wool gown and drew her white cashmere shawl more tightly about her shoulders as they moved down the cold gallery. "But, Chace, this is dangerous. Surely we should stay with Mary and Edward."

"I know we should." He was distressed as he hurried her toward the gallery. Using the secret panel and descending the narrow staircase, Emma soon found herself in the library and very much alone with Chace. A tidy fire was burning in the grate as he drew her near the blaze. Taking both her hands in his, he held them tightly against his chest.

Emma drew in her breath sharply. He had never appeared more handsome to her than in that moment, with his face etched with concern. "I fear for your safety," he said quietly, his voice wondrously resonant.

"As I fear for yours," she whispered in response.

"Oh, Emma," he said, leaning close to her, his breath warm on her lips. At the same time, he slipped one arm about her waist. "I believe I've been a fool these past several years."

"Yes, you have," she returned, smiling softly and lifting her face up to him.

"I have so much I want to say, but I would much rather do this." Slowly, he placed his lips on hers, giving her a kiss that felt as though he had never kissed her before. The warmth, the tenderness of the moment, flowed over Emma in a gentle wave of growing love and pleasure.

When he had kissed her before, passion had seemed to rule the moment. But now, as he continued to hold one of her hands to his chest, as his lips remained soft and tender, an entirely new sensation surrounded the loving salute—of respect, of a wish for the future, of safekeeping.

Emma stood very still, allowing the strength of her feelings to become centered exclusively on the kiss she was sharing with Chace. Silently, she spoke to him of her admiration for him, of her thankfulness that he had stood by her all last night and tonight, of her hope that they would both survive to kiss and to be kissed again.

He released her hands. She let her fingertips slide down his chest, the blue superfine fabric soft beneath her fingers as she slipped her arms about him. He embraced her, holding her tenderly against him. His kiss grew fuller, warmer, more demanding.

In the distance, she heard a crying-out.

She drew back from Chace slightly. "We should return to the others now." Suddenly she began to feel dizzy.

He nodded and would have drawn her back to the secret staircase, but she stopped him, throwing her arms tightly about his neck. He could not resist her embrace and kissed her hard in return.

Emma felt the familiar dizziness and leaned into the viscount. She loved Chace so very much.

No, not Chace, she thought, the other one, the one who seemed to be in her mind now. Tendrils of longing began curling about her brain. She held Chace more tightly still, a violent passion rising within her. How exquisitely he began to assault her. She moaned and began clutching at his coat, pulling hungrily at the fabric, sliding her hands to the buttons in front and jerking them from their moorings.

Chace, too, seemed caught up by her need, by her desire for him. Freed from the coat, she tugged at his neckcloth. He laughed and unwound it from his neck. She felt so strange, so powerful as she touched his bare throat. Excitement and hunger shot through her. She kissed his neck and sank her teeth into his throat.

"Emma, stop!" he cried. "You're hurting me!"

She heard him cry out, but she was mad with a desire that had overtaken her mind. She felt hands and arms tugging at her, one set pushing her away, the other pulling her away. She didn't understand what was happening, only that she didn't want to let Chace go. Not now, not when a terrible thirst was upon her. She needed Chace. She needed him now. She wouldn't live unless she . . .

As the horrifying thought finally reached her brain, she let Chace go and the arms pulling her backward sent her flying to the carpeted floor of the library. She lay cringing, her mind reeling. Her thoughts had been a vampire's thoughts.

She looked up at the viscount, who was now doubled over and holding his throat in a painful grasp. The St. Austells stood between them. Mary was crying, Benedict watched her solemnly and Edward looked as though his heart had been torn from his chest.

"Dear God," he exclaimed.

Emma knew her complete senses had not yet returned to her as she rose unsteadily to her feet. Even as she looked at Chace, she felt no compassion for the pain she had inflicted on him. She felt dead inside, lifeless, drained of all emotion.

"What happened," Chace asked hoarsely. He was still doubled over, his eyes narrowed in pain as he looked back at Emma.

Emma couldn't speak.

"Lansallos," Mary said quietly, stepping away from Emma. "He took hold of her mind. Let me see your throat."

Chace released his hand, revealing a large bruise on his neck. Emma wanted to cry for some reason as she saw the bruise. She felt disconnected from the people about her, yet at the same time she wanted to know why they were so distressed and what had happened to Chace. She squeezed her eyes shut, trying to clear her mind, but her mind didn't seem to be part of her anymore.

Her chest contorted suddenly with the same longing she had known before, only this time Chace was not the object. She turned toward the doors of the library and lifted her arms up and outward.

"Come to me," she called. She closed her eyes and felt her mind and spirit drifting away from her body. At the same time, she knew that she was suddenly surrounded by bodies. But why? To what purpose would these simpletons try to keep her from the one she loved, the one she must know and have, the one to whom she would give her soul for all eternity.

The door of the library opened. He was there, the one who would love her forever, who would keep her safe, who would protect her.

The throbbing in Chace's neck dropped to a faint hum. For a moment, when Emma had held his throat firmly between her teeth, he had known a pain so excruciating that he had almost fainted. When the St. Austells came to his rescue, he understood what had happened, that Lansallos had begun his first attack, that he had made the possession of Emma's mind his primary weapon.

He turned now to view his enemy.

How odd to see what appeared to be merely a well-dressed man, a man whose costume even Beau Brummell would have approved of. He was in every sense immaculately groomed, as though he might have stepped out of a ballroom in Grosvenor Square instead of a vault in the castle dungeons. His hair was brushed in the simple Brutus fashion, his evening pantaloons and dress tails were of an elegant black superfine, his waistcoat was a brilliant white, his slippers of a fine black silk. His shirt points were moderate and neatly starched, his white neckcloth was tucked into an array of careful folds.

Realizing that the count had not made an earlier appearance because he was attending to his toilette seemed so absurd to Chace that some of his fear dissipated. He straightened his shoulders and observed Lansallos carefully. He did not seem so formidable now. Chace began to prepare himself. If Lansallos thought he would turn Emma so easily, he was greatly mistaken.

The count's gaze was fixed solely on Emma, whose expression became more animated. Mary, Edward, and Benedict surrounded her, keeping her safe by imprisoning her within the tight circle of their arms and bodies.

"Lansallos," she murmured, leaning toward him, reaching out to him, her arms stretched over the shoulders of Edward and Mary.

Lansallos extended a hand to her and Emma began to moan, trying to push Edward away, trying to get to the vampire.

Chace circled behind the struggling St. Austell family, who forced Emma to stay safe within their circle. Lansallos appeared to ignore him as he sauntered into the chamber, his hand still extended toward Emma.

"Help me, Lansallos!" she cried. "Help me! Release me!"

His black eyes never strayed from her face. Chace watched him closely, noting that his concentration was so fierce that the veins at his temple and jawline pulsed steadily. He glanced back at Emma and was astonished by the longing on her face and in her lovely hazel eyes. A tightness closed about his heart and his breathing began to accelerate. Rage suddenly ripped through his chest—the rage of jealousy.

How dare Lansallos force his way into Emma's mind and overpower her? Emma's mind belonged to him. Her soul belonged to him—now and forever.

Having no thought but to drag Emma's soul back from the brink of obliteration, he leapt at Lansallos, landing squarely on his back and bringing him hard to the floor. He was pounding the back of his head with his fists and suddenly felt himself thrown backward. A whirl of painful blows fell on him as though a flock of birds were batting their wings at his face, arms, shoulders, and chest, over and over.

He closed his eyes as the thrumming and beating of wings robbed him of breath and of his senses. He took several blows to his mouth, cheekbones, and chin. He felt himself falling as though he were dropping hundreds of miles into the earth. Then nothing.

Emma blinked, then blinked again. A terrible chill had robbed her of the ability to make sense of where she was and what she was doing. She was shaking feverishly as though a strong ague had taken possession of her body. She couldn't move, she couldn't speak, she couldn't think. She wasn't even sure what the strange blur in front of her was. She thought she saw wings flying this way, then that, but how? Why? Nothing made sense to her. Where was she? What was happening?

Castle Breage. Her knees gave way. She sank to the carpet, to her knees, and wrapped her arms tightly about herself in an attempt to stop the shaking.

Where was Lord Chace?

Lord Chace. Yes, now she was starting to remember. She took a deep breath, blinking again and again. Her vision began to clear and at the same time she saw that several people with strange wings were beating at one another and at the carpet in front of her.

Suddenly, one winged creature took flight passing through the door into the cold, stone entrance hall beyond.

She was in the library. She had been kissing Chace. She began hurting him.

Lansallos! She gasped and placed her hands over her face. "Dear God," she cried. "I almost—I would have—"

As though a deep, thick mist had kept her mind trapped, suddenly she came to her senses and the sight that met her eyes caused tears to roll down her cheeks. Mary, Benedict, and Edward St. Austell were lying on either side of Chace, their clothing torn, their faces marred by bruises. None of them moved. They all breathed in ragged gasps.

Edward rolled to his side, holding his stomach and coiling into a ball. "Benedict," he murmured.

"I'm here, Papa." Benedict had been caught beneath Chace's legs and his father's torso.

Emma glanced at Chace. He was lying very still and she couldn't see whether or not he was breathing.

She rose to her feet, crossed to him, and leaned down to touch his back.

"He's all right," Mary said, her breathing still harsh and uneven.

Emma dropped next to Chace and placed her hand on his neck. She saw that his throat was horribly bruised. More tears streamed down her cheeks as she realized she had done as much to the man she loved. She leaned toward him and placed a kiss on his neck. She felt the pulse of his heartbeat, and another swell of tears brimmed over her lids to trickle down her cheeks.

"Chace," she said to him. He groaned, and she turned him over gently, but his eyes remained closed.

She straightened up and met her cousin's worried gaze. "When will Lansallos return, Edward?" she asked, fearing to hear the answer.

"We have an hour, perhaps two. He is weakened, but only a trifle, I'm sure." He covered his face with his hands. Emma heard him sob and saw his shoulders shake. "I thought we could vanquish him!" he cried. "Have we come home without the smallest ability to see him in his final grave?"

"Hush, Papa," Benedict said kindly, moving to sit beside Edward. "He has had far more decades in which to learn his craft, but we are not finished yet, not by half!"

Edward looked at his son and smiled weakly. "You have more confidence than I," he said, "but I do thank you, my son."

"We—must set—a trap—for him."

"Chace!" Emma cried, turning her attention fully to the viscount. "Are you all right? Speak to me!"

He lifted an arm to pat her shoulder gently. "Of course I am," he responded through swelling lips. "Do you think I can be slain by a mere vampire?"

She laughed, but even the laughing was a matter of great pain for her. There was nothing amusing about their situation.

"What happened?" Chace asked after a time, glancing toward Mary. "I felt as though wings were beating at my face and arms, but how could that be?"

Emma also turned to look inquiringly at Mary, who had risen to her feet.

Mary did not at first answer, but glanced at Edward and Benedict, both of whom remained silent. "We—" she began, but broke off, her brows drawn together in a worried frown. Emma wondered why she found it difficult to continue.

Emma tilted her head. "I saw large, winged creatures. Or thought I did. My vision was blurred, and even though I blinked a dozen times, I couldn't quite—"

"We can metamorphose," Mary said at last, unable to meet Emma's gaze.

Emma shook her head, rising to her feet at the same time. In a sympathetic gesture she touched Mary's arm. "Animals? Birds?"

"Predatory creatures mostly," Mary responded. "Kestrels, vultures, bats." Only then did she lift her gaze to Emma's. Her eyes had become black and pulsing. Her nostrils flared. "Please don't touch me. The warmth of your flesh—" She broke off and turned away from Emma. "I must go into the woods. I will have no strength left in two hours, unless—unless I find some nourishment."

Even as she spoke, she began moving toward the doors of the library.

"Wait, Mama," Benedict called after her. "I'll come with you."

Chace struggled to sit up. Emma helped him and afterward assisted him in rising to his feet. Edward, however, remained sitting on the floor, his shoulders slumped. He appeared utterly dejected.

When Chace was settled on the moss-green velvet sofa,

Emma turned back to her cousin. "Edward?" she asked quietly. "How can I help you? Is there nothing I can do?"

Edward slowly gained his feet as well. "I couldn't save my family sixty years ago, Emma," he said, "and it seems I won't be able to save you either. Was a poorer specimen of a man born than I?" He dropped into a chair near the sofa and again sank his head into his hands.

Emma went to him. "We are not finished yet. Chace is right. We must create a trap for him—something! It is our wits that shall win the day, not our force. And a man can always prevail with his wits. If only we could—" She stopped, an idea striking her.

Edward lifted his head. "If we could what, Emma?" he asked. "Almost you give me hope."

"Well, I have been thinking of the extraordinary fact that last night—or you might say early this morning—Lansallos was almost slain by the dawn. I shall never forget the piercing scream he emitted when the faintest light touched his eye. In fact, it was so faint that I was sure dawn still eluded me."

Edward shuddered. "You can have no idea the pain such an event can bring. And on the eye." He shuddered again.

"But don't you think it odd that he didn't know dawn had arrived?"

"Now that I think on it—not odd at all," he said, hope lighting up his bruised features. "He is but just arrived in England, and there is a time lapse. You may have something there. I'll wager he is still slightly disoriented, which might just prove to be his undoing. If we can keep him occupied until dawn, then we, that is he, could meet his fate in the light of day."

"Precisely!" Emma cried.

"But how do we keep him occupied?" Chace interjected. "Unless we could subdue and bind him. Can he be bound? Can ropes hold such a creature?"

"Yes," Edward said quickly. "He may be strong, but not strong enough to break out of a sturdy rope and carefully tied knots."

Because of Lansallos's vow that he would not seek the blood of any victim before he tasted of Emma's, it was decided that she must serve as bait for their trap. When Benedict and Mary returned from their foraging expedition, Emma was startled to see that their bruises had healed completely. She put her hand to her mouth, barely suppressing a gasp as she turned away from her relatives. How horrible to think that the nourishment they sought in the woods had had the power to repair their wounds.

Directing Emma to explain their plan to Mary and Benedict, Edward left to take his own turn hunting.

Two hours later, at a quarter past three o'clock in the morning, Emma stood at the top of the stone stairway, waiting for Count Lansallos to collect his prize. She was nervous, of course, but more so because Lansallos was late. Fifteen minutes late. Had he seen through their ruse? Would he catch her off guard? Would she be lost before they had even begun? For one thing, if he captured her at the top of the stairs, their plan would be ruined. For another—she commanded her thoughts to cease. There could be no use in torturing herself with potential pitfalls.

She smoothed out the skirts of her high-waisted gown of forest-green silk, embroidered across the bodice in seed pearls. She had dressed specifically to appeal to the fastidious count. Glancing down at the lovely fabric, she smiled, thinking that at least Lansallos could not be put off by her appearance—Mary had seen to that. She had helped Emma choose precisely the gown that would appeal to Lansallos the most, and had dressed her hair according to her knowledge of his preferences. The gown bore puffed sleeves of a fine, sheer tulle and several rows of ruffles of the same tulle about the hem of the dress. Her thick black hair was drawn up into a knot of curls atop her head. She wore no necklet about her throat—naturally. What vampire wouldn't prefer his victim bare-throated? White gloves and dark green matching slippers completed her ensemble. The shift beneath her gown was of a delicate wool in protest against the dankness and frigidity of the castle. Over her elbows she carried a shawl of elegant merino wool in a pale yellow. She was as prepared as she could be for Lansallos.

Her heart thumped in her chest as she awaited his arrival. She glanced at the armory decorating every wall of the enormous stone entrance hall. In particular, she scrutinized each of two suits of armor flanking the bottom of the stairs. Would Lansallos remember these suits had not originally been placed in their present locations?

She trusted he would not.

Only, where was he?

Earlier, Benedict had reported his audience with the count. He had sought out Lansallos in the castle dungeons, directly below the twelfth-century towers, where he had found the vampire nursing his wounds and changing his garments. The count had merely lifted a brow at his arrival. Benedict had then told Lansallos that he and his parents were conceding their stupidity in trying to brook the count's rights to convert Emma. He informed Lansallos that if he were willing, they would present her to him as an offering for their misdeeds at three o'clock in the entrance hall. Would he consider accepting Emma as a peace offering? They were certain she could be made willing to oblige them all—her mind, as Lansallos already knew, was easily turned and tricked. He begged the count to consider their offer. They didn't want war, and their attempt to disrupt his corruption of Emma had been foolish in the extreme.

Lansallos, though eyeing him suspiciously, had finally agreed to the scheme as well as to meet them in the entrance hall at three o clock, at the bottom of the stairs.

But now the count was late and Emma was nervous. She heard a faint brushing sound behind her, then another. Without turning around, she instinctively took a step off the landing and began a quick descent of the stairs to the half-landing.

"Why do you run away?" she heard Lansallos call from behind her.

Emma gasped and turned around, only to find that the count was at the top of the stairs. If she hadn't moved when she did, he would have caught her and assaulted her then and there with no one to help her. Why had they assumed he would be arriving through the tower dungeon stairs or through the library? They had misjudged him. How many more times before the night was through would they misjudge him?

"There you are," she said, attempting a light tone she did not feel. She smiled, but turned to take several more steps down the stairs, toward the suits of armor. "I had begun to wonder if you meant to come to me," she added, hoping to distract him by her congeniality. "Edward and Mary explained how foolish our resistance to you has been. I am prepared now to do as you bid me."

Lansallos called out. "Stop at once."

Emma felt his mind dart within hers and tug on her thoughts as though he were drawing in the reins of a horse. She paused. He had control of her—she could feel it. Five steps to the bottom. She tried to move her feet, but she couldn't.

At that moment Mary emerged from the doorway of the library into the entrance hall. "She is a lovely prize," she said, sauntering into the center of the hall. She had exchanged her gown as well and was now wearing a beautiful, elegant ball dress of rose silk covered with a spangled net. Her blond hair was dressed prettily in curls at the crown of her head and she wore a necklet of diamonds.

"Faith, but you always were beautiful," Lansallos called to her, his eyes glittering. "But I sense mischief afoot." Emma turned to look at him, still frozen by the command he had over her mind. He wore a new, unscarred black coat and a burgundy brocade waistcoat, black silk knee breeches, and white silk stockings. His silver-buckled shoes clicked as he descended the stone steps. He was a decidedly handsome vampire.

"No mischief," Mary said. "Merely, we've come to our

senses. At least I have." Emma heard the hard note in her voice and thought that Mary St. Austell would have made a marvelous actress. She continued. "The truth is, Lansallos, my husband is a weakling and I should have listened to you a dozen years ago when you begged me to travel to India with you and to leave Edward behind. What a fool I was not to have done so, for now I fear his incompetence will get me killed."

Emma felt Lansallos release her mind, unwittingly perhaps, but again on instinct she remained where she was as though he still controlled her. She watched him draw near her, but his black gaze was not fixed to her but to Mary. A terrible lust was in his eye.

"You have come to your senses," he said, addressing Mary. "I should have killed Edward the night I converted you. Perhaps I have been as great a fool as you."

When Lansallos drew abreast Emma, she turned and looked at Mary. Mary's gaze shifted to Emma for only a fraction of a second.

"What the devil!" Lansallos cried.

Emma knew what she had to do. As Lansallos reached out to grab her, she slipped under his arm and half fell, half scrambled down the remaining five steps. Lansallos leapt after her and Chace, concealed in the suit of armor to the right of the steps, swung his mace into the chest of the vampire, knocking him backward on the stairs. Edward, hidden in the second suit, to the left, struck Lansallos over the head with his metal arm. The vampire lost complete consciousness.

"My God!" Chace cried. "He is so strong! An ordinary man would be dead by now!"

"Hurry!" Mary cried. "You must bind him now! You haven't but a minute or two—I promise you! Benedict—come! Hurry!"

Benedict ran in from the library, carrying a coil of heavy rope in his arms. Together, Emma and Mary began binding his arms and legs as Edward and Chace removed their armor with Benedict's help. When Chace was free, he saw to the completion of Lansallos's binds. The two men carried him up the stairs, into the ballroom, and onto the balcony overlooking the Spanish chestnut trees.

As before—clearly since Lansallos's arrival in Cornwall—a thick mist cloaked the hills, trees, and shrubs about Castle Breage. Thirty feet beyond the castle, nothing was visible. Not that it mattered, because all they had to do now was wait for the dawn. Even a heavy fog could not prevent the dawn nor the light that would end Lansallos's reign forever.

Five

Emma's slippers moved, slid, and skipped easily along the wood floor of the ballroom. Her heart was lighter than she could ever remember it being. She was safe and Chace was guiding her smoothly and skillfully about the ballroom floor to the sounds of Mozart floating from the pianoforte. Benedict had made at least some useful employment of his vampirish years and had learned to play the pianoforte with great skill. Edward and Mary also made their way about the ballroom, dancing with lively enjoyment the form of the English contre-danse.

In some ways it felt odd to Emma to be dancing, especially when she had been in so much danger so recently. At the same time, she thought it appropriate that they celebrate their hard-earned victory by moving joyously through the practiced steps of a dance.

Emma glanced at Chace and smiled

"Better?" he queried. His face still bore a bruised appearance both from his encounter with Lansallos on the night before and from the strange battering the vampires' metamorphosed wings had given him earlier. His neckcloth covered the bruise on his throat.

"Much better, thank you," Emma responded.

Now that Lansallos was bound firmly and stretched out on the balcony awaiting the light of day, Emma could return her thoughts to the future and to Chace. In a twinkling she recalled to mind all of their forbidden kisses and embraces of the past two days. She felt a blush rising on her cheeks.

"Why do you smile so?" he asked, his green eyes sparkling.

Emma knew that her blush was deepening, but because only three candelabra lit the large chamber, she was certain he could not detect the pink flush on her cheeks. Smiling more fully, she responded, "I am thinking, my lord, of how frequently you have taken complete advantage of me over these past hours and days. You've behaved shamelessly."

"I? What of you?" he suggested. "Is it possible that you, Miss Keverne, have been equally as culpable in the matter?"

"That is the worst of it," she responded almost gaily. "I believe I have."

The country dance came to an end and in its place, Benedict struck up a waltz. Gladly, Emma entered the circle of Chace's arms and with the pronounced rhythm of the new music began to whirl with him about the ballroom floor. But the waltz, so much more intimate in its style than the country dance, altered and deepened their previous conversation.

"Benedict read my mind," Chace said, smiling down on her. Up and back he guided her, around and around. "He must have, since I have wanted nothing more for the past half hour than to be waltzing with you like this."

Emma sighed happily. How wondrously dizzy she felt. She began to giggle and then to laugh. She was beyond happy. She was exhilarated.

Chace looked into her youthful, pretty face, and found himself enchanted, as he had been, if the truth be known, from the night of her come-out ball. In the dim, glowing candlelight, her hazel eyes were almost brown but sparkled as though they were blue. For a moment he took pleasure only in holding her gently in his arms and whirling her up and back, around and around.

Their scheme had worked to perfection. Lansallos was defeated, now and forever. Only an hour, perhaps less, was needed to see the task completed. Dawn could not be far away.

He sighed contentedly. The past two nights had been so strange—so full of danger, yet of passion as well. There had even been several times during Lansallos's siege when he had begun to fancy himself in love with Emma, to the point that marriage had actually crossed his mind. But now that the danger was past, he realized that only the fright of the situation had tricked him into believing he could bring himself to beg for her hand. Thank heaven he hadn't been such a fool as to have offered for her during a moment of weakness.

Besides, he thought roguishly, he had Emma entirely in his clutches. After tonight, he was convinced he could do whatever he wished with her. The scandalous nature of having shared a bed, however innocently, would be enough to blackmail her if he had to. But he didn't think that would be necessary, not after she had professed her true feelings for him. She had said she loved him and there was nothing preventing her now from becoming his mistress—save a little propriety which he had small doubt a few seductive kisses could help set aside.

If Edward and Mary had not been present, he would have begun at once, kissing her, teasing her, enticing her to give full expression of her love for him. But since the St. Austells were quite interested in Emma's welfare, no such tryst would be allowed and certainly not condoned. Regardless, he felt as he had a dozen times before when he had pursued a lady and knew himself within an inch of possessing her—exhilarated. Completely, utterly exhilarated.

"I don't think I've ever seen you quite so content, Lord Chace," Emma said as they turned, and turned again.

"I can see the future," he said, whispering the words rakishly into her ear. "We shall be together, you and I, for a long, long time. Paris first, then Venice, and later, Rome. Perhaps we shall follow Princess Caroline's lead and sail about the Mediterranean on a yacht. Would you enjoy that?"

Emma slid her ear away from his tantalizing words and caught his gaze. She wanted to see his warm, loving expression.

She wanted to hear the words she had been waiting three years to hear.

But when she looked into his eyes, she knew something was amiss. No warmth and affection glimmered in his expression, instead a familiar teasing glitter gazed back at her, a glitter she found too reminiscent of Count Lansallos's expression to make her in the least comfortable.

Her heart sank. So Chace had not changed, not really. At least twice, perhaps more, during the past hours and days, she had experienced a tenderness in Chace's company that had not been there before, a tenderness that had caused her to hope that their flirtation had deepened into love. But no such love filled Chace's green eyes.

In a quiet voice she responded to his query. "I have always wanted to travel, to see the beautiful cities of Europe about which I have only read. But, Chace, you are not describing our honeymoon tour, are you?"

She could see by the sudden lift of his brows that she had startled him, and she had her answer. He missed his steps. They both stopped in mid-twirl and he offered his arms to her as though to resume the dance, but she placed her hand to her temple and said, "I've been a simpleton, I can see that. I had thought when you spoke of your sentiments earlier, of *falling* in love with me, of your belief you had been a fool these three years and more, that you naturally meant we were to be married." She glanced toward the balcony where Lansallos was held captive. "Rather silly of me, wasn't it? But now that our adventure has drawn to a close, I believe I shall seek my bed. It has been a most trying evening, to say the least. Good night, Lord Chace."

She slipped by him and walked quickly toward the door before he could stop her.

Chace could have kicked himself. He had erred—mightily. What a halfling he was, misjudging the moment as though he were still in his salad days!

"Emma," he called to her. "Wait. I shouldn't have said such things to you." But Emma did not pause in her steps.

Mary and Edward drew near him. "Is she all right?" Mary asked. The music stopped as Benedict left his post at the pianoforte and joined them.

"Yes, I'm sure she's fine. It's just that I offended her by something I said. Perhaps I ought to go after her, bring her back."

But before he could take a step, a long, terrifying scream shot through the ballroom. Twice. Then a third time.

Emma.

"My God!" Chace cried. His feet were pounding across the wooden ballroom floor before the last of her screams died away. He entered the hallway, looking up the corridor toward the east tower, then down toward the antechamber leading to the back stairs. He had no way of knowing from which direction the sound had come.

Edward and Mary arrived shortly after him. "Which way?" Mary cried. "What do you think has happened?"

Edward turned back to his son, "Make certain Lansallos is still bound and find out whether or not he remains unconscious."

"Yes Papa." Benedict darted toward the windows. From the balcony he called out, "All's well. He's tied up snugly and still hasn't awakened. Perhaps Emma stumbled on the stairs."

Chace thought this possibility as reasonable as any other and headed toward the staircase that led to the second floor and therefore to Emma's bedchamber. But when he arrived, she wasn't anywhere to be found. He glanced down the stairs to the entrance hall. The suits of armor were still in a state of disarray from the earlier assault on Lansallos. He listened intently for sounds of movement, but nothing returned to his ears.

He crossed the landing and checked the drawing room, the dining room, and the gallery, then descended to the library through the secret passageway, but he found no sign of Emma. He made the long journey back up the two flights of stairs to her bedchamber, scratched on the door once, then twice. When he received no answer, he opened the door, scrutinized the room and her dressing room, but she was not there.

He retraced his steps and found Edward and Mary in the drawing room. "I couldn't find her. Have you seen even a whisper of her skirts brushing round a corner?"

They both shook their heads, bemused.

A strange look overcame Edward's face. "Oh, God, no," he breathed. "The ballroom. I can feel what is happening. Lansallos!"

Emma had never felt anything so wondrous as the sensation of the count's teeth pricking her neck. Desire, pleasure, ecstasy, seemed all rolled into one. How clever of Lansallos to have led her away from the ballroom, prompted her to scream, then to have led her back. How could she ever have wanted to resist him, when such pleasure was nearly beyond bearing? She felt dizzy and light-headed.

Then he withdrew his teeth and began kissing her. "Dear cousin," he murmured into her ear. "Your pleasures are only beginning this night. I have waited for you for so long and I was right in thinking that you might be the best of all those who have come to me over the centuries. We will go to the Continent. You have but to breathe the words that you want to be with me, to be like me, to join me, and the deed is done."

He pulled away from her slightly, enough for Emma to look into his black eyes and to think that she had never been happier or more content in her entire existence. She would find great joy and love in this man's arms, sharing his life, his travels, his bed. She understood now what she wanted—to become one of the dead among the living. What was a mere mortal's life anyway? Drudgery, discontent, death always hovering about? But with Lansallos, she would know nothing of these. Death couldn't touch her.

"You hesitate, my dear?" he queried in the softest voice.

Again his teeth pricked her neck. She could feel her life flowing into him. She could feel him becoming stronger. His thoughts were rich in her mind. Her intentions became unified with his. "Yes, Lansallos," she began, "I want to—"

Suddenly, his teeth bit at her flesh as he was dragged away from her. She saw another man who she recognized vaguely as a man she had known at one time, a long time ago. Oh, yes. Lord Chace. The man she thought she loved. But she hadn't known real love until Lansallos had touched her and kissed her. She watched Chace struggle with the count. She felt faintly amused. How silly for the viscount to battle a man of such powers as Lansallos. He had his hand around Chace's throat. How red the viscount's face became.

She glanced across the ballroom floor. The St. Austell child was where Lansallos had left him—unconscious near the pianoforte. The others arrived and approached Lansallos, but he lifted a mere hand and they were thrown backward as though by a strong wind. All three of the ineffectual St. Austells now lay prone and unconscious on the ballroom floor.

Her gaze shifted back to the count, and she saw, much to her surprise, that Lord Chace was slumped against him and that Lansallos was sinking his teeth into his neck. She watched the vampire's complexion become healthy and vibrant as he drank. She thought, *This is what I'll be doing.*

Somehow these words shook her to the depths of her soul. She blinked. Her mind grew clear. She could see by the whiteness of Chace's complexion that he would be dead soon.

"Dear God, no!" Emma cried.

Lansallos removed his spiked teeth and, as though intoxicated, looked back at her.

"Don't be a fool," he said, his voice low and commanding. "You want this. I know you do."

Several thoughts raced through Emma's mind. She had to do something. She knew he cared nothing for Chace, that he was only caught up in the act of draining the lifeblood from his victim. She also knew that he wanted her more than anything.

"I shan't do it," she stated flatly, and slowly began her exit, walking nonchalantly across the ballroom floor as though she hadn't a care in the world.

When she had crossed the room halfway, and stepped over Mary's inert form, she glanced back at Lansallos. She saw the indecision on the count's face as he held Chace with one arm.

"You aren't as strong as you think you are!" she cried hotly. "Maybe you've killed Chace, but you'll never have me!"

When he let Chace fall in a heap on the wooden ballroom floor, Emma began to run. Entering the hallway, she ran toward the kitchens and descended first into the scullery, then back up the opposite stairs into the dining chamber. She paused to catch her breath, listening hard for sounds of Lansallos. She heard his laughter coming from the stairs she had just mounted.

Leaving the dining room, she went into the drawing room, then into the gallery. She moved into the secret passageway, but instead of returning to the library, she ascended to the towers, which she felt to be a desperate mistake. She had never been there before, at least not through the secret stairs. She found herself spiraling up and up on a narrow and dangerous flight of stone steps. When she reached the wooden door to the tower, she found it latched, but there was no light to reveal the location of the latch.

She heard Lansallos's laughter behind her. She felt all over the door. Splinters began slicing into her palms. "Dear God! Dear God!"

"Did you think to escape me!" His voice floated up to her. "Don't be a goose, Emma. You are meant for me."

She felt that horrible familiar dizziness and shook it off. He wouldn't take her mind this time. Not this time. Not if she hoped to save Chace.

The latch. She felt it beneath her palm. A hard turn, a push, the door sprang open. She vaulted through, then whirled around to close the door, barring it with another latch inside the tower room. She heard the count reach the opposite side of the door and begin to pound. "Damn you!" he cried. "Enough of this nonsense, Emma. The hour is getting *early,* as you well know. Surrender! Now! For if you don't, I shall torment you badly tomorrow night, and any who love you!"

"Go to the devil, you monster!" Emma cried.

She heard him begin to descend the staircase and knew she had but seconds to beat him to the entrance hall or he would catch her and either kill her or turn her completely to his horrible ways.

She was about to throw open the door of the tower room, when she remembered the second tower and its link to the second floor. She passed into the hallway connecting the tower chambers, then descended the second tower to the floor on which her bedchamber was situated. She felt for the cross in, the pocket of her gown, only to remember she had changed gowns. She needed at least one of her crosses if she had any hope of withstanding even part of the count's attack.

When she reached her bedroom, she hunted on the royal blue Aubusson carpet and found one of them. She hurriedly gained her feet and ran into the dressing room, intending to retrieve the second cross from the pocket of her gown, when Lansallos suddenly emerged through the secret door, vaulted toward her, and threw her backward.

He was on top of her, His teeth again sinking into her flesh. As before, a wave of profound pleasure rolled through her. She felt the cross biting into her hand, burning her own hand. But, why?

"Oh, God, no!" she cried as awareness dawned on her. With all her might she jammed the cross into his cheek. She heard the searing of his flesh. The scream that resulted was unearthly. He rolled off her and into a ball at the far side of the dressing room. She scooted herself backward, holding tightly to the silver cross. She finally gained her feet and was about to run, when she caught sight of the clock on her mantel. The hour was nearly seven. Surely dawn had come.

She whirled around and felt his mind taking hold of hers as it had time and again. She watched him emerge slowly from the dressing room, the arrogant smile on his face as beckoning as ever. She felt the cross fall from her hand. She backed toward the draperies. He was on her again. His teeth, sharp. Immense pleasure. She had hardly any strength left to her. She tried to tug on the drapes to pull them down, but she had no power in her to do so.

She was in a strange place of metamorphosis. She felt her soul divide into two parts. Within her mind she was looking at herself. She felt as though she were poised on a rope and suspended high in the air. If she fell to the left, she would join him. To the right, she would die. Was there nothing she could do?

Her hands were still clasping the velvet. She gathered up the fabric with both hands, making use of what wretchedly little strength was left to her. She leaned backward so that his weight was more completely on her.

He withdrew his teeth for a bare second and said, "Will you come with me?"

Emma let herself slide down the wall, taking the drape with her. He toppled awkwardly over, falling on top of her. "No," she muttered inaudibly.

There was no great glow of dawn to shine on his face. No shimmering sun just peeking over the distant hills to burn his skin, no orange sky to blind him. But there was a grayness that struck his face which held him in a fast embrace of pain and terror. Edward had been right. Lansallos had not been careful of the hour.

Dawn had come.

The shrieking that ensued was more than Emma could bear. She covered her ears and rolled onto her face. Minutes went by. Still the creature shrieked as if in horrible pain.

Finally the air in her bedchamber was still. She lifted herself slightly and saw not some burnt-up creature unfit for burial as she expected to see, but the form of a man whose expression was so peaceful in death that Emma began to cry.

"Dear cousin," she murmured as she rose to her feet and looked down at him. "It's over, forever."

"Emma?" Mary called to her from deep within the recesses of the dressing room.

Emma turned to find the vampire family huddled together near the secret entrance. She could see that they were shivering and in pain.

She rose quickly to her feet and drew the drapes fast across the window. She entered the dressing room and closed the door behind her.

"Is he—?" Edward queried, trembling.

Emma nodded. "But he seemed so peaceful in the end. Not the horrid man who had tormented all of us over the past two days."

"I saw it once," he said, glancing toward the door. "A friend of mine had erred, the palest sunlight struck him and he died. The culmination is peaceful, however, just as you've said, which is what we've come to tell you."

Emma searched his face, the light from the single candle in the dressing room barely sufficient to reveal the subtleties of his emotions. Edward clapped a hand on her shoulder. "We have come home to die," he stated simply.

Emma drew in her breath sharply. Somehow she hadn't expected this eventuality even though now that she thought on it, she had suspected their motives from the time she watched Mary and Edward descend the gangplank in Falmouth. The sadness that had hung about them then, and that still existed in every glance shared among the small, unhappy family, had been sufficient warning.

Still, she had just made their acquaintance, these odd cousins of hers. To lose them now, now, when they had all suffered so much together, was a loss that struck her deeply.

Mary glanced toward the bottom of the door from which the thinnest line of light could be seen. She winced and averted her gaze. "However will we be able to do this, Edward?" she said, her voice panic-stricken. "Even when I look at the light, the pain I feel—"

"I know, I know," he murmured, tears in his eyes. "I feel it as well."

At that moment the door to the secret entrance opened slowly and Chace, his hand sliding down the length of the door, toppled into the small chamber. "I didn't—know—if I was needed," he said, collapsing onto the floor. His complexion was a chalky white.

Emma went to him immediately and helped him to recline on her lap. "You needn't fear, Chace," she said gently, stroking his forehead, which felt cold beneath her touch. "Lansallos is dead—at last."

She felt him sigh even though the sound of his breath didn't pass his lips. Emma looked up at Edward. "Will he be all right? I mean, he has not been permanently—" The thought of Chace becoming a vampire sent a horrible chill through her body.

Edward smiled. "He is perfectly safe. To become a vampire, one must be asked to join the brotherhood and agree to it. Chace was neither asked nor agreed. Lansallos's intention had been strictly to—to take his life."

The thought of losing Chace again sent a shiver through her body. She looked down at him and continued to pet him and to rub his arms, chest, and shoulders, hoping to warm him up a little.

"We must say good-bye now, Emma," Edward said quietly.

She looked up at him and lifted a hand to him. "Good-bye, Cousin. Godspeed."

He took her hand and gave it a squeeze. Benedict dropped quickly down beside her and placed a kiss on her cheek. "I wish we could have stayed with you longer. But we have all agreed that if we don't do this thing now, we'll never have the courage again. Even for the undead, life is still preferable to the unknowns of the afterlife."

"I'll miss you," she said. "You played the pianoforte better than anyone I've ever known."

He chuckled. "I had more years to practice."

She smiled but not for long. Mary took up Benedict's place beside her and embraced her. "Good-bye." She released her, then shook a finger at her. "I know you haven't been considering as much, but don't even think of going to the Continent with Lord Chace except as his wife." She then narrowed her eyes as though looking into the future. "You will have six children, equally divided, boys and girls. They will be a blessing to you."

She then rose to her feet. Together the family looked down upon her and upon Chace, who lifted a hand in a gesture of farewell. As one they murmured their good-byes again, then turned toward the door, linked arms, and strode bravely into her bedchamber.

"Have I understood them?" Chace inquired.

"Yes," Emma replied. "They are going home." Just as she spoke the words the shrieking began and Emma let the tears flow down her cheeks.

"Good God," Chace whispered.

"I know," she said. "But you'll see. In the end they'll be all right."

Emma struggled to awaken as from a deep fog. Nightmares still haunted her, of strange beings that drank the blood of life in order to survive, who battled one another for predatory rights, who transformed into grotesque winged creatures. Her whole body felt on fire as she strove to open her eyes. Something was chasing her—it was the strongest creature of them all, a man named . . . what was his name? Lansallos. Yes, Lansallos.

She screamed and thrashed about, trying to get through the fog.

Finally, she awoke with a start. Her eyes flew open and she looked quickly about her. Where was she?

Oh, yes. Her bedchamber. She leaned back into her pillows.

"You're awake now," a cheerful voice called to her.

Emma turned to her right and watched dear Aunt Powler rise from a rocking chair beside her bed. Emma tried to speak, but her throat felt swollen and dry. "Have—have I been ill?" she asked. "I don't feel very well."

Aunt Powler seated herself on the side of the bed and took Emma's hand in her own. "Quite ill, m'dear. We feared you would not survive. But here you are. You suffered a crisis last night, the fever broke, and we all began to breathe more easily."

Only then did Emma notice the dark circles beneath her aunt's eyes. "Aunt!" she asked, startled. "How long have I been so sick?"

"A week, my dear. I suspect you should not have gone off into that mist the night of your masquerade ball—kissing Chace beneath the chestnut trees just about cost you your life."

"Did—did Chace leave?"

Aunt Powler's brows lifted in surprise. "Well, no. But of course there was no way you could have known. He was taken up dreadfully ill himself. Your head groom found him in the stables as pale as death. But he is recovering. It would seem he was attacked by some animal. His clothes were torn, his body was cut and bruised, and he had a terrible bite on his neck." She gave Emma's hand a hard squeeze. "But the surgeon assures me he is well, so you mustn't worry about him."

Emma wasn't worried. She knew what had bit him. Or did she? Was it possible that she had only imagined the existence of the St. Austells and Count Lansallos?

"When did I fall ill?" she asked. "I know it must seem odd to you, but I can't seem to remember."

"It wasn't the night of the ball, or the next night. It was the following morning. When your maid called at your door, you didn't answer. She found you in bed, in your nightclothes, but you had been overtaken by a terrible fit of the ague. You weren't in your right mind."

"Was there—I mean, was no one else in my room when she found me?"

"No," Aunt Powler said, giving her head a shake. "But no more talking. You've been very ill and I daresay your mind will need a few days to adjust itself and then you will be fit as a fiddle."

Emma nodded. She was beyond tired. Perhaps Count Lansallos had only been a character in her dreams, the St. Austells too. She felt as though every muscle in her body had been pummeled for several hours by very strong fists. She fell asleep and did not awaken until dusk. The afternoon of rest left her feeling stronger and better able to recall the events following her masquerade ball. She knew that she hadn't imagined, or merely dreamed up, such terrible events, but she had been so ill that many of her memories were hazy. By the next morning, however, everything was clear to her.

When the vampire family had died, she had bid Chace rest and had gone to the kitchens to fetch a little bread and milk for them both. Exhaustion ruled their bodies and a little sustenance was needed in order for them to perform a much-needed task before the servants were due to return later that afternoon.

Summoning what little strength remained to her, she had fed and cared for Chace until he recovered sufficiently to help her conceal the bodies of Count Lansallos, and of Edward, Mary, and Benedict St. Austell in the dungeon crypts. Afterward, with dawn having broken fully across the hills to the east, Chace asked her to stand on the balcony with him and to welcome the sun, a symbolic gesture that gave her a great deal of peace. He kissed her gently on the forehead and sent her to bed, saying that he intended to harness his team to his curricle himself and to drive back to Trevisgate in order to protect her reputation.

She now realized that he must have been terribly ill when he left for the stables and that evidently he had fallen unconscious before he had gotten even one of the horses harnessed to his carriage. Had the ague not overtaken her, she would have learned as much later that day.

Three days later she saw Chace for the first time since the death of the vampires. He was in the library and had begged to speak with her privately, having sought Aunt Powler's permission first. Emma recalled the last words Mary St. Austell had said to her about making certain she did not acquiesce to his roguish scheme of taking her to the Continent as his mistress, a scheme she had been wondering if she ought to accept.

She entered the chamber in a warm woolen gown of soft ivory, a cashmere shawl in the palest of pinks draped elegantly over her elbows. She wore pearls about her neck and matching drops upon her ears. Beneath her gown her shift was of a warm doeskin so that she was comfortably protected against the November chill. Her black locks were drawn up into an elegant chignon and a fluff of curls graced her forehead. She wanted him to see in her coiffure, her gown, and her demeanor that she would tolerate none of his nonsense. But when she caught sight of him and how thin he was, some of her purposeful composure deserted her.

He smiled crookedly as he rose to his feet to greet her.

"You are still not well," she said sympathetically as she extended her hand to him. He took it gently in his clasp. The bruises on his face had still not healed completely.

"I am perfectly well," he insisted, his green eyes twinkling.

When he lifted her hand to his lips and kissed her fingers quite warmly, she chuckled softly. "I can see that you are," she said.

He stood looking down at her for a moment, his gaze holding hers steadily. "And I can see that you are recovering well, but I was worried when Aunt Powler told me you had not been in your right mind for days."

Emma shook her head. "The ague, only. But your illness was something far worse."

He chuckled. "Not at all. According to the surgeon, the blood replenishes itself remarkably quickly."

Emma shuddered and tried to withdraw her hand from Chace's, but he wouldn't permit her to do so. Instead, he held her fingers more tightly, then simply drew her into his arms.

"There, there. It's over. Truly. Now and forever. You have nothing more to fear—only from me."

His last words made her laugh. "Are you still intent on taking me to Europe?"

"Yes," he said. "Paris first, then Venice, then Rome."

She slipped her arms about his waist and held him fast. "I can't go," she said boldly. "Unless you marry me."

He rocked her a little and sighed. "What a taskmaster you are," he said, sighing resignedly. "Well, if I must go to the guillotine, I expect I could do far worse."

She drew back and looked up at him reproachfully but did not take her arms from about him. "I fear you will strain yourself, m'lord, in making such pretty love to me," she said facetiously. "So many enchanting words and all at once—how do you bear it!"

He looked down at her and grinned. "How do I bear it?" he asked mockingly. "Because I love you. Dear God, I love you to the point of madness. I don't ever wish to be separated from you again. When I was held in that monster's clutches, all I could think was *How will I bear not being with my Emma again?* Quite an odd thought to have, don't you think, when you are being killed?"

"The whole of this is so macabre, I don't know what to say."

"Say you'll be my wife."

"I have wished for nothing more these past three years. You must have known as much."

"In some oddly disjointed way, I suppose I did. But I enjoyed teasing you so much that I couldn't seem to bring myself up to scratch. And during our last waltz with the St. Austells I made a complete mull of it. Later, seeing Lansallos readying you to become his mistress, drove any idea of a clandestine life together straight out of my head!"

Emma laughed outright. "It took only an attack of a vampire to bring you to your senses. I don't like to mention it, my lord, but if you prove as recalcitrant in marriage, we are likely to brangle quite often."

"I depend upon it, Miss Keverne," he whispered, leaning toward her meaningfully.

He placed a warm kiss on her lips and all the tension of the past fortnight seemed to drain out of her with the pressure of his gentle salute. Happiness flooded her, replacing the fright and the pain of the previous days' suffering. She returned his kiss in full, and after a moment pulled away from him slightly.

Looking into his eyes, she queried, "How do you feel about six children—three boys and three girls."

He eyed her oddly. "I was just thinking about that very number and what a perfect assortment it would be."

Emma smiled and kissed him again. Perhaps Mary St. Austell had looked into the future. Perhaps.

"What do you say," she said after a time, "shall we have a Christmas wedding?"

"Yes, if you wish for it. But I insist on a bower of mistletoe over our pillows."

She slapped his wrist. "Can you think of nothing else?"

"Nothing."

"You will always be a rogue. Of that I am convinced."

"Would you have me any other way?" he said, pulling her down with him to sit beside him on the sofa.

Emma smiled up into his face as he slipped his arm about her shoulders and held her closely to him. "No," she murmured, resting her head on his shoulder. "I expect not." He had agreed at last to become her husband. She would fill both their bedchambers with mistletoe if he truly wished for it. Rogue or not, Lord Chace was the man she loved and would always love.

He kissed her again, quite passionately, a salute that was brought to a sudden conclusion by Aunt Powler's entrance.

"You go too far, Chace!" she exclaimed. "I demand that you wed my niece for having taken advantage of her here in the library." Her chin was set firmly, her lips compressed, her blue eyes narrowed.

Chace sighed and shook his head, appearing again as though he were being marched to the guillotine. "Have it as you will," he said. "I know I have behaved badly and I will accept marriage as the proper atonement for having accosted Miss Keverne in the library."

Emma watched her aunt and couldn't keep from smiling at the expression of astonishment on her face. It was clear that Aunt Powler truly did not know whether to believe Chace or not.

"It's true, Aunt," Emma said at last when her aunt remained mute. "Chace and I are to be married. It is all settled between us."

When Aunt Powler finally came to believe that her fondest wish for her niece had actually come true, she took up a seat beside Emma and took hold of one of her hands. Her congratulations and well-wishes flowed for a full quarter-hour, until suddenly her brow grew furrowed.

"What is it, Aunt?" Emma queried. "Do you have some concern for our future happiness? Though I promise you—"

"No, no, it's not that," she said. "In fact, my thoughts have taken an entirely odd turn. When I first came to the library to seek you both out, it wasn't to harass Chace into making a declaration, rather to discover, if I could, why it was you dismissed all the servants the night following the ball. And what relatives of yours did you fetch from Falmouth? One of the stable boys told your head groom of his having taken you and Chace to Falmouth and of having brought back to Castle Breage an odd but apparently charming couple who had emerged from a ship called the *Victory*."

Emma glanced at Chace, who held her gaze for a moment. How much of the truth, if any, ought she reveal to her aunt? Though she didn't really want her aunt to know what had transpired, she didn't see what else she could do but tell her all that happened.

She took a deep breath, and began. "Have you ever heard of a man by the name of Count Lansallos?"

Mrs. Powler smiled as though she were very pleased. "Of course. I met him at your Halloween ball. I danced with him as well. What a delightful man. He said he was a cousin of yours, only whyever didn't you tell me about him? He and I enjoyed the most delightful conversation while you were with Chace beneath the Spanish chestnut tree." She sighed gustily. "Such a handsome man, exceedingly well bred and such a delightfully well-turned leg. If I were but ten, well, twenty years younger—"

Emma bit her lip as she listened to her aunt prattling on about Lansallos. She had intended to tell her the truth, but now she felt certain a whisker or two was in order. Perhaps she would say the couple was a friend of the count's and that the three of them had left early the next morning for London. As for why she dismissed all the servants, she supposed she could blame it on her illness, or a whim, or something. Something. Anything.

Anything but the truth.

No, the truth wouldn't do. Not by half.

About the Author

Valerie King lives with her family in Glendale, Arizona. She is the author of sixteen Regency romances, including *A Summer Courtship* and *Bewitching Hearts,* and two historical Regency romances—*Vanquished,* now on sale at bookstores everywhere—and *Vignette,* to be published in April 1997. Valerie is currently working on her next traditional Regency romance, to be published in November 1997. She loves hearing from her readers and you may write to her c/o Zebra Books. Please include a self-addressed stamped envelope if you wish a response.

ZEBRA REGENCIES
ARE
THE TALK OF THE TON!

A REFORMED RAKE (4499, $3.99)
by Jeanne Savery

After governess Harriet Cole helped her young charge flee to France—and the designs of a despicable suitor, more trouble soon arrived in the person of a London rake. Sir Frederick Carrington insisted on providing safe escort back to England. Harriet deemed Carrington more dangerous than any band of brigands, but secretly relished matching wits with him. But after being taken in his arms for a tender kiss, she found herself wondering— *could* a lady find love with an irresistible rogue?

A SCANDALOUS PROPOSAL (4504, $4.99)
by Teresa DesJardien

After only two weeks into the London season, Lady Pamela Premington has already received her first offer of marriage. If only it hadn't come from the *ton's* most notorious rake, Lord Marchmont. Pamela had already set her sights on the distinguished Lieutenant Penford, who had the heroism and honor that made him the ideal match. Now she had to keep from falling under the spell of the seductive Lord so she could pursue the man more worthy of her love. Or was he?

A LADY'S CHAMPION (4535, $3.99)
by Janice Bennett

Miss Daphne, art mistress of the Selwood Academy for Young Ladies, greeted the notion of ghosts haunting the academy with skepticism. However, to avoid rumors frightening off students, she found herself turning to Mr. Adrian Carstairs, sent by her uncle to be her "protector" against the "ghosts." Although, Daphne would accept no interference in her life, she *would* accept aid in exposing any spectral spirits. What she never expected was for Adrian to expose the secret wishes of her hidden heart . . .

CHARITY'S GAMBIT (4537, $3.99)
by Marcy Stewart

Charity Abercrombie reluctantly embarks on a London season in hopes of making a suitable match. However she cannot forget the mysterious Dominic Castille—and the kiss they shared—when he fell from a tree as she strolled through the woods. Charity does not know that the dark and dashing captain harbors a dangerous secret that will ensnare them both in its web—leaving Charity to risk certain ruin and losing the man she so passionately loves . . .

Available wherever paperbacks are sold, or order direct from the Publisher. Send cover price plus 50¢ per copy for mailing and handling to Penguin USA, P.O. Box 999, c/o Dept. 17109, Bergenfield, NJ 07621. Residents of New York and Tennessee must include sales tax. DO NOT SEND CASH.

ZEBRA'S REGENCY ROMANCES
DAZZLE AND DELIGHT

A BEGUILING INTRIGUE
(4441, $3.99)
by Olivia Sumner

Pretty as a picture Justine Riggs cared nothing for propriety. She dressed as a boy, sat on her horse like a jockey, and pondered the stars like a scientist. But when she tried to best the handsome Quenton Fletcher, Marquess of Devon, by proving that she was the better equestrian, he would try to prove Justine's antics were pure folly. The game he had in mind was seduction—never imagining that he might lose his heart in the process!

AN INCONVENIENT ENGAGEMENT
(4442, $3.99)
by Joy Reed

Rebecca Wentworth was furious when she saw her betrothed waltzing with another. So she decides to make him jealous by flirting with the handsomest man at the ball, John Collinwood, Earl of Stanford. The "wicked" nobleman knew exactly what the enticing miss was up to—and he was only too happy to play along. But as Rebecca gazed into his magnificent eyes, her errant fiancé was soon utterly forgotten!

SCANDAL'S LADY
(4472, $3.99)
by Mary Kingsley

Cassandra was shocked to learn that the new Earl of Lynton was her childhood friend, Nicholas St. John. After years at sea and mixed feelings Nicholas had come home to take the family title. And although Cassandra knew her place as a governess, she could not help the thrill that went through her each time he was near. Nicholas was pleased to find that his old friend Cassandra was his new next door neighbor, but after being near her, he wondered if mere friendship would be enough . . .

HIS LORDSHIP'S REWARD
(4473, $3.99)
by Carola Dunn

As the daughter of a seasoned soldier, Fanny Ingram was accustomed to the vagaries of military life and cared not a whit about matters of rank and social standing. So she certainly never foresaw her *tendre* for handsome Viscount Roworth of Kent with whom she was forced to share lodgings, while he carried out his clandestine activities on behalf of the British Army. And though good sense told Roworth to keep his distance, he couldn't stop from taking Fanny in his arms for a kiss that made all hearts equal!

Available wherever paperbacks are sold, or order direct from the Publisher. Send cover price plus 50¢ per copy for mailing and handling to Penguin USA, P.O. Box 999, c/o Dept. 17109, Bergenfield, NJ 07621. Residents of New York and Tennessee must include sales tax. DO NOT SEND CASH.

ELEGANT LOVE STILL FLOURISHES —
Wrap yourself in a Zebra Regency Romance.

A MATCHMAKER'S MATCH   (3783, $3.50/$4.50)
by Nina Porter
To save herself from a loveless marriage, Lady Psyche Veringham pretends to be a bluestocking. Resigned to spinsterhood at twenty-three, Psyche sets her keen mind to snaring a husband for her young charge, Amanda. She sets her cap for long-time bachelor, Justin St. James. This man of the world has had his fill of frothy-headed debutantes and turns the tables on Psyche. Can a bluestocking and a man about town find true love?

FIRES IN THE SNOW   (3809, $3.99/$4.99)
by Janis Laden
Because of an unhappy occurrence, Diana Ruskin knew that a secure marriage was not in her future. She was content to assist her physician father and follow in his footsteps . . . until now. After meeting Adam, Duke of Marchmaine, Diana's precise world is shattered. She would simply have to avoid the temptation of his gentle touch and stunning physique — and by doing so break her own heart!

FIRST SEASON   (3810, $3.50/$4.50)
by Anne Baldwin
When country heiress Laetitia Biddle arrives in London for the Season, she harbors dreams of triumph and applause. Instead, she becomes the laughingstock of drawing rooms and ballrooms, alike. This headstrong miss blames the rakish Lord Wakeford for her miserable debut, and she vows to rise above her many faux pas. Vowing to become an Original, Letty proves that she's more than a match for this eligible, seasoned Lord.

AN UNCOMMON INTRIGUE   (3701, $3.99/$4.99)
by Georgina Devon
Miss Mary Elizabeth Sinclair was rather startled when the British Home Office employed her as a spy. Posing as "Tasha," an exotic fortune-teller, she expected to encounter unforeseen dangers. However, nothing could have prepared her for Lord Eric Stewart, her dashing and infuriating partner. Giving her heart to this haughty rogue would be the most reckless hazard of all.

A MADDENING MINX   (3702, $3.50/$4.50)
by Mary Kingsley
After a curricle accident, Miss Sarah Chadwick is literally thrust into the arms of Philip Thornton. While other women shy away from Thornton's eyepatch and aloof exterior, Sarah finds herself drawn to discover why this man is physically and emotionally scarred.

Available wherever paperbacks are sold, or order direct from the Publisher. Send cover price plus 50¢ per copy for mailing and handling to Penguin USA, P.O. Box 999, c/o Dept. 17109, Bergenfield, NJ 07621. Residents of New York and Tennessee must include sales tax. DO NOT SEND CASH.